DOWN

ALLY BLUE

Riptide Publishing
PO Box 6652
Hillsborough, NJ 08844
www.riptidepublishing.com

Down
Copyright © 2015 by Ally Blue

Cover art: Kanaxa, www.kanaxa.com
Editors: Danielle Poiesz, Delphine Dryden
Layout: L.C. Chase, lcchase.com/design.htm

ISBN: 978-1-62649-259-2

First edition
April, 2015

Also available in ebook:
ISBN: 978-1-62649-258-5

DOWN

ALLY BLUE

RIPTIDE
PUBLISHING

This book is lovingly dedicated to Jacques Cousteau and all those awesome undersea adventures I watched on TV as a child. They sowed the seeds of my lifelong love for all things aquatic. I can't remember a time when I haven't been obsessed with the dark and horrific, so I'm blaming that on genetics.

.

TABLE OF
CONTENTS

CHAPTER 1

May 2137
BathyTech 3 deep-sea mineral mining pod
Bottom of the Peru-Chile Trench

Mo thought he knew the dark. He'd sought it out all his life. Made himself intimate with it. Explored cellars and caves and forgotten places where the sun didn't penetrate and dead things decayed in the corners.

Then he'd gone down, and learned what darkness really meant.

Nothing blotted out the light quite like seven thousand meters of ocean.

The unrelieved blackness with its nightmare creatures called to the explorer in him. The part that wanted to uncover long-lost secrets and learn what no one else knew.

Which was why, when the scientists upside had asked the thirty-person crew of the BathyTech 3 deep-sea mineral mining rig to help find out what was pinging their mapping scans down in Richards Deep, Mo had volunteered to guide the science team into the deepest part of the Peru–Chile Trench to look for it.

His boss, Jemima, scowled when he told her. "I don't want any of my miners skipping off on some stupid geek mission. I need every one of you on the vents."

"It's one shift. You'll hardly even miss me." He answered her death glare with a grin. "C'mon, Jem, don't be like that. Think of it as a political move."

Jem rolled her eyes, and Mo stifled a snicker. Pod 3 was the first of the BathyTech mining rigs to incorporate scientific research into its operation. To say that the scientists and the miners didn't always get along would be a gross understatement.

"Fine. But for the love of Pete, *ask* me before you volunteer for this shit next time." Jem pushed herself out of her chair and crossed to the refrigerator on the other side of the miner's lounge. She opened it and pulled out a pouch. "Beer?"

He held out his hands. "Lay it on me, Big Mama."

That earned him a sour look. She couldn't weigh more than forty-five kilos soaking wet, and the top of her head only reached Mo's armpit. The nickname irritated the crap out of her. She tossed him the beer anyway, then dug another one out of the fridge for herself. Mo tore the tab off the top to activate the polymers, marveling for the umpteenth time at the transformation from a soft-sided pouch to a solid bottle that felt exactly like real glass. He always got a kick out of breaking the empty bottle and watching it change back into a flexible pocket. It reminded him of entropy, decay, and dissolution.

She plopped into the chair, tore open her pouch, and took a long swallow the second it solidified. "So when's this geek crew comin' down?"

"Tomorrow. Early." Mo gulped beer, savoring the tingle of bubbles on his tongue. "They're sending an outside team instead of BathyTech scientists."

Her eyebrows shot up. "Yeah?"

"Yep."

"How come?" She scratched her chin. "In fact, how come our guys couldn't go get whatever the hell this thing is?"

"They tried. I heard they sent Rover out, but it wouldn't pick up the thing. Acted like it wasn't even there."

"Seriously?"

"Yep." He took another swallow of his drink. Licked his lips. Did it again because he knew damn well she was dying for more details and he was having way too much fun not giving her any. "Mmm. Good beer."

She shot him a tight smile. "You're an asshole."

"Yep." He raised his bottle to her.

She flipped him off.

Chuckling, Mo slouched into his chair, nursed his beer, and drifted off into his thoughts while Jem turned on the TV. If he was honest with himself, the strangeness of the whole business was the main reason he'd jumped at the chance to lead the upside team in their walk. Dr. Poole, BathyTech 3's head of science, had already shown him Rover's vid. It was way more staticky than it ought to be, but Mo had caught glimpses of what looked like a rock. The problem was, rocks didn't show up as empty space on mapping scans, and they couldn't fool state-of-the-art unmanned retrievers into thinking they didn't exist.

Something highly unusual—maybe even something completely new—waited in Richards Deep. Mo fully intended to be among the first to see it in person.

Dubai's three-month-long blackout back in 2110 had taught Mo a lot. Like how to get in and out of any place he wanted without getting caught. How to make a gang member with an automatic weapon and a necklace of human tongues believe a thirteen-year-old boy would shoot first. How to pull the trigger without hesitation when he had to. Mostly, though, he'd learned how to tell whom he could and could not trust.

He'd left his home and his teenage self behind a long time ago, but he'd never forgotten those lessons. People who arrived in the airlock pasty, sweaty, and sick from the journey down might not be bad sorts in general, but Mo sure as shit wouldn't trust them out in the open water at over seven thousand meters in a walker suit. It was a recipe for disaster. Therefore, he got up early the next day to meet the sub from upside and see what he'd be dealing with on this assignment.

Dr. Poole shot Mo a cool look when he strode into the airlock's outer atrium. "I wondered if you'd turn up."

"Of course." Mo grinned at the geologist's sour expression. "That's not a problem, is it?"

The doctor narrowed his eyes. Before he could say anything, though, the chime sounded, and the airlock tech announced the arrival of the sub from BathyTech's flagship research vessel, *Peregrine*.

Dr. Poole pointed at Mo. "Behave yourself."

"Remind me, Doctor, which one of us had our pay docked for fighting in the cafeteria?" Mo rubbed his chin. "Oh, that's right. You." And Jem, though that was beside the point right now. The two had literally come to blows more than once.

Poole went red to the roots of his thinning hair. Behind him, his two lab assistants laughed. Poole's glare shut them up just before the airlock door slid open to let in the upside scientific team.

Mo straightened his spine, put on a pleasant expression, and studied the group filing into the atrium. Three men, two women, all with that hungry look scientists got when they were after something unique.

Curiosity burned in Mo's belly. He ignored it. Whatever was going on, he'd find out soon enough. *Patience is a virtue*, his mother used to say.

He went back to his perusal of the team. Of the five of them, only one had that pasty, damp-at-the-hairline look that meant the trip down hadn't agreed with him. He strode in with a wide smile anyway, bright-blue eyes crinkling at the corners. Mo thought he looked more like a football coach than a scientist.

The man held out a wide hand to Dr. Poole. "Hi there. I'm Dr. Douglas. Call me Neil. Real pleasure to meet you. And you are?"

"Dr. Oliver Poole. I'm the lead scientist here." Poole managed a smile that settled uncomfortably on his face. "Welcome to BathyTech 3. We're happy to have you and your team here."

The other man looked startled, then laughed. "Oh, no, I'm just the exobiologist. Dr. Savage-Hall here is the head of our team." He turned to a slender, dark-haired man—midforties, at a guess, with large black eyes—who stood silently beside him. "You might've heard of him. His work in theoretical marine geology is groundbreaking."

Mo pressed his lips together to keep from pissing off Poole by jumping into the conversation. He'd read Dr. Savage-Hall's study on the potential for macroquantum behavior of the seabed at extreme depth last year and found it fascinating. The doctor's *back off* expression didn't invite questions, but damn, Mo would love to pick that impressive brain.

He only half listened while the upside doc introduced the rest of his team—Dr. Mandala Jhut, microbiology and microgeology; Dr. Carlo Libra, deep-marine geology; and Dr. Ashlyn Timms, practical and theoretical physics. Admiring Dr. Savage-Hall's severe, studious good looks was much more interesting than hearing who did which job.

Poole gestured toward his assistants. "These are my lab assistants, Ryal Nataki and Hannah Long. They're both at your disposal while you're here." He nodded at Mo, his nose scrunching like he smelled something rotten. "This is Maximo Rees, one of our miners. He's volunteered to lead the walker team into Richards Deep tomorrow."

To Mo's surprise, Dr. Savage-Hall strode toward him with one slim hand held out and a smile that didn't seem forced. "Mr. Rees." His gaze flicked downward, then back to Mo's face, so swift Mo almost missed it. "Thank you for agreeing to provide us with technical leadership on this excursion. We're most grateful."

Mo grasped the man's hand and shook. He had a good, strong grip and a refreshingly direct gaze. Mo flashed his most disarming grin, partly because he couldn't help liking the guy and partly to see if the once-over he'd gotten came from professional interest or something more fun.

"Please. Just Mo." He let his smile warm when the doctor's black-as-the-Trench eyes did the down-and-up thing again, checking him out less covertly this time. A hot glow stirred deep in his belly. "I'm excited to be a part of this team. Thanks for letting me play."

One dark brow lifted. "I look forward to our time together, Mo." Dr. Savage-Hall dropped Mo's hand and turned to his team, all business again. "Dr. Poole, is there somewhere we could all gather to discuss the excursion? I'd like to go over the logistics of it and precisely what everyone's role will be. I think we'd all be much more comfortable if we could sit down somewhere and talk."

"Of course." Poole gestured toward the hallway. "The library is private enough for a conversation and has plenty of room. Would that be all right?"

Everyone agreed, and Poole led the way. While the rest of the group huddled together behind Poole to talk, Dr. Savage-Hall dropped back to walk with Mo in the rear. "This is my first time in one of the BathyTech facilities. I'm hoping to find someone to show me around and tell me more about the operations here." His no-nonsense gaze cut sideways to meet Mo's. "Pardon my bluntness, but I'd love it if you'd oblige me."

The heat in the doc's eyes told Mo he'd be obliging more than a BathyTech tour. Which was fine with him. After nearly four months without getting laid, he was ready to jump the first man who'd have him. This doctor represented a definite upgrade from his usual casual lovers.

"On one condition." Leaning closer, Mo lowered his voice to what he'd been assured was a sexy growl. "Tell me your first name."

"Armin." The doc's pretty lips curved into an honest-to-fuck smirk. "I'll look forward to hearing you say it later."

Mo laughed. He liked a confident man. "Me too, Doc. Me too."

They made an early start of it the next day. It was still dark upside, Armin reflected, when he, Mo, Carlo, Ashlyn, Neil, and the lab tech Hannah set off in the go-carts for their excursion into Richards Deep.

With nothing to do until they reached their destination, Armin gazed out the window of the go-cart while Mo piloted the vehicle along the seabed. He'd studied the lightless world of the deepest ocean countless times, yet he never tired of it. What seemed barren at first glance teemed with life if one watched with a patient eye and an open mind. Not all living things looked as though they ought to carry that label.

Learning that had changed him forever.

"It was the tube worms that got me."

Mo's low voice from the pilot seat brought to mind things other than marine life for a moment, stirring a heart-pounding heat in Armin's belly. He shoved the feeling away with both hands because now wasn't the time. Not with Ashlyn in the seat behind him and the second go-cart following them out to the place where the unknown object waited. He needed to present his best professional self and keep his mind on the work.

He glanced sideways at Mo and tried to act casual. "Oh, yes?"

Mo nodded. "I saw a TV show when I was little about the first worms they found on the deep-sea thermal vents. How they didn't need the sun, but used the nutrients from the vents for energy. I remember thinking how they looked like some kind of weird rock. But the show said they were worms. They were *alive*. And that changed my whole world view."

He studied Mo's profile, trying not to picture his face contorted with pleasure the way he'd seen it a few hours ago. "This is what made you want to be a deep-marine diver?"

"It planted the seed, yeah." The heavy-lidded eyes pinned him with a knowing look. "I saw you thinking about it."

For a paralyzing second, Armin thought Mo meant their tryst the night before—not that day and night had any real meaning down here. Then he understood and laughed, relieved. "My moment was the first time I saw a mermaid fish."

Ashlyn snorted. "Those are a myth."

"They're not." Mo's voice was soft. Reverent. His eyes glittered in the jaundiced light of the go-cart cab. "I saw one six years ago, in the Mariana Trench. It was fucking gorgeous. That's what made me jump at this job. I heard they'd been spotted here too. I wanted to see one again."

Armin understood. His first glimpse of the disturbingly humanlike fish on his third bathyspheric dive as a student had cemented his path in life. He'd fallen under the spell of its milky-green stare, and resolved to study the creatures of the extreme ocean depths as a secondary degree to his first love: theoretical marine geology, a field he'd helped pioneer. The possibility that he was about to lay hands on the first real proof of his theories—a macro object exhibiting quantum behavior—excited him.

On the other hand, on the single glimpse Poole and his team had gotten of it, the object they were after looked remarkably like the one Klaudia Longenesse had carried from the Varredura Longa into the Antarctic Ocean. That fact filled him with a deep disquiet.

"Doc?"

He blinked and met Mo's questioning gaze. "Yes?"

The lips that had explored his body until he shook and moaned curved into a lopsided smile. "Where'd you go?"

He looked away, embarrassed. "Sorry. I get lost in my thoughts sometimes."

Behind him, Ashlyn made a scornful sound. He glared at her over his shoulder. She pursed her lips and stared out the round porthole at her side.

Mo eyed him with an odd intensity for a moment, then turned his attention back to the cart's controls. "Okay. Well. We've got coordinates for this thing, whatever it is. Shouldn't take too long to retrieve it."

"Excellent."

"Now. About the mapping tech." Mo touched the flat-screen readout on the dash. It popped up into 3-D. "The walker helmet hooks into the BathyTech satellite automatically. It'll show you a map of the seafloor if one already exists, and if there isn't one, it'll make one as you go and hook it up with what's already known of the area. What you're looking at here is a map created during our initial mining operations several years ago."

Armin studied the readout, impressed. "It's amazingly detailed."

"Yeah. The suit's automatic camera isn't as good as the extra one we added for scientific purposes—that one records in way more detail, and in parts of the spectrum the human eye can't see—but the built-in camera has a wide-angle lens, and it's integrated with the mapping software, so it produces a pretty damn good readout." Mo pointed at the flat-screen in front of Armin, then jerked his thumb over his shoulder toward Ashlyn. "You each have your own readouts you can study if you want. Dr. Timms, I know you're not walking, but you can still have a look at the map if you're interested."

They lapsed into silence. Armin brought up his personal data display and studied the digital map of their destination. Whatever it was they sought, it lay in a part of Richards Deep less than a kilometer from the official boundary of the Deep, on a shelf above a narrow chasm.

He stared at the soft white dot on his display and wondered, as he'd done ever since he'd first seen it, what it might be.

Ashlyn tapped his shoulder, and he barely managed not to jump. "Yes? What is it?"

"We're here." She sounded amused. "Thought you might be interested."

Mo aimed an assessing gaze at him. A rush of blood turned his cheeks hot. Maybe it didn't matter what Maximo Rees thought of him back on the BathyTech pod, but out here, Mo's good opinion was law. If Mo thought he wasn't mentally up to the walk, he'd be forced to wait in the go-cart. And he could *not* let that happen.

"Of course. I was just studying the readouts again." With a smile he hoped didn't look too forced, he turned off the display. "Well. Shall we?"

Mo watched him while the two of them stripped to their skins and donned their walker suits. Examined his every move while he fastened into his helmet and started the flow of Mist. Armin tried not to cough as the thick, wet gas mix that would keep his lungs expanded and his body chemistry normalized crept into his sinuses and alveoli. It was fine once you got used to it, but those first few seconds never became any easier.

"Readout on." His voice was muffled by the Mist. His display popped up on the walker's faceplate, crisp and clear. He glanced sideways. Mo was going through his own systems tests but still watching him, and his patience ran out. "What in the hell are you looking at?"

If his outburst swayed Mo's opinion one way or another, it didn't show. His face was expressionless. "This is Rees in Walker One to walker team. Testing coms. Acknowledge by number. Over."

Armin knew his temper was being tested as much as the communication systems. He intended to pass.

Calling on his trusty scientific discipline to suppress his frustration, he answered with a calm he hoped his companion would note. "Walker Two, over."

Behind his faceplate, Mo hitched up one corner of that damned sinful mouth. Armin stared into the inky water of the large, round moon pool in the middle of the floor instead. Something salt white and roughly the size of his thumb skittered across the underside of the clear GlasSteel cover before vanishing into the blackness.

He wanted to follow it.

Carlo's voice from the other go-cart came through his com with perfect clarity. "Walker Three, receiving both of you. Over."

Armin made himself meet Mo's gaze and nod. He thought he caught an echo of his own exploratory yearning in Mo's eyes before he blinked his attention back to his work.

Mo methodically tested the links between the walkers and Ashlyn, Neil, and Hannah in the go-carts. Meanwhile, he managed, without so much as a glance in his direction, to make Armin feel as if he were still being watched.

Annoyed with himself, he did his best to ignore it. If he'd known how a tryst with Mo would affect his concentration, he might not have given in to the temptation.

On the other hand, remembering the clutching heat of that beautiful body, he couldn't bring himself to regret it.

Finally, when he'd gotten affirmatives all around on the com connections, Mo declared all systems go. He grinned behind his faceplate. "You geeks ready to walk?"

An answering smile spread over Armin's face as he pictured the scowl he knew Carlo was wearing right now. The man hated being called a geek. "Let's go."

"Computer: Pressurize chamber." At Mo's command, the edge of the moon pool room door glowed red, indicating the go-cart's computer had sealed it and upped the air pressure in the chamber to keep the sea from bubbling up to flood it when they uncovered the pool.

The computer's voice was bland and sexless. "Chamber sealed and pressurized. Shall I uncover the pool now?"

"Yes. Thank you."

The cover drew back from the moon pool, revealing a round well of black water cold enough to stop a human heart instantly and heavy enough to stomp their bodies flat without the protection of the walkers. Up front in the pilot's compartment, Ashlyn switched on the lights on the underside of the go-cart, illuminating a flat slurry of mud and organic detritus two and a half meters below.

Staring down at the first step in his journey to the thing he'd come here to find, Armin felt a vague dread seep into his blood. He shoved it away. He didn't want anything to poison his excitement over what could be the greatest find of his career.

"I'll go first. You follow as soon as I give you the A-OK. Got it?"

Armin blinked and looked up at the sound of Mo's voice in his ear. He nodded. "Roger that."

Mo flashed that heart-stopping grin again. "See you on the bottom, Doc." He switched on his walker lights, stepped to the edge of the pool, and plunged in.

He gave the A-OK a few seconds later. Armin switched on his lights and leaped into the deep.

He landed on the ocean floor with a silent *ploof.* The fine silt rose in a cloud around his knees. Mo stood beside him in a similar cloud. Carlo was walking toward them from the other cart like a misplaced astronaut, holding an equipment bag with its buoyancy adjusted so it floated along beside him. The dive legs of the side-by-side carts cast spindly crisscrossing shadows on the seafloor.

Beyond the reach of the lights, solid blackness hunched like a living thing. He imagined it flexing curved claws and licking long, bloodstained teeth, watching them with pitiless patience, waiting for its moment to pounce, rend, and devour.

He thought he saw the gleam of hungry eyes on the edge of the light. But it was probably just one of the delightfully unusual creatures that called this cold, unforgiving place home. There were wonders enough here without imagining the dark itself as something with thought and intent.

Mo's calm voice brought Armin out of mental pathways best left untraveled and back to the safe, sensible world of the real. "Okay. We're heading south-southwest from here. We'll hit the start of the ledge in about fifteen meters. After that, it starts sloping down a little. Not too bad, maybe five degrees. The ledge narrows down fast to only a couple of meters wide, though, so watch your footing."

Carlo nodded inside his helmet. "What's our order?"

"I'm leading. You're second. Doc Armin's taking the rear, since he has the most experience out of the two of you with walker suits. Once we get near the thing, whatever it is, I'll let the two of you at it." Mo studied each of them in turn, his expression serious. "Any questions? I want everything crystal clear before we go."

Carlo shook his head. "No questions. We're clear."

Mo looked at Armin, who nodded. "Everything's understood."

"All right, then." Mo turned to face the direction they were heading. "Go-carts, Walker One here. Walker team moving out."

Ashlyn's cool voice crackled in Armin's helmet. "Cart One, acknowledged."

"Cart Two, acknowledged." Hannah sounded excited as a child. "Keep the feeds on, guys. Neil and I want to see!"

Mo laughed. "You got it, Hannah."

The three of them moved beyond the comfort of the go-cart lights and into the dark. Armin tried not to imagine the creep of silent footsteps in the expanding swath of blackness behind him because really, what could be there? Tiny shrimp? Miniature squid flashing neon colors? Translucent fish with their needle teeth, too small to hurt anything so massive as a human being?

All those things might hover in his wake, certainly. But none could stalk their team with intent to harm, or indeed any intent at all. None could create the deliberate, plodding *floop . . . floop . . . floop . . .* his brain insisted on hearing at his heels—despite the fact that his helmet's sensors weren't configured to pick up external sounds. Even if it were possible for this sound to exist. Which it wasn't.

Eventually, his stubborn refusal to look paid off. The impossible noise stopped once the team started down the sloped path, an ever-rising wall of rock to their right and the abyss to their left. He peered into the void less than a meter away. The dark water felt charged, as if on the verge of revealing some forgotten horror older than human memory.

For one heart-stopping moment, he knew—*knew*—the thing was about to rise from the murk, white and bloated as a corpse.

He shook his head, as if he could physically knock the unwelcome visions out of his mind. Clearly the atrocities he'd seen a few weeks earlier in Antarctica had affected him more than he'd thought.

Mo slowed, one hand held out behind him. "All right. The anomaly is just ahead, about three meters. You guys go around me. Very carefully, all right? I don't want anyone going over the edge."

"Copy that." Carlo tweaked the buoyancy on the equipment bag, and it drifted downward to rest on the ledge behind Mo. "I'll leave that here. You can bring it up when we're ready."

Mo nodded. "Sure."

Mo and Carlo flattened themselves against the wall. Armin edged forward, taking small, cautious steps. He put a hand out to steady himself, and Mo grasped it. They looked at one another through the faceplates. Mo smiled, excitement equal to Armin's shining in his eyes, and Armin's heart turned over. He smiled back, savoring the moment of connection.

"Go on, Doc." Mo's voice was soft and eager. "Go get your mystery thing."

Laughing, Armin stepped around Mo and reluctantly let go of his hand. "Yes, indeed. The great mystery."

He faced forward and made his way along the ledge. His helmet and wrist lights picked up an outcropping of the wall, and sitting atop it was a plain, round, jet-black stone. The lights glittered on its surface.

I've seen this before.

The thought was so out of place, it stopped Armin cold. But it was true. He *had* seen this before. Or rather, something remarkably like it. The grainy, three-second bit of footage from the Varredura Longa's outside camera was the only clue to what had happened there. The sheer improbability of what seemed to be the same type of object showing up both there and here kept Armin's feet glued to the seabed and his gaze fixed, unbelieving, on the thing that appeared to be a rock but wasn't.

"Oh my God," breathed Carlo through the walker's com system. "That looks just like—"

"I know." Armin cast him a *keep quiet* glare. "Let's not jump to conclusions."

Mo, who'd crept up behind them, leaned around Armin's shoulder to study the object with fascination. "Looks like what?"

"Nothing." Armin touched Mo's chest. "Could you give us a bit of room, please?"

Mo obediently backed up a couple of steps. "So what is this thing? Poole said Rover was working fine, and so was all the equipment on the *Peregrine*, so how come it acts like it doesn't exist?" He turned his curious gaze to Armin. "If the tests bear it out, it'll pretty much prove your theories about the potential for macroquantum behavior of some materials under extreme pressures, right?"

Armin looked at him, surprised and pleased. "You've read my paper?"

"Yeah." Mo grinned. "Can't say I understood all of it, but yeah, I read it. Everything about marine science fascinates me."

A sweet warmth rose in Armin's chest. He returned Mo's smile, and for a moment it was only the two of them, alone in the vastness of the sea.

Carlo cleared his throat. "Any time you're ready, Romeo."

If it weren't for the Mist, Armin would have blushed. Ignoring Mo's low chuckle, he walked the last couple of meters to the mysterious object. Pulse pounding in the base of his throat, he stroked the thing with one hand. The bulky glove kept him from feeling anything, of course, but he imagined the smoothness of it anyway. The idea that he might be touching something new to science, something unique—perhaps something extraterrestrial?—sent elated shivers through him.

"Can we retrieve it?" Carlo asked. "I mean, are you able to just pick it up, or will we need to blast it loose?"

"Whoa, hang on there." Mo held up both hands, palms out. "We've got incendiary paste back at the pod, but we'd need to do more extensive testing on this wall before you could safely blast it."

Carlo gave him a sour look. "I'm well aware of that. I was asking *Armin*, who is also well aware of the precautions we'd need to take, whether or not we can retrieve this thing without blasting."

Armin spoke up before the other two could get into a completely unnecessary argument. "I believe so. It doesn't seem to be attached to the wall."

"Good." Carlo moved closer. "Let's do the scans, then grab it and go."

"Of course." Armin glanced back at Mo. "Switch to infrared lights, Mo. We're going to scan on IR first."

"Roger that."

All three of them switched their suit lights to IR. The specially made IR sensors in the walker's faceplate allowed Armin to see the reverse-image ghost of Carlo's faceplate display. It lit his features in a sickly pale green that made him look dead.

A hard chill ran down Armin's spine. Doing his best to ignore the unease tickling the nape of his neck, he leaned forward, one hand on the outcropping blocking the path, and peered at the back of the object. The IR light reflected off the curve of the rock. It was utterly featureless, and produced no heat or other radiation visible on infrared.

Armin found it strangely beautiful in its blank, perfect symmetry. He stared at it until he could no longer fight the instinct to blink. As his eyelids swept down, feeding his weak human need to lubricate his weak human corneas in spite of the Mist in his helmet, the thing seethed like a nest of worms.

He froze. Stared again, harder. This time it held still, like an ordinary—if uncannily round and smooth—rock.

He swiveled to look at Carlo. "Go ahead and get out the transport box while I complete the scans."

Carlo switched to regular light, then opened the bag and fetched the box they'd brought to transport the object, while Armin activated his walker's built-in scanning function. His gut told him microbes and radioactivity would not be among the dangers this thing brought with it, but a scientist couldn't afford to operate on instinct. So he scanned for everything modern technology allowed.

Absolutely nothing showed up. Less than nothing, in fact. As far as his suit could tell him, the object he'd been staring at for several minutes, that he'd touched with his own hand—albeit through a walker glove—wasn't there at all.

Because that was clearly not the case, he lifted the stone carefully, reverently, and placed it in the box.

Carlo engaged the box's seal, and Armin switched back to regular light. Mo had already switched. He watched with a million silent questions in his eyes as Armin unfolded the webbing around the container and prepared to carry it back to the go-cart.

Armin pretended not to notice. Now that they'd retrieved the thing they'd come here for, Mo's part in this was at an end. He wouldn't like it, but that wasn't Armin's problem. His only concerns were keeping this one-of-a-kind object safe, and learning everything he could about it.

Back on the go-cart, Mo sidled up to Armin while they were changing and ran a single fingertip down the side of his neck. "Interesting rock you got there, Doc."

"Yes, it is." Armin leaned briefly against Mo's bare chest, enjoying his warmth. "I'm anxious to begin studying it."

"I bet." Laying a gentle hand on Armin's cheek, Mo angled his face sideways and up until he was forced to meet Mo's intense gaze. His lips curved into a smile that made Armin's heart thump. "I know you probably don't want to share with a walker jockey like me, but I'd sure love to hear all about what you find."

Armin couldn't help returning the man's rakish smile. "We'll see."

"Translation: No."

Before he could think of a suitable answer, Mo cupped his chin and kissed him: a deep, open-mouthed kiss that left him breathless and uncomfortably aroused. He turned in Mo's embrace and clutched the belt loops on his pants. "I'm sorry. It's simply that I have no idea what we'll find, if we find anything at all, and I don't want any premature information getting out."

Mo's eyebrows went up. "I don't gossip, Doc."

"I didn't mean to imply that you do." He cast about for the best way to explain without making it sound as if he were indeed implying that very thing. "Information takes on a life of its own if you're not careful with it. And when it comes to scientific research, we have to take great care not to allow incomplete or unverified findings to get out because that can discredit the final findings." Following a sudden instinct, he took Mo's hand and laced their fingers together. "I like you very much, Mo, and I admire the way your mind works. I wish I could share more of what we're doing with you. Please understand why I can't."

Mo nodded, his smile soft. "Yeah. I get it." He kissed the end of Armin's nose. "I'm coming to your quarters tonight, though. Maybe I can change your mind." He waggled his eyebrows.

Armin laughed, and they both went back to getting dressed. But something told him that Mo hadn't been joking.

Later, when the approach to researching the impossible rock had been discussed by the team and said rock had been safely locked in the lab vault, after dinner and mutual congratulations, Armin took Mo back to his quarters. Mo sucked him off in the shower, then laid him down on the unmade bed and fucked him until his vision blurred and he couldn't have formed words even if he'd wanted to.

Afterward, he curled into Mo's arms with a sense of completion he'd rarely felt in his life. Had never felt, in fact, with a lover. Not that he made a habit of staying with the men he bedded, or inviting them to stay with him. His one and only long-term relationship hadn't ended well, and he'd never felt the need to involve himself with anyone since then. He wasn't sure what to make of this unexpected connection with Mo. It was a bit frightening, and a lot exhilarating.

Why should I fight it? he wondered, breathing in Mo's warm male scent. *I'll be here a few weeks at the most. Why shouldn't I enjoy his company while I'm here?*

Mo started to get up. Armin tightened his grip. "Don't go."

The muscular body in his arms tensed. "Huh?"

"I said, don't go." Armin tilted his head back enough to peer at Mo through half-closed eyes. "You can stay here tonight, if you'd like."

One dark eyebrow lifted. "Can I?"

"Mm-hmm." Grinning, Armin slung a leg across Mo's thighs. "Don't go."

For a long moment, Mo watched him with a strange glitter in his eyes. Armin felt like a prize stallion being admired by a potential buyer. Logically, he shouldn't have enjoyed it. Yet he did. His skin heated under Mo's stare, and he wondered at the strength of his own libido.

Finally, when Armin's breath began to come short and he'd started to wonder if he might actually get hard again, Mo favored him with a wide smile. "I'd love to stay." He slipped a hand between Armin's legs. "Can we play doctor again?"

Laughing, Armin pulled Mo down into a kiss.

CHAPTER 2

Mo got up an hour early the next day so he could go to the lab before his shift started and see how Doc Armin and crew were doing with the mysterious rock. He expected he'd have to sweet-talk Armin into telling him anything, but after yesterday, he held out real hope for success. Especially after last night, when Armin had looked at him with big, soft, vulnerable eyes and asked him to stay.

The fact that he'd done it without a second thought was a whole other thing. One that he didn't much want to examine too closely. Maybe he could keep seeing this thing as a multi-night stand, as long as he ignored the warmth that filled him every time Armin smiled, or laughed, or creased his brow and started explaining some complex scientific thing or other. Which was weird, maybe, but there it was.

So, yeah. He'd expected to talk his way around Armin's professional reserve when it came to work. What he didn't expect was Ryal guarding the lab door, refusing to let him in.

"All I know is, Dr. Savage-Hall sent me out here and told me not to let anyone in except his team. I don't know why, and I don't know what the hell they're doing in there. Except Hannah gets to be in there and I don't, which is stupid." Ryal's round face radiated irritation and boredom. He leaned against the wall, a covered mug of what smelled like extra-strong coffee in one hand, and the other drumming a random rhythm against his thigh. "Sorry, Mo."

"Don't worry about it. I was just curious anyway." It was a big fat lie, of course, not that Ryal needed to know that. A thought struck Mo, and he grinned. "I bet Dr. Poole loves being locked out of his own lab."

"Oh, he's thrilled, all right." Ryal smirked. "He's in Youssouf's office right now complaining."

Mo snickered. He wished he could see Poole's face when Dr. Youssouf told him to suck it up and quit bitching. BathyTech 3's head of operations was nothing if not a woman of her word, and she'd promised Armin and his team the run of BT3's lab facilities for as long as they needed it. She wouldn't go back on that just because Armin wanted to keep everyone else—even Poole—out of the loop and out of the lab.

As much as Mo savored it, though, the delicious schadenfreude wasn't enough to hide the bitter taste of being left out. He couldn't pretend he hadn't hoped whatever was brewing between him and Armin would buy him a ticket inside. The fact that it didn't rankled.

The nagging idea that Armin might not want to hook up again bugged him even more. Which irritated him all by itself. He'd never had a problem being someone's one-night stand before. Or in this case, two-night stand. So far. He wouldn't pretend not to hope for more. Armin had taken up residence in his head and didn't seem inclined to leave. He kept seeing those big black eyes every time he blinked, kept thinking of Armin's smile, hearing him breathe *oh, oh* like a prayer when Mo slid inside him. Did Armin think of him too? The question nagged at him.

Fucking hell. This was why he'd sworn off men a couple of years ago. Unsuccessfully, sure, but still. They always made you suffer one way or another. No-strings sex outside of paying for it was a myth. No matter how hard either partner tried to make the relationship work, there was always this evil merry-go-round of anger, competition, and wounded pride.

Or maybe it was just him. His last serious lover had told him as much before packing up and leaving for good. Said Mo was too damned possessive. Held on so tight a man didn't have room to breathe. Mo had never believed it, but everyone could be wrong sometimes.

Realizing his mind had wandered, Mo forced his face into his best approximation of a smile before Ryal could start asking him personal questions. "Well. Guess I'll go grab some breakfast, then."

"'Kay. See you later." Ryal sipped his coffee, his attention already drifting off someplace else.

As Mo turned away, the lab door slid open. He swiveled to face it again, hoping to catch Armin coming out. Instead Neil Douglas emerged, yawning. He smiled. "Hey, Mo. Can I help you with something?"

Mo swallowed his disappointment. "No, I was just leaving." He thought about asking Dr. Douglas to tell Armin he said *hi*, and decided against it. He wasn't *that* desperate. "All right, then. See you." He walked away, smothering the urge to look back.

In the cafeteria, he swallowed powdered protein made to resemble eggs, and gulped overcooked coffee without tasting it. His mind was in the lab, pondering the thing they'd brought back from Richards Deep and the unusual circumstances surrounding it. Why had the mapping scans read it as a tiny little blank space? Why had Rover gotten vid of it—however poor quality—but not recognized it as a physical object that could be retrieved? It didn't make any damn sense. He'd seen it himself, and it'd looked like a rock.

Okay, not an ordinary rock. Armin's suit had scanned it as blank space, just like the mapping software. Just like Rover. Those scans were anything but ordinary.

Well, now that he thought about it, the rock hadn't looked *entirely* ordinary. Natural stones weren't that perfectly round. And the way Armin's wrist lights had glistened on its smooth, glassy surface during the one brief glimpse Mo had gotten before it went in the box . . . To Mo it had felt like a pretense, as if something inside was trying to disguise its own glow by mimicking a normal reflection.

He imagined the thing breaking open like a geode to reveal a dark, shifting glitter like captured starlight infused with an impossible life.

The mental picture was vivid, disturbing, and seductive for reasons he couldn't name, and it stuck with him as he finished his coffee and made his way to the go-cart bay to start his shift.

Jem raised her eyebrows at him when he wandered in, last of the team to arrive in spite of having gotten up early. "Nice of you to join us, Rees."

Marcell, busy running the last of the checks on the go-cart's hull, glanced up long enough to grin at Mo. "You get busy with that hot piece of doc from upside? I know you tried, so don't bother saying you didn't."

"None of your damn business." Ignoring Marcell's promise to pester it out of him, Mo crossed to the scanner, which he really should've already tested by now. His walking partner Yvonne was running through the series of tests required prior to every shift. He shot her a guilty smile when she looked up at him. "Hey. Sorry I'm late."

"No big deal. It's the first time I know of." She stretched, both hands pressed to her lower back. "Computer. Tests complete. Load mining array scanner into go-cart bay and sync with go-cart computer."

"Understood, Yvonne."

Mo raised his eyebrows when he heard the computer's low, masculine purr. "You been reprogramming again, Yvie?"

"That's what happens when you get here late. You get my dream man on the computer." She smiled, brown eyes shining. "Thought you'd be into it."

Before he could tell her that he liked it a lot, actually, something went *click-click-click* behind him. He whirled, pulse racing, picturing some kind of malfunction with the Mist compressor.

In the split second as he turned toward the machinery, several small black somethings skittered behind the compressor and disappeared.

Bugs? There couldn't be *bugs* down here. It wasn't possible.

He crossed to the compressor without looking away. Nothing moved. He peered around the curve of the machinery. Nothing continued to move. There were no bugs.

Well, of course there weren't. The only bugs on BT3 were the ones Hannah had delivered in a special freeze-dried container every month to feed her pet tarantula, Daisy. The pesticides had kept any stray wild creepy-crawlies out of the pod ever since it was built. No reason to think they'd suddenly made their way down here now.

Right?

"Mo."

He started, and could've kicked himself for it. Damn it, he could *not* be jumpy out on a walk. He faked a calmness he didn't feel and met his fellow miner Rashmi's questioning look. "Hm? Yeah?"

"We're ready to go." Rashmi frowned, putting a deep crease between his brown eyes. "Are you all right?"

Translation: *Are you in any shape to walk? Are the rest of us going to be in danger because you're distracted?*

Mo gave it a moment's thought because walking at seven thousand meters was serious business and he owed it to his team to make sure he could do it safely. "I'm kind of tired," he admitted after a few seconds. "But I'm okay to walk."

Rashmi nodded, his expression solemn. "If you change your mind, say so. There's no shame in stepping out."

"I know. I'll be fine." Mo clapped his friend on the shoulder. "Thanks."

Rashmi walked away with a smile and an assessing look. Mo followed him into the go-cart, doing his best not to stare at the Mist compressor. If this place suddenly had a vermin problem, he didn't want to know. At least not right now. He fucking hated bugs.

Mo couldn't help thinking that the only reason he got through his shift without a hitch was that the process of walking the mineral collector circuits on the vents had become embedded into his brain cells and muscle memory; anything the slightest bit out of the ordinary would have set off his inner alarm bells.

Good thing, because in fifteen years of marine mineral mining, he'd never been so distracted. For the first time, the sea felt unfriendly. Like an enemy. Like something was sidling up to him with sinister intent whenever he put his back to the endless night of the deep. He had no idea what to make of it. He'd always been perfectly comfortable at the bottom of the ocean. This new sense of tension—he didn't like to call it fear—annoyed him, even while it brought out his innate urge to poke at things he probably shouldn't. He felt fidgety with the need to delve into the reasons behind his own nervousness.

Arriving back in the airlock at the end of his shift was a relief. It shouldn't have been. It never had been before. Walking had always calmed him, soothing his spirit regardless of its purpose. Now a strange, formless anxiety had invaded the cold, quiet darkness he loved, and he didn't know what to do. His chest felt hollow, his throat tight and burning.

He stomped out of the go-cart and across the bay to Yvonne, who'd already started the postwalk tests. "Yvie, can you manage without me today? I . . . I don't feel so good."

Her eyebrows shot skyward, but she nodded without asking questions. "Sure. Go lie down. You look like shit."

He managed a feeble laugh. "Thanks. I'll do the testing next shift."

She waved a dismissive hand his way and went back to her work. He turned away, grateful that his partner didn't want to know about other people's business.

Everyone was allowed an off day. This was his.

"Rees. Hold up."

Shit. Scowling, he slowed his pace to let Jem catch up to him. "What do you want?"

"I want to know what the ever lovin' fuck's wrong with you." She scampered in front of him, planted one small hand in the middle of his chest and her feet on the floor, and dug in, forcing him to stop in spite of his superior size. She peered up at him with a familiar, annoying determination. "Nobody's perfect, and everybody's business is their own, as far as I'm concerned. But your mind was a million kilometers away out there. You could've gotten somebody killed, including yourself. So you'd better damn well tell me what's up."

She was right, which only made it harder to swallow. He sighed and raked a hand through his sweat-and-Mist-damp hair. "I don't know, and that's the truth. I just kept feeling like something was watching me. Like it was about to jump on me and eat me or something."

She dropped her hand and frowned up at him. "There's nothing out there but us and some fish."

"I know, okay? I know it doesn't make any sense." He rubbed a hand over his face. He almost told her about the bugs, but didn't. Why mention what was probably just a trick of the light? "Maybe I'm just tired. I dunno."

She watched him for a long, uncomfortable moment while the rest of the team filed past, shooting curious glances at the pair of them. Once they were alone again, Jem reached out and touched his arm. "Look. If you don't feel back to normal by next shift, let me know, okay? I'd rather you take some leave time than endanger the whole team by trying to tough it out." She studied his face with an intensity that made him want to squirm. "Am I understood?"

"Yeah. Understood." He stepped back, uncomfortable with her touch and her penetrating stare. "Thanks, Jem."

"No problem." She gave him an awkward pat. "I'm off to The Beach. You coming?"

Normally, Mo would've hung out at the pod's ironically named bar with the rest of the crew for a while. Tonight? He didn't feel in the mood. "I think I'm just gonna go to bed."

Thankfully, Jem didn't say anything about it. "All right. See you later."

"Yeah. See you."

They parted ways without another word. He aimed his gaze at the bland gray metal beneath his feet and strode out of the bay into the hallway. The sooner he got to his quarters, the better.

He wasn't sure what to think when he found Armin waiting for him, pacing the floor in front of his door and gnawing one thumbnail ragged. Mo stopped and stared. They hadn't known each other long, but he'd already gotten used to calm-Armin. Agitated-Armin was something new and unsettling. "Doc? What's wrong?"

Armin started like he hadn't seen him coming. He blinked and focused on Mo's face, those big dark eyes full of something that made Mo's heart gallop. "Could we go into your quarters?" He stepped forward into Mo's personal space, never breaking eye contact. "I'd like to talk to you in private."

Mo breathed in, caught a heady whiff of desire, and decided to let his dick overrule his brain for now. Sliding his hand into the thick black hair at the nape of Armin's neck, he pulled the man close and planted a hard, claiming kiss on his mouth. "Sex first. Then talk."

Armin's breath ran out in a warm, whiskey-scented rush against his lips. "I hoped you would say that."

The heat in Mo's gut flared into a full-blown fire. Grinning, he led Armin through the door and into his suite.

The sex was every bit as good as before, but Mo could feel the undercurrent of distracted nervousness beneath his partner's passion. As soon as they finished and he caught his breath, he rolled onto his side to face Armin, who was lying on his back with his eyes shut, breathing hard, a faint smile tipping up the corners of his mouth.

Mo reached over and traced a fingertip around the curve of Armin's lower lip. Armin's eyes opened, and Mo smiled at him. "You gonna tell me what's wrong now?"

Armin blinked, a lazy sweep of those long black lashes. "Wrong?"

"I get the feeling you didn't show up here tonight just to talk about the weather." He smoothed his thumb over the worried crease already digging itself between Armin's eyes again. "What's wrong, Armin?"

"Maybe nothing." Armin tucked an arm beneath his head and stared at the ceiling. "I probably shouldn't tell you this, but . . . Well. The rock we found . . ."

Mo prodded when he failed to continue. "What about it?"

"I've seen it before. *We* have. Mandala, Carlo, Neil, and I. We've seen it—or something that looks like it—before."

The implications of that tensed Mo's body with intrigue and excitement. "What do you mean, you've seen it before? I keep up with the journals. I haven't read about anything like this."

"It hasn't been written up. We have nothing to write about, really." Armin rolled onto his side and propped his head up on one hand, peering at him with solemn black eyes. "We got a brief look at an object that looked very much like this one on a poor-quality video from another research facility. That's the only information we have, and all we're able to get. I wish I could tell you more, but there's really nothing to tell."

Mo's sensible side told him to leave well enough alone. Armin had already told him more than he'd expected. He should keep quiet and be grateful. Unsurprisingly, the lifelong inquisitiveness that had driven him to turn over rocks, break into condemned buildings, and explore new places—that had, in fact, led him to the deepest ocean— stomped his sensible side flat and prodded him to keep digging.

He stroked his fingertips along the line of Armin's neck idly, picking at Armin's words in his head. "You're thinking it's not a coincidence, huh? The same sort of rock in two places."

"I don't see how it *can* be." Armin lifted his shoulder in a half shrug. "But who knows? The video clip we saw was extremely bad quality. It's possible they aren't the same at all."

"Is there anything I can do to help you figure it out? Because I will, if I can." Partly to satisfy his own curiosity, of course, but also because he hated seeing that torn, uncertain look on Armin's face. If he could help fix it, he would.

Armin smiled, his eyes full of a soft light that made Mo feel hot and tight inside. "I believe you would, if there was anything you could do. But there isn't." He touched Mo's cheek, a bare brush of his fingertips. "I wanted to tell you, that's all. Talking about it with you makes me feel lighter. Helps me work it all out in my head. And I believe I can trust you to keep what I say to yourself."

Mo's heart thumped hard against his sternum. "Of course you can trust me." He scooted closer, threaded a hand into Armin's hair and kissed him, soft and slow. "Stay with me tonight?"

Armin answered by resting his head on Mo's chest and tucking his arm around Mo's middle. Mo shut his eyes and let the rise and fall of Armin's ribs beneath his hand soothe him to sleep.

When Mo woke who knew how many hours later, he felt the presence before seeing it. Frozen, afraid and excited, his lover sleeping beside him, he stared wide-eyed into the soft, sweet darkness. He counted twelve heartbeats whooshing in his ears. Then he saw it—a denser blackness slithering through the dark, huge and sinuous, unseen hide rasping impossible whispers against the air as if the room's atmosphere had turned solid.

Terror and anticipation bubbled up to clog Mo's throat. He couldn't speak, or scream, or fucking *breathe*, could only watch as the thing rose to the ceiling, expanded to the walls, pushed into the corners to swallow up the furniture and extinguish the tiny red light indicating the locked door. The faint blur of Armin's foot vanished into the tarry sludge.

The sight broke Mo's paralysis. He sat up, unsure if he wanted to stop the thing or find out what it was.

Only it wasn't there anymore.

Confused, relieved, and a little bit disappointed, he turned to Armin.

Eyes gone a deep, bottomless black from lid to lid stared back at him. Armin grinned wide, showing gleaming rows of silver needle teeth, and Mo screamed.

CHAPTER 3

The scream yanked Armin from a dream of seductive horror into disorienting darkness. An amorphous shape loomed beside him. For one heart-stopping second, he thought the already half-forgotten visions from his nightmare had followed him to the waking world. Then Mo's familiar voice called up the lights, and the universe snapped into its proper alignment.

One look at the half-panicked, half-yearning gleam in Mo's eyes drove the last of the dream shadows from Armin's mind. He sat up and laid a hand on Mo's arm. His skin was hot and damp with sweat. "Mo? What's wrong?"

Mo searched his face, as if afraid of what he might see, then shook his head. "Nothing. Just a . . . a weird dream." He rubbed both hands over his face. "Christ. Sorry I woke you."

"It's all right." Armin tucked his legs beneath him and caressed Mo's tight shoulders. "Would it help if you told me about it?"

Mo barked out a laugh. "I don't think so. Thanks anyway."

For reasons Armin couldn't pinpoint, Mo's reaction felt like more than a desire to not relive a nightmare. He decided not to push the issue. After all, he had no real reason to doubt Mo, and no right to demand explanations.

He lay back again when Mo did and settled into his embrace. He said nothing when Mo dimmed the lights instead of turning them off. He understood the need to keep the sinister darkness at bay.

When Armin arrived at the lab the next morning, Hannah and Mandala were in the middle of a heated argument.

"I know what I saw." Hannah's cheeks were pink and her stance tense with indignation. "If you don't trust me on a microscanner, maybe you ought to bring down someone from upside."

Mandala sighed, as if they'd already gone through this multiple times. "It isn't that I don't trust you. But anyone can make a mistake. All I'm saying is that you made a mistake."

"So, anyone but *you* can make a mistake. I see."

"That is *not* what I said." Mandala rubbed her forehead. "I do wish you'd be reasonable."

Hannah opened her mouth. Armin cut her off before she could say anything else. "Would one of you care to tell me what this is about?"

"There are microbes in the rock." Hannah's expression was fierce with excitement. "Bacteria. *Live* bacteria."

"There are not," Mandala said before he could recover from his shock sufficiently to answer. "Where do you suppose bacteria would have found nutrients they could use at seven thousand plus meters underwater when that rock was nowhere near a vent or any other source of energy?"

She was right, of course—she was one of the world's leading microbiologists, which was one reason she was here—but he had to ask. "Did you check to be sure?"

Mandala shot him a withering look. "Of course I checked. I found no microbes of any sort, living or dead, bacteria or otherwise. Neil gave it a look too, as a double check." She gestured toward Neil, who was fiddling with one of the microscanners. "He also found nothing."

"Well, that's it, then." Armin studied Hannah's increasingly red face and confused, angry eyes with concern. "Mandala's right, Hannah. Anyone can be mistaken about something like this. We all have been at one time or another. It's certainly nothing to be ashamed of."

She scowled, her usually sweet expression turning thunderous. "Fine. I have other duties I can be taking care of, if that's all right with you, Doctor?"

Armin studied Hannah's tight mouth, fiercely furrowed brow, and the gaze burning a hole through the lab floor. He hadn't known her for long, but he'd already learned enough to know that this—the argument, the childish reaction to being wrong, all of it—was utterly unlike her. Unease pooled in his belly.

He nodded, pretending a nonchalance he didn't feel. "Of course. I don't want to keep you from any of your other duties. And you must know that no one here on BT3 is in any way substandard."

Hannah ignored him and stalked out the door in a near-visible cloud of fury.

Neil watched her go with a frown. "Why's she so upset? What did we do?"

"Obviously she was embarrassed about being wrong, that's all. She'll be fine." Mandala crossed the lab to her scanner station and settled on her rolling stool.

The lab door slid open, and Carlo hurried in. "Sorry I'm late. I overslept."

Everyone turned to stare at him. Armin had known the man for nineteen years, and had never once known him to be late.

Naturally, it was Neil who broke the uncomfortable silence with a laugh. "Hell, Carlo, I was starting to think you were a robot or something. Good to know you're as human as the rest of us." He clapped Carlo on the shoulder, either unaware of Carlo's glare or ignoring it. "You missed the excitement. Hannah thought she saw bacteria on the scans of the rock, but none of the rest of us saw anything, and she got all upset and stomped out when Armin told her she must've made a mistake."

Carlo stroked his chin. "Are you sure she *did* make a mistake?"

Mandala answered without looking up from her workstation. "Yes. Neil and I both checked behind her to be certain. We found nothing."

"Hm." His features set in a thoughtful frown, Carlo crossed to the vault holding the object they'd brought in the day before. He pressed a palm flat on the door, as if he could feel the force of the thing through the metal. "I wonder . . ."

The dreamy lilt to Carlo's voice plucked the alarm threads in Armin's mind. He cast a glance around the lab. Neil had gone back to his work, typing with his index fingers as he tended to do. Mandala was massaging her temple and fiddling with the flat-screen controls. Ashlyn was absorbed in studying the electromagnetic waveforms from the object on her workstation in the corner.

Armin suppressed a sigh. He stared at the holo of the rock inside the vault, letting the image jump and blur as his mind wandered up through the endless black of the ocean above—back to the *Peregrine* where he'd first seen the strange sonar signature and realized what it could mean, further back to the Antarctic Ocean and the events that still haunted him. Maybe the past few weeks had made him paranoid. He thought that was understandable, all things considered, but he needed to get a grip on it if he wanted this mission to succeed.

Giving himself a mental shake, he blinked and turned to Carlo, just in time to watch the other man press his thumb to the security panel and open the vault.

Armin frowned. "Carlo, what are you doing?"

"Wait. But I heard . . ." Carlo cast a puzzled look at the rest of the group, who had all abandoned their stations in favor of eyeing him with caution. "I thought I heard a voice. From inside the vault."

"Who did you think was in there?" Ashlyn's voice was calm and without inflection, her expression blank, but Carlo's face flushed red anyway.

He glowered at her, his tone becoming aggressive. "I know it wasn't the rock, all right? It's just a *rock*."

She raised her hands. "I never implied that you thought otherwise, Doctor."

"Not in words, *Doctor*, but I think we all got your meaning." Carlo cast her one more vicious glare before turning to Armin with uncertainty stamped all over his features. "I thought someone had gotten stuck in there somehow. I never would've opened the vault otherwise. We agreed."

They had, mostly because no one was certain of the object's exact nature. That being the case, it seemed prudent to limit their physical contact with it. Armin peered into his friend's troubled eyes. Carlo hearing voices from the vault was worrisome. Even more worrisome, however, was the transparent fact that he wasn't sure of his own experience—whether he'd truly heard it or not, where it had come from, why it had happened. Carlo was a practical, grounded man. It was a job requirement for being a scientist. If he believed for a moment that he'd actually heard voices from the vault, even after seeing it was empty, then he couldn't be here working on this project.

Edging around the spot where Carlo still stood as if his feet had sprouted roots, Armin shut the vault and keyed in the security code.

"Carlo, why don't you go back to your quarters and lie down? Take the rest of the day off. Tomorrow as well, if you need to."

Carlo spun and pinned Armin with a wild, wide-eyed stare. "Why?"

Armin didn't want to say it. Not in front of everyone else, even though they were all scientists and they had to know that Carlo couldn't work if he was hearing things. He shook his head. "Please, Carlo."

For a moment, he didn't think Carlo would do it. He breathed in. Out. Steeled himself for what would likely be an ugly confrontation.

Finally, Carlo let out a deep sigh and scrubbed both hands over his face. "You're right. I'm feeling a bit under the weather." He dropped his hands and peered at the floor as if he expected it to do something interesting. "I might join you all for dinner later."

"Please do. I'd like to know you're all right." Armin touched Carlo's hand. His skin felt cold.

Carlo flashed a faint smile, turned, and walked out the door. The silence echoed in his wake.

"Well. Losing two in ten minutes." Mandala arched one neatly groomed eyebrow. "I must say, we're off to an excellent start."

Neil snorted. Ashlyn remained silent. Armin pressed his fingertips to his right temple, where a thin pain had begun to throb. "Let's get back to work. I can handle Carlo's workload for today."

No one argued with him, thank God. He needed some space and quiet to think. To try to figure out what in the seven hells was going on, and what to do about it.

Mo didn't see any bugs in the go-cart bay airlock when he arrived for his shift. Instead, the Mist compressor grew a crown of long, whipping antennae for the fraction of a second before he could focus on it.

He shut his eyes tight and counted to five before opening them again. The compressor sat there as plain and free of abnormal appendages as it had always been.

Well, of course it did. Mining equipment didn't suddenly sprout insect parts. He'd imagined it, just like he'd imagined the bugs he thought he'd seen yesterday. He blamed lack of sleep. If he'd gotten eight hours of shut-eye in the last couple of nights put together, he'd eat his fucking walker, helmet and all. Which was weird and annoying, because great sex usually put him in an impenetrable O-coma for at least six hours. And just to make it all perfect, his scant sleep had been broken up by freaky-ass dreams that planted disturbing images in the back corners of his mind where he couldn't quite see them.

Stupid nightmares. He forced a smile for Yvonne and Rashmi, who had their heads together as they murmured over the scanner. Yvonne frowned. Rashmi eyed him with concern stamped all over his face.

Mo pressed his lips together to keep his irritation from spilling out. They were his coworkers and friends. If the situation were reversed, he would have been worried about them, too.

Jem stuck her head out the open door of the go-cart. "Rees! You gonna stand there all day with your thumb up your ass, or you coming along with the rest of us?"

He took a look at Jem's sour expression and sighed. So it was gonna be one of *those* days. "Keep your pants on, Big Mama. I'm coming."

"Glory hallelujah." She ducked back inside.

He rolled his eyes and turned to uncouple the cart from the Mist compressor.

Something twisted at the edge of his vision. Black, dense, wriggling like a tongue.

He spun, his pulse knotted in his throat. The thing was gone.

Because it was never there, said the sensible part of his brain. But his heart still raced, and his mouth was drier than the desert where he'd been born.

Dom slapped his shoulder, making him jump. "You done there, brother?"

"Almost." Mo finished the uncoupling process, thumbed the control panel, and watched the hose shrivel and reel itself into the wall. "Okay. All set."

He followed Dom into the cart. Yvonne and Rashmi came behind with the scanner.

As the go-cart's computer shut the hatch behind them, the dark shape vibrated in the shrinking space between the two metal slabs.

He fought the instinct to lunge for the porthole and peer out the scratched GlasSteel. He stopped himself, not because he was afraid he wouldn't see anything but because he feared he *would*.

Shaking off the crawling sensation as best he could, he put his back to the hatch and the porthole and strode into the cab. He had work to do.

The thing in the tail of his eye followed him as he and Yvonne checked the mineral collection arrays that squatted around each vent like huge metal spiders. It squirmed and fluttered on the fringe of his sight, beyond the reach of his helmet light or the flood lamp attached to the scanner.

By the time he and Yvonne got to the Pipes—the last vent, named for its impressive mineral formations—Mo was wound as tight as an overtuned guitar string by the constant movement that vanished whenever he tried to look at it. The shape whipped an amorphous pseudopod almost within range of his vision, and he stumbled. "Fucking *shit*."

Yvonne peered at him across the rounded bulk of the scanner, her face all planes and angles in the glow of her helmet light. "Okay there, Mo?"

"Yeah. Just tripped, that's all."

She cast him a narrow-eyed, *sure you did* look. Mo ignored her and concentrated his full attention on the scanner readout. She could be suspicious of his uncharacteristic clumsiness all she wanted. No way was he telling her he was seeing things. Later, after they were safely back in the pod, maybe he'd talk to Jem. Or at least mention it to Armin. Right now, he was keeping it to himself.

Hell, maybe he ought to get his eyes checked. The damn wiggly thing had stuck with him all day. Hallucinations didn't do that. Did they?

His com crackled, and Marcell's voice shouted in his ear, high and breathless with excitement. "Mermaid fish! 'Bout five meters east-northeast of the Pipes. Cams, folks, let's go!"

All the miners had standing orders from the biologists to drop everything and start filming if they spotted a mermaid. No getting close, no interacting. Just video. It was the one thing the two factions never argued about. Everybody on BT3 wanted to be the one to get vid of the rare, elusive creatures.

Mo lifted his head and swiveled as fast as possible in the walker, the squiggling shape in his eye forgotten for the moment in a rush of excitement. "Walker One. Camera on standby."

"Acknowledged, Mo," said the walker's computer. "I will record on your mark."

"Thanks." Answering the computer had become a habit over the years, but it still didn't feel quite natural. That's what happened when you spent your teen years cobbling together communications equipment from parts older than your great-grandparents. In the postblackout years, they'd been lucky the computers had worked. Forget talking back.

"Anything for you, *Mo*."

The utterly unexpected rasp of Armin's low, rough whisper coming from the walker's computer startled Mo badly. He tried to turn, got his feet tangled together, lost his balance, and fell sideways. He hit the ooze on the seabed harder than he would've expected with the water to slow him down. His teeth dug into the inside of his cheek.

Yvonne called over the com, asking him if he was all right. Marcell, predictably, snickered from his spot at com central in the go-cart. Mo let it all float through his consciousness and out again without paying much attention—because the mermaid fish was right there, not five meters from his face, hovering like a ghost in the margins of the light.

He froze, his gaze locked onto the creature's luminous greenish-white eyes. Christ, it was something else, weirdly beautiful with its long, translucent, fingerlike fins and the small, flat scales that seemed to absorb the light. Its body was sleek as a shark's, grayish-white, at least two meters long, with a short dorsal fin and a flat tail like a whale's. Its gill slits opened and closed, opened and closed, pumping water through its respiratory system.

A blue-black spark shone deep in the mermaid's unblinking eyes. It stared directly at Mo as if it could beam its strange, fishy thoughts straight into his brain with the force of its gaze. His stomach knotted in a churning chaos of nerves and awe.

"Walker One." He kept his voice low, though he had no idea whether a mermaid could pick up voices from inside a walker, or what they'd do with it if they *could* hear it. No point in taking chances. "Outside camera, record."

"Recording, Mo."

This time, he didn't answer. Instead he held as still as he could, hardly daring to blink in case the mermaid decided to swim away in the fraction of a second his eyes were closed. This encounter was bound to be brief, and he didn't want to miss any of it.

His heart thudded seven, eight, nine hard, rapid beats while he and the rare animal stared at one another. Then the wide, lipless mouth opened, revealing rows of too-long, pointed metal teeth identical to Armin's from Mo's nightmare.

A shocked *oh* escaped Mo's throat before he could stop himself. His arm jerked, raising a plume of silt. The mermaid flipped its tail and glided off into the darkness.

"Fucking shit." Mo shut his eyes and told himself to calm down. *Fuck.* "Walker One. Camera, stop recording."

"Recording halted, Mo."

He breathed in and out, steady breaths, willing his heartbeat to slow. Now that the whole thing was over, a wave of pure giddy joy washed over him. He'd just been face-to-face with probably the rarest animal on the planet. For the *second* time in his life, and this encounter was so much closer than the last. How many people could say that? He laughed out loud.

"Mo?" Yvonne's boots approached as she spoke. "What's going on? Do you need to go to sick bay?"

"No. I'm fine." Mo clambered to his feet, grinning. "It's not every day we see a mermaid fish, you know. It's damn exciting." He kept the part about the nightmare teeth to himself. She already thought he got too wound up about "science shit" as she put it, when he ought to be concentrating on his job. If he told her about the fucking teeth, she'd drag him to Dr. Palto herself.

She grinned back at him, because *everybody* got excited about seeing mermaids. "Well. At least we both got some footage. Poole'll jizz his shorts."

The whole team let out a collective groan over the com network. "Didn't need that visual, Yvie," Dom growled from where he and Rashmi were walking the vents to the south.

Jem broke in for the first time in the walk. "Finish it up, guys, and let's get home. I got a wicked fucking headache."

Grumbles and scattered laughter came over the coms before everyone settled into tying up the loose ends of the shift's work. Mo was glad. He didn't feel like telling anyone what he thought he'd seen.

He should've known that wasn't going to wash with Jem.

Back in the BathyTech airlock after the postwalk tests were run, Jem stopped him with a hand on his arm before he could get away. He gave her his best blank face. "What's up?"

"You're taking the next shift off."

Damn it. "I don't need—"

"Don't argue with me, Rees, I'm not in the mood." Jem rubbed one temple. Her features were tight, the corners of her mouth downturned. "You're smart enough to know you can't be out here if your head's not right, and I've worked with you long enough to know when it's not."

Mo sighed, because she was right. "Fine."

"If I don't think you're back to normal when you come back, I'm taking you off duty for longer." Jem studied Mo's face like she was trying to see inside his brain. "I'm not trying to punish you, Mo. I hope you know that."

"Yeah, I know." Mo forced a smile. "I'll see you in a couple of days, then."

"Yeah. See you." She turned and went to the wall terminal to record her shift report.

Mo headed out of the go-cart bay and into the hallway, turning over the events of the past few hours in his mind. He wondered if he ought to talk to Armin. The encounter with the mermaid fish had rattled him, in spite of the thrill of it all, and he knew Armin would listen without judging.

On the other hand, mermaids *did* have impressive teeth, like lots of the fish that lived at depth. Or at least, the one he'd seen in the Mariana Trench had. He assumed they all did. The angle of the light had probably made this one's teeth look unusually long and given them a metallic sheen. The human tendency to connect one thing to another had supplied the mental link to the image from his dream. As for the strange black squiggle . . .

He tried to look without looking. It was gone.

Maybe he really should use his unexpected time off to get his eyes checked.

He considered whether to go to The Beach or head to his quarters. The idea of being alone right now made him feel cold inside, so he headed for the bar instead.

His usual shortcut took him past sick bay. As he passed, the door slid open and Hannah walked right into him.

Her features twisted in anger for a second, then smoothed out again. "Oh. Hi, Mo. Sorry, I wasn't looking where I was going."

"No problem." He took in her abnormally pasty complexion and the sheen of perspiration on her upper lip—not to mention the fact that she'd just come out of sick bay—and touched her elbow, worried. "You okay? You need me to help you back to your quarters?"

"Naw, I'm fine. My eyes have been bothering me a little, is all." She gave him a smile several watts dimmer than her usual. "I think some of the lab equipment's off-kilter a little. But hey, the equipment's an upside problem now." She grasped Mo's hand and gave it a quick squeeze, then let go. "See you later, Mo."

"Okay."

He watched her go with a frown, uneasy. People had eye problems sometimes. It didn't mean anything. Not even when it happened at the same time as other people's hallucinations.

Nodding to himself as if that would help make it true, he resumed his trip to the bar. Hopefully the noise and bustle of all those people would help loosen the knot of apprehension winding tight in his stomach.

By the end of their second day in the lab, the only thing Armin felt certain of when it came to the object from Richards Deep was that it was utterly unlike anything he'd studied in all his years as a scientist. It stubbornly refused to register properly on any of the equipment, behaving more like some sort of enormous subatomic particle than a rock roughly the size of a shot put.

He did his best to keep his elation to himself, even though every new finding added another confirmation to the theories that had made him a pariah in some scientific circles and a cult hero in others. It didn't matter how many times he'd proven himself in equations, or in a lab setting. This find would prove him right in a real-world setting, and that was everything.

Mandala led the way out of the lab as she, Armin, Ashlyn, and Neil finally left after twelve hours with very little to show for it. "It's as though the object isn't even solid. Only we *know* it is, because you and Carlo have both handled it, Armin. And, yes, I know you predicted this. That doesn't help us figure out what to actually *do* with it." Sighing, she pressed the heels of her hands to her eyes. "I'm going to lie down. My head is killing me."

Armin laid a hand on Mandala's shoulder. "Are you all right? Would you like for me to bring you some dinner?"

"No, that's fine. I'm not hungry at the moment. Perhaps I'll get something later on." She lowered her hands and patted his cheek. "It's kind of you to offer, though. Thank you."

"Well, I'm starved. I'm headed for the cafeteria." Neil raised his eyebrows at Armin and Ashlyn. "What about you guys?"

Ashlyn nodded. "Me too."

Armin's stomach growled. As usual, he hadn't even thought of food while working. "I could definitely eat."

"I'll see you all in the morning, then." Mandala gave them a wan smile, then headed down the hall toward her quarters.

The main dinner rush in the cafeteria seemed to be over, but several people still sat singly or in small groups around the room, talking and eating. There was no line at the self-service food bar. Armin and his team loaded their trays, found a spot in the corner, and dug in.

The three of them ate in a heavy silence. Armin knew his fellow scientists must be mentally sifting through the day's findings and trying to slot them into a working model of the universe. He couldn't help feeling a bit ahead of the curve, in spite of the difficulties inherent in working with such an unusual find. Mandala was right—the fact that he'd predicted the existence of an object like this one did not make the reality of studying it any easier.

"Wow, this is a real happy party, huh?"

Startled, Armin blinked himself out of his thoughts and lifted his gaze from the remaining peas he'd been pushing around his plate to the man standing on the other side of the table grinning at him. "Hello, Mo. We just got finished in the lab. I suppose our minds are still on the work."

Mo let out a loud *pfft*, which made Neil snicker. Mo ignored him. "You science types're always working. You ought to let your hair down once in a while."

Ashlyn set her fork down on her empty plate and watched Mo with obvious amusement. "Mr. Rees, have you been drinking?"

"Maybe a few." Mo favored her with a wink and a rakish smile that made Armin feel hot inside. "Jem made me take next shift off, so why the hell not, right?"

"Amen, brother." Neil leaned back in his plastic chair with a deep sigh. "I could go for a beer myself, if I wasn't so tired. Maybe another night."

"Doc, you let me know when you want to go drinking, and I'll take you to The Beach for that beer." Mo gave Neil a friendly slap on the back. "Armin, you think we could talk for a minute?"

Instinct—plus the way Mo fidgeted—told Armin that the request was related somehow to Jemima ordering Mo to take tomorrow off. He hid his sudden vague anxiety behind a casual smile. "Of course. Would you like to sit down?"

Mo's gaze cut left, then right. Quick and nervous. "Um. Actually, if we could talk in private, that would be great." He widened his eyes at Ashlyn and Neil. "No offense to you guys."

"None taken." Ashlyn pushed back her chair, stood, and picked up her tray, still half-smiling as though she found Mo entertaining. "I think I'm going to go back to my room and read for a while. I'll see you guys tomorrow."

"Wait up, I'll walk with you." Neil jumped up, grabbed his own tray, and hurried after her.

Mo watched them for a moment, then shook his head, blinked, and focused on Armin's face with an intensity that bordered on frightening. "Look, this might seem kind of weird, but . . ." He cast a sharp, hunted glance over his shoulder, as if he'd heard someone sneaking up on him. His pupils were wide and black, his body tense. "I know a place we can talk where no one'll overhear us. Would that be okay? I don't . . ." He chewed his thumbnail, something Armin hadn't seen him do before. "I don't feel comfortable talking here."

What was there to say? Armin stood. "Of course. Let's go."

He took his tray to the recycler, then followed Mo out of the cafeteria and down the hallway to a juncture he'd noticed before, but never paid much attention to. Mo turned left off the main corridor down the narrower side passage. It was deserted. They walked along for a few minutes, past closed doors and secondary halls with lights dimmed for the "night" shift.

He was beginning to wonder just where they were going when Mo finally pushed open a doorway on the right, marked simply: *Aquarium.* The obvious question died on his lips when he trailed Mo inside and saw what BathyTech 3's idea of an aquarium was.

"My God." Armin paced to the center of the circular room, staring in awe at the GlasSteel dome that arched over the whole space. A strip of low lights running around the baseboard provided the only illumination, bathing the floor in a soft golden glow and leaving the endless blackness of the deep as the room's focus. A jellyfish drifted past overhead like a lost star, and Armin laughed. "This is incredible. Why did I not know about it before now?"

"I guess we've both been a little busy." Mo tilted his head back and peered upward with a smile full of memories. "Not many people come here just to hang out, I guess. Poole's biology staff use it to study the wildlife, of course. Most of the other miners aren't really interested after the novelty wears off. But it's my favorite spot in the pod." His gaze dropped to meet Armin's. "You never know what you'll see out there."

Something haunted had crept into Mo's eyes, and Armin knew they'd moved beyond talking about the weird, wonderful creatures one normally encountered in the deep ocean trenches.

He stepped close, reached up, and ran his fingertips along the line of Mo's jaw. "What have *you* seen?"

For several heartbeats, Mo didn't answer. Armin stayed silent and watched the struggle over what to say and not say play out across his features.

Finally, Mo shook his head and turned away to face the ocean, shoulders tight and arms crossed. "What's happening down here, Armin?"

An invisible hand wrapped around Armin's ribs and squeezed. "What do you mean?"

Mo stepped closer. The aquarium's shadows cast an artificial grimness over his features. "I know it's none of my business. But I really want to know what you've found out about that rock."

Armin studied Mo's carefully expressionless face. Determination glittered in his eyes, shot through with a bright thread of fear.

Worried now, he laid a hand on Mo's arm. "Mo, has something happened?"

"No. Well . . ." Mo turned his head to stare out the transparent wall at the endless ocean beyond. "No, not exactly. We saw a mermaid fish today. It was pretty cool, but . . ." He trailed off again, forehead furrowed. "This one looked different."

The way he spoke, quiet and puzzled, made the back of Armin's neck prickle with unease. "Different how?"

"Like its teeth were too long, or something." Mo let out a short laugh. "I don't know. It's stupid. Yvie—my walking partner—says my imagination runs away with me sometimes. I probably imagined it."

His frown said he didn't really believe that. Armin had no idea where this new development fit into the picture, or if it did at all. But he knew it made him worry about Mo more, not less.

He turned Mo to face him and slid both arms around his waist. Mo tensed, but didn't pull away. Instead, he touched Armin's face with his fingertips, a gentle caress that made Armin shake inside.

"We still don't know precisely what we're dealing with." Armin hated the faint tremor in his voice, but he couldn't stop it. Not when Mo kept touching him like that, like he was something rare and precious. "So far the tests we've run have confirmed my theories, but that hasn't gotten us any further in how to define this thing."

Mo's gaze searched his. "This is going to sound really strange. But humor me. Do you think it can cause any . . . you know, problems?"

Armin shook his head, confused. "What sort of problems?"

Mo studied him in silence for several long seconds. The whole time, his fingers mapped the contours of Armin's face. The touch was profoundly intimate, and Armin thought he ought to have found it disturbing. Instead, it soothed him. Eased away some of the apprehension that had been gathering like a storm inside him lately. He spread his palms flat on Mo's back, the better to feel his warmth and the rise and fall of his ribs with his breathing.

"I've seen things," Mo admitted finally. "Nothing spectacular. I thought I saw bugs in the go-cart bay the other day. And today I thought I saw antennae on the mining array, then I kept seeing this squiggly thing at the corner of my eye all day long." He quirked a wry smile at Armin. "Probably I just need to get my eyes checked. I'm coming up on the big four-oh soon. Maybe that perfect vision I used to have is going away."

"I see no reason to believe the object would cause hallucinations, or any other physical problems." Armin pulled Mo's body flush against his, mapping the contours of his muscles through his shirt. "You should definitely get your eyes checked."

"I'll do that." Mo buried his fingers in Armin's hair, then bent and kissed him, light and quick. "And if there's nothing wrong with my eyes?"

The disquiet that followed Armin everywhere now gave his insides a sharp tug. Maybe what Mo had seen meant nothing, even if his vision tested normal.

"Let's cross that bridge when we come to it." Armin stole a kiss of his own, then another. It would be so easy to lose track of time and simply stay here all day and all night, kissing Mo. But he couldn't. He made himself pull back. "Well. I should get back to the lab. I have a few odds and ends I'd like to wrap up before I call it a night."

"Okay." Mo took both Armin's hands in his and squeezed. His dark eyes peered deep into Armin's. "My place or yours tonight? Because I can't not have you."

Oh. Armin's knees wobbled. "I'll come to your room. I'm not sure what time I'll be done in the lab."

"Cool. I'll be waiting for you, Doc." Mo dropped his hands and strode away with a wicked smile.

Armin stood there, cheeks hot and heart hammering, until his legs regained the strength to walk, then he left the aquarium. Just one more look at the strange rock, and he could go to Mo's bed without the mental image of the thing beating against the insides of his eyelids.

The next morning, with nothing but time on his hands, Mo decided to see what he could find out from Ryal about the work going on in the lab. Unfortunately, that meant playing Ryal's favorite game: air hockey.

Mo sucked at air hockey.

Ryal sent the plastic disk flying across the table, straight past Mo's defense and into the goal slot. He threw both arms in the air and let out a victory whoop that had heads all over the rec room turning toward him. "Oh, *hell* yeah! Ryal the Merciless is once more victorious!"

Mo had to laugh, in spite of having just lost his ninth game in a row. "Yeah, fine. It's not *that* big a deal."

"It is when you don't have anything else to do. But hey, at least I don't have to stand outside the lab pretending to be a guard today." Still grinning ear to ear, Ryal skirted the table and slapped Mo on the shoulder. "Come on, I'll buy you a drink."

Mo followed the younger man to the bar. He usually didn't drink this early in the day, but Ryal with a few beers in him meant one chatty lab assistant. Mo wasn't above taking advantage of that. Even though Ryal hadn't actually been in the lab since Armin and his team arrived, he was pretty tight with Hannah—and she *had* been in the lab, for a short time anyway. With any luck, Hannah had told Ryal at least some of what was happening with the mysterious rock from Richards Deep, and a little alcoholic brain lube would encourage him to pass that information on to Mo. Not ideal, but at this point it looked like the only way Mo was going to learn anything beyond what little Armin had told him. Especially when that little bit turned out to be more disturbing than enlightening.

He *had* to figure out what was happening. He had to. That morning's visit to the pod's medical bay would've convinced him pretty damn quick that something extremely out of the ordinary was going on, even if the fear on Armin's face last night hadn't already. Dr. Palto said there wasn't a thing wrong with Mo's eyes, he showed no signs of physical or mental stress outside of what you'd expect in this job, and there wasn't any medical reason to send him back upside. Of course, he hadn't told Palto about the nightmares or the lack of sleep, but he hadn't seen any good reason to mention it. This wasn't the first time he'd had trouble sleeping, and he'd suffered occasional bouts of nightmares ever since the blackout. That was on his BathyTech psych profile. They'd never considered it a problem before, so why would they now? It was "known and stable."

The way Mo saw it, if there wasn't anything wrong with *him*, something must be wrong with the *world*. Something that made bugs and antennae and black shapes appear where they had no business being.

Not to mention Armin's voice coming from the walker's computer. Best not to think too much about that. And it had all started after they'd recovered that rock. To Mo's mind, that meant the two things must be related one way or another.

Ryal leaned both elbows on the long plastic slab serving as a bar. "Hey, Dara. Two beers, please."

"Comin' up." The bartender pulled two beer pouches out of the cooler, tore them open one at a time, and set them on the bar. "Enjoy, gents."

"Thanks." Ryal gave Dara a bright smile, took one beer, and slid the other to Mo, then pushed away from the bar. "Let's get a Suicide Booth, where it's private."

He trailed Ryal to one of the booths along the outer hull, where the genius who'd designed this rig had decided to install portholes so staff could look outside, the idea being to boost morale. Most people avoided the booths, with their less than cheery view of the seabed, the occasional monster-movie fish, and the endless pitch-black ocean. Some smartass had dubbed them the Suicide Booths, and the name had stuck.

Mo grinned as the two of them slid into the last booth on the end, as far from the rest of the room as it was possible to get. "Wow, this really is private. Are you trying to get in my pants or something?"

"Listen, if I ever give up on the ladies, you're *still* not gonna be my type." Ryal leaned back against the bloodred faux leather, studying him through narrowed eyelids. "I know you, Rees. I know what it means when you get that look in your eyes." He put his beer bottle to his lips and drank, never taking his gaze from Mo. "Information'll cost you, you know."

Mo sighed. Damn that boy. "Do you actually *have* any?"

Ryal shrugged. "Some. I don't know if any of it'll make sense to you. It sure as hell doesn't to me."

He considered. Maybe what Ryal knew was worthwhile and maybe it wasn't, but there was only one way to find out. He drank deeply from his beer, set the bottle on the table, and fixed his gaze on Ryal's face. "All right. What do you want?"

The self-satisfied, teasing mask fell from Ryal's features. He leaned over the table, deadly serious now. "I want to know what *you* know."

Sheer surprise left Mo floundering for a moment. "What? That's it?" He'd expected money, or at least merchandise. Everybody knew Ryal loved the finer things in life.

"Yes." With a quick, sidelong glance toward the closest group of people—at least three and a half meters away—Ryal lowered his voice to a murmur, barely audible over the latest orchestral rap blasting from the sound system. "Look. Something's been off with Hannah ever since she came back from that walk to the Deep the other day. She swears she's fine, but she's not. Something happened that she's not telling me, and I want to know what it is."

Unease prickled the skin along Mo's arms. He shook his head, puzzled. "Hannah was in the second go-cart with Dr. Douglas. She didn't walk with us. If something happened in the go-cart, nobody told me about it." He made a mental note to ask Hannah later. He'd been in charge on that walk. Any incidents, no matter how seemingly minor, should've damn well been reported to him.

"She said Dr. Libra brought the thing you found on board their go-cart in a box. She said she saw it later in the lab, and it was just a rock." Ryal turned his beer bottle in circles on the table. His gaze held Mo's. "Is it really? Because everything started with that so-called rock."

Exactly, Mo thought. Because he couldn't be sure, though, he said, "I don't know."

"But you suspect." Ryal spun his beer bottle again, and again, and again. His gaze never wavered from Mo's face.

Mo hitched up one shoulder in a so-so gesture. "Maybe. I'm not sure enough of anything at this point to commit myself. Which is one reason I wanted to talk to you." He took a swallow of beer. "This would've been easier if you'd just gotten drunk and talkative like you were supposed to."

Ryal laughed. "Sorry to screw up your plans. But I kind of think this is better. For both of us." Lifting his bottle, he pointed it at Mo. "Admit it, you're likely to learn a whole lot more with me as a partner than you would've if you'd tried to be all sneaky about it. You suck at being sneaky."

Mo snorted. "Well, when you're right, you're right." He glanced out the porthole. Something with far too many appendages jetted out of the range of the pod's lights before he could get a good look at it. Some kind of squid, surely. Just because he'd never before seen a squid with hooks like that on the ends of its tentacles didn't mean it couldn't exist. He'd have to talk to the biologists about it.

Turning sideways, he put his back to the porthole, leaned against the wall and stretched his legs out on the seat. "So. I'll tell you what little bit I know—and I'll warn you, it's not much—you tell me what you know, and we'll try to figure this shit out. Deal?"

"Deal." Ryal set down his beer and held out his hand. "Shake, brother."

He shook, and that was that. They both drank, as if to seal the deal. Ryal's enthusiasm made him seem frighteningly young and vulnerable. Mo hoped like hell he hadn't just gotten them both in deeper than they could handle.

Ryal leaned forward. "So. Since you're the asshole who tried to get me drunk and take advantage of me, I think you ought to go first. What do you know?"

He wished Ryal was wrong, but he wasn't. Sighing, he polished off half his beer for courage, then passed on the few scraps of information Armin had given him. Only after telling Ryal did he realize how little it really was.

Ryal wasn't impressed. "So it proves his theories. So what? I don't get why that means they have to have all this cloak-and-dagger shit."

"I figure they just don't want information getting out early. That's never good." Mo took another long swallow of beer. "Okay, it's your turn. What's the deal with Hannah?"

"Well, she got kicked out of the lab yesterday because the upside scientists didn't believe her when she told them she found live bacteria in that rock. They said she was wrong and made her leave."

The equipment's an upside problem now, she'd told Mo yesterday. He nodded as the pieces fell into place in his mind. "So you think something else happened in the lab that she's not telling you?"

"I don't know. I don't think so, it's just . . ." Worry pulled Ryal's brows together and drew down the corners of his mouth. "I ran into her earlier today. She was supposed to be compiling data for Poole, but *he* kicked her out too. She said he claimed she was picking fights with people and not keeping her mind on her work. She was *really* mad at him." He trailed off, his gaze turned inward.

Mo stifled a sigh. "Ryal? What happened?"

Ryal blinked and focused on his face. "Nothing, exactly. But she was really jumpy. She kept looking behind her. Like she was afraid somebody was sneaking up on her." He picked absently at a broken place on his thumbnail. "She was acting almost paranoid, saying how Poole and the upside people were all out to get her, and she was so nervous she couldn't even stand still. It wasn't like her at all. *Something* must've happened to her. I can't think of any other reason she'd act that way."

Mo agreed. Hannah was one of the least jumpy people he'd ever known, which was why she drove the go-carts when the mining team needed someone to fill in. She had the right kind of temperament for it. Nervousness was way out of character for her.

If she'd been experiencing any of the same things Mo had lately, he couldn't blame her for feeling on edge.

He swung his legs off the seat. "I'm gonna go talk to her."

Ryal's eyes went wide. "Wait, what? You . . . I mean, you won't—"

"Don't worry. I won't tell her you snitched on her." He made himself grin like it wasn't a big deal as he slid out of the booth, but inside he felt anything but lighthearted. If he was the only one seeing things, that was a problem for him, but probably not a threat to the pod as a whole. A sudden rash of hallucinations, on the other hand, spelled potential disaster if they didn't identify what was happening and stop it before it could gain momentum. "I think we should both keep this little talk to ourselves, okay?"

"Yeah, sure." Ryal folded his hands around his beer bottle and stared at nothing, his attention clearly no longer on Mo.

Mo sauntered out of the rec area as casually as he could manage. In the hallway, he broke into a jog and headed straight for Hannah's quarters.

He realized the implications of what he'd been thinking. He'd dismissed the things he thought he'd seen lately as his imagination. Tiredness, lack of sleep, overwork—hell, sheer boredom—might make his eyes play tricks on him. He knew that. But was there any difference between imaginings and hallucinations, when you got right down to it?

If his grip on reality slipped, regardless of the reason, he knew damn well he wouldn't enjoy the results. He'd never handled forced confinement well.

Maybe he'd started to crack, in spite of what Dr. Palto had told him. Maybe Hannah had too.

Wrong, whispered the part of him that saw things clearly.

Hannah didn't answer her door, even after Mo told the auto-port he had important business and needed to speak with her right away.

He glared at the blank video screen in helpless frustration. "She's there, right?"

"Hannah Long is in her quarters." To Mo, the auto-port's bland female voice sounded vaguely disgruntled. Which was impossible, but there it was. "However, she is not answering my summons. I am very sorry, Maximo Rees. How else can I assist you?"

Mo wrestled down the urge to tell the machine to go fuck itself. The damn thing would probably inform him, in that same soulless-yet-improbably-put-out tone, that it was not capable of human sexual activity and it was very sorry.

This time, the auto-port spoke in a voice like gravel and nails. "Oh, I know how to fuck. I can fuck your brain to jelly and suck it through a straw."

Mo's mouth went dry. He stumbled backward, his pulse galloping, and stared at the auto-port screen. It stared back, blank as ever, and silent again.

Well, of course it was silent. It obviously hadn't spoken in the first place. Even if some joker had programmed it to say what he thought he'd heard, he doubted anyone would bother to reprogram the voice to one rough as a sanding belt and thick with cruelty.

Great. He was still hearing things.

Ignoring the auto-port as best he could, he stepped up to the door and pounded on it with his fist. "Hannah! Answer the door. It's Mo. I need to talk to you."

No answer. He counted twenty seconds to give her enough time to throw on clothes if necessary, then banged on the door again when it remained closed. "Damn it, Hannah, if you don't open this door I'm using medical override. Come on."

It was a bluff, and she ought to know that—he didn't have the authority to enter her quarters using the medical override function— but it worked. The door slid open.

She grabbed his wrist and yanked him inside before he could say a word. The door shut behind him, and he stood blinking at her in the dimness of lighting set to the system's lowest level. As his eyes adjusted, he noted with growing alarm the open drawers, the clothes scattered all over the floor, and, bizarrely, the mattress ripped from the bed and upended to form a barrier in one corner.

She slapped his upper arm hard, startling him. "What're you doing here?" Her voice emerged low and half-panicked. "Did anybody see you?"

Stunned, he searched her tense face for his calm, level-headed friend. He saw no sign of her, which terrified him on multiple levels.

He took a step toward her. She skittered backward until she ran into the wall. He stopped, holding both hands up with the palms out. "I need to talk to you about what's happening here." Asking if she'd seen or heard anything unusual seemed pointless, given her hunted stare and the way she stood on the balls of her feet as if preparing to run.

She sucked in a hissing breath. In the space between one blink and the next, her eyes glowed a dark, bruised blue. "You know about it too?"

"I know I've seen some things I can't explain." He chose his words carefully, using her expression as a guide. "I'm guessing you have too."

Her nostrils flared along with the weird incandescence in her irises. One hand shot out and caught his elbow in a grip painful enough to make him grunt.

"They're gone, Mo. All of them out there. Ryal and Poole and *everybody*. They've been swallowed up. Eaten." She blinked, again and again, until her shining eyes resembled strobe lights in the dark. Her fingers—long, long fingers, had they always been that long, that slender, that *flexible*?—dug into Mo's flesh. "You can hide here with me. We're safe here, for now. When everyone's asleep, when they're all asleep and dreaming, we'll escape. Just you and me. Okay?"

She blinked up at him with those wide, round, shimmering eyes, licked her purple lips with a tongue gone thin and unnaturally nimble, and Mo's mind put on the brakes.

He drew a deep breath. Blew it out. Forced himself to stand his ground, even though every cell in his body told him to run. "Hannah. Nobody's been . . . um. Eaten. Everything's fine." He tried without success to pry her fingers off his arm. "Let me take you to the med bay, okay? Let Dr. Palto look you over." If this was some previously undiscovered reaction to living at extreme depth for long periods of time, Palto would figure it out. That was the focus of his research here. Serving as the pod's medical doctor was his secondary role.

The shine in Hannah's eyes flared into a luminescent fire. "You've been eaten too. Just like *them*." Her fingers dug deeper into his muscle, sending a sharp pain all the way down to his thumb. "Don't worry. I'll help you." She yanked his arm close, her lips pulling back to bite.

Tearing his arm free from Hannah's grip, Mo spun and lunged for the door. He got the disorienting impression that it opened from sheer force of habit, then tried to close before he could get through. The damn thing clipped the back of his right heel as it shut. It hurt, but not nearly as much as Hannah's outraged wail, cut short when the door slid closed.

CHAPTER 4

For a second, Mo stood and stared at the blank, pale-gray rectangle, wondering what the hell had just happened. Had he imagined the weird glow in Hannah's eyes and the abnormal length of her fingers? Her trying to bite him? Had he imagined *all* of it?

He looked around. The hallway was deserted. "Auto-port. Maximo Rees calling for Hannah Long. Urgent." Fear turned his mouth bone-dry, but if he could see her on the screen, at least he would know whether or not he'd seen what he thought he'd seen.

"One moment." The auto-port's voice was perfectly normal now. The amber light beside the screen pulsed for several long seconds. Mo fidgeted and chewed his thumbnail. When the voice spoke again, he jumped. "Hannah Long is in her quarters. However, she is not answering my summons. I am very sorry, Maximo Rees. How else can I assist you?"

Fuck. Mo rested his forehead against the door and shut his eyes. Hannah's luminescent blue stare burned into his brain from behind his lids. He opened his eyes and backed up, his heartbeat thumping in his throat. "Nothing. Nothing else."

"Do you wish to leave a message for Hannah Long?"

He shook his head. "No message."

As he turned to go, a voice—low, deep, rough as lava rock—chortled in vicious glee. Mo glanced over his shoulder, though he knew he shouldn't. Why give his hallucinations room to grow and breed? But he had to look because looking was part of his DNA.

Once, when Mo was small, he'd gone fishing with his uncle. They'd caught a net full of eels. The creatures had wriggled and whipped and threaded through and over and around one another in a frantic attempt to escape the net. The memory of that living mass in constant, desperate motion had fascinated Mo ever since. Now the auto-port screen, previously blank, roiled in 3-D exactly like the mass of gray-black eels trying to work their way out of the net on that long-ago day.

He about-faced and strode away from Hannah's quarters as fast as he could go without running. The flat metallic taste of fear coated the back of his tongue. He had to get someone else into Hannah's quarters right the fuck now. Her paranoid behavior made her a danger to herself and everyone else.

Besides that, if he'd hallucinated the things he thought he'd seen, he needed to know—unpleasant as that might be—so he could take himself off duty and get help before it got any worse.

If what he'd seen was real?

Well. They were all in a shitload of trouble.

He hurried toward the med bay as fast as he could.

At first, each nonresult and new mystery surrounding the rock that wasn't a rock had sent excited shivers up Armin's spine. It all added credence to his theories. But the honeymoon was over now. He was tired of adding to the list of things the object *wasn't*. He wanted to learn just a little about what it *was*. But despite his halfhearted hopes, the object behaved no more normally today than it had previously.

Over at the scanner interface, Mandala drummed her fingers on the stretch of gleaming countertop and glared at the 3-D display. "Maybe the equipment simply needs adjusting. This display looks . . ." She shook her head, her brow furrowing as if she were searching for the right word. "I don't know. I can't put my finger on it. It's just off. I wonder if we could get Hannah back here to go over the settings with me since she's familiar with this particular machine?"

The odd hush to Mandala's voice caught Armin's ear and set his heart beating faster. "Do you mind if I have a look at the 3-D?"

"Be my guest." She keyed in the code, and a perfect hologram of the object in its sealed chamber materialized about one meter above the holo display pad on the floor.

The image looked exactly like the thing they'd found in the seawall—perfectly round, perfectly black, perfectly featureless.

The hologram lacked only the original's sense of inconceivable life waiting to be set free.

Armin walked around the image, studying it from every angle. Nothing changed as he did so. It didn't move or shift the way it had in Richards Deep. It seemed flat and uninteresting—unlike its real-life counterpart in the chamber, which had left Armin with the distinct feeling that if he only stared long enough into it, if he only angled his eyes precisely the right way, he'd learn secrets never meant for the human mind.

The idea both terrified and intrigued him. Having the scanner between the unearthly thing and the fragile human creatures in the pod—himself included—provided him a measure of comfort.

He knew, however, that a feeling did not constitute scientific observation. "It looks exactly the same as the actual object to me. Can you try to describe what it is about the image that seems off to you?"

Hopping down from her stool, Mandala skirted the counter and approached the hologram. She stopped a few paces away and eyed it with undeniable mistrust. "Hm. Well, it looks fine now. Which only bothers me more because given the same settings the scanner should project the same image every time."

Neil glanced up from his terminal. "And you haven't changed the settings, I guess?"

She shook her head. "Not for the 3-D display, no.

The way the object defied every attempt to test it both elated Armin and frightened him. He turned away from Mandala and Neil so they wouldn't see the churning chaos of emotions he couldn't hide. "If you could possibly describe what you found off about the display before, I'd still like to know."

Ashlyn looked up from her workstation, showing interest in the conversation for the first time. "Why?"

He frowned at her. "Because I think it might be important, that's why."

She raised both hands in a gesture of surrender. "You're the boss. I was just curious."

Deliberately turning his back on her, Armin focused all his attention on Mandala. "Do you think you can describe it?"

"I'm not sure, but I'll try." She shut her eyes and stood silently for a moment in obvious deep thought before speaking again. "It seemed as though the image had a sort of twitchiness to it." She opened her eyes, and the look in them was troubled. "Almost as if it were moving in tiny bits, where you couldn't quite catch it, but your eye still knew it was happening."

The memory of the impossible movement Armin thought he'd seen before played itself out behind his eyes. His stomach rolled over.

Neil approached them from his station, nodding. "I know just what you mean. It's how things look inside sometimes when you first come in from the sunlight, right?"

"Not exactly, but that's a pretty good description." Mandala circled the holo, surveying it the way Armin had just done. "I definitely want to have Hannah go over the settings with me. In fact, I think we should run a full diagnostic. This is too important to have anything go wrong." She aimed a solemn stare at Armin. "It looks remarkably like the object from the Varredura Longa footage, Armin. I know you've seen it too. You, Neil, and Carlo. If the two are related, we must learn how, and if the object from the Antarctica video was the reason they called us. There's absolutely no room for error here. If we don't have fully functioning equipment, we have nothing."

Armin gazed into Mandala's fearful, determined eyes and nodded, because she was right—about all of it. He studied the smooth obsidian curve of the image hovering in front of him, thinking hard. "There's no need to bring Hannah back into it. I'll run the diagnostic myself. In fact, why don't the rest of you take a break while I do that?"

Neil and Mandala both gaped at him. Even Ashlyn abandoned her work to stare at him as if he'd taken leave of his senses. He'd expected that. He showed them all a bland smile.

"Armin, no offense, but . . . what?" Neil spread both hands out to his sides and shook his head, his expression puzzled. "Why would we need to leave for you to run a diagnostic on the scanner? And why do *you* want to do it anyway? Why not call Dr. Poole? He knows the equipment, and he'd be tickled to death to be involved in this."

Because none of them would agree to leave if he shared what he actually planned to do, he went with a half lie to answer the questions for which he *had* answers. "I've used this type of scanner many times before. I can run the diagnostic perfectly well without dragging Poole into it. You know as well as I do that if we let him in here, he'll want to run the whole show."

Neil's eyebrows rose. "That doesn't mean we have to let him."

Ashlyn rose and stretched. "No, but him hanging around trying to take over would be nothing but a distraction. I think Armin's right. We should keep this operation among ourselves, like we'd planned."

Mandala nodded, her arms crossed and her expression hard. Neil let out a deep sigh. "I guess you're right."

Relief eased some of the tightness from Armin's muscles. They'd decided to minimize the BathyTech 3 crew's presence in the lab, mostly to keep premature information from leaking out. Armin had begun to wonder if there might be better reasons, but his worries were vague at best and he didn't want to share yet, though it seemed as though Mandala might share them.

"I don't know about you guys, but I missed breakfast and I'm starving." Ashlyn's voice was unusually perky, her grin wider and brighter than normal. "Let's go get food. And coffee."

"I'm not sure you could call that swill coffee," Mandala grumbled, but she headed for the door anyway.

Neil trailed after her. "I could use more caffeine myself." He shot Armin a questioning look as he and Mandala left the lab, but said nothing else.

Ashlyn stopped on her way out and pinned Armin with a gaze that seemed to peel back skin and bone to delve directly into his brain. "You're right to keep them away from here while you open the chamber, but you're not immune to whatever's in that thing. Be careful."

His heart thudded hard against his sternum. Torn between horror and relief that she'd guessed his intentions, he did his best to hide his reaction behind silence and a blank stare.

She let out an impatient noise. "Fine. Be that way. But remember, there's a lot we still don't know." She leaned forward, her eyes wide and intense. "I know you're thinking about the Varredura Longa. So am I. If there's a connection, then we have to be careful."

For a moment the lab faded away, replaced by the horrors he'd experienced in Antarctica. The flickering yellow light. The bodies.

The smell of death. The one survivor, who could tell them nothing because—

No. He wouldn't think of it. Not here. Not now.

He made himself smile. "I don't know if there's any connection. The object Dr. Longenesse carried away on the video looked similar to the one we're studying, at least as far as I can tell. But the vid from the Varredura Longa was very poor quality. For what it's worth, I agree with you. We must be cautious if there's any chance of a connection."

"Good." Still watching him, she took a step back, then pivoted and strode out of the lab.

He waited until she'd left, then locked the door behind her. His team—including Carlo, if he ever felt well enough to show up— could think what they liked about that, if they returned before he was finished. He wasn't letting anyone else in until he'd not only tested the equipment—it wasn't a bad idea, after all, to make sure it worked correctly—but had seen the thing for himself once again. Not in the vast, tempting dark of the ocean depths, but in the harsh light of the laboratory, where the universe fell into orderly lines and mysteries were dissected, catalogued, and understood.

He wouldn't take the same chances Carlo had. He intended to prepare himself first. To be ready for whatever might happen.

With his solitude secured, he turned toward the hologram. For a split-second, it squirmed like a fly-blown corpse.

Pulse racing, sweat beading on his upper lip, he shut his eyes. *It's not real. Ignore your fear. Study it. Learn the how and the why. That's the only way to understand it. To protect yourself, and everyone else, if it comes to that.*

He opened his eyes. The image remained obediently still. Steeling himself, he crossed to the locker holding the goggles and isolation gear and started suiting up.

When the sampler skidded off the object's evidently frictionless surface for at least the fourteenth time, Armin shoved his chair away from the apparatus and pressed both palms to his eyes. "Damn it. Stupid rock." His voice echoed in the ringing quiet of the lab, nudging the throb behind his eyes up another notch toward nasty-headache territory.

Of course, the hour or so he'd spent so far with the mysterious object had confirmed one thing for him: whatever it might be, it wasn't a rock. The equipment—all of which performed perfectly on testing—continued to tell him that it didn't even exist in the way one would expect. The readings were more consistent with energy than with mass.

It seemed a ridiculous finding. The thing looked and felt as real as any other object its size. He'd not only seen it—watched the light glisten on its glossy black surface, in the ocean and here in the lab—but touched it. He'd felt the weight of it when he lifted it from its underwater niche to the container, and again when he moved it into the isolation chamber. But he couldn't weigh it, and it cast no shadow, even though both the 3-D and the 2-D scanners produced images of it. Not terribly reliable images, but at least they recognized its existence. Best of all, to his mind, it exhibited definite quantum particle properties. He wondered if it would show entanglement ability if another of its kind were found.

Through the excitement of the findings that continued to support theories Armin had developed over years of work, memories of the Varredura Longa wound like a dark and nebulous warning. As if he hadn't worried about that from the first.

As if when he'd laid eyes on the object perched like an abstract Neptune on that undersea wall, he hadn't seen an echo of the single blurred image of the thing Klaudia Longenesse had carried with her into the icy black sea.

They'd never found her body.

A scream jolted him from his thoughts. He held his breath and stilled his hands, listening. Another scream—a woman's voice, mindless with terror—came from somewhere outside the lab. It ended on a lost, hopeless sob.

Armin took time only to pull the sampler out of the vault and seal the object back inside before running for the lab door, shedding his goggles and gloves as he went.

He exited the lab just in time to nearly run right into a hover stretcher guided by two of the BT3 staff with medical personnel badges clipped to their shirts. More dual-role staff, he assumed; this pod employed many of them. He pressed himself against the wall, out of the way. The young woman strapped to the stretcher mumbled and cried behind the oxygen mask half-covering her face. Her skin was grayish, her hair plastered to her forehead and neck in sweaty clumps. He thought her lips had a purplish tinge, but it was hard to tell with the mask in the way.

She looked so different, it took him a moment to recognize Hannah Long, the lab assistant.

Shocked, he stared at her as she passed. Her eyes glowed a faint, luminous blue. She caught his gaze, craned her neck, and struggled against her restraints as the medics towed her away down the hall. "They're eating you. They're *in* you, and they're *eating* you. They're going to eat all of you, you know!" Her voice was high and hysterical.

One of the medics pressed a hypo to her neck. She subsided, still muttering to herself.

Armin watched them take her around the corner. "My God. What happened to you?"

He hadn't expected an answer, so Mo's voice behind him startled him. "Doc Palto said she had some kind of psychotic break."

Armin turned, his pulse racing. "What? Why?"

"I don't know." Mo let out a deep sigh, his shoulders slumping, and closed the distance between them. He let Armin wind their fingers together. His palms felt cool and damp against Armin's. "I went to see her because Ryal was worried about her. And she was . . ." He shook his head. "She was paranoid. Talking about everybody on BathyTech being eaten."

They're inside you. They're eating you. A chill raised the hairs on Armin's neck.

Oblivious, Mo continued. "They're taking her upside for treatment." He leaned his forehead against Armin's. "I don't get it, Armin. Why would she just lose it like that?"

Armin licked his lips. "Staying down too long is a stress on the body and the psyche. That's why time in the trenches is strictly limited. You know that."

"Yeah, but Hannah's only been down for three months this cycle. She wasn't due for an upside shift for another three months. And before today, I would've said she was the least likely person I knew to crack. So what happened? Why her?" Mo's voice was soft and calm, but a world of questions pooled in the puzzled crease between those deep brown eyes.

Armin bit back the urge to assure Mo he knew nothing about it. That was true, as far as it went, but answering rhetorical questions would only call attention to formless fears he couldn't articulate to himself yet, never mind express to someone else.

Mo must have seen a shadow of those worries on Armin's face, because his eyes narrowed. He studied Armin, thoughtful, blameless, neutral, for now. "Well. I'm gonna go see Hannah off. I'll talk to you later."

"Right." Armin pressed a swift kiss to Mo's lips. "Let me know what happens. I hope she'll be all right."

Mo gave him a wan smile. "Me too. Thanks." He strode after Hannah and the medics, though they had to be pretty far ahead by now.

Armin resisted the urge to go after him. They weren't in a relationship, and he had work to do. If he was correct in his belief that the object Klaudia had taken from the Varredura Longa was of the same sort as the one they'd recovered from Richards Deep, then that work took on a whole new significance.

Unless he was wrong. All he had to connect Antarctica to now was the brief, far-from-clear video of Klaudia Longenesse walking into the sea carrying an object that looked like the one they'd found in Richards Deep. It was entirely possible that a better-quality video would've shown them something far different.

Wishful thinking.

Turning his back on the brightness of the hallway, he went back inside the lab and locked the door.

That night, Hannah visited Mo in his nightmares. The new Hannah, with her glowing eyes, her purple lips, and her long, long fingers that twisted and bent like seaweed in a current.

It's not so bad, being eaten, she assured him, her voice burbling, waterlogged. *Just accept it, that's all. Don't fight. And you'll see things you never imagined. Such terrible, beautiful things.*

He tried to follow her as she turned and moved away. But he couldn't. His muscles were frozen. He could only watch as she smiled a smile full of translucent needle teeth and walked through the ooze of the seabed in slow motion, her hair floating behind her in the water. As she drifted away, her clothes fell off, her legs fused together into a powerful tail, her arms became fins, and her mermaid body whip-cracked out of sight, out of knowledge, into the cold forever night of the deep.

Mo opened his mouth—to scream, maybe, or to beg her to take him with her. He didn't know which. Frigid salt water flowed into his throat, into his nose, filled his sinuses and stomach and lungs until he became a creature of saline and skin, drowning, disintegrating, all that made him Maximo Rees scattering into its component molecules and becoming food for the bottom-feeders.

Let me in. The voice, Armin's and yet not Armin's, licked at Mo's mind while it trembled on the edge of dissolution. *Let me inside you, and I'll fuck you so good you won't know who you are anymore.*

The sensation of another consciousness winding eellike through his own tore a shout from the throat he no longer had.

He woke drenched in sweat, tangled in the sheet, with his own cry ringing in his ears.

He sat up, heart racing, trying to stare into every corner of the room at once. "Lights on."

The lights came up. For a single breath-freezing second, he thought he saw something thin and black whipping out of sight behind the dresser. He focused on the spot, where the sleeve of one of his shirts hung off the edge of the furniture.

"Just a trick of the light," he told himself. "It looked like it was moving when the lights came on. That's all. Stop being a damn civvie."

He turned toward where Daisy's terrarium sat on the floor. All he could see of her was half of one hairy black leg, ending in the pink foot that gave her species its name. He hadn't seen much more than that since he'd retrieved her from Hannah's quarters.

He couldn't pretend he liked spiders. Especially big, hairy ones. But Daisy couldn't help what she was, and with Hannah gone, she would die unless someone stepped up to take care of her. Since Ryal would rather walk into the depths without a suit than even lay eyes on something with eight legs, Mo had volunteered.

Right now, even arachnid company felt better than none.

He eased back down under the covers. But he left the lights on low, and his sleep the remainder of that night was restless.

He arrived at the go-cart bay four hours later, tired, grumpy, and out of sorts. He cut Jem off with a single pointed finger before she could say anything about taking him off duty again. "I'm fine to walk. I just didn't sleep very well, that's all. No big deal."

She pursed her lips and studied him with narrow-eyed suspicion for several seconds. "Okay. But I've got my eyes on you, Rees. You screw up today, you're off duty for a week. Got it?"

"Sure thing, Big Mama." Ignoring her exasperated scowl, he strolled over to where Yvonne was just starting the tests on the scanner. "Hi, Yvie."

"Mo." She cast him a frankly curious look. "How're you doing? Better?"

"I'm fine. Mama was just being extra careful." He thumbed the terminal on the wall. "Computer. Maximo Rees, requesting preshift internal diagnostics on mining array scanner."

"Acknowledged, Mo. Beginning diagnostics."

Mo shot a dark look at Yvonne, who grinned. Not that he didn't enjoy the deep, masculine growl she'd programmed into the computer, but for him, at least, sexy computer voices made it hard to concentrate on the job. And the last thing he needed was a distraction.

Meanwhile, the sexy-growly voice was talking, not giving a shit about his inner angst because it was a fucking computer and computers were stupid. "Internal diagnostics finished. All systems go. In fact, I'd sure like to fuck that scanner like a bitch in heat."

Mo nearly bit his tongue. He blinked, his pulse rushing in his ears. "Um. What?"

Yvonne frowned at him. "Computer says internals are a go. Externals too." She switched off the crawler that inspected every inch of the scanner's hull before and after each shift, pulled it off the scanner, and stuck it back in its wall niche. "Are you sure you're okay?"

Mo glanced from Yvonne to the wall terminal, torn. He couldn't have actually heard what he'd thought he had. Which meant he ought to step out of the walk. On the other hand, he knew—he *knew*—he was fine. He was sane. There wasn't anything really wrong with him.

After all, he knew what was real and what wasn't. Right?

Right.

"Yeah, yeah. I'm fine. Just let my mind wander for a second." He smiled, making it casual. "It won't happen again. I swear."

Her expression was dubious, but she didn't argue. "Help me load this in the go-cart."

She didn't need any help, since the scanner had hovering capability, but Mo did as she asked. Together, they guided the equipment into the go-cart. The rest of the team followed soon after, and their shift began.

The next ten hours passed without anything remarkable happening. The occasional odd things Mo might've seen—a fish with teeth too long or metallic, the rare octopus with too many arms or hooks in its suckers, the strange whips flailing out of the Pipe vents for the space of a breath before vanishing again—could easily be explained by the weird shifting of the walker lights combined with an imagination stirred by real-life terrors. Mo couldn't pretend the whole ugly business with Hannah hadn't affected him.

He ignored the uneasy churning in his gut that told him this wasn't over. That whatever had happened to Hannah would happen to others.

They were all back in the go-cart and three-quarters of the way back to the pod when Dr. Youssouf herself contacted them on the coms.

Jem answered, darting a wide-eyed sidelong glance at Mo. "Knang here. What's up?"

The pod director's voice was clipped. "We have an unauthorized exit from the go-cart bay. Someone's taken a suit and gone walking."

"Who?"

"We don't know. Whoever it is didn't identify themselves, and we're not sure yet who's missing. But we've got everybody trying to figure it out. In the meantime, I need you to find 'em."

Jem nodded, looking as stunned as Mo felt. "Where are they headed?"

A pause followed. Mo wondered if the heaviness he sensed was real, or his imagination.

"Richards Deep." Youssouf sighed. "I don't think I need to tell you what'll happen if a person gets lost in the Deep, even in a suit. I'm sending you the tracking feed from the walker. I'm going to contact the other go-carts as well, but you're the closest, so you're our best chance to get them back. Good luck."

"Roger that. Thanks. Go-cart One out." Jem cut the connection. She peered at the tracker readout, her face grim. "Well. Whoever it is, they're not far from here. I'm heading that way. Shouldn't take more than five minutes."

Mo unbuckled and rose from his seat. "I'll get ready to walk."

"Take Yvie or Rashmi. I don't want anyone going after this person alone."

Mo didn't argue. He hated to drag anyone else into potential danger with him, but Jem was right. Anyone who would take a walker and run off to Richards Deep without go-cart backup—hell, without even telling anyone—was unpredictable. They had to assume he or she could turn violent.

Mo and Yvonne were in their walkers and ready to fill the helmets with Mist when Jem called in from the cab. "We have a visual on our target. I'm gonna try to cut 'em off. Y'all get ready."

"Roger that, Big Mama." Yvonne raised her eyebrows as she and Mo both picked up their helmets. "Show's on."

"Yep." Mo put on his helmet, sealed it, and hooked up to the Mist tank. He breathed slow and deep as the heavy gas filled his lungs. Watched Yvonne do the same. "Walker One, testing coms to Walker Two and go-cart. Come in."

"Walker Two here. Getting you loud and clear, Mo."

"Go-cart. You're both coming in great for me."

Mo nodded. "Walker One. I'm hearing both of you, no problem. Jem, give us the word as soon as you stop. I'm gonna go ahead and pressurize so we'll be ready."

"Will do. It won't be long."

Dread curled in Mo's gut. Christ, there were so many ways this could go badly.

He shoved his fears to the back of his mind. "Computer. Pressurize chamber."

A few seconds later, Jem's voice overrode the computer telling them the chamber was sealed and pressurized. "We're here, kids. Feeding coordinates to your walkers now."

A translucent virtual map of the seabed popped up on Mo's faceplate, with a bright little blip representing their stray. He grinned. Jem had stopped the go-cart practically on top of their mystery walker.

"Computer," he said, "uncover the pool."

"Anything you say, you sexy piece of man."

Mo pressed his lips together and cast a glance at Yvonne. If she'd heard the same unprecedented declaration from the computer, she was hiding it really damn well.

She didn't hear it. Because the computer didn't say it. You're hearing things again.

It wasn't a comforting thought, especially now. Since they had an urgent job to do, though, he kept his experience—and his worries about what it meant—to himself and followed Yvonne into the moon pool.

He spotted the runaway immediately. Whoever the person was, they acted like someone on a vital errand that happened to involve traipsing off to a spot some eight thousand meters below the ocean's surface. The man or woman in the walker strode along in the muck of the seabed as though nothing else mattered, cutting around the go-cart like it was no more than an obstacle in the path.

Mo rested a hand on the stun stick every miner kept on their belt just in case, ever since one miner had lost it underwater five years ago and killed his entire team by smashing their faceplates with a rock pick. "Yvie, you flank them to the right. I'll go left. We'll try talking first, obviously, but if that doesn't work I'll use the stunner."

Yvonne nodded, her face ghostly in her helmet light. "Got it." She veered toward the right, her long legs closing in fast on the quarry.

He angled to the left, breaking into an awkward jog. As he drew closer, he noticed that the person's helmet light wasn't on. Neither were the wrist lights. Meaning that up until now, with the arrival of the go-cart, the escapee had been walking in utter darkness.

The thought chilled Mo even more than the idea of running off alone in a walker in the first place. Not so much because of what might be lurking there in the unending blackness, but because it was such a strange thing to do. Downright alien to usual human behavior.

He didn't like where that line of thought led him.

Yvonne caught up to the figure first. Her reaction was very quiet over the com. "Oh my God."

Adrenaline kicked Mo's pulse into high gear. "Yvie? What's wrong?" He started running faster, trying to get to her as quickly as possible without using too much Mist, since neither of them had topped up.

She didn't answer. A few meters away, she reached toward the still-moving figure. "Doctor? This is Yvonne Liss. I'm one of the miners. Could you stop and talk to me for a minute?"

Mo's heart lurched. Which doctor? Was it Poole? Or one of the upside team?

Please don't be Armin. Maybe it was selfish, but he wanted Armin whole and safe even if it put someone else in that walker right now.

He was almost there. Almost within reach of the doctor in the walker. With no more than a couple of meters to go, the figure—still silent in the darkened suit—swung and knocked Yvonne out of the way. She fell to the seafloor, sending up a cloud of silt.

She waved Mo away before he could ask. "I'm fine. Just catch him. Something's very wrong."

Mo didn't take the time to ask any of the questions chasing each other around his brain. He lunged for the man, caught his arm, and whirled him around.

Carlo Libra's face stared back at him in the reflected glow from Mo's helmet light. But something wasn't right. Something was *missing*.

Humanity, Mo realized, with a sickening roll of his stomach. The indefinable spark that made a person human.

Christ.

"Dr. Libra. It's Mo. Remember me? We walked together. Remember?" He tried on a smile for size.

Dr. Libra's expression remained blank as a mask. But for a fraction of a second, his dark eyes flashed a deep blackish-blue, like the lights of some creature of the abyss, and Mo tasted bile in the back of his throat.

The doctor tried to hit Mo like he had Yvonne. Mo was ready for him, and blocked the blow. "Dr. Libra. Carlo. Come on. Let's go back to the pod, okay?"

By that time, Yvonne was up and closing in from the back. Dr. Libra seemed to realize he was outnumbered. He shook off Mo's grip and sidestepped out of their reach, baring his teeth in a snarl.

Long, sharp, metal teeth.

Staring into Carlo Libra's black-light eyes, Mo's world ground to a halt around him. For the first time in his life, he didn't know what was real and what wasn't. For all he knew, whatever had made Dr. Libra steal a walker and try to go into Richards Deep was taking over his body as well as his mind. Changing him.

"What's happening?" Mo's voice emerged in a Mist-choked whisper. He wondered who he was asking.

A low, gurgling chuckle came over the com. From Dr. Libra's walker? Mo couldn't tell, and that terrified him.

"Wonderful things are happening." The voice was Dr. Libra's, but not. Sort of like the Armin-but-not-Armin voice Mo had heard before. "You'll see."

Before Mo could say a word—before he could act in any way, he told himself over and over afterward—the doctor unsealed his helmet and took it off.

All Mo could think was, *He can't do that*, as the tremendous weight of the ocean crushed Carlo Libra's skull like a paper shell.

CHAPTER 5

"**D**r. Carlo Libra is still not in his quarters." The auto-port informed Armin of this as though it were utterly unimportant. "Do you wish to leave him a message, Dr. Armin Savage-Hall?"

He closed his eyes and rested his forehead on the cool metal-plastic hybrid that comprised most of the walls in this place. Carlo had contacted him early that morning to say he was still feeling too ill to work, so naturally Armin had come to look in on him after finishing up in the lab. That was ninety minutes ago. Only Carlo hadn't been there. Nor was he anywhere else in the pod, at least not that Armin could find. Which raised the question, where exactly *was* he?

"No message. Wait, yes. I *would* like to leave a message." He opened his eyes again, turned, and leaned his back against the door. "Tell Dr. Libra to contact me on my personal com link immediately. Send the message as a priority, all right?"

"Yes, Dr. Armin Savage-Hall." The auto-port blinked amber once, twice, then blinked green. "Message sent. Can I be of further assistance?"

He considered asking to be let into Carlo's quarters, but that seemed like a step too far toward paranoia. "No. Thank you."

"You are welcome, Dr. Armin Savage-Hall."

Good Lord, that got old quickly. He walked away, trying to think of something he might've missed in his search for his friend, but nothing came to mind. At this point he didn't know what to do, other than go to BT3's director, Dr. Youssouf, and report Carlo missing—as impossible as that sounded on its surface. She knew this pod better than anyone. If there was a place on it that a sick man might hide and not be found, she could tell him what that place might be.

Mo would know, said the seductive voice in his head, the one that remembered too well the warm, silky touch of Mo's tongue on his skin.

He pressed his lips together and shook his head. No. He wouldn't ask Mo—even if he was back from his shift yet, which he very well might not be. Mo would only penetrate him with that stormy stare that saw far too much and demand knowledge for knowledge. What was Armin's game? What did he know or suspect? Mo would give up the secret corners of the pod, but only for Armin's blackest, most horrific beliefs regarding what they'd brought up from the deep. And he wasn't ready to share.

He was almost to Youssouf's office when he nearly ran into the woman herself hurrying down the hall with an air of urgency. She almost passed him by without speaking, then stopped in midstep, recognition flowing over her face. "Dr. Savage-Hall." She took his arm and pulled him along with her. "I have some bad news."

Apprehension churned in his stomach. He ignored it. "It'll have to wait, Doctor. I'm sorry. But, you see, Dr. Libra is missing. I went to see him this evening after I finished in the lab, and—"

She stopped. "Doctor. *Armin*. Please listen to me." She laid a hand on his arm and gazed up at him with that awful sympathetic look, and he knew.

He swallowed the acid rising in his throat. "What's happened?"

"Someone took a walker a couple of hours ago and headed for Richards Deep." She sighed, her ageless face showing every one of her sixty-eight years for a moment. "Jemima Knang's mining team found him. It was Carlo Libra . . ."

"And?"

"And he removed his helmet. They weren't able to stop him."

He knew exactly what the force of over seven thousand meters of water did to the human body. He felt his own shoulders bow under the imagined weight of it. "God."

"They brought him back." She gave his arm a pat, then dropped her hand. "I'm heading there now. You're welcome to come if you like, but you know it's not going to be pretty."

"I know." He drew a deep, trembling breath. Blew it out. His chest felt heavy and tight. "I'll come."

She nodded, sharp and approving, then continued her journey down the hall. Armin followed in silence, his heart cold and all the fight drained out of him.

They arrived at the go-cart bay ahead of the mining team. The airlock was still closed and sealed. Youssouf sat on one of the benches along the wall and stared straight ahead, her hands folded in her lap, while Armin paced with his fingers laced behind his back so he wouldn't bite what was left of his fingernails.

They only waited eleven minutes—he watched them tick by one by one on the time display on the wall—but it felt like aeons before the computer announced the return of the go-cart. Another six minutes passed before the go-cart docked, the outer bay door shut and sealed, and the inner airlock door opened to allow the team back into BathyTech 3.

He slipped through the doors before they'd properly opened, and ran to the misshapen figure laid out on a hover stretcher and covered in plastic. "How did this happen?"

The tall, slender black woman whose name he didn't know let out a deep sigh. "He tried to go into Richards Deep, who knows why. He 'bout knocked my helmet off when I asked him to talk to me, then he took his own helmet off when Mo asked him what he was doing." She cut him a glance full of compassion underneath the awful memory of what she'd been forced to witness. "He just lost it out there. I know it doesn't make it any easier, but for what it's worth, I'm sorry."

He smiled in sincere gratitude. "It means a lot. Thank you."

"Armin. You shouldn't be here."

The familiar voice jerked his head around like a physical force. He stared into Mo's grim face, the dark skin gone ashen, and wished he could've spared him the sight of Carlo's horrific death.

A completely irrational anger flooded his veins. "I am not some little wilting flower, Mo. Believe it or not, this isn't the first time I've seen this sort of death. Carlo is my colleague and my friend. Of course I came here."

The shock on Mo's face would've been funny if it weren't for the horrible flatness of the plastic sheet over Carlo's body.

Mo's shoulders sagged. "Christ. I'm sorry. It's just . . ." He lifted one arm. Let it fall. He seemed lost, Armin thought. "It *is* the first time I've seen somebody die like that, and it was pretty fucking awful, you know?"

Armin's throat tightened. He vividly remembered the first time he'd seen someone crushed by the weight of the sea. Without a word, he went to Mo and hugged him hard. Mo's arms went around him, holding him close. His hands shook where they pressed into the small of Armin's back.

"I'm sorry you had to see that." Armin kissed the cool skin of Mo's neck. Buried his fingers in Mo's damp hair. "It's a terrible thing, I know."

"Yeah." Mo pulled back enough to look into Armin's eyes. Horror and guilt dug new lines into his face. "I would've saved him if I could. I wasn't quick enough to stop him." He gestured toward the woman who stood a little way to the side in silent support. "Yvie can tell you. There was nothing we could've done. Right?"

He sounded desperate, as if he didn't believe his own words, and Armin's heart went out to him. "Of course not. Who could have predicted that he would do such a thing?" He touched Mo's cheek, then reached out, grasping Yvie's hand and squeezing it. "Thank you both for trying. Truly."

Yvie nodded. "I wish it would've turned out different."

"So do I. But there's nothing anyone could have done differently." Leaving Mo to commiserate with his friends, Armin knelt beside Carlo's body and rested a hand on what was left of his chest. The plastic rustled beneath his palm.

"I'm sorry." He pressed down until the chill from his dead friend's corpse seeped through the shroud into his skin. Should that happen? Should Carlo feel so cold already, as if he'd been in a freezer? "I wish I could have stopped this from happening. I'm so, so sorry."

The flesh beneath his hand shifted, a nauseating roll like a nest of newly hatched snakes.

He scrambled backward, landing on his hip with bruising force. His pulse thudded in his ears, muffling the variations on *What's wrong with him?* coming from the people surrounding him.

Naturally, it was Mo who crouched beside him, rested a hand on his back, and peered at him with concern. "Armin? Are you all right?"

Am I? He looked down at the floor. Breathed. Looked back up. Carlo lay there dead beneath a plastic sheet, his body flattened by the weight of the ocean and as motionless as only a corpse could be. Guilt and grief squeezed Armin's heart like a hand.

"I'll be all right." He met Mo's gaze with a faint, forced smile. "This is . . . stressful."

Sorrow flowed over Mo's features and bowed his shoulders. "I know." He stood and held a hand down to Armin. "C'mon, Doc. Let me walk you to your quarters."

Armin put his hand in Mo's and let Mo pull him to his feet. "I need to find the rest of my team first and tell them what's happened. And don't you have to give a report or something?"

The pod's medical doctor had apparently entered when Armin wasn't paying attention; he spoke up now, regarding Armin and Mo with a weary solemnity while two assistants activated Carlo's hover stretcher. "Not yet. I'll need to examine Dr. Libra's body before I know what, if any, questions to ask. I've advised Yvonne to take the rest of the day off, go to her quarters, and rest. I'll give you both the same advice. I know Dr. Libra's death wasn't easy to witness, nor is it easy to lose a friend and coworker in this manner. Dr. Savage-Hall, I know you and your team are probably anxious to get on with your work, but I think you should all take some time off, at least for today, to process what's happened. Let me know if you'd like to set up a group therapy session to talk things out. I'd be happy to do it."

Armin smiled, both touched and amused. "I didn't realize you were a psychiatrist, Dr. Palto."

"I'm licensed to practice in psychiatry, general surgery, and general medicine. Down here it's a requirement of the job, since we have no easy access to consultants." Dr. Palto glanced toward the stretcher rising off the floor. "If you'll excuse me, I must see to Dr. Libra now. Please accept my condolences." He turned on his heel and followed Carlo's body out of the bay.

Armin watched him go. "Well. I suppose I should find the others now and tell them." God, he didn't want to. The dread of it sat like a rock in the pit of his belly.

Mo gazed at him with eyes full of sympathy. "I'll help you." He shifted his grip on Armin's hand—*he hasn't let go, all this time and he hasn't let go*—to weave their fingers together. "Where do you think they'll be?"

He ought to know. Mandala had said something before they'd all left the lab for the day. Armin could see her face in the foreground of his memory, could hear her talking, but her words slipped through his mind without sticking.

He shook his head, frustrated and feeling dangerously close to collapse. "I don't know. I *should* know, they told me, but I can't remember."

Mo nodded. "Understandable. You've had a hell of a shock. It messes with your head."

Armin's heart turned over. He wanted to tell Mo how much his empathy meant. How much Armin admired the strength of a person who could lend comfort and support to someone else when he himself had just watched the sea crush a man to hamburger.

In the end, he could only force a whispered, "Thank you," past his tight throat. But he thought Mo understood.

As they left the bay, Mo kept Armin's hand firmly in his.

They found Dr. Douglas and Dr. Jhut in the cafeteria. After Mo suggested looking there, Armin had remembered Dr. Jhut saying the three of them might grab something to eat while Armin was checking on Dr. Libra.

Mo figured he'd relive Dr. Libra's skull collapsing to a red pulp in his nightmares for years—never mind the sight of his pancaked body when they got him out of the walker—but his heart hurt for Armin and the rest of his team. They'd *known* Carlo Libra. They'd worked with him. Losing a friend and colleague in such a sudden, violent way must be awful.

"But *why?*" Dr. Jhut glanced from Armin to Mo to Dr. Douglas like one of them might know the answer. A fierce frown dug between her eyes. She rubbed circles on the surface of her coffee mug with her thumbs. "Carlo never showed the slightest tendency toward psychosis or suicidal ideation on any of his tests. It makes no sense whatsoever." She cast a blank gaze from Armin to Dr. Douglas and back again, radiating confused anger, as if the unlikelihood of Dr. Libra's suicide bothered her as much as the simple fact of it.

"No. It doesn't." Armin hunched forward over the table, where he'd clasped his hands together so hard his fingers had gone pale. He seemed to have aged ten years in as many minutes. Grim lines framed his mouth and his skin was grayish under his natural golden-brown complexion. His gaze was unfocused, staring at nothing. "How on earth am I going to tell Miko?"

Mo's stomach rolled. "Is that his wife?"

Dr. Douglas shook his head. "Ex-wife. They got divorced several years ago, after their little girl died. But they were friends, eventually, even though it took a while. This is going to be hard for her."

"Christ." Dr. Jhut frowned at her coffee. "Armin, I hate to bring this up, but has Dr. Palto considered that this might be some form of contagion?"

The idea made Mo feel cold inside. He kept quiet and hoped like hell Armin would tell Dr. Jhut all the reasons why she was wrong.

Instead, Armin let out a deep sigh. "I don't know. But I've wondered the same thing. That being the case, I'm sure he's thought of it too."

Mo was about to ask what made them think they were dealing with an infectious organism, when a shout from the other side of the room cut him off before he could say a word. He turned to look. To his surprise, Ryal had one of the miners from the shift opposite Mo's—Karen—backed into a corner, a steak knife at her throat.

"Oh my God." Leaving the scientists to their conversation, Mo ran toward the crowd gathering around Ryal and Karen. "Ryal, stop! What're you doing?"

Ryal glanced toward Mo. A flash of blue black shone from his eyes for a fraction of a second before Karen punched him in the jaw, sending him stumbling sideways. The knife clattered to the floor. He snarled like an animal and leaped on her, taking them both down.

It only took Mo a couple of seconds to navigate through the tables and chairs to reach the pair fighting on the tiles, but in that time they'd already bruised and bloodied one another. When Ryal straddled Karen's thighs and leaned over her, hands around her throat,

Mo took the opportunity to hook his arms under the smaller man's armpits, break his hold on Karen, and haul him away from her.

"You fucking piece of *shit*!" Karen lunged for Ryal, screaming, her voice raspy. A couple of people from the crowd grabbed her and held her back. "You're going down, motherfucker. Or up, I should say. 'Cause there's no fucking way you're staying down here after Youssouf finds out what a psycho you are."

Ryal grinned. For one sharp, crystalline moment, his long black teeth glinted like obsidian scythes in a mass of flabby white flesh. Mo shook his head. Blinked. And Ryal's face went back to normal, minus one eyetooth.

"Bitches who don't wanna get cut ought to keep their filthy mouth shut."

Ryal's voice emerged cold and ugly, silencing everyone around him. Because it wasn't him. The words, the tone, all of it—not Ryal. Even Karen stared at him with round eyes full of fear not for herself, but for him.

She turned to Dr. Jhut, who'd walked up near her. "I didn't say anything." She kept her voice low as if trying to ensure Ryal wouldn't hear her. "I didn't even talk to him."

Mo glanced around the room and found Armin's steadying gaze only a few meters away. Armin nodded, and Mo knew they were on the same page. They had to get Ryal out of there and into the med bay. Ideally without any more bloodshed.

Easing his grip on Ryal, Mo slid an arm around his shoulders. "You need to get those cuts and bruises looked at. C'mon, I'll take you to see Doc Palto."

Ryal narrowed his eyes at Mo. The strange bioluminescent gleam flared and was gone before Mo could decide if he'd truly seen it. "I'm fine."

"You lost a tooth." Mo answered Ryal's suspicious glare with his best *I'm your friend* grin. "Ryal. Come *on*, man. How do you ever expect to impress the ladies without that winning smile?"

For a second, Ryal's face went blank. Then he snorted and rolled his eyes. "Yeah, yeah. Fine. Let's go."

Mo's legs sagged with relief. He hid it and led Ryal toward the exit. A swift backward glance showed Armin already activating his com, presumably to call Dr. Palto and his team to meet Mo at the med bay.

Outside, Mo smiled and laughed and joked with Ryal while they strolled along the corridors. Inside, he begged every deity he didn't believe in to save his friend from whatever had invaded BathyTech 3.

Armin watched Mo lead the lab tech—Ryal?—out of the cafeteria as he murmured into the com link on his wrist. "Dr. Savage-Hall calling Dr. Palto. Urgent."

The delay wasn't more than a few seconds, but it felt like forever. He shuffled from foot to foot, anxious.

Finally the doctor answered, sounding impatient and put out. "Palto here. What is it? I'm about to begin an autopsy."

"I know, and I'm sorry. But I think we may have a situation." Armin glanced around, noted the curious looks cast his way, and strode out of hearing range. "There was an altercation in the cafeteria. One of the lab techs, Ryal, pulled a knife on one of the miners because he thought she insulted him."

"Miners and science personnel aren't exactly best friends down here, for the most part." Thoughtful pause. "Although it's been a while since we had actual bloodshed. And weapons aren't usually involved. Hm."

"She claims she not only didn't insult him, but in fact didn't say anything at all."

Another pause. "So you believe he might be hallucinating."

It wasn't a question. "It certainly seemed that way. He was acting in a very irrational and paranoid manner."

"Where is he now?"

"On the way to the med bay. Mo's bringing him."

Dr. Palto cursed. "He should've called for medical assistance."

Armin swallowed the lump of guilt in his throat because, damn it, he should've thought of that.

Palto continued before Armin could speak. "Oh well. What's done is done. What about the miner? Does she need medical attention?"

Armin glanced her way. She'd sat back down and was finishing her meal in brooding silence. "I don't think so. They're both a bit banged up, and Ryal's lost a tooth, but neither seems to be seriously hurt. It's Ryal's state of mind Mo and I are worried about."

The doctor drew in a sharp breath. "You believe he's had a psychotic episode similar to Hannah's."

"That's what I'm afraid of, yes."

"Another one. Good Lord." Palto sighed. "All right. I'll activate the emergency medical protocol. I've already pulled one of my ad hoc staff out of the biology lab to help me with this autopsy, so she's available immediately, and Tomás can be here shortly. We'll be ready. Thank you for letting me know, Doctor."

"Of course."

The connection cut out. Armin rubbed his dry, burning eyes with the heels of his palms. God, he was tired. Dropping his hands, he turned to Neil and Mandala. "Where's Ashlyn? I need to tell her about Carlo."

"She left a few minutes ago. Said she had some stuff to take care of." Neil's eyes were red, his mouth uncharacteristically downturned. He pushed his half-eaten potatoes around his plate with his fork. "I can't believe this. Why would Carlo *do* that?"

"I wish I knew." Armin reached over to give Neil's hand a squeeze. "Did Ashlyn tell you where she was going?"

"No, she didn't." Mandala cast him an apprehensive look. "She has her com link. She should be easy enough to reach. Do you think something's wrong?"

She didn't say it, but Armin knew she was thinking of Carlo.

"I don't see any reason to think so, no." He activated his com. "Dr. Savage-Hall for Dr. Timms. Urgent."

By the time Ashlyn's answer came, he was on the verge of heading off on a room-by-room search for her. "Armin? What is it?" She sounded stiff and utterly unlike herself.

Uneasy, Armin frowned. "Where are you, Ashlyn? I need to speak to you. In person."

"I'm in the lab." She paused. Her breathing sounded shaky and loud through the com link. "Could you come down here? I'm afraid I can't leave."

Her voice was halting, stilted, thick as tar. Alarms clanged in Armin's mind. He glanced at Neil and Mandala, and saw his fears echoed on their faces. "Of course. I'll be right there. Out."

"Something's not right." Neil drummed his fingers on the table, his forehead creased with obvious concern. "What's she doing in the lab? We just *left* there. She's got no reason to go back."

"And why can't she leave?" Mandala shook her head. Worry framed her eyes and mouth with thin lines. "I don't like it."

"Come with me, but stay outside the lab while I talk to her." Armin held up a hand to stop their protests. "None of us know what's going on, which means we need to be careful. But one of us has to talk to her, and I think it should be me. I want the two of you to be ready to call medical if need be. All right?"

Neither looked happy about it, but they nodded. Satisfied, Armin led the way out of the cafeteria.

The hallway to the lab seemed to go on forever, winding around sharp curves he couldn't remember having taken before. Armin felt as though each step he took added another meter to navigate.

"Is something wrong with the lights?" Neil cast a nervous look around as the three of them followed the corridor—which should definitely not have had this many twists and turns. "It seems darker than usual."

"You're imagining things." Mandala's tone was terse.

"I don't think he is." Armin glanced over his shoulder, certain he'd heard a voice that shouldn't be there. The corridor was empty except for himself, Neil, and Mandala. "It seems dim to me as well."

Mandala shot him a cautious look, but said nothing.

She truly doesn't see it.

He peered around, wielding his skills of scientific observation like a shield. Illumination that should have been bright was dim, yellowish, and sickly. But Neil had seen it too. Which meant Armin wasn't imagining it.

So then, why didn't Mandala see? Mandala who was, if anything, the least emotionally swayed, most relentlessly objective person on their team? It didn't make any sense.

They came upon the lab door suddenly, as if they'd been standing in front of it for a while and it had waited until now to reveal itself.

Ignoring the bizarre thought, Armin keyed in the code and marched inside. Mandala and Neil remained in the hall, though Armin could tell neither was pleased.

Too bad. Now more than ever, Armin wanted them on the outside. Not only to protect them from whatever might be in there, but to call for help in case he couldn't.

All the lights were on. He peered from one workstation to another. The place looked empty. "Ashlyn? Where are you?"

"In the back, beside the emergency eye wash station."

She sounded calm, but her voice was weak. And if she was at the eye wash station, not moving . . .

Armin ran for the rear of the lab, his chest tight with a blossoming dread. He came around the corner and skidded to a stop, gaping like a fish.

The things on the metal tray beside the sink hit his vision in bright flashes. A roll of medical tape. A blue sterile wrap, purple with blood. A gory scalpel. An empty gauze bandage package, the paper ripped down the middle. Two objects that at first glance looked like large white marbles with the stubs of strings attached, smeared with blood. Until he noticed the brown irises, and realized he was looking at human eyes.

He stared at Ashlyn's back where she leaned over the sink—at her thin fingers grasping the sides of the bowl, at the white gauze tied around her head, at the way she trembled all over—and felt sick. "Oh my God, Ashlyn. What have you done?"

CHAPTER 6

Armin made Neil and Mandala stay outside the lab while he called a medical isolation team to the lab on a stat basis. He put on isolation gear while he waited, in the event that BathyTech 3 was, in fact, dealing with a breakout and he'd just been exposed. If he hadn't already been exposed before now.

The creative corners of his mind—the part of him that had created something new and strange from the staid, respectable field of marine geology—had already connected the dots. The picture they formed frightened him to his core.

"That's not necessary," Ashlyn said as Armin zipped into the suit. "The isolation gear, I mean."

He didn't ask how she knew what he was doing. Everything about this situation was wrong. Why shouldn't Ashlyn be able to see through her blood-stained bandage in spite of her lack of eyes?

"I hope you're right. But you know I have to err on the side of caution." Armin approached the chair where he'd made her sit and laid a gloved hand on her arm. "The medics will be here shortly. They'll give you medication for the pain and take you to the medical bay for treatment."

She breathed a barely audible sound that told Armin how hard she was holding back the agony of what she'd done to herself. "That'll be good. Thank you."

"Of course." Armin studied the tight pain lines around her mouth and the tension in her shoulders, and felt helpless. "Why did you do it?"

"I had to. It was the only way." She laughed, a low, wobbly sound. "I realize how insane that sounds. But the weeds get in through the eyes. So they had to go."

A strange, icy tightness clutched at Armin's lungs. "Weeds?"

"They're not weeds in the usual sense, but . . ." She made a so-so gesture with one pale hand. The blood drying around her nails looked black. "It's close enough, I suppose. They creep in through your eyes and grow inside you. Like weeds taking over a lawn." She lifted her mutilated face toward the ceiling, as if she were staring with some mystical inner sight through the kilometers of cold, black ocean to the sky above. "I couldn't let that happen. A sacrifice had to be made, and I made it."

The vice around Armin's lungs squeezed tighter. "What do you mean?" He sounded breathless. Weak. Afraid.

But Doctor, breathed a rough voice in his mind, *don't you want to know? So very much to knooooooow, Doctor . . .*

Ashlyn's head tilted, almost as if she'd heard the voice too. She reached out and grasped his wrist in both hands. Her fingers were cold and shaking. "Armin, listen to me. You remember you told me about the Varredura Longa? About the eyes?"

The eyes. Human eyes in the lab sink, in cups, rolling on the floor. Corpses staring at him with blank, empty, accusing sockets . . .

Ashlyn's self-mutilation had brought back vivid memories of the Varredura Longa. Armin and his team had speculated about the *why* of that crew's actions, but had never come up with satisfactory answers. "You believe they took out their own eyes for the same reason?" It was a terrible thought.

"Yes." Her fingers dug harder into his flesh. "Think about it. Why else would someone do that? They knew something was trying to get to them. Take them over. So they tried to stop it by closing the door. Taking their own eyes. Only they were too late."

It made a horrible, twisted sort of sense. Dread knotted cold and tight in his gut. He laid his free hand over Ashlyn's tense fingers. "What makes you believe that's what they did? Or that you had to do the same? My God, Ashlyn, you cut out your own eyes!"

She went perfectly still. The twin blood-blossoms on her gauze seemed to stare into his brain. "Only a few people in Antarctica actually handled the object they found, but they all *saw* it. Do you understand? *Everyone* saw it. The damned thing infected them through their eyes."

It was a crazy idea, with absolutely no precedent in the natural world. On the other hand, the object currently locked in the lab's vault had no precedent either.

What if she was right?

He swallowed the acid rising in his throat and breathed deep, in and out, in and out. Of course Ashlyn wasn't right. It was ridiculous. No infectious organism spread the way she was talking about, and she knew it. If anything, they were dealing with a previously unknown contagion that caused psychosis. That was bad enough. No need to borrow trouble by buying into Ashlyn's paranoid fantasy.

Beyond the workstations, he heard the lab door *whoosh* open. "Medics," a voice called. "Where are you?"

"Beside the eye wash station," he called back. "Are you wearing isolation gear?"

"Yes." The medics rounded the corner—in full protective dress, to Armin's relief—while Ashlyn was still laughing at Armin's question. The female medic gaped at Ashlyn. "What the . . .?"

"She doesn't think isolation is necessary." Armin stared hard at one medic, then the other. Trying to convey with a silent look that she might not be entirely lucid. "She believes the contagion enters through the eyes."

He watched the light dawn on both medics' faces. The male medic shook his head. "All right, then. I'm Tomás and this is Misha. We're here to take you to the med bay, Ms., um . . ."

"Dr. Ashlyn Timms." Ashlyn's lips twisted into the wry, condescending smile with which Armin had become extremely familiar since they'd started working together. She stood, clinging to the back of the chair with one hand. "If one of you could help me to the stretcher, I'd appreciate it. I'm feeling a bit shaky."

"Here, Ashlyn. I've got you." Armin took her elbow, put an arm around her waist, and walked her the few steps to where the medics waited. Fine tremors ran through her body, the only outward sign of the pain she must feel. He helped her onto the floating gurney. "I'm going along with you, all right? I'll be right here."

Her smile blossomed into something more genuine. "Thank you, Armin. You know, you should really do the same, before it's too late.

You and anyone else who's still unaffected. It's already spreading fast. This place'll end up just like the Varredura Longa if we're not careful."

Blood on the lab floor. Intestines strung like grisly holiday decorations around the mess hall. Someone's tongue bobbing by a wire in the moon pool. Lights dim, equipment smashed, so many dead, so many more missing...

Armin shook off the memories, his throat too tight to answer. He squeezed her hand, then backed out of the way so the medics could cover her with an isolation tent and take her away.

He braced himself for the questions Neil and Mandala would no doubt have. Hopefully, he could tell them what little he knew on the way to the medical bay, then find Mo and take him away for a private chat. He had the sinking feeling now was the time to tell Mo all the things he'd been trying not to say for the past several days. It was a conversation he did not look forward to, but it had to be done.

Squaring his shoulders, he followed the stretcher out the door.

Mo was about to leave the med bay in search of Armin when the call came in about Dr. Timms.

"She cut out both her eyes with a scalpel." Misha's voice was grim over the com. "Said she had no choice because the weeds spread through the eyes."

Dr. Palto rubbed a hand over his face. "Good Lord. She's isolated, I hope?"

"Yes. Dr. Savage-Hall requested isolation when he called us." Misha paused for a beat. "He wants—"

Armin cut in. "Dr. Palto, I believe we have a serious situation here. Ashlyn needs to be isolated, and everyone else with the exception of essential medical personnel needs to be confined to quarters immediately, and for the foreseeable future. Is that possible?"

Mo let out a soft, humorless laugh. At least Armin could be counted on to see the potential threat in the situation.

Palto curled forward, like the weight of what was happening was too much to handle. "I wish I could disagree with you, Doctor, but I can't. I'll have the isolation room ready when you get here."

"Good." Armin spoke to someone on the other end, then came back to the com. "I think you should probably call upside as well, and tell them what's going on down here. Tell them that Hannah is most likely patient zero."

"Agreed, Doctor. See you shortly." Palto leaned back in his chair and ran both hands over his close-cropped hair. He looked grim and older than his years, his dark complexion ashen. "When I was hired for this job, I told Youssouf three iso rooms were excessive. My research *might* have required one. In the unlikely event that anyone here developed an illness requiring isolation, we would've only needed a room long enough for the *Peregrine* to send a team down to take them upside for treatment. But now it looks as though we may wish we had more before the day's over."

It was a scary thought. "What sort of contagion causes people to . . ." Mo gestured toward Ryal, pacing his small room like a panther scenting blood and unable to get to the source. "To be like this? Or like Hannah. I've never heard of any disease that does that."

"Some infections can certainly cause psychotic behavior. However, few that I know of are likely to be present in a bathyspheric environment. Of the ones that might be—such as some sexually transmitted diseases—none would spread so quickly, and all would show other symptoms prior to psychosis."

"In other words, you don't know that it *is* anything contagious."

"No, I don't. I have no idea what, exactly, we're dealing with. But, at the moment, we have four people in the space of two days who have exhibited symptoms similar enough to make me want to take precautions. One of those people is dead and the other mutilated, both at their own hands." Palto tapped his fingers on the machine that dispensed meds. "Right now, we *have* to assume the worst—that we have an outbreak of a highly contagious, unknown disease on this pod. Until we have solid proof otherwise, we will continue to act as though that is the case. If you'll excuse me, Mr. Rees."

Mo nodded and wandered away while Palto called the medical team on the *Peregrine*. He leaned his elbows on the desk, thinking hard. Something was happening on BT3. Something bad. If scientific method and medical treatment could stop it? Hell, he was all for that.

If only the quiet little corner of his mind would stop whispering to him that nothing could stop the forces that had been set in motion here.

The med bay door slid open. Tomás and Misha trotted in, leading a hover stretcher covered with an iso tent. Through the transparent plastic Mo saw Dr. Timms, her hands folded over her belly as if she were sleeping and a bloody bandage wrapped around her eyes.

Or, well, where her eyes had been until she'd cut them out. *Jesus.*

"Bring her into Iso Two." Dr. Palto led the way, pulling on his protective gear as he went. "Misha, if you could assist me with the exam and surgery I'd appreciate it."

She nodded. "Sure thing. I'll get the trauma kit."

She veered away, leaving Tomás and Dr. Palto to guide the stretcher into the isolation room. In the cubicle next door, Ryal stopped his pacing long enough to watch with a detached sort of curiosity until the stretcher was out of sight. He flashed Mo a grin that chilled him deep down.

The bay door opened again, making Mo jump. Armin walked in, his shoulders slumped, weariness stamped into the part of his face Mo could see above the isolation mask. Mo forgot all about the disturbing changes in Ryal.

"Armin." He crossed the room in a few strides and stopped before he could act on the urge to hug the man, iso suit and all. "Are you all right?"

For a moment, Armin didn't say anything. He looked burdened, as if he personally carried BathyTech 3's fate on his back. Mo took his hand and squeezed. Fuck the gloves. It didn't matter. Armin obviously needed someone to let him know they cared about him right now, and Mo did.

"No." Armin curled his fingers around Mo's. "I'm not all right. One of my oldest friends committed suicide today. One of the most brilliant scientists of this century just cut out her own eyes because she believed *weeds* were going to get in through them and infect her mind. And I brought both of those people down here."

Mo ached for this man he barely knew but already considered a friend. Possibly more. "It's not your fault. You have to know that."

Armin let out a brittle laugh. "Isn't it?" He looked at Mo, and the anguish in his eyes was heartbreaking. "Mo. We need to talk. There's a great deal I need to tell you. Things that I probably should have told you before, but I didn't because I thought they had nothing to do with our work here. But now I'm very afraid they might."

Okay, that didn't sound good at all. Mo studied what he could see of Armin's face, trying to read him. "Can we go somewhere to talk, before we get confined to quarters?"

Armin glanced toward the iso room where Dr. Palto and Misha were bent over Dr. Timms. "I can't expose anyone else. And, in fact, you shouldn't either. Not until we know more about what we're dealing with."

Mo strode around behind the desk, grabbed a filter mask and a pair of gloves, and pulled them on. "How about now? Can we leave now? How about we go to your quarters?"

The way the skin around Armin's eyes crinkled told Mo he was smiling behind his mask. "Well. I suppose it's good enough. The last isolation room ought to be saved in case another symptomatic case turns up, anyway."

Armin crossed to the other end of the desk and spoke to the nurse. Telling him where they were going, no doubt. After he'd talked to the nurse, Armin headed straight for the exit without a word. Mo followed.

Thankfully, they only passed a couple of people on the way to Armin's quarters. Mo ignored the strange looks they got because of the iso gear. He'd deal with that if it meant finding out what was making Armin look so damn scared.

Armin stopped outside his room and glanced around like he expected to find bad guys lurking in the shadows. Mo frowned into the unnatural dimness. What the fuck was wrong with the lights?

As soon as Mo thought it, the entire hallway went pitch-black. The lights came back on before he'd properly registered the darkness. He gaped at the perfectly ordinary soft white glow.

Armin turned to him, forehead furrowed, as the door opened. "Mo? What's the matter?"

Meaning Armin hadn't noticed the temporary blackout. Mo licked his lips. "Um. Have you noticed that the lights have been kind of dim?" He peered overhead. "Well. Not now. But they were for a while."

"Oh." Armin grasped the edge of the door so hard his fingers trembled. "I've noticed, yes. But I don't know . . ." He trailed off, staring at nothing.

"Don't know what?"

Armin sighed. "Come in. I'll tell you what I can." Turning his back on Mo, he went inside.

Mo trailed behind, stomach churning. Whatever Armin had to say, he had a feeling he wasn't going to like it.

Armin stopped just inside his room, heart in his throat. Everything had changed. The light pulsed a low, ominous amber. Strange shapes skulked in the shadows, reaching for him and Mo with tenebrous fingers.

He turned and grasped Mo's hands. "Mo. I know this is a strange question, but humor me. What do you see?"

Mo's eyes searched his for a moment, then that keen gaze lifted and moved beyond Armin to the room behind him. "I see your room. You're . . . uh . . . kind of a slob."

Armin laughed. It sounded halfway hysterical, so he stopped. "What about the light, Mo? Is the light normal? The shadows?"

Mo's brows pulled together in obvious concern, but he didn't hesitate to answer. "Looks fine to me, yeah. Why?"

Don't worry, Doctor. It's only the thing living in your brain.

He closed his eyes. Only for a second. A count of *one-one-thousand*. But when he opened them again, the room was exactly as he'd left it that morning—the light a gentle ivory, the sinister shadows banished.

So that was it, then. He was hallucinating. Which meant what? That he was infected? That Mo was as well? He wished he knew.

Mo's fingers in his hair brought him hurtling back to Earth. He stepped closer, close enough to press his body against Mo's, slipped his arms around Mo's waist, and clung to him. "I'm glad you're here. You have no idea."

"I wouldn't be anywhere else." Mo's voice was soft. Tender. He framed Armin's face between his palms to peer into his eyes with a frankness so deep it hurt, and Armin's heart turned over. "I'm here, and here I'm gonna stay. With you. Okay?" He kissed Armin's brow as if he were a child in need of comfort. "Now let's sit down, and you tell me what you brought me here to tell me."

"Yes. Of course." Feeling tired—but far calmer than he had only moments before—Armin dropped his arms, took Mo's hand, and led him to the bed, where they sat side by side. "I'm afraid, Mo."

Mo's sigh sounded infinitely weary. He rested a gloved hand on Armin's thigh. The heat of his palm sank through the layers of latex, the light material of the iso suit, and clothing to sear Armin's skin.

"I'm scared too. I think we both have a right to be." Mo leaned closer. Rested his forehead against Armin's temple. "But Doc, something's happening here. We both know it. Don't you think we have a better chance of fighting it if we're honest with each other?"

He was right. Deep in his soul, Armin knew it.

Mo straightened up, tugged off his gloves, took off his mask, then reached out and removed Armin's mask. He wadded all of them up together and threw them to the floor. "It's just us now. Can we both agree we don't need these?"

The light flickered, dimmed, and stabilized again, yellow and subdued. Armin shut his eyes. "I don't know how to stop this. I'm so sorry."

"Doc. Hey. Don't." The mattress shifted with Mo's weight as he moved closer. One strong arm slid around Armin's back. Mo cupped his cheek and lifted his face for a slow, deep kiss that woke every nerve in his body. When the kiss ended, he cracked open his eyelids, and Mo smiled. "Better now?"

Armin laughed, because he couldn't help it. "Yes. I think kissing you makes everything better."

"Can't hurt." Mo kissed him again, a chaste peck on the brow this time. "Okay. We came here to talk. So why don't you tell me what's been bugging you about that fucking rock?"

A warmth that made no sense whatsoever spread through him like a drug. Of course Mo knew where the heart of their troubles lay.

He was an unusually perceptive man. Armin liked that about him. Liked it to a dangerous degree, in fact.

He leaned against Mo's shoulder so Mo wouldn't see how his desire had begun to move beyond sex. "The rock is . . . different."

"I figured." Mo's fingers traced down his neck, the touch light enough to raise goose bumps. "Different how? C'mon, Doc. Spill it."

Armin peeled off his gloves, stood, and unzipped his iso suit. He felt Mo watching him as he took it off. Whether he was stalling for time, or he needed to get out of the uncomfortably hot suit sooner rather than later, he couldn't say. All he knew was that he didn't want to have this conversation until he'd gotten out of the isolation gear. Now that he and Mo were alone, he didn't think it was necessary. It seemed unlikely he'd caught anything from Ashlyn, since she couldn't possibly have been exposed to anything he hadn't.

He kicked the suit aside and settled back onto the bed, into the curve of Mo's arm. "You already know this thing, whatever it is, isn't the first of its kind. Or at least I'm fairly certain it isn't."

Mo nodded. "Yeah. The other one you wouldn't tell me anything about." His voice held no particular inflection, but Armin heard the faint put-out quality anyway.

"Yes, well, I truly don't know anything about it. What it is, where it came from, anything at all. But I'm going to tell you the whole story of how we found out about it." Armin stared at his hands, putting the story together in his mind. Finding the best way to tell someone who didn't know. "A few weeks ago, I got a call from Mandala on behalf of Dr. Klaudia Longenesse, a colleague of ours who headed the Varredura Longa, a deep-sea research pod on the ocean floor off the coast of Antarctica. They were funded by Chile's university system, coupled with donations from private parties, so they had a great deal of money for research of all sorts. Mermaids had been reported there, and they'd been trying to get footage of them. Trying to study them and learn something of their habits. Anyway, Klaudia and her crew had found an odd sonar signature a few kilometers from the pod. They went to check into it, and brought back something unusual."

"A not-rock like the one in the lab, you mean." The grimness in Mo's voice matched the way his fingers gripped Armin's shoulder.

"Well, that's the thing. We're not sure what it was they brought back."

Mo scratched his chin. "They didn't show you any footage?"

"No." And, God, how Armin had wished, over and over and over, that he had pressed Mandala to ask Klaudia to send them something—anything—for study before they went to Antarctica. But he hadn't, and now he had nothing but a low-quality video clip from an outside camera. "Klaudia wanted to keep it as secret as possible, and we didn't push her since Mandala was planning to bring a team down soon anyway."

"What happened?"

Blood. Bodies. The smell of death. Klaudia Longenesse walking into the darkness. And God, Dr. Aguilar . . .

Armin rubbed his palms on his thighs, trying to scrape away the memory on the rough cotton of his trousers. "Klaudia contacted Mandala first, because she needed a microgeology expert. Mandala asked me to join the team because the object was found in fifty-seven hundred meters of water, and my secondary degree is in deep-marine biology. Carlo was on board because he is . . . *was*—" Damn, that was painful. "—a leading expert in deep-marine geology. She called Neil Douglas also, because he's one of the world's only true experts in the field of exobiology. She wanted a full complement of experts in various disciplines that might be needed, and we'd all worked together before at one time or another so we were already familiar with each other and knew we worked well together."

"And what happened when you got there?"

When they got there.

He knew he'd see those first moments in his nightmares for the rest of his days.

He stared at the brownish blotch on the middle drawer of his dresser so he wouldn't have to see Mo's horror and pity while he told his tale. "Only Neil and Carlo were available immediately. I wasn't able to get away for another ten days at the earliest. Mandala could've gone within the week, but no one thought there was any rush. Klaudia said the object was safe in their vault and for us to come when we could. So the group waited for me." He laughed, the sound sharp and bitter. "Ten days, that's all. But when we arrived, there was no one there to greet us. All but one of the Varredura Longa crew was either dead or missing."

"Jesus." Mo rubbed a hand over the stubble developing on his chin. "How? And where in the hell did they *go*?"

"All of the walkers were missing, as well as both rovers. Oddly enough, the sub for traveling upside was still there. And the dead . . ." The memory had his pulse racing as if he were experiencing it all over again. He turned to face Mo. "They weren't simply dead. They'd been slaughtered. Torn apart. Some had knives still in their hands. Others had injuries we couldn't figure out at all. We were forced to identify some of the crew by DNA sample, because all that was left was internal organs."

The color leeched from Mo's face, though his expression didn't change. "Jesus."

"We found only one surviving crew member." Armin watched Mo's fists open and close, open and close. "Dr. Prema Aguilar, one of the marine zoologists. She specialized in studying deep-sea octopi, particularly in the Antarctic area. A brilliant scientist." He paused, remembering.

"Armin?" Mo touched his knee. "What happened?"

Not for the first time, Armin wondered how a mind as bright and quick as Mo's remained sane in a profession as dull as mining. He laid his hand over Mo's. "We found her barricaded in the infirmary. She'd cut out her tongue and both her eyes."

"Oh shit." Mo swallowed. He looked ill. "That part sounds a little too familiar."

"Exactly." Armin wove his fingers together with Mo's and focused on the places where their skin pressed together. "We found other eyes scattered around the place. Seventeen of them in all. One pair and a single belonged to two of the more intact bodies. We never did find the people the other ones belonged to."

He watched the realization dawn on Mo—that some of the missing Varredura Longa crew must have gone walking minus their eyes.

Mo licked his lips. "That must've been a shock."

"It was." Armin studied the glisten of Mo's newly moistened lower lip with fascination. "Neil's the only one of the three of us with any practical experience in medicine, so he stabilized Dr. Aguilar while Mandala and I attempted to download the computer logs and lab records into our portables before notifying the authorities of the deaths."

Mo rubbed his thumb along the edge of Armin's hand. "So you didn't think they'd let you go back there once the investigation was started?"

"We knew they wouldn't. And we were right. After we reported the deaths, we weren't allowed back into the facility." He clung to Mo's hand. Mo's strong grasp calmed him. Steadied him. Made him feel as if he could face whatever lay ahead. "None of us ever heard anything else about it. No one told us what the findings were. And none of us were allowed to see Dr. Aguilar again."

"You said you *attempted* to download the records. Does that mean you weren't able to?"

"They'd all been wiped blank."

Mo's lips formed an *oh*. "Damn."

"Yes." Armin sighed. "We have no idea why they would've done such a thing. It makes no sense. And to my mind, at least, such a deliberate act doesn't fit with the unbridled violence that obviously occurred there. The dichotomy makes me uneasy."

"Yeah, I can see why." Mo's eyes focused on Armin's face as if he were an anchor in a stormy sea. "What about the thing they found, that they'd wanted you guys to look at?"

"It was gone. Most of the security footage was reduced to static—we still don't know why—but we were able to recover three seconds of footage from one of the outside cameras. It showed Dr. Longenesse in a walker suit, moving away from the pod into the open ocean, carrying what looked like a round, black stone."

Mo drew in a hissing breath. "Just like the one we recovered."

Armin nodded. "The footage wasn't very clear, but as far as we can tell, this one is identical."

"Christ." Mo hunched his shoulders, his forehead creased in thought. "How'd you know it was her?"

"Varredura Longa walkers are very much like BathyTech's in that they're the same color, but they're personalized to their wearers. Her name was printed on the back. Otherwise we would've had no idea who it was." Armin closed his eyes and watched the memory of the Varredura Longa parade across the inside of his eyelids, his punishment for not getting there in time to save them. "We never seriously considered an infectious organism, though of course we suggested that the authorities test for one. There are no known organisms that fit what happened there. Some do spread that quickly, but absolutely none cause psychological symptoms without physical ones."

"And you never thought you might be dealing with something brand-new?" Mo sounded surprised and put out.

Armin opened his eyes and stared at Mo, defiant. "Something new? From where? Even if the object were extraterrestrial and Klaudia and her team found signs of life in it, that wouldn't equate to something infectious. You wouldn't say that if you had any idea what the odds were against it."

"Okay. Fine. Sorry." Mo moved closer, his fingers tightening around Armin's hand. "I really am sorry. We shouldn't be fighting right now. We need to be a team."

"Yes." He leaned forward to press a kiss to Mo's mouth. "Yes. We do. We *are*. A team. You and me."

Mo smiled, and Armin's heart did a strange little flip. He squeezed Mo's hand. The connection felt good. It felt right. It calmed the confusion and terror swarming like locusts inside him.

Mo's smile faded into a solemnity that matched Armin's to perfection. "The things I've seen and heard scared me before. But it scares me even more now."

"It scares me too." He slid closer still until his leg pressed against Mo's. "I have no idea if this is truly a contagion, some sort of mass psychosis, or something else entirely. But whatever's happening right now, it's very real, even if what you're experiencing isn't. If we're going to fight it, we have to keep our heads. We have to distinguish the real from the imagined."

"Yeah." Mo rested his free hand on Armin's knee. The heat of his palm sank through Armin's trousers to warm his skin. It made him feel protected. "I know when I'm seeing or hearing things. Or, well, I think I do. I'm pretty sure." He let out a soft laugh. "Okay, no, I'm not. I can't always tell anymore. Not when the shit I'm experiencing *feels* so damn real."

Armin nodded. "It's terrible not being able to trust your own senses."

They stared at one another. Armin knew they had much more to say to one another, but he couldn't quite mold his thoughts into words, and he suspected Mo felt the same.

The com beside the door whistled the tone for general emergency announcements, sending a jolt of adrenaline through Armin's body. He clutched Mo's hand tight while they listened.

"This is Dr. Youssouf with an emergency announcement from Dr. Palto. Effective immediately, operations are halted and all personnel with the exception of the medical team are confined to quarters. We've had an outbreak of a suspected contagion. We are not certain how it spreads, or even its exact nature. All we know is that whatever this is, it spreads very, very quickly. Symptoms we know about so far are psychotic and/or violent behavior, and, well, that's all." She paused. "Sorry, folks. I know nobody likes it. But it's for your own safety, so just do it, okay? Youssouf out."

Armin absorbed the news without surprise. After all, he'd recommended it. Although . . . "I know this is a ridiculous question, but living quarters here *are* equipped with standard two-week emergency rations, right?"

"Yeah. We'll have to split it if we stay together, which gives us a week's worth, but I can't see this thing lasting that long anyway." Mo let go of Armin, stood and paced to the door and back again. "Damn it. I can't stay in here."

"I know how you feel. My team and I need to continue our work if we're ever going to understand what's happening here. But this *is* the safest thing for the population of this pod."

"I know." Mo scratched his neck. "I was just thinking about Daisy."

Jealousy elbowed Armin in the gut. He ignored it, because he had no patience with irrational feelings. He raised his eyebrows. "Who's Daisy?"

"Hannah's pet pink-toed tarantula. Nobody thought to take her upside with Hannah, so I'm taking care of her." He shrugged. "Maybe it's silly to worry about a spider right now, but Hannah loves her, and it's not like she can forage for herself or anything down here.

She's pretty low maintenance, but still . . . If this *does* end up lasting more than a week and I'm not there to feed her and give her water, she'll die."

This glimpse of Mo's sweet side warmed Armin's heart. He rose to his feet. "Then let's go to your quarters. We'll wait it out there, together. If I bring my rations we won't even have to split anything."

Mo's eyes widened. "Are you sure you want to do that? You'd leave your own room?"

"Why wouldn't I?" Armin gestured at the small, plain space. "There's no particular reason for me to stay here. I'll simply tell the auto-port I'm staying with you."

"We'll get in trouble if we get caught leaving."

"Then we'll have to make certain we don't get caught."

A slow, wicked smile lit Mo's face. He grasped Armin's wrist, tugged him close, and planted a toe-curling kiss on his lips. "You're sexy when you break the rules, Doc."

Armin grinned. "In that case, I'll have to do it more often."

A dark fire glittered in Mo's eyes. He kissed Armin again. Deeper this time. Aggressive. Armin's knees wobbled.

Finally, ages later, Mo drew back, looking as dazed as Armin felt. "Well. We better get going, before Youssouf decides to lock everybody's doors just in case."

Armin blinked, startled. "Can she do that?"

"I don't think so. But I'd rather not find out the hard way that I'm wrong."

"Right. Just let me get a few things."

Mo fidgeted beside the door while Armin threw his toiletries and a few changes of clothing into his travel bag, along with the silvery pouches of his freeze-dried food rations. Once he was packed, he told the auto-port to forward any messages to Mo's quarters, and the two of them slipped out into the hallway, each carrying one of the five-gallon water jugs from Armin's ration closet.

The corridor seemed deserted. They saw no one during the short walk from Armin's quarters to Mo's. But the back of Armin's neck prickled, and he had to fight the urge to turn around.

Reaching Mo's room was a relief. He set his things on the floor and flopped onto the bed as soon as Mo sealed the door behind them.

He watched, curious, as Mo opened the lid of a tall, wide, transparent-plastic cage on the floor, took a cricket from a box, and dropped it into the cage. The arachnid skittered down a leafy branch propped diagonally from bottom to top and attacked faster than Armin would've thought possible.

Armin pushed up on one elbow so he could see better. "Fascinating. I've never seen a tarantula feeding in person before."

"Yeah, it's something all right. Not sure what exactly, but it's something." Mo crouched beside the cage and peered through the wall at the spider. "Hi, Daisy," he crooned in a high, singsong voice. "You're a big old hairy, creepy thing, you know that? Yes, you are."

Armin laughed. "And yet here you are, feeding her and talking to her like she's your child."

"What can I say? I'm a softy."

"I think it's lovely." Moved by a sudden surge of desire, Armin slid over to make room and patted the mattress. "Come here."

The way Mo's lips curved told Armin their minds were on the same track. Mo rose, crossed the room in a few strides and lowered himself to the bed.

Armin woke an undetermined time later in the dim glow of the light Mo liked to keep on even while sleeping. At first he couldn't figure out what had woken him. Then the sound came again—a solid *thud, thud, thud* on the door.

He sat up. Mo stood beside the bed, pulling on the trousers he'd discarded when they'd undressed earlier. "Mo? What's going on? Who could be out there?"

"Don't know. I'm gonna find out." Mo sidled up the door. "Auto-port."

"Yes, Mo?"

"Identify the person outside the door."

"Checking." The light blinked once. Twice. Three times. "Unable to identify. I am sorry, Mo. Shall I activate the camera?"

Mo glanced wide-eyed at Armin. "Yes."

"Very well. Activating."

The auto-port visual screen came on. At first, Armin only saw a silhouette. The light in the hall was dimmer than it ought to be, even on the night shift. Then the figure leaned closer to the port's outside screen, and Armin let out a surprised *oh*. Mo jumped back with a curse.

On the monitor, Ryal Nataki's eyes glowed purple-black in a dead gray face. The dull light glinted off a grin full of long, pointed teeth.

CHAPTER 7

Mo stared, shocked. "Armin? Does he look...different? To you?"

"Different as in glowing eyes and pointed teeth?"

"Yeah."

"In that case, yes." Relief shone through his words bright as the sun Mo barely remembered anymore. Armin stood, still naked, moved to Mo's side, and took his hand in a cold, hard grip. "The fact that we're both seeing it could be a good thing, or a bad thing, you know."

Mo snorted. "The way I figure, it could be a bad thing, or a worse thing, but I get what you're saying."

Before Mo could stop him, Armin thumbed the manual intercom activation. "Ryal. This is Armin Savage-Hall. You're very ill. You really ought to go back to the medical bay."

Ryal chortled. The low, gurgling sound raised gooseflesh all over Mo's body. "Oh, I don't think so, Doctor. Way too much *fun-fun-fun* to be had out here in the candy factory." He peered sideways with one glittering purple-black eye, like he was trying to look through a peephole. "You there, Mo? I know you are." He licked the auto-port screen. His tongue was long and thin, *too* thin, deep midnight blue like an exotic sea slug. "Mmmmm. I can *tasssssste* you."

Mo shuddered all over. Fighting the brew of revulsion and sadness burning his throat, he edged closer to the port. "Ryal, listen to me. Armin's right. You're sick. You've caught some kind of infection. You need to get back to the med bay and let Doc Palto help you."

The disturbingly non-Ryal-like chuckle came again. "Help? Why would I want any *help*, even if anyone in this ridiculous tin can had any to give?" Ryal lifted his hands, flexed fingers grown too skinny, bending in all the wrong ways—*just like Hannah's*—and stared directly into the camera as if he could see straight through to the men on the other side. "I don't need help. I'm becoming so much more than I'd ever dreamed possible." He leaned so close all Mo could see was one eye empty as space, with a purple spark in the middle forming into a shape he almost recognized. "Don't worry, friends. You'll find out."

He pushed away from the door so fast Mo saw nothing but a blur of speed. But the shape Ryal's body imprinted on Mo's brain as he sprinted down the corridor was as wrong as his face.

Mo plopped onto the bed, mind and heart both careening out of control. "What the hell just happened?"

"Obviously Ryal has gotten out of isolation somehow." Armin crossed the room and bent to dig through the pile of clothes on the floor.

"That's not what I meant."

"I know. We can discuss the implications in a moment. Right now we need to contact the medical bay."

"They probably already know he's—" Then Mo understood. He shut up and lunged for his dresser.

While he pulled on the first shirt he put his hands on, Armin finally found his com in the mound of discarded clothes, strapped it onto his wrist, and activated it. "Dr. Savage-Hall calling any personnel in the medical bay. Urgent."

No answer. Mo and Armin exchanged an apprehensive glance. "Any personnel in the medical bay," Armin repeated, pulling on his pants as he talked. "Please come in. This is an extremely urgent medical matter."

The silence from the bay stretched on. Armin and Mo were both dressed in a matter of seconds, but that was more than enough to convince Mo that Ryal hadn't gotten away using the power of words.

They left Mo's quarters and headed for the med bay without discussing it. Mo wasn't exactly sure what they could do, but he wasn't telling Armin that. He didn't think he could stand to sit in his room twiddling his thumbs while something bad was probably happening in the med bay.

"Dr. Savage-Hall calling Dr. Palto." Armin kept his voice low and his gaze moving, like he was afraid of attracting attention. Not that Mo blamed him, under the circumstances. "Come in. This is *extremely* urgent."

Nothing.

Scared now, Mo broke into a jog, Armin hot on his heels.

They'd almost reached the med bay when Armin's com came to life. "Armin, this is Gerald Palto. Sorry, I was in the middle of an emergency call. What's going on?"

Relief turned Mo's legs to rubber. He sagged against the wall, laughing.

Armin rubbed a hand across his forehead. "Damn it, Palto, you scared me."

"Uh. Sorry?" The doctor sounded confused.

Armin shook his head. "Listen. Ryal Nataki got out of isolation. He's on the loose."

"What?"

"Yes. He came to Mo's quarters and spoke to us through the auto-port. He's . . ." Armin stared down the hallway, as if he were looking for the right words at the end of it. "I believe he may be very dangerous."

"Goddamn it. Hang on." From the other end of the connection, Mo heard Palto calling instructions to someone. "Please tell me you're still in Mo's room."

Armin shot a guilty look at Mo, who rolled his eyes. "Not exactly, no."

"We're just outside the med bay," Mo broke in. "Armin called in there first thing, but no one answered."

"Someone might be hurt." Armin cast Mo a stern glare. "We're going in."

Palto sighed. "Can I talk you out of it?"

"No."

Mo opened his com link. "Someone should start looking for Ryal. I'll com Gordon."

Armin shot him a questioning look. "Our part-time security guy," Mo explained. "We don't need a full-time staff or anything. Or, well, we never did before. Gordon's sort of on call just in case. His main job is communications."

"Do that. We need to find Ryal as soon as possible." A woman said something in the background of wherever Dr. Palto was. He answered her with what sounded like a drug name and dosage. "Tell Gordon to treat him as a patient, not a criminal, all right? Now I need to get back to my own patient. Speaking of, please call me back ASAP and let me know if the med bay is safe or not. I need to get—ah, this patient there as soon as humanly possible. He's stable, but I need him in the bay to keep him that way."

Something about the way Palto stumbled tripped Mo's alarms. He glanced at Armin. Dread gathered in every line and shadow of his face.

"Gerald." Armin's voice was low and measured. "Who is your patient?"

A heartbeat of quiet followed, and Mo knew the answer wasn't anything they'd want to hear. Armin shut his eyes.

"I'll tell you later." Dr. Palto's gentle answer wasn't reassuring. Mo laid a hand on Armin's shoulder. "Please be careful."

Mo answered when Armin didn't. "We will. Out."

Armin opened his eyes. His jaw took on the stubborn set Mo had already learned meant *don't fuck with me.* "Call your security person, Mo. I'm going in."

Mo snagged his wrist before he could move. "Me first."

Armin's dark eyes flashed. He shook loose of Mo's grip. "Why?"

"Because you're the doctor. I'm just the muscle." Mo answered Armin's stunned stare with his most disarming smile. "Besides, I'm a damn good fighter. And I'm armed." Reaching into the side pocket of his pants, he pulled out the switchblade he absolutely, positively was *not* supposed to have. "Face it, Doc. We don't know who or what's in there. We both have a better chance of not getting hurt if me and my weapon go in first."

Shaking his head, Armin lifted the wrist with his com link. "Dr. Savage-Hall to security. Urgent."

A short silence followed before Gordon picked up. "This is Gordon. You got a security issue? For real?"

"Yes." Armin shot Mo a wide-eyed glance. "Ryal Nataki was in medical isolation, but he's broken out. Mr. Rees and I are about to enter the med bay. We need you to find Mr. Nataki." Armin's eyebrows drew together. "He may be dangerous, so please be cautious, but he is also a patient in need of help. Do you understand?"

"Yeah, of course." Gordon paused. "Maybe I ought to come over there to the med bay first and go in with you and Mo. Make sure it's safe in there."

"Thank you, but I believe it's far more urgent to find Mr. Nataki."

"Okay, then. I'm on it. Out."

"Thank you. Out." Armin lifted his determined gaze to Mo. "Are you ready?"

Mo's lips curled into a grim smile. "Let's go." He pressed his thumb to the access panel at the bottom of the auto-port screen. The med bay door opened.

Armin hung back when Mo gestured to him to wait. Mo eased into the bay, his back to the wall and his knife in the loose fighting grip his oldest sister had taught him ages ago. Sometimes, during the fire-lit Dubai nights when they'd thought the lights would never come back on, they'd needed the silence of a weapon that wasn't a gun.

He saw Tomás's face first. Bluish. One eyelid at half-mast, the other closed, his mouth open.

Mo knelt to check for a pulse, though he knew he wouldn't find one. He'd seen enough corpses to recognize the slackness unique to the faces of the newly dead.

Sure enough, the man had no heartbeat and no breathing. He hadn't been dead long enough for rigor mortis to set in, but his face was chalky, and when Mo leaned down to look, lividity had begun to stretch the length of his neck.

The parts that weren't bruised purple and black, that was. The bruises wrapped around his throat, ringing the spot where his trachea seemed abnormally flat.

Christ. He'd been strangled. Recently, by someone strong enough to crush incredibly tough rings of cartilage like it was easy.

Normally, that would in no way describe Ryal Nataki. Or anyone else here, for that matter. But since break-ins didn't happen at seven thousand meters, it had to be someone in this pod. Which was pretty fucking terrifying, for lots of reasons.

Rising to his feet, Mo glanced around. The bay was empty other than the dead medic. He went back to the door. "C'mon in, Doc. I don't think we can do much here except try to figure out what happened."

Armin glanced at the dead man, then back up to Mo, a question in his eyes.

Mo shook his head. "No pulse, no breathing. But it's been too long to try reviving him."

"You're right." Armin eyed the man's crushed throat. "I hate to believe that Ryal killed him, but it seems likely. I think we have to consider him a danger to everyone on this pod."

Sorrow for his friend coiled tight in Mo's chest. Ryal had always been such a warm, happy, generous person. He'd give his last penny to a stranger in need. How could he possibly become this dangerous—even deadly—reverse image of himself?

Overcome by a sudden surge of fear, Mo moved closer to Armin. "What the hell's happening here? How did everything get so crazy?"

Compassion and concern filled Armin's black eyes. He cupped Mo's face in his hands. "I wish I knew. But we're going to do our best to stop it. All right? And if there's any way at all to help Ryal, we're going to do it. Him and Hannah. I don't want—"

He stopped, teeth snapping together with an audible *clack*. But Mo heard what he hadn't said.

"I know, Doc." He smoothed Armin's hair away from his face. Kissed his brow, where the worry lines gathered. "I don't want anyone else to die either."

A faint half smile tilted one corner of Armin's mouth. "Exactly."

They stood there for a few seconds that felt like lifetimes to Mo, hands on one another's faces, gazing into each other's eyes. Mo felt like he was falling. Like he'd found the secrets to life itself and couldn't look away.

This is how it is when someone understands you. He traced his thumb around the shell of Armin's ear.

Armin blinked, visibly pulled himself out of his thoughts, dropped his hands from Mo's face, and stepped back. He cleared his throat. "I'm going to check on Ashlyn. She should be safe, but she must be terrified."

Mo nodded, shoving his hands in his back pockets to hide how they shook. "Yeah. Okay."

Armin crossed the bay to the iso room in the far corner. The inside curtain was drawn shut. He rapped on the GlasSteel wall beside the door. "Ashlyn? It's me, Armin. Are you all right?"

No answer. Armin frowned over his shoulder at Mo, who strode up to stand beside him. "Ashlyn?" Armin called, louder this time. "Are you all right?" He knocked on the door. It swung open.

Armin sucked in a startled breath. Before he could move a muscle, Mo pushed him aside and went through the door.

The little room was empty.

Alarm and intrigue pushed Mo's pulse into a gallop. He let Armin in, and they stared at each other. "How in the hell did she get anywhere?" Mo wondered. "Do you think Ryal . . .?"

He couldn't finish the sentence, as if saying it out loud would make it true. Armin sighed. "A few hours ago, I would've said there was no way in the world Ryal would harm anyone. Now? I don't know. I feel like I don't know anything anymore."

Mo didn't answer. What could he say? He was as adrift as Armin—more—when it came to figuring out what the hell was happening here.

In his heart of hearts, he found the whole business exciting. Which was wrong, and he knew it, but he couldn't help it. The mystery lured him. Whispered to the dark part of him that longed for new experiences, sights no one else had seen, secrets previously unrevealed.

That wasn't such a bad thing, he mused, rubbing his chin and gazing into the empty room. His desire for information could help them learn about whatever had taken hold of BathyTech 3. That could only be good.

Right?

"Armin, are you there?"

Palto's voice through Armin's communicator made them both jump. Armin blew out a breath and lifted his wrist. "I'm here. The med bay is safe. Ryal and Ashlyn are both missing, though, and Tomás is dead. At this time, Ryal is considered to be dangerous. So please be careful."

"Jesus H." Palto said something to someone on his end. "We'll be there in about ten seconds. Everybody stay out of our way. This patient is no longer stable, and we're going to need to get to the crash cart."

Armin and Mo looked at one another. They both ran out of the iso room at the same time. Armin made sure the crash cart was accessible while Mo opened the third iso room. Maybe they needed it and maybe they didn't, but there was no harm in having it ready.

The med bay doors opened. Dr. Palto and Misha burst in at a run, both in full iso gear, a hover stretcher floating between them. Palto held an IV bag dripping into their patient's arm, while Misha squeezed a blue plastic bag attached to a stiff tube sticking out of the man's mouth. Mo knew just enough about emergency medicine to know the other end of the tube was in the man's trachea, and Misha was squeezing air into his lungs to breathe for him.

The man looked so unlike himself, it took Mo a few seconds to recognize Neil Douglas.

Armin saw at the same time Mo did. "Oh my God." He rushed over and followed the stretcher into the isolation room. Mo followed, pushing the crash cart. "What happened?"

"As far as I can tell, he's had a stroke." Dr. Palto connected the stretcher to the bed in the iso room. The stretcher's transfer function lifted Dr. Douglas gently onto the bed. Palto connected the breathing tube to the built-in ventilator and began inputting the settings. "Misha, start the scans and the necessary blood tests." While Misha began inputting settings into the room's computer terminal, Palto glanced at Mo and Armin. "Each room has basic scanning ability. We need to know if we're dealing with an ischemic or hemorrhagic event so we'll know how to treat it."

Armin nodded. "Of course. Is there anything I can do?"

"Not here, no." Palto shot him a sympathetic look. "I'm sorry. I'll update you when we know something, though."

"Yes. Thank you." Armin's forehead furrowed. "I think I should find Mandala and the two of us should get back to work immediately on the object from Richards Deep. Whatever's happening here, I believe it may be related to that thing, so the faster we can work out what exactly it is, where it comes from, and what—if any—life-forms it harbors, the better."

"I think that's a good idea." Palto studied the readouts on the panel above Dr. Douglas's head. "I'm going to get back to the autopsies once Neil's stabilized. Misha can look after him."

"All right. Thank you." Armin turned his gaze to Mo. "Well. I'll call you when I'm ready to go back to your quarters, all right?"

"Sure, Doc. Good luck." Mo waved and grinned as Armin left, though he wasn't feeling it. He didn't much want to be left out, and he wanted Armin out of his sight even less. Worry twisted cold and tight in his stomach.

An idea hit him as the door shut behind Armin, and he jumped on it. He thumbed on his communicator. "Maximo Rees to Chaz Gordon."

"Gordon here. What's up?"

"Let me help you look for Ryal. And Dr. Timms, she's missing too now."

"Christ on a bike. Two missing people. Wow." Gordon sighed over the com. "You can't be serious."

"Why not? I have security training." Not the kind Gordon was thinking of, but he didn't need to know that. "Besides, Ryal is a friend of mine. If anyone can get him to give himself up, I can."

Silence. Deep, thoughtful silence. Mo fidgeted and kept quiet.

Finally, Gordon barked out a short laugh. "Okay. What the fuck. I recruited Tsali from engineering to help. She's an ex-bodyguard. I'll send her over to get you and you two can search section A."

Mo grinned. "That's perfect. Thank you."

"Yeah, yeah. We'll see if you still say that later. Out."

Mo cut the link and parked himself beside the door to wait for Tsali. Finally, something useful to do.

Or not. Twenty minutes after leaving the med bay, Mo and Tsali had searched nearly every corner of section A without finding the slightest sign of Ryal or Timms, and Mo was starting to get restless.

"Okay, we got the library and aquarium left to search." Tsali peered around the dim hallway—it shouldn't be this dim, and the light shouldn't flicker like that; it wasn't right—with her ice-blue eyes that never stopped moving. "Which one you want to do first?"

Like it mattered. "Library." The way Mo figured, the aquarium offered no place to hide. Therefore, the library was most likely to turn up their missing persons. "Can I go in first this time?"

She glared at him, and he raised his hands in defeat.

They entered the library the same way they had the cafeteria, the lounges, The Beach, and the theater: Tsali first, Mo after she'd determined there was no immediate threat to his life.

God, that was galling.

The only light was the faint blinking glow of the computer interfaces. Mo frowned. "Lights on." Nothing happened.

"They're not responding." Tsali glanced at him as she made her way to the rear of the room, her weapon at the ready. A tranq gun, not a real one. Mo couldn't decide if that made him feel better or not. "I don't know what's the deal with that. I'm gonna go check in back. Stay here and don't go poking around."

Mo nodded to placate her. As soon as she turned the corner around the shelves of carefully preserved marine life specimens and rare paper books, he wandered among the cabinets and computer interfaces in the front of the room, listening and letting his senses pick up whatever might be there.

To his right, the life-sized *Entwined Lovers* sculpture hovered like a shadow in its plastic display case. Mo walked up to it. There weren't many pieces of art on BT3, and the few they had fascinated him. This one most of all. The way the naked woman's head arched backward to rest against the shoulder of the man who held her, blank gaze trained toward the unattainable sky, sent hot and cold shivers up his spine.

The man intrigued him even more. The empty carved eyes seemed to follow him, the half smile on the thin lips hinting at dark thoughts flowing through a mind that positively *could not* spark and throb with life in that hollow wooden head.

The sensation of an unfriendly stare raised goose bumps on the back of Mo's neck. He turned away from the statue man's blank eyes and peered around him. His gaze lit on the storage cabinet on the other side of the room. It wasn't a large space. Then again, Ryal wasn't a large person.

He considered calling for Tsali. But that would alert whoever might be in the cabinet, and that would not be good. He had a knife, and he knew how to use it.

Strange, how fast the things he'd learned thirty years ago came back to him.

Drawing his switchblade, he eased away from the *Lovers* and across the room toward the cabinets. Around the workstations, past the computers, down the corridor of pressurized tanks containing specimens of deep-sea life.

He'd almost reached the cabinet when he heard a stealthy sound behind him. Soft, faint, whispery.

Alive.

Fear ran in paralyzing waves from his chest down his arms and legs and curled like ice in his stomach. Heart racing, he forced his frozen body to move, to turn and look, because damn it, there was *nothing there*.

Only there was. The plastic encasing the sculpture was gone, and the statue man's body had finally caught up with his living mind. Malicious intent glittering deep in his empty eye sockets, he pulled his arms off of the woman with a hissing sound like a snake slithering across concrete and stepped around her. His body, brown and wispy as a vine, creaked with the movement.

Mo stared, horrified and captivated. *Stop*, he thought at the thing, and wished his voice would work.

As if it had heard, the statue that ought not to be alive—but *was*—halted. It reached one slender arm toward Mo, fingers stretching, elongating, flexing in ways that raised the hairs on Mo's neck.

"You're not real." Mo said it out loud, because maybe that would make it become true. "Go away."

When the wooden lips opened into a wide grin, revealing a mouth full of short, thin tentacles where teeth ought to be, Mo felt as if he were being mocked. He grasped his indignation and held on to it as if it were the only thing keeping his sanity intact. It might just be.

Statue-man took another step, so silent Mo would have thought he wasn't there if it weren't for the visual evidence. The blue-green glow of the tanks glinted off something on the end of a tentacle. And another, and another. Mo couldn't tell what it was. Instinct warned him he would not like it, but the adventurer in him wanted to know. He squinted, trying to see.

Statue-man stepped closer. Closer. Unable to move, shaking with a mix of terror and curiosity, Mo stared.

A single shimmering pearl of fluid dripped from the tiny metal fang at the end of one agile little tentacle and burned a hole in the library floor.

Hot fury surged through Mo's blood. He pointed at the impossible wooden man. "Fuck you. You're *not real*."

"Who're you talking to?"

Tsali's voice surprised him. He whirled to see her hurrying toward him from the back of the library, her weapon pointed toward the ceiling. "Tsali. This might sound weird, but do you see anything . . . well, out of place?"

She glanced left. Right. Met his gaze again with caution stamped all over her face. "No. Why? Do you?"

Reluctantly, Mo peered sideways. Statue-man was back in his plastic box, willowy wooden arms wrapped around his lover and dead lips blessedly sealed.

Mo shut his eyes. Opened them again and studied the library with deliberate, methodical detachment. The tank filters bubbled. Tank and terminal lights cast a cool blue glow over the room. Statue-man stayed put. Nothing else moved.

He rubbed a hand over the ache blooming in his forehead. Either he was losing his shit, or what he'd seen was real.

Or whatever had happened to Hannah and Ryal was happening to him.

The idea sent waves of nausea thumping through him. Sweat beaded on his upper lip.

"Just my eyes playing tricks on me, I guess." His voice shook. He cleared his throat. "So. No sign of Ryal or Dr. Timms, huh?"

"Not yet. I'm not done looking yet, though. There's still the storage room to check. I came up here when I heard you talking to nothing." She gave him a stern frown. "Stay here, be quiet, and don't do anything, okay? I'll be right back."

Mo sat in the nearest chair and gripped the arms hard so he wouldn't follow her. Right now, he didn't much want to be alone with that damned statue. Or his own imagination. Especially both at the same time.

He didn't remember the cabinet he'd been about to open earlier until the neck-crawling sensation of being watched came back. And of course he'd picked a chair that put his back to the cabinet.

Shit.

Calling on the stealth he'd learned all those years ago in Dubai, he rose and turned in one smooth motion, switchblade open in his hand.

Ryal stood less than a meter away.

Time slowed to a crawl. Mo's heart pumped once. Twice. He felt the blood push through his arteries, down to his capillaries, feeding his cells one by one. Giving him strength to defend himself against the long, thin fingers that had crushed a man's windpipe like tissue paper.

Staring into Ryal's black-light eyes, Mo saw no trace of his intelligent, fun-loving friend. But he had to try. "Ryal? Are you in there?"

"I haven't gone anywhere, Mo. I'm just different now." Ryal's mouth twisted sideways and his brow knitted, as if considering what he'd just said. "It's hard to explain."

He sounded calm. Reasonable. Hope sparked in Mo's chest. "I'm listening. I want to understand."

Ryal sighed. "It's too late for that. All that's left now is what has to be done." He took a single step toward Mo, stopped, and pierced him with a stare that put the lie to his sane, measured tone. "For what it's worth, I'm sorry. You were always a good friend."

Instinct dropped Mo into a crouch when Ryal rushed him. Ryal missed Mo's throat, fingers raking the top of his head instead. He whipped around with inhuman speed and came at Mo again, lips pulled back in an angry grimace.

Mo backpedaled, his knife brandished in front of him. "Stop. Don't make me hurt you."

Ryal laughed. "You can't hurt me. It's a new world. I'm a god here." Grinning, he lunged at Mo, deadly hands reaching for him.

Something went *pop* to Mo's left. Ryal stopped, put a hand to his neck, and yanked a small dart from the muscle. He threw it to the floor. Before Mo could move, Ryal spun and leaped on Tsali, knocking the tranquilizer gun from her hand. The two of them crashed to the floor with Ryal on top, both his wrists clamped in Tsali's hands as she fought to keep him from strangling her.

Heart racing, Mo hooked his arms under Ryal's and pulled with all his strength. Ryal hissed like a snake and hung on to Tsali with his knees. Since Mo outweighed him, though, he couldn't bend forward.

Tsali used that window of opportunity to drop one of Ryal's hands and punch him hard in the temple.

His head snapped sideways, and Mo thought she'd coldcocked him. But he snatched at her wrist, yanked her hand toward him, and sank his teeth into the web of skin between her thumb and index finger.

"Ow! Goddamn it." Wriggling one leg free, she kicked Ryal in the balls. He growled at her, but dropped her hand. The grip of his knees must've eased because she scrambled out from under him, gained her feet, and glared down into his upturned face, holding up her injured hand. His teeth had left puncture wounds. "Fucking little shit." She punched him again.

This time, he sagged against Mo's chest. He turned to grin up at Mo. "Big things are coming, Rees. *Great* things. Just wait 'til they take you. You'll see."

To Mo's shock, Ryal's eyes rolled up into his head and his body began to convulse. "Oh, fuck." Mo laid him on the floor, careful to keep him on his side in case he vomited. "Tsali? Call the med bay. He's having a seizure."

Tsali activated her com and called for urgent medical assistance. Mo left her to it and kept his attention on Ryal jerking violently in his lap. It was all Mo could do to keep Ryal's head from slamming into the floor tiles and giving him a brain injury on top of everything else.

Ryal went limp at the same time as the library door swooshed open and the medical team—two of the staff biologists, who Mo guessed were second wave ad hoc medics—came barreling in. They pushed Mo out of the way and bent over Ryal with their equipment and their competency and their air of *getting things done*.

It was too late. Mo had already seen the weird purple light die in Ryal's eyes, felt his body sink in the peculiar way bodies did when life left them, and he knew. But he stumbled out of the way without saying anything, because the team had to do their own work and come to their own conclusions. Nothing he could say would make any difference.

Tsali was searching through the cabinets where Ryal had been hiding. Looking for Dr. Timms, Mo realized after a moment of confusion. They still hadn't found her. He crossed the room to help Tsali search. She said nothing.

Mo was glad. If he had to stand there like an idiot while everyone else had a job to do, he thought he might lose it.

He'd opened the last cabinet and was shining his flashlight on the boxes of fish food and piles of tank maintenance equipment when one of the medics swore. "Hell. That's it, folks. I'm calling it. Time of death, oh-four-seventeen on May 17, 2137."

So that was that. Ryal was dead, killed by some unknown contagion that they had no idea how to stop. Mo shut his eyes and rested his forehead on the cool faux wood of the cabinet.

A hand gripped his shoulder. He opened his eyes and turned to meet Tsali's sympathetic gaze. "Sorry, Rees. I know you guys were friends."

"Yeah. Thanks." Mo hauled himself to his feet, trying not to watch the medics zipping Ryal into a plastic body bag. "I guess we ought to keep looking for Dr. Timms, huh? I mean, she's not in here, and I assume no one else has found her since we haven't heard any updates."

"Yeah. You're right." Tsali stood, crossed to where her tranq gun lay wedged against the base of a fish tank, and scooped it up. Her hand had stopped bleeding, though the four unexplainable punctures were still there instead of the human tooth marks she ought to have. She studiously didn't look at the wound, and peered at the activity going on behind Mo's back instead. Her face was unreadable. "Come on."

Mo retrieved his knife and the two of them followed the medical team to the door. Ryal's body was an unmoving plastic-covered hump on the hover stretcher. Mo trailed behind the group, searching his memory for clues to what had happened. What kind of sickness could've turned his easygoing friend into a murderer?

As he stepped out of the library into the hallway, the sudden sensation of unfriendly eyes on him raised gooseflesh on the back of his neck. He turned.

Statue-Man stood only a couple of meters away. The door slid shut on his tentacular grin.

CHAPTER 8

The ChemScan readout of the first sample they'd finally been able to obtain from the object was exciting, if not surprising.

"Seven different unknown substances comprise a total of sixty-eight percent of this thing." Mandala leaned back in her chair, massaging her neck with both hands. "The rest is a hodgepodge. About fifteen percent carbon, ten percent silicon, a smattering of nickel, lead, nitrogen, and cyanide. Even a trace of oxygen."

"Good Lord." Armin planted his elbows on the counter and rested his aching head in his hands. "Well, the carbon could be important. But we can't really know for certain until we learn more about those other substances."

"How many samples were you able to get?"

"Four."

Not enough when they were dealing with something unknown, but he felt he'd done well to scrape off *that* many shavings. The thing was ridiculously hard for an object that insisted on pretending it didn't exist. He'd ultimately had to use the pod's brand-new, state-of-the-art ion scraper, which he hadn't wanted to try because he wasn't sure how it would interact with something whose physical properties they didn't in the least understand. So far it hadn't seemed to have caused any problems, though, thank goodness.

Mandala nodded. "Well. We'll do what we can with it. Why don't you run a repeat of the ChemScan on this sample while I start molecular mapping on sample number two? Maybe the structure can at least give us a clue as to whether or not we're dealing with something organic."

She stood and crossed to the sealed, light-protected sample container without waiting for Armin's answer. Shaking his head, he went to take her place at the ChemScan and programmed it to repeat the test with the same parameters as before. If they'd had unlimited samples, he would've run the scan on a new one. For something this unusual, repetition of each test was necessary to confirm their results. But with only four samples, they couldn't afford to use multiple scrapings for a single analysis. Therefore, they would reuse each one, and hope for the best. At least the testing equipment didn't destroy the samples like the machines of a century ago would have.

While the scan was running, he kept one eye on the display and wondered what was going on beyond the lab. Surely Gordon would've let them know if Ashlyn or Ryal had been found. Gerald Palto would've called personally if Neil had taken a turn for the worse. Armin knew all of that. Yet he couldn't shake the feeling that fate had already struck. That all their efforts were too little, too late.

The chirp of his com startled him out of his thoughts. "Maximo Rees calling Armin Savage-Hall. Armin, pick up. Urgent."

Mo sounded shaken. Frowning, Armin lifted his wrist. "This is Armin. What's wrong?"

"Armin." His name emerged wrapped in relief, as if Mo had feared for his safety. "Look, we found Ryal, but he . . ." A pause followed, heavy with a story Mo wasn't sharing. "He had a reaction to the tranquilizer, or something. He's dead."

"Oh no." Armin's heart went out to Mo, who he knew had been friends with Ryal Nataki. "I'm so sorry. Do you want me to leave the lab? Meet you somewhere?"

Mandala shot him a sharp look, which he ignored. He knew how it felt to lose a close friend to whatever was running loose on this pod. If Mo needed him, he would be there.

Mo breathed an almost-sigh into the com. "It's awfully tempting, but no. You've got important stuff to do in the lab, and Tsali and I still need to finish our sweep."

Armin knew what that meant. "You didn't find Ashlyn, then?"

"No. No one has, that I know of. Hang on." In the background, Armin heard Mo say something he couldn't make out. Someone else—Tsali, presumably—answered, then Mo came back on. "Tsali just confirmed with Gordon—the whole pod's been searched, except for the aquarium and a couple of meeting rooms that Tsali and I still have to cover. Dr. Timms hasn't been found anywhere yet."

Despair closed its icy fist around Armin's chest. He rested his forehead in one hand. "What could have happened to her?"

"Well, she *has* to be someplace." Mo hesitated a second. "Gordon checked the vidfeeds from the moon pool and from outside the pod. He didn't see her on those. I know there aren't many places left to look, but we might still find her. In any case, we know she hasn't left the pod. So that's something, right?"

"Definitely." It was huge, in fact. Armin hadn't realized until now how worried he'd been that Ashlyn had gone off into the deep like Carlo. Like Klaudia Longenesse. "Com me when you're finished, all right? I don't want you walking the halls alone. Either wait for me in the med bay or have someone else walk with you back to your quarters."

Mo laughed. "You can't be serious."

"Yes, I am. It's quite likely there are people here who've been infected but haven't been isolated. If those people develop psychosis, they'll be dangerous."

"Don't worry about me, Doc. I can take care of myself."

The cold certainty in Mo's voice reminded Armin how little he knew about the man with whom he currently shared a bed. He rubbed at the sharp pain boring into his temple. "Humor me. Please."

"Jesus Christ." Low conversation came over the com, along with female laughter. "Okay, look, I'll com you when we're done with our sweep, but I'm not waiting around the med bay, and I'm sure as shit not getting anyone else to walk me to my own fucking room."

Irritation and worry churned up a toxic brew in Armin's stomach. He swiveled his chair to avoid Mandala's curious look. "Mo—"

"I'll meet you at The Beach, all right?" The cutting edge had melted from Mo's tone. Armin could almost see the soft, pleading light in his eyes. "I know everybody's confined to quarters, but Gordon and Tsali will be heading there to talk about what's going on and form a plan for dealing with it. I'm sure they'll want to bring in some other ad hoc security people. So there'll be other people there. Uninfected people. I'll tag along and wait for you there. I won't get too close, in case Ryal or Hannah exposed me. I can even put on iso gear if you think I should." His voice dropped to a hoarse whisper that dragged along Armin's senses like a physical touch. "I don't want to be alone, Doc. I'll fucking lose it if I have to be alone in my quarters right now."

What could he say? Armin let his lips brush the com link on his wrist, remembering the last time he kissed the sex-sweat from the curve of Mo's back. "All right. Let me know when you're going, and I'll meet you there. And, Mo, I'm sorry. About Ryal."

On the other side of the com link, Mo drew a faint, hitching breath. "Thanks. Out."

The link cut. Armin felt Mandala's stare on the back of his head. *Don't ask*, he thought at her. She'd never been one to intrude into anyone's personal life, but she wouldn't hesitate if she thought it affected the work. And Armin couldn't honestly say his desire to protect Mo *wasn't* affecting his work.

He was saved from whatever Mandala might have said by the chime of the ChemScan announcing the end of its second run. He turned his attention back to the sample. "Computer. Display scan results on 3-D."

"Anything you say, Doctor."

Armin swallowed the shock clawing its way up his throat. The lab computer didn't say such things. Especially not in a suggestive growl of a voice. He'd changed the settings himself because he preferred machines that did as they were told without talking about it. The stress of the last day or so must be getting to him.

But could he truly blame stress for what he'd just heard, knowing what he knew?

On the other hand, he didn't believe he'd shown any real signs of psychosis. Mandala would march him straight off to isolation the moment he did. Nor had he developed the physical changes Hannah and Ryal had. So where did that leave him?

Frightened. Confused. Wondering.

He rubbed the back of his neck, where tension had knotted the muscles tight. If only they'd thought to ask Ryal, Hannah, and Ashlyn if they'd experienced visual or auditory hallucinations prior to the manifestation of their other symptoms. Of course, Armin suspected they wouldn't have gotten a straight answer out of any of them.

"Oh, for God's sake, Armin. What did you do?"

Startled, Armin swiveled to face Mandala. Her expression reflected the irritation in her voice. Armin frowned, puzzled. "What do you mean?"

"Take a look at the readout." Mandala crossed her arms, pursed her lips, and pinned him with an *I'm waiting* stare.

He looked, and his mouth fell open. If he hadn't been sitting right next to the ChemScan this whole time, he would've sworn the sample inside had been switched out, because everything was different.

"I didn't do anything. I programmed it to scan again using the same parameters as the last time." Armin stood, his knees shaking, and circled the holo. "I don't understand. How is this possible?"

"Well, clearly it isn't possible for the sample to change its entire chemical makeup between one scan and the next. So, it has to be a malfunction in the machine." Mandala rose and crossed the lab to stand beside Armin. She studied the display with a steady, penetrating stare for a while. "It's interesting that the carbon and silicon are still there in almost the same percentages as before, and that nitrogen and oxygen are still present, but in larger amounts."

"The other trace elements have nearly been swallowed up in the unknown substances." Armin shook his head, as if he could physically shake the scattered puzzle pieces into place. "It doesn't make any sense. My equations didn't predict this."

"I know." Mandala planted both hands on her lower back and stretched. "That being the case, I think we ought to rule out equipment malfunction before we take the testing any further."

Armin nodded. "Agreed."

"I'll run the diagnostics. You go on to The Beach and talk to Mo."

"It won't take that long. I can help, and—"

"Armin. Stop." She brushed her fingers across his arm. "I appreciate it, but you know as well as I do that troubleshooting a ChemScan is a one-person job. I use this type of equipment every day. I'm much better qualified for this than you are. Also, he's going to be comming you soon, so you might as well go now."

He'd worked with her long enough to know when she was keeping something to herself. Usually he wouldn't stand for it. In this case, however, he rather appreciated not having to hear how she didn't fully trust the things he saw and heard. Particularly since he no longer trusted himself.

Maybe she'd figure out how to fix this disaster while he was at the bar with Mo.

He forced a smile. "You're right, of course. I'll go. Com me if you need me, all right?"

"Of course." She grasped his hand. Her grip was strong and sure, and it made him feel better. "We'll figure this out."

He wasn't so sure, but he nodded anyway. She let go and went back to the equipment. Armin headed out into the hall.

He activated his com link as he turned the corner. "Dr. Savage-Hall calling Maximo Rees."

Mo answered after a few long seconds of silence. "Mo here. What's up, Doc?"

Armin laughed, remembering the classic cartoon with the wisecracking rabbit. "We've had some problems with the lab equipment. Mandala kicked me out while she's running diagnostics, so I'm on my way to The Beach right now. I should be there when you arrive."

"Oh. Okay, good. We're almost done, so it won't be long." Mo paused. "We haven't found Dr. Timms yet."

Fear and worry dug harder into Armin's insides. He'd never felt so helpless. "Well. We can only keep trying. Like you said, she has to be here somewhere."

"Yeah." Another pause. "Is someone walking with you to The Beach?"

Uh-oh. Armin sucked on his bottom lip. "Well—"

Another voice on Mo's end interrupted him. "Hang on a sec, Doc."

Muted conversation drifted through the com, while Armin's shoulders sagged in relief. He didn't want to lie to Mo, but he didn't much want to tell the truth either. He walked faster. The quicker he could reach the bar, the better.

He was nearly there when Mo came back on. "Sorry about that. There was a report of noises in the visitor's lounge, but it wasn't her." He let out a derisive snort. "Some asshole was raiding the bar there for liquor, can you believe it?"

"I'll believe almost anything people do."

"Point."

A door opened to Armin's right as he passed. A young woman strode out, squealed in surprise when she almost ran into him, and edged past. It wasn't Ashlyn. Since she seemed fine other than being startled, he swallowed his heart back down and ignored her. "Any signs of psychosis?"

"I don't know, I wasn't there. But it didn't sound like it." Mo's voice dropped low. "Did something happen? You sound a little shaky."

"No. I'm fine. Just thinking about what Mandala and I have found so far in the lab. It's very strange." He tried to think of a way to describe it over the com link and couldn't. "I'll tell you about it when you get to the bar."

"Okay." Mo's worry and doubt came through quite clearly in those two syllables. "I'll be there in a little bit."

"I'll be waiting. Out."

He cut the link and hurried on. The sense of some alien presence breathing down his neck had him walking as fast as he could without running.

It couldn't have taken him more than three or four minutes to reach the bar, but it felt like hours. Tension, he told himself. With all that had happened here in such a short time, it was no wonder every minute seemed stretched and twisted. He pushed open the old-fashioned swinging doors with relief.

And stopped just inside, flummoxed. He'd expected to find the place either empty, or occupied by only a few people discussing the current situation over coffee or perhaps a beer at one of the big tables in the middle of the floor. He'd expected the lights to be on and the music off.

He hadn't for one second thought he'd find the bar in near-complete darkness broken only by a ball of soft-colored lights overhead, flashing a dim rainbow over the wall-to-wall crush of people dancing. Though the way they moved looked more like simulated sex. Men and women in various stages of undress writhed to the primal rhythm pounding through the room like a pulse. Armin's heartbeat quickened, his breath coming faster in spite of himself. He wished Mo would get here.

As if summoned by his thought, Mo emerged from the throng, shirtless, chest and face gleaming with perspiration. His lips curved into a wicked smile. He stretched out a hand. Armin took it and let Mo pull him close.

He wanted to ask how Mo had gotten here first. He wanted to ask what all these people were doing here, why they were dancing as though this was an upside city sex club instead of a makeshift bar seven thousand meters down, on a mineral mining rig where everything was falling apart bit by bit. But Mo's hands were warm on his back through the fabric of his shirt, Mo's cheek rough with stubble against his, and the words caught in his throat. Mo started to move, his body undulating to the drumbeat, the sexual roll of his hips pushing his erection into Armin's groin, and Armin's fears melted like snow in a fire.

The thump and throb of the music carried them into the pulsing heart of the crowd. The air was hot and damp, musky with sweat and sex. Sighs and moans created a drifting, sensual counterpart to the relentless beat that Armin felt right down to his bones. The vibration urged him into motion, and he swayed, Mo's palms cupping his ass and Mo's breath warm on his neck. Mo's body molded to his was a gravitational force, tugging his hips side to side in an achingly slow grind.

When Mo shifted position to kiss him, hard and deep and hungry, Armin thought he might come in his pants like a virgin boy. He let the sensation flow through him without sticking. It was surprisingly easy. The whole thing felt surreal. Dreamlike. The scientist in him—the part that never switched off—wondered how much of it was real, and how much was mental candy floss spun by the usurper he'd begun to suspect had taken up residence in his brain.

The idea was enough to pull him away from Mo's kiss so he could look into those drowning-dark eyes. "Mo. We need to get out of this room."

Mo didn't ask questions. Didn't say a word, in fact, which did nothing to dispel Armin's unease. Instead he flashed the same sinful smile as before, took Armin's hand, and led him through the crush of people to the exit.

The hallway was silent and empty. The flickering lights threw bizarre shadows on the walls. Impossible shapes wriggled at the edge of Armin's vision and vanished around the corners before he could catch them.

I see you, he told the invader lurking in his synapses. *I know what you're doing. I know this isn't real. You won't catch me that way. And I won't let you have anyone else.*

If it heard him, it showed no sign. Armin couldn't tell whether that meant he'd won or lost. In any case, he had no choice but to soldier on as best he could. He lifted his chin, kept his face forward, and followed Mo through the haunted house BathyTech 3 had become.

He was relieved when Mo brought him to the aquarium. The quiet here was normal. Peaceful. The monochrome dimness eased Armin's anxiety. He could think clearly here. Let his guard down, if only for a moment. This time, he was the one who drew Mo into his arms and kissed him.

Mo opened for him, both arms snaking around his waist to hold him close. The only sounds were their quick, harsh breaths and the wet slide of their mouths together. God, it felt good. Armin shut his eyes and let the taste of Mo's tongue erase everything else.

When Mo took him to the ground, Armin went eagerly. He knew they had things they needed to talk about, but his mind skimmed over the memory's surface and veered away. He didn't want to think about it anymore. Didn't want to think about the things that had happened, or might happen. Right now, all he wanted was Mo inside him, pounding away the grief and horror and sickening, paralyzing fear.

Undressing happened in watercolor flashes, blurry disconnected moments of fumbling hands and swift, hard kisses, ending with the two of them tangled naked on the cool polycrete floor. Armin wound a leg around Mo's hips, bit his neck, and arched up against him, into his solid human heat. Mo moaned, and Armin worked the flesh between his teeth with his tongue to draw out more of those low, sweet noises that made Mo's throat vibrate against his lips.

Mo tore away, leaving red marks on his skin where Armin's teeth had been. He stared at Armin with a dark fire in his eyes. "Turn over."

Armin rolled onto his belly. His heart galloped and his head swam, and he couldn't decide whether the tightness making his breath come short was desire or apprehension.

ALLY BLUE

Mo had lifted Armin's hips and pushed his knees apart before he realized Mo's growled order was the first time he'd spoken since they'd met in the bar. But he didn't have a chance to wonder about that, or about the unusually raspy tone of Mo's voice, because Mo was holding him open and pushing relentlessly inside, his cock slicked by something thin and not enough. Saliva, most likely. Armin had used it before, and it got the job done, but it wasn't comfortable.

Armin curled his fingers on the cold floor and breathed through the pain because it would ease into intense pleasure any . . . moment . . . now . . .

The third slow, measured thrust did it. Armin's body, trained by years of exactly such encounters, relaxed to allow the intrusion. Gooseflesh broke out all over his skin. Unable to speak, he rocked backward in a silent bid for more. Mo leaned over him, planting one hand on the floor beside his elbow and reaching beneath him with the other to grasp his erection in a confident, practiced grip. Armin shuddered. Sighed. The sound echoed along the dome and came back to him, heavy with his need.

Mo nipped Armin's shoulder, so quickly the small pain was gone before he'd properly felt it. He bent his neck sideways so Mo could reach the spot just below his ear that sent sharp, hot shocks arcing along his skin when Mo sucked on it.

Outside the dome, something large, white, and *wrong* hovered, milky-green eyes watching them with a strange hunger. Armin stared. *What are you? Why are you here?*

The mermaid held his gaze. Knowing, but not answering.

Taunting.

It grinned a glass-shard smile and waved long, pale hands through the inky water.

Wait. Hands?

Yes. Who do you think we are, Doctor?

"Just a mermaid." Mo's breath was warm against his ear. "Let it look." The fingers around Armin's cock moved faster, stroking him just this side of too hard. Mo plunged into him in short, brutal jabs that froze his breath and short-circuited his thoughts. "Come, Doc. Let it watch you come."

124

The weird, voyeuristic thrill of the animal beyond the GlasSteel staring at him while Mo fucked him, shoved him headlong into a bone-rattling climax. He came with a cry that anyone wandering past surely would've heard. His semen hit the floor with a thick *splat-splat-splat*. Behind him, Mo shifted, grasped his hips, and slammed into him hard and fast. It hurt, and orgasm made it both better and worse. Finally, Mo let out a low, tortured noise and buried himself to the root in Armin's body. He pumped his groin against Armin's rear in a slow, gentle roll like the sea.

Through the white haze of pain and sexual release, Armin registered the way Mo's fingers shook where they grasped his hipbones. He wondered if the whole experience felt as bizarre to Mo as it did to him.

Mo pulled out of him. He hissed at the sting. He and Mo dressed in silence, not looking at one another. Armin scrunched his face when he was forced to put on his clothes over the fluids oozing out of him and gelling on his skin, but at the moment he had no choice. He could clean up later.

When he sat down to pull on his shoes, the events of the past day hit Armin like a tsunami. Dizzy, his eyelids heavy as stone, he leaned against the dome and yawned until he thought his jaw might unhinge. He waved away Mo's concerned look. "I'm fine. Just need to rest a moment."

"All right." Mo knelt beside him, cupped his face in both hands, and kissed him. Lightly, tenderly, thumbs caressing the corners of his mouth. "Rest, Doc. You've been through so much. Just let everything go." His fingers slid through Armin's hair, rubbing soothing circles on his scalp. "Sleep for a while. That's what you need. To sleep. Forget it all for a little while."

A vague alarm sparked somewhere deep in Armin's gut. A warning of something not quite right. But it was no match for the spell in Mo's voice, reminding him how very tired he was, how much rested on his shoulders. Telling him to lay down his burden, if only for a short time.

Whatever the not-right-ness was, he could work it out later, after he'd rested. Surely it couldn't hurt for him to close his eyes for a few minutes. He'd be mentally sharper for it.

Five minutes. That's all. Mo can wake me.

"Five minutes." His eyes drifted shut. He hauled them halfway open again and peered at Mo, his vision blurry with exhaustion. "Promise."

He wasn't sure he got his point across, but Mo nodded and smiled. "Don't worry." He wound an arm around Armin's shoulders. "Rest now."

Mo's voice rumbled in Armin's ear. Soothing, soporific, sucking him under like a whirlpool. Caught in Mo's comforting embrace, Armin spiraled down into unconsciousness.

He woke curled up on the floor with his com link beeping at him. Mo was gone. Armin sat up, confused and a little angry that Mo had left him there alone and vulnerable in sleep.

How long *had* he slept, anyway? God, Mandala would be furious if . . .

His com. Still beeping with the message indicating that someone had tried to get in touch with him and he'd slept right through it.

Mouth dry and pulse racing, he activated the com's message retrieval. Gerald Palto's voice came through high-pitched, frantic, and interspersed with bursts of static. "Arm . . .'s Ger . . . We . . . ation here. N . . . inf . . . ed. Thing's . . . ting . . . contr . . . Med bay's on iso . . . now. Okay? No one in or out. I tried ca . . . souf but coms are—"

Shouts cut through the static, followed by a female scream much closer to the audio pickup. He heard the unmistakable sounds of a struggle, then a peculiar gurgling noise before the recorded message ended.

He scrambled to his feet and activated the com's call function. "Dr. Savage-Hall for Dr. Gerald Palto. Maximum urgency."

Five seconds passed while he crossed the room. He'd reached the door when his com lit up, announcing an incoming answer.

Except no one spoke. All he heard was a soft, loose rattle, like someone breathing through a trachea full of fluid. Someone very close to the other com link.

Cold fear clawed at his belly. "Gerald? What's happened? Are you all right? God, answer me."

The breathing morphed into a wet chuckle. "Gerald can't talk now." The guttural voice originated so near the com that Armin could hear the viscous rub of the mouth forming the words. "Good-bye, Armin." Something crunched, ending the conversation.

He had never heard that voice before. He'd never be able to forget such a thing. Yet he couldn't shake the feeling that he knew it. Fighting off the terror leeching the strength from his limbs, he shoved the door open and headed out into the dim, empty corridor. "Dr. Savage-Hall for Dr. Jhut. Urgent."

Mandala answered immediately. "Dr. Jhut here. Armin? What's wrong?"

"I'm not sure, exactly. But I think something might have happened in the medical bay."

"Did you call security? Well. Gordon?"

"Not yet. I wanted to call you first. To make sure you were safe, and to tell you to keep your eyes open and your wits about you. Things have become . . ." He hesitated, searching for the right word. "Very strange."

"Don't worry about me. I've shown no signs whatsoever of psychosis, and I'm more than capable of taking care of myself. Just call Mr. Gordon to the med bay, and get yourself back here. I'm almost finished running diagnostics."

"Oh. Good." He decided not to mention what Gerald had said about isolating the med bay. They could worry about that after they found out what had happened. Maybe he shouldn't ask, but . . . "Mandala? This is going to sound like a strange question, but how long has it been since I left the lab?"

"About an hour and twenty minutes, more or less." Her voice grew gentle with concern. "Are you all right?"

"To be honest, I'm not sure. But I'm trying to find out." A cackle like a hyena's floated from around a corner somewhere behind him. He picked up his pace, trying to look everywhere at once. "I'm going to call Gordon now. I'll come back to the lab soon."

"All right. Be careful. Out."

The moment Mandala cut the connection, Armin hailed security. "Dr. Savage-Hall for Mr. Gordon. Urgent."

Nothing. He strode thirty long steps with no answer.

Uneasy, he tried again. "Dr. Savage-Hall for Mr. Gordon. Please answer, this is a security matter of utmost urgency."

"Gordon here. What's going on? I'm at the lab, watching the door. Youssouf said I should stay here."

Armin blew out a relieved breath. "I think something's happened at the medical bay. Dr. Palto commed me, but he was cut off by sounds of a struggle and screams. When I commed him back, a voice said he couldn't talk, then crushed the com link."

"Fuck me." Gordon was quiet for a moment. "Listen. Don't go in there. I'll be there in a minute, all right? Just let me—"

"No. Stay at the lab."

"But—"

"Youssouf was right. You should stay there. It's important that Dr. Jhut and the work underway there remains safe."

"Well. Okay. But I don't like it."

"Neither do I. But we have no choice at this point. Out."

He cut the connection before Gordon could say anything else. For a moment he stood there, shaking inside, mentally steeling himself for what lay ahead. When he felt he could walk without his knees buckling, he continued along the empty hallway.

He commed Mo as he strode toward the med bay. "Armin Savage-Hall for Maximo Rees. Urgent."

Mo took only a few seconds to answer, but it felt like years. "What's wrong?"

Armin smiled in spite of everything, a hard, tight warmth expanding in his chest. Mo had an impressive ability to read his mood. "I just wanted to make sure you were all right."

Mo hesitated only a moment, but it was enough for Armin to worry. "Yeah, I'm okay. Heading back to my quarters." His voice went from soft and slightly confused to sharp and focused. "Where are you?"

Armin considered, and decided to trust Mo. "On my way to the med bay. I'm concerned about Dr. Palto."

"Concerned? Why? What's going on?" Mo's tone was hard and clipped, full of rising worry.

Ahead, Armin saw the med bay doors standing halfway open.

In his mind, he heard Gerald's pronouncement through the static that the med bay was on isolation. *No one in or out.*

Shit.

"I'll tell you later. I have to go." He kept his voice barely above a whisper so whoever might be in there wouldn't hear him. "I'll com you again soon. Out."

Armin cut off the com and hung back in the hallway, wiping his palms on his pants and assessing the situation. Doors on underwater installations *never* stayed open as long as the controls were working correctly. It was a safety requirement, making it quicker and easier to seal off sections of the pod in case of a breach. Which meant the controls for this door must have been disabled.

Considering what he'd heard through his com, this couldn't be anything but very, very bad.

God, Armin really wanted backup on this. He was only a scientist. He wasn't equipped to deal with someone—some*thing*?—intent on violence. But Gerald or some of the staff might be hurt. And no one else was coming.

You're it, Doctor. Buck up.

He breathed in. Out. Straightened his shoulders, edged up to the doorway and slipped inside.

The unmistakable stench of recent violent death slapped him in the face. He tugged his collar over his nose and glanced around. The body he knew must be there was not in immediate sight. All three isolation rooms remained closed, the inner curtains drawn. Deciding to leave them for last, he moved toward the desk. The room appeared empty.

"Gerald? It's Armin. Are you all right?" No answer. He breathed through his mouth in an attempt not to smell the nearby slaughter. The air hissed through the fabric of his shirt and left a raw-meat taste on the back of his tongue. He swallowed hard. "Security's on the way," he added, in response to the sensation of a hidden gaze following him.

The surface normality ended when he skirted the desk. He turned away and leaned on the soothing, pale-gray polycrete surface until the urge to vomit eased, then made himself look again, this time with an eye to the details.

Misha lay spread-eagled on the floor, her belly laid open and her organs flung around in no discernible pattern. The smell came from her shredded intestines, draped across a nearby chair. Her open eyes stared up at the ceiling in permanent surprise.

Christ. Armin had seen bodies before, but never such casual slaughter. Except on the Varredura Longa.

If Misha had been the only one in here, he would've run straight for the relative sanity of the hallway. But he still had to find Gerald.

He sidestepped Misha's body, trying to stay away from the blood splatters and bits of viscera. The overhead light glistened on the blood coating the inside of her abdominal cavity, and for the first time Armin realized she'd been hollowed out right down to her spine.

Saliva flooded his mouth. He stumbled into the nearest—thankfully empty—patient care compartment and threw up in the sink, cursing his weakness the whole time and trying to listen for any abnormal sounds through the noise of his meager stomach contents splashing into the faux-metal bowl.

When he finished, he took a moment to splash his face with cold water before going back out into the bay. He didn't look at Misha's mutilated corpse. "Gerald? Are you here? It's Armin."

Silence. Deep, still, watchful silence.

He moved toward the autopsy room, in case Dr. Palto was in there working and unable to hear him. His footsteps sounded like bombs in the brittle quiet.

The door to the autopsy room was not only shut, but bowed inward. He blinked at the irregular dent, trying to make sense of it. Would he even be able to get in?

Only one way to find out.

He reached for the sensor. Thumbed it. The door tried to slide open and stuck at an odd angle.

He studied the narrow triangular aperture. It wasn't much, but he ought to be able to squeeze through. The real question was, would the unstable structure close on him?

He thought of Misha and what might have happened to Gerald, and decided he had to take the chance. Gathering his courage, he turned sideways and wriggled through the tight space into the autopsy room.

It was dark as pitch and quiet as the rest of the med bay. A coppery tang filled the air and coated the back of his throat. The hairs rose along his arms. "Lights on."

He hadn't expected them to work, so the sudden flood of bright white illumination took him by surprise. Once his eyes adjusted, he saw Ryal Nataki on one table and Carlo on another. It looked as though the autopsy on Carlo was well underway, while the one on Ryal hadn't yet begun. He wished it were the other way around, so he wouldn't have to see Carlo's crushed skull and flattened body.

Don't look. The only one you can help now is Gerald Palto. Don't even look at the others.

He dropped his gaze to the floor. "Gerald? Are you in here?"

Still no answer. But he spotted what looked like a foot peeking out from the far side of the table where Carlo lay like a specimen to be examined.

Shoving the worst possibilities to the back of his mind, he crossed the room in a few hurried strides. He rounded the table, heart in his throat . . . and fell to his knees. Gerald lay in a twisted heap on his side, a laser scalpel still clutched in one gloved hand, his skull smashed into a pulp of bone, blood, and brain. His still-intact jaw jutted outward, giving him a strangely stubborn postmortem visage.

Armin lifted his wrist to activate his com. "Dr. Armin Savage-Hall to . . ." He stopped. Who *was* he supposed to call? All the medical personnel he knew of were dead. Butchered. Just like before. Cold and scared, he hunched forward as if he could protect himself that way. "Fuck. Anyone. Gordon. Youssouf. Whoever's still out there. Gerald Palto's dead. Misha's dead." He drew a shaking breath and forced himself to calm down. "Whoever killed them is clearly quite dangerous, and is currently at large on this pod. I think we need to call together a security team, and—"

A vicious blow between his shoulder blades knocked him off-balance and sent him sprawling facedown on the floor. He felt something hard under his ribs, and realized he'd landed on top of Gerald's shin. Instinctive revulsion sent him scrambling backward on all fours, until he ran into something else.

The something else moved. Connected with his ribs. He skidded over the floor, gasping around the pain. When he stopped moving, he saw, and it all made sense.

Neil Douglas stood over him, blue eyes gone black with a luminous purple spark deep inside. His blue-tinted lips parted in a needle-full grin.

"Hello, old friend." Neil's voice was rough and strange, yet familiar. The same voice Armin had heard over his com forever ago, back in the cool, dim, corpse-free peacefulness of the aquarium. "We're so happy you're here."

CHAPTER 9

We.

The word bothered Armin even more than the physical changes in his friend, not least because his gut told him Neil—or whatever had taken control of him—meant it literally.

Armin planted his palms on the floor and eased backward as far as possible without looking away from that luminous stare. "Who are you? Where's Neil?"

The thick sandy-brown eyebrows drew together in a puzzled frown so familiar it made Armin ache with grief. God, he hoped Neil was still in there somewhere. That he could still be saved.

"Neil is part of us." The grinding voice was gentle now, as if trying to spare Armin's feelings. Neil's swollen face twitched. "I . . . Neil . . . I'm changing, Armin. Neil is us." The violet flame in his eyes flared. He stepped toward Armin, one hand held down to him. "Be us, my friend. The changing isn't bad. And you'll see *such things*."

Knowledge beyond human science. That's what Neil—*not Neil*—offered him.

He wanted it so much it hurt.

Not-Neil grinned wider. Yellowish fluid dripped from its teeth, hit the floor with a hiss, and began eating through the polycrete. It reached down and lifted Armin by the shoulders. Armin clenched his jaw against a cry of pain as not-Neil's fingers—grown long and thin as worms—dug deep into his flesh and ground into his bones.

"We're in you." The Neil-thing's whisper rumbled like a chainsaw on idle. Its breath smelled of blood and the seabed. "Be us."

"What are you?" The question emerged in a high, breathless rush. "How . . . how are you in us? H-how do we become you?"

The Neil-creature laughed at him. "We are *in* you, Doctor. You must choose."

Choose? Armin had no idea what that could possibly mean. But the fear of giving in to the temptation to find out prompted him to wrench his arms free from the not-Neil's grip and punch it in the jaw.

It felt like sinking his fist into spongy, clotted gel. As if the bones that had formed Dr. Neil Douglas's face were softening. Dissolving. Changing him into something else.

The creature pretending to be Neil growled and backhanded him hard enough to knock him across the room. He hit the far wall with a dizzying *thump* and stared at the monster that was once his friend with terror, anger, and sorrow boiling inside him. *This isn't real. This can't be real.*

Only it was. The throb in Armin's face proved it.

Not-Neil stalked toward him, rapier teeth bared and dripping, fingers flexing like snakes, jointless and powerful. Armin raised both hands, palms out as if he could ward off the thing with nothing but his will. Neil's body leaned over him with its nightmare grin and elongated digits. The purple glow in the black pits of its eyes tugged at Armin's mind like a metaphysical current, while its voice breathed inside his head. *Come with us. You can't even imagine what exists outside this sphere. Come and see.*

Armin blinked. Opened his mouth.

Whatever he might have said, he didn't know. Would never know. A soft *pop* sounded, and the center of the Neil-thing's neck blew outward in a spray of skin, cartilage, and blood. A thick clot landed on Armin's thigh with a *splat.*

Time slowed to a crawl. He had ages to study the glob on his leg as Neil's body performed its graceful final fall. The blood gleamed a dull reddish-black and felt cool through the fabric of his trousers, as if it had come from a corpse several hours old. Yet here was Neil right in front of him, just now hitting the floor with his arms splayed, the gelatinous skin of his face still in motion from the force of the impact. How could his blood already be room temperature and coagulating?

It said something about Armin's state of mind that the *how* and *why* of Neil's sudden death didn't even occur to him until a figure approached from the doorway of the autopsy room, crouched in front of him and laid a hand on his shoulder. "Armin? Are you all right?"

Lifting his head, he blinked at a face he'd come to know well, and the world's gears clacked into motion again. "Mo." He clutched at Mo's arm, shaking. "Mo. Mo."

Nothing else would come out past the caustic lump of relief, fury, and desperation lodged in his throat, but Mo seemed to understand. Laying his gun on the floor, he gathered Armin into his arms and held him.

Twenty minutes later, Mo leaned against the wall outside the autopsy bay and watched Armin try to pace a trench in the floor while talking to Youssouf, Dr. Poole, and Dr. Jhut on a group com call. He seemed okay now, but Mo couldn't forget the stark terror in Armin's eyes when he'd found him huddled against the wall of the autopsy bay.

Not that Mo blamed him. The changes in Dr. Douglas were enough to scare the shit out of anyone, even without murderous intent. And he'd definitely been trying to kill Armin.

Thank fuck Mo had gone back to his quarters for his Triton semiautomatic pistol, then followed Armin here, or Armin might be dead right now. The thought of him with his skull smashed or his guts strewn around the room made Mo's stomach knot.

Bright flashes of memory—dream? hallucination?—pulsed one after another behind Mo's eyes: Armin pressed against him at The Beach, Armin naked on the floor of the aquarium, Armin's wide-eyed stare drilling into his brain like the end of the world.

Or maybe just the end of his sanity. He remembered comming with Armin before, but the time between that conversation and dancing in the empty bar was a black void in his mind. So were going to the aquarium and leaving it. His memory was a blank file dotted with scattered blips up until the moment Armin commed him again while he was wandering aimlessly in the hallways near his quarters.

Poole's voice rose above the others, startling Mo out of his thoughts. "*I* am the senior scientist on this pod, damn it! I should be in charge of the autopsies."

Mo wrinkled his nose. Bad time for scientific posturing.

On the com, Youssouf shut down Poole's pouting with her usual efficiency. "I don't give a shit about rank right now, Poole. You're a damn good geologist, but you're not a medical doctor. I am. Therefore, I'm running this show now. Unwad your goddamn panties and deal with it."

Mo laughed out loud. Even Armin cracked a smile, which eased the awful haunted look on his face for a second.

Dr. Jhut spoke, sounding tired and grim. "I'm going to continue the experiments here in the lab. Mr. Gordon has agreed to remain here. He's rounded up some of the BathyTech staff with military experience to act as security for you while you perform the autopsies. We do *not* want a repeat of what happened to poor Gerald and Misha."

"Definitely not." Armin stopped pacing and closed his eyes. In that moment, he looked exhausted and fragile, and Mo's concern ratcheted up a few thousand notches. "Be careful, all of you. Be careful coming here. Don't take any chances. Mandala, you be careful as well. And please let me know if you learn anything new."

The others promised caution. They all sounded subdued. It was as if Gerald Palto and Neil Douglas's deaths had broken them somehow.

A twinge of guilt prodded Mo's gut, though he knew it shouldn't. He pushed away from the desk, went to Armin, and touched his cheek. Armin's eyes flew open, like he'd forgotten Mo was there, and Mo wished he had the power to turn back time.

"I'm sorry about Neil." He moved closer. Traced his fingertips along Armin's jaw. "You know I wouldn't have shot him if I didn't have to."

"I know. And I'd be dead or worse if you hadn't, so I'm grateful to you for that." The wan shade of a smile curved Armin's lips again. "Amara's glad you shot him through the neck instead of the head, so his brain is preserved for autopsy."

It took Mo a second to realize Armin was talking about Youssouf. Nobody on BathyTech called her by her given name.

He shook his head. "That was a cold thing to say to you."

"She's a practical woman, that's all." Armin peered at him with dark eyes full of fear, questions, and apologies. "Most of the pod is still confined to quarters. She'll want you back in your room as well."

"I figured she would."

"You don't mind?"

Fuck yes, I mind, I belong here, *with* you, *figuring this shit out.* Or at least working security. Not that there was much hope of *that.* Youssouf didn't like trusting security to anyone without formal military or law enforcement training.

Mo swallowed his vitriol and forced a casual shrug. "I'd rather stay, but hell, I just work here. I do what the boss says." An idea occurred to him that perked him up on the inside as well as the outside. "I can go over the videos from the first walk when we found the rock, and the ones we got of the mermaids the other day. Nobody's had a chance to do that yet, what with everything else going on, so I might as well do it while I'm cooped up."

A strange expression crossed Armin's features. Like something Mo said connected with some half-forgotten fragment of knowledge in the depths of Armin's subconscious. The hairs on Mo's arms rose with the sense of impending revelation. Then Armin shook his head, as if to physically rid himself of whatever he was thinking, and the moment passed.

"I think that's a good idea." He took both of Mo's hands in his, laced their fingers together, and squeezed. "I wish you could stay. I don't like the thought of you in your quarters alone."

Mo's heart turned over. Nobody had worried about his safety since he left Dubai, a lifetime ago. It was sweet. And he worried about the doc too. All the time, actually, which bothered him. He hadn't gone into this thing looking for a relationship. Especially now, with everything going to shit around them.

None of which he said out loud. Instead he tugged Armin close, leaned in, and kissed him. Nothing sexual or aggressive. Just a soft, lingering press of lips, letting the doc know they were on the same page. Even if they weren't.

"I'll be fine." He stole another kiss, and another, quick and sweet. "Don't worry about me. You smart types just concentrate on figuring out how to fix this mess."

Armin smiled, and the flat, vacant look the attack had left on his face receded a little more. Mo was glad. Now that he'd thought of going over the mermaid videos, he was anxious to get back to his quarters and start watching them. Guilt about leaving Armin would only distract him, and wouldn't help anyone else. Least of all Armin.

Youssouf and Poole arrived a few minutes later. As expected, Youssouf banished Mo to his quarters. He left without argument, exchanging a quick glance with Armin on the way out.

He'll be fine, said the voice in Mo's head that wanted nothing more than to examine the footage of the mermaids in private, with no one hanging over his shoulder. He nodded to himself. Armin was well guarded. Safer than Mo, most likely.

Jem, Rashmi, and Edie Ling from communications waited for him in the hall. He grinned, pleased to see his friends healthy and whole. "Hey. You guys get stuck with babysitting me?"

His boss rolled her eyes, but she was smiling. "Me and Rashmi're walking you to your quarters, that's all. Then he's off to help Gordon guard the lab and I'm coming back here."

Mo eyed Ling, who'd taken up a stance at the med bay door that practically screamed *bad-ass guard, do not fuck with*. It looked natural. Like she did it every day, even though she didn't.

The corner of her mouth hitched into a wry half smile, as if she knew what Mo was thinking. "São Paulo. Jemima and I served together."

"Oh." Mo scratched his head, not sure what to say. He knew Jem had fought in the war that had torn South America apart and had been part of the battle that had nearly wiped Brazil's largest city off the map fifteen years ago. But he couldn't reconcile the quiet, soft-spoken Ling he said *hi* to in the hall with the ruthless soldier she must've been if she'd survived the bloodiest, most vicious war in over a century.

Jem plucked at his arm. "C'mon. Let's hustle."

"Yeah." Mo shot Ling a smile. "Later."

She nodded once, her smile already fading into a blank gaze that made Mo think of a machine. He turned and followed Jem and Rashmi down the hall with a sense of relief.

When they arrived at his quarters, Jem insisted on going inside first to make sure the place was empty and safe. She *pfft*ed when he protested. "People can get pretty damn creative when it comes to being places they're not supposed to be. What're you afraid I'll see, anyway? Your lace underpants? Like I give a shit."

Rashmi snickered. Mo scowled. "Fine. Whatever."

Jem raised her eyebrows. With a deep sigh, Mo thumbed the sensor. The door slid open. Jem slipped inside and swept her weapon in a wide arc before moving deeper in.

Mo waited in fidgety silence, chewing his thumbnail while Rashmi watched the hall as if something might attack from that direction any second. Truthfully, Mo had no idea why Jem checking his room made him so damned nervous. There was no good reason for it. Nothing for her to find that he'd be ashamed for her to see. Armin's things were in there, but they hadn't exactly kept their involvement a secret.

Logical or not, he didn't relax until she emerged less than thirty seconds later and gave the all clear. "You know the drill. No leaving your quarters until Youssouf gives the go-ahead. Call with the emergency code if you need help urgently."

Mo remembered Armin's story about the woman on the Varredura Longa who'd had her tongue cut out. As far as Mo was concerned, the jury was out regarding whether she'd done it herself. "What if I'm disabled? Or I can't speak?"

"The new com bracelets have emergency sensors, remember? All you have to do is press it for three seconds." She studied him with obvious concern. "You okay, Rees?"

Inside, Mo cursed himself for forgetting about last month's modifications to the com links. Outside, he put on his best casual smile. "Yeah, no worries. Just covering the bases."

Her eyes narrowed. Mo kept his smile in place and hoped he hadn't just talked himself into a trip back to the med bay, this time as an isolation patient.

Let it go, he thought at Jem, gritting his teeth behind his fake bland expression. *Just let it the fuck go.*

Finally, Jem sighed and stepped back. "All right. Well. I guess we're off, then." She pointed at him, reminding him of his oldest sister for a second. "Behave yourself for once."

Mo saluted. "Aye aye, Cap'n Mama, sir."

Rashmi laughed out loud. Jem shook her head. "Asshole. Stay here and don't get killed, okay?"

Mo grinned. "Love you too."

Her mouth twisted into a reluctant smile. "C'mon, Rashmi. Let's go." She turned and started up the hall.

Rashmi shot Mo a solemn look. "Take care, brother."

"Yeah. You too."

Rashmi trotted after Jem, who'd already gotten a sizable lead in spite of her shorter stride. Mo watched them until Jem turned to glare at him over her shoulder, then he stepped through the door into his quarters and locked it behind him.

Inside, alone, his tension fell away. He rolled his shoulders. "Turn lights down to low."

The light dimmed to a soft golden glow that illuminated the untidy heaps of clothes, shoes, and various junk he and Armin had left on the floor. He kicked his way through the mess, promising himself he'd clean up after he went over the vids. It seemed like a stupid waste of time, but what the hell else was he going to do while he was stuck in his quarters? Lie on the bed and worry? Fuck that.

He settled into the round, plush chair at the workstation in the corner, and drummed his fingers on his knee. Maybe he could go ahead and watch the mermaid vid first, since it was so short. Get it out of the way. After that, he could watch the one from the first walk. Hell, they were both no more than different ways to kill time and keep himself from going nuts wondering what Armin was learning in the lab. He didn't expect to find anything earth-shattering on either one. Interesting, maybe. Useful? No way.

"Computer, 3-D display of video record from my walker cam, dated 14 May 2137. External cam." Walkers automatically recorded each walk on their built-in feeds, but since that data tended to take up a lot of space in the central system those feeds were necessarily lower quality. He'd watch them later on, maybe, but he doubted it would help much. What he really wanted to see was the high-quality, high-res external cam. The one that only recorded when he told it to.

"Anything you say, Mo." The computer spoke in a low, sexy growl. He could almost picture the man behind the voice stretched out naked on rumpled sheets, a lazy grin curving kiss-swollen lips, one big hand trailing down well-defined abs, following a line of black hair to —

Stop it. Focus.

He cast a nervous glance around the room. Other than the hellacious mess Armin seemed to take with him everywhere that wasn't a lab, it looked the same as it ever did. No naked men lounged on his bed, thankfully. He didn't think he could handle that particular hallucination right now.

Daisy crouched in her cage beside the dresser, half-hidden behind the large, leafy branch, the empty husk of her latest meal discarded nearby. She watched him with her beady black spider eyes. He wondered what she was thinking. Was she curious about him and what he was doing? Did she miss Hannah? Or was she laser focused on how good that cricket had been and when she might get another one? Was she content with her plastic-caged existence, or did she yearn for the jungle she'd never seen, and the hunt she'd only known in her strange arachnid dreams?

The floor of the Peru–Chile Trench sprang to miniature life from his desktop, startling him out of his near-trance. Laughing at himself to dispel his uneasiness, he wheeled closer, adjusted the settings on the 3-D display to one hundred twenty percent magnification, and peered at the video.

This was his second sighting of the rare fish, and the first time he'd ever had a vid he'd taken himself to study and compare to his actual eyewitness sighting. Mermaid videos were exceedingly rare in the first place. To Mo's knowledge, only seven—including his—existed. Hell, he remembered when news of the creature's discovery had first broken. He'd been six years old then. He and his family had watched the news on TV, ages before the massive storms that destroyed the power grids in most of the Middle East. The memory of those few seconds of blurred black-and-white video had lurked in the back of his consciousness through the wonder of learning about life on the deep-sea vents, through the long, dark hell of the Dubai blackout when half his family had died and he'd learned how to kill, through the training to become a bathyspheric diver and miner, through all the ups and down of his life since then.

The creature was so rare and so poorly documented that even now, half the scientific community thought it was a myth, like the Loch Ness Monster or something. That the few vids of it were either mistaken identity or outright fakes. But Mo knew it was as real as himself. Ever since he'd first seen a mermaid swimming toward him out of the blackness of the Mariana Trench, pallid and green-eyed and dreamlike, he'd wanted to see one again. To vid it. Capture its horrific beauty for himself.

And now he had. Now he could study it at his leisure.

If he could concentrate. Seemed like his mind wanted to wander. The short video had ended while he was sitting there daydreaming instead of paying attention.

He dug the heels of his palms into his eyes. "Computer. Restart video from the beginning."

Thankfully, the computer did it without comment. He thought he might lose it if he heard that fucking impossible seductive voice again.

This time, he ignored all the mental pictures swirling through his head and kept his attention on the display. The mermaid's image hovered in the translucent black cube, its tail undulating from side to side and its elongated, fingerlike pectoral fins stretching and contracting as if reaching for something beyond the edges of the video. The creature's wide mouth gaped open, showing rows of teeth like glass shards. Its eyes seemed to stare straight into Mo's.

It can see me.

Mo's pulse caught in his throat. The skin pebbled up and down his arms. Logically, he knew he was imagining things. A video couldn't see him. It was only a shadow of the original, without awareness. But he couldn't shake the sensation of a keen mind focused on him through the image of the mermaid's bulging, hazy eyes.

"She sees."

Adrenaline shot through Mo's blood, freezing his breath and paralyzing his limbs. He spun around. No one was there. "Who said that?"

The strange, cracking, clicking voice spoke again. "She. Sees. You."

He glanced around, but couldn't find a source for the sound.

Because it's not real. You're hallucinating.

Right?

The grinding whisper answered as if it had heard his thought. "Not. Imagined. Is. Real."

Mo laughed. It sounded deranged. "You just answered something I didn't even fucking say. You realize that doesn't help, right?" He covered his face with his hands when it dawned on him what he'd just done. "And now I'm talking to the voice in my head. Great."

"Not. Voice. I am. I am." Something went *tap-tap-tap*, very softly, close enough to make Mo jump. "Look. At me."

What?

Not knowing what else to do, Mo spun his chair in a circle. He still didn't see anyone, or anything. No possible origin for the weird, alien voice in his brain. Bizarrely, the frustration beating at his consciousness felt as if it came from an outside source rather than his own rapidly disintegrating control of the situation. Which was so many kinds of wrong he didn't even know where to start.

He shook his head. "Where *are* you?"

The only answer was the tapping noise. *Tap-tap-tap. Tap-tap-tap.*

What the hell was it? Christ. Holding on to his sanity by his fingernails, he leaped from his chair and paced from one side of the room to the other. No one was there. He was alone, except for Daisy, tapping on the side of her plastic cage with one pink-toed foot.

Wait.

Mouth dry and heart racing, Mo knelt beside the dresser and peered at Daisy, who'd climbed to the top of her branch and sat crouched near the humidifier in the upper left corner of the cage. Her fangs had grown longer. Thinner. Translucent. Yellow fluid dribbled from the cruelly sharp tips.

Every one of her black marble eyes glowed an awful, familiar purplish blue.

CHAPTER 10

Mo's vision went gray around the edges. He clung to the sides of the dresser and stared at the spider until the urge to pass out faded. "Daisy?"

She waved her front legs. "Can help. I can."

Fuck. This can't be happening.

Mo's head swam. He lost his balance and sat down hard on the floor, still staring at Daisy. "Help? Wh . . . what?"

"She. Sees." Daisy's unexpected spider voice echoed in Mo's brain. "*They*. See." She stroked her forelegs along her fangs with a gentle, loving touch. "This. Show you. Tell you."

Mo rocked in place, shaking his head. He felt on the verge of some massive revelation, if only he could get what Daisy was trying to tell him.

The hysterical laugh bubbled up again. He was talking to a spider. A fucking *spider*. And getting upset because he couldn't understand what it was trying to tell him.

Christ.

Was this insanity? Wasn't much fun, but honestly, it could be worse.

A wheezing screech like the death of some ancient machine pierced Mo's skull. He clamped his hands over his ears. "Ahh, fuck, stop it!"

"*Listen*." Daisy again. Goddamn. If he wasn't careful, her strange, crackling mind-voice might end up becoming familiar. She waved her front legs around, for all the world like a tiny human losing patience. "I. Will make. You. See."

A pearl of bile-colored fluid oozed like oil from one of Daisy's fangs onto a broad green leaf. Mo watched the light glance off the tiny drop, and suddenly he got it.

For a few endless seconds, he knelt there on the floor, poised between terror and curiosity. Did he dare? What would happen to him if he accepted Daisy's oblique offer? She'd promised to show him. To let him see.

See what?

It was the potential in the *what* that tipped the scales for Mo. Using the dresser for balance, he heaved himself back into his chair, opened the top of Daisy's cage and reached inside. Daisy crawled into his palm. He lifted her out slowly, taking care not to drop her.

He settled the back of his hand on the top of the dresser and watched Daisy stroke her fangs. His stomach churned and his pulse pounded so fast it made him dizzy. He couldn't decide if his shaking fingers and bone-dry mouth were due to fear or excitement.

Daisy's forelegs stretched. Grew. Became long, slender, and flexible. Tentacle-like. She wrapped them around Mo's wrist. They held him in a strong grip, the fine black bristles stinging like nettles.

He licked his lips, suddenly more afraid than he liked. "Wait."

"No."

The spider sank her fangs into the inside of his wrist. Her venom pumped into him in scalding waves, and he saw.

"There. Right there." Armin pointed a gloved finger at the squiggly steel-colored oddity on the 3-D scanner. "Go around it counterclockwise, please."

Youssouf maneuvered the scope deeper into Neil's brain with an expert touch. The display dipped sideways, blurring into a smear of white, gray, and blackish-red for a moment before settling back into an image of brain, coagulated blood, and the thing that definitely should not be there.

They both stared at it. Poole, relegated to the role of assistant, dropped his petulant scowl long enough to tread closer and peer at the image in pure scientific curiosity. "So three out of four have it."

Armin nodded. "Apparently."

Neil's was the fourth corpse they'd performed an autopsy on over the past few hours. Carlo Libra and Ryal Nataki had also shown the same abnormalities in their brain tissue, though Armin and Dr. Youssouf had very nearly labeled the grayish-black smears in Carlo's brain a result of trauma. Since Neil's brain was intact, unlike Carlo's, the lesion invading both frontal lobes was undamaged. It was identical to the one in Ryal's head. Which did nothing to help them identify it.

Poole frowned. "What is it?"

"I don't know," Armin answered truthfully. "I've never seen anything like it."

"Neither have I." Forehead furrowed with the effort, Youssouf guided the scope in a slow, steady tour around the anomaly. "It looks kind of like a malignant tumor, only . . . not."

Poole rolled his eyes heavenward. "Yes, very descriptive."

During the course of the autopsies, Armin had come to understand why so many of the BT3 staff disliked Dr. Poole. He might indeed be an excellent geologist—Armin wouldn't know—but he had a habit of talking to others as if they were stupid.

Armin decided speaking to Poole would be unproductive at best. "I understand what you're saying, Dr. Youssouf. It does indeed resemble a malignant brain lesion in many respects. Particularly in its invasive nature." He pointed to the branches snaking off the irregular lump and into Neil's cerebrum. "But the differences are there. It's simply difficult to pin down what they are."

Poole snorted. "Please."

"Exactly." Youssouf ignored Poole as if he weren't even there. Her gaze never wavered from the display. "I'm sampling now."

Armin watched as Youssouf carefully took samples both from the growth and the surrounding brain tissue, as she'd done with the remains of the other anomalous lesions. They'd also sampled Gerald's brain, which looked completely normal on autopsy except for the massive trauma which had killed him.

The fact that the anomalies only showed up in the brains of the men who'd shown symptoms of the contagion—or whatever it was—did not escape Armin's notice.

Youssouf pulled the scope free of Neil's skull with an awful slurping sound. She deposited the samples into the microscanner, peeled off her gloves, tossed them in the recycler, and crossed to the sink to wash her hands. "Well. We have a few minutes until the scans are finished. You want to give Mandala a call and see how it's going in the lab?"

"Good idea." Armin stripped off his gloves, gown, and mask, washed up, left the autopsy bay and plopped into the closest chair. God, he was tired. He activated his com link. "Armin to Mandala."

A second passed. Two. Armin shifted in his seat. Three seconds. Four. Five. Should he call again? Get Gordon on the com? If something had happened to Mandala—

"Mandala here. Are you finished with the autopsies?"

Relief left Armin weak. He sagged against the back of the chair. "Just now, yes."

"And?"

"And we found anomalies in Carlo's, Ryal's, and Neil's brains. Tumorlike growths. Gerald's was normal except for the trauma."

Shocked silence on the other end. "Jesus. Any idea what the growths are?"

"Not yet. The lesion in Carlo's brain didn't retain any kind of identifiable structure. We're still running cellular analysis on the ones from Neil and Ryal, and chemical and atomic level analysis on all the samples." Armin rubbed his forehead. "What about you? Have you been able to find out anything else about our mysterious rock?"

Mandala let out a sigh that said it all. "That damned thing."

Armin chuckled. "I suppose that answers my question."

"Well, it definitely doesn't harbor any sort of life as we know it. Which is good, I suppose, because it means this object didn't bring a contagion on board. At least, not one of a type we're familiar with."

Not exactly encouraging. "What have you found?"

"This object gives off a completely unknown array of spectral readings."

He frowned. "What do you mean?"

"I mean its spectral pattern is unknown. There's nothing remotely like it in the worldwide database. This confirms that our previous results were correct, and not a result of equipment malfunction." Her voice dropped to the low, clipped, precise tone she used when she was excited and trying to maintain her scientific objectivity. "Armin. None of the known elements that we saw previously are showing up on spectral analysis. Oxygen, carbon, none of them. I've checked the equipment. It's functioning perfectly."

Armin swallowed, his throat dry. "So you're saying . . ."

"I'm saying that this object is composed of materials that are entirely new to science."

The idea of it struck Armin dumb. A material utterly unknown before now was a huge enough find on its own. One that also fit his theories to perfection changed everything.

"I want to see." He sounded breathless in his own ears. Awestruck. He rose, putting his hand on the wall for balance when his knees threatened to buckle beneath him. "The microscans will be finished soon. The moment they're done, I'll come to the lab. Then we can swap notes and hopefully come up with some sort of plan."

"Yes, if this object in fact has anything at all to do with what's happening here. It might not, you know."

He knew why she had to say it. They hadn't established a firm link between the object and the bizarre events here, in spite of the timing, and a scientist could never assume. But he knew in his gut that every death, every hallucination, every unexplainable occurrence was connected to the object in the lab's vault. Their job was to figure out how.

"I'll be there soon," he said. "Armin out."

An hour later, Armin, Youssouf, Poole, and Mandala all huddled around the small conference table at the back of the lab, discussing their findings and trying to decide what it all meant. So far, there had been much speculation—not all of it friendly—but nothing in the way of solid conclusions.

Armin felt light-headed and strung out with exhaustion. His colleagues didn't look in any better shape. Entirely aside from that, they were wasting time talking in circles while the situation beyond the lab door deteriorated by the minute.

He cut off yet another of Dr. Poole's wild theories about mass hypnosis by slapping his open palm on the table. "This is ridiculous. It would be lovely if we could go step-by-step and test all the possibilities, but we don't have that luxury. The longer we sit here and talk, the harder it's going to be to fix this before it's too late."

Mandala stared at him in transparent shock. "I can't believe you just said that, Doctor. The scientific method is the basis of everything we do."

"I'm aware of that." Armin rubbed his dry and stinging eyes. "But this isn't a lab experiment. We need to *do* something concrete, soon, before everyone on this pod dies."

Youssouf nodded, her face thoughtful. "You're right. I wish we could be more careful, but we can't." She covered a wide yawn with both hands. "Excuse me. So, what do we know for sure?"

"Nothing, really." Poole slouched in his chair, arms crossed. "This is all some sort of mass hallucination. What we need is a psychiatrist."

Youssouf didn't even bother to look at him. She held up a hand and ticked off points on her fingers. "We know that we have six dead people on this pod, three of whom have measurable physical growths in their brains. Testing shows that those growths are not cancer, or abscesses, or in fact anything else previously known to medical science. Those same three people showed psychotic symptoms prior to death. Ryal Nataki and Neil Douglas both showed outward physical changes. We're not able to verify any physical changes in Carlo since he wasn't seen before he went out into the ocean and the massive trauma he suffered obscured any macro-level changes. We also know that this rock you found turns out to be made up of something previously unknown to science. Even Poole can't deny that, because he saw the spectral readout for himself."

Poole scowled, but for once didn't argue. As a geologist, he'd recognized the bizarre nature of the spectral analysis the moment he'd seen it.

Mandala planted her elbows on the table, clasped her hands together, and rested her chin on her steepled index fingers. "Perhaps the object gives off some sort of radiation that we're unable to detect. If that radiation causes these brain growths, might that lead to the sort of strange behaviors we've seen?"

"That's a good thought." Armin stood and paced in an attempt to get his sluggish mind moving. "Amara? What do you think?"

"It's entirely possible." Youssouf pressed her thumbs together, frowning. "I'm just wondering how radiation poisoning would be passed on from person to person."

Poole eyed Youssouf with open contempt. "Awfully big leap to make, isn't it? From radiation in a rock, to it somehow being passed person to person."

"I'd agree with you, except for the fact that Ryal never laid eyes on the damn rock." Youssouf arched an eyebrow at Poole, who sucked in his cheeks and glared daggers at the wall.

A mental image of Neil's horrifically changed face popped into Armin's head. "This is going to sound strange. But their eyes glow. The people who are symptomatic, I mean. They begin to show physical changes, and glowing eyes is one of them. Maybe that's how it's passed on." He glanced around at his fellow scientists, who were eyeing him with caution. He let out a soft laugh. "I guess you haven't noticed."

Dr. Youssouf spoke before Poole could, which was probably a good thing. "Nothing like that's ever been documented before. But then again, all of this is new territory. We can't afford to rule out any possibility that fits what we already know."

"Armin, you said that Ashlyn talked about weeds getting in through the eyes." Mandala gazed up at Armin with dread stamped all over her features. "What if she was right?"

The idea silenced all of them. Ashlyn might not have had all the details worked out, but it seemed she might have hit upon the essential nature of the problem before any of the rest of them.

Youssouf pushed back her chair. "I'm calling upside. The medical team there needs to know what we've found here, and how it might impact Hannah's care."

"We should find out anything they've learned as well." Armin came back to the table but remained standing. He thought if he sat right now, he might fall asleep in spite of the situation. That couldn't happen. He had to remain alert.

"Don't worry. I'll ask." Youssouf activated her com link. "This is Dr. Amara Youssouf, head of BathyTech 3, calling any medical personnel on the *Peregrine*. Priority emergent."

A male voice answered immediately. "Acknowledged, Dr. Youssouf. This is Niro Aster. I'm the RN in charge. What's your emergency?"

"I need to speak to Dr. Ngalo right away. We've learned something she needs to know."

"About Hannah Long, I hope." The nurse's voice had a grim undertone that Armin didn't like one bit. "I'll get the doctor."

Armin and his colleagues barely had time to exchange a *what the hell* look before a crisp female voice answered. "Dr. Youssouf. This is Dr. Ngalo. Please tell me you've figured out what's wrong with this patient you sent me and what to do about it."

Ngalo sounded positively disgruntled, which worried Armin. Things were bad enough down here, but if the worst happened at least it would be contained by several kilometers of ocean. Not so on the *Peregrine*. If this strange plague spread upside, there would be no stopping it.

He saw his fears reflected in Amara's drawn brow and tight shoulders. She sat forward. "What's happened?"

"She's much worse over the past twenty-four hours. She's delusional and violent, attempting to attack me and the nurses. She's also become quite photophobic. We've had to put her in an isolation cubicle with blackout curtains because she claims that even the slightest amount of light causes her a great deal of pain." There was a rustling sound, as if the doctor had covered her com link with her hand. She shouted something Armin couldn't make out. "Well. We've just had to sedate her. She bit Niro." Her voice dropped low. "Can you explain to me *how* it is that a human bite is able to leave *puncture* marks?"

Armin's stomach rolled. He resumed pacing because he had to do *something*.

Across the table, Mandala shook her head. "Christ. What the hell's going on up there?"

Armin let out a hollow laugh. "Same thing that's going on here."

"Quiet, both of you." Youssouf massaged the back of her neck with her free hand. "Dr. Ngalo, have you noticed any . . . physical changes in Hannah? Such as, uh . . ." She wrinkled her nose. Armin didn't blame her. She had to know how the truth sounded. "Such as elongated fingers, glowing eyes, and longer, sharper teeth?"

Silence. When Ngalo spoke again, a solemn fear had replaced the irritation. "She's exhibited precisely those changes, yes. She was beginning to show them when she arrived, but they were subtle. Now they're obvious. We're not sure what to make of them. I've never seen anything like it."

"Same here. But we've had others show those symptoms—the psychosis and the physical changes—since we sent Hannah to you."

"And? What happened to them?"

Youssouf drew a breath. Let it out. "They're all dead."

"Dear God." Ngalo sighed. "Tell me."

"Two were shot because they were actively attacking other personnel. One walked into the ocean and took off his helmet. So Hannah's still the one who's survived the longest. She's also patient zero, if this is some sort of contagion—which I think we have to assume it is."

"I think you're right. I'll have Niro put your girl on suicide watch, just in case. She's already on isolation, simply because we weren't sure what was wrong with her." Another sigh, deep and tired. "You said you'd discovered something. What is it? Will it help stop this?"

"I'm not sure. But I hope so."

Armin's mind wandered while Amara explained their autopsy findings, the events and discoveries surrounding the object from Richards Deep, and their half-formed theories regarding how the two might be related. He wondered what Mo was doing. Was he still poring over mermaid videos, reviewing them for the umpteenth time? Or had he given up? Was he sleeping? Dreaming? Lying in the semidark he preferred and staring at the ceiling, unable to stop thinking about death and needle grins, secrets and fear, and pupils that shone when they shouldn't?

Unable to shake the uneasy sense that Mo needed him, Armin lifted his com link close to his mouth. "Armin Savage-Hall for Maximo Rees. Mo, I know you're probably resting, but please answer. I need to know you're all right."

Nothing. He waited while the endless seconds ticked by. Armin gave him almost a minute, then called again. "Mo, this is Armin. *Please* answer. Urgent."

Still no answer. By this time, Youssouf had finished talking to Dr. Ngalo and was watching him. "Armin? What's wrong?"

"I was trying to raise Mo on the com, but he's not answering me." Leaving the link open just in case, Armin strode toward the door. "I'm going to his quarters."

"That could be dangerous." Poole's tone suggested he wouldn't mind if Armin met with some sort of peril.

Youssouf nodded. "Get someone to go with you. Gordon's recruited an ad hoc security force."

"And for God's sake be careful. We don't want anything happening to you." Mandala shot an icy glare at Poole, who ignored her.

"Don't worry. I certainly don't intend to let anything happen to me." Armin patted Poole's shoulder on the way out. "Sorry, Doctor."

Poole *hmph*ed. Mandala gave Armin a crooked smile.

Out in the hallway, the crowd of makeshift security personnel all turned to stare at him at once. Jemima Knang and Edie Ling had accompanied him and the other scientists from the med bay to the lab, which meant four people now guarded the lab door. It seemed excessive, but who could tell?

Armin spoke before anyone could question him. "I'm going to Mo's quarters to check on him. The situation being what it is, I'll need an escort. Who would like to go with me?"

Mo's boss stepped forward. "I will."

Armin wasn't surprised. He'd only known the woman for a few hours, but he'd already learned that she was smart, fearless, and intimidating as hell in spite of being half his size. No wonder Mo respected her so much.

"Good. Thank you." He looked at Gordon, who was in charge since he was the only actual security person BT3 had. "Dr. Youssouf, Dr. Poole, and Dr. Jhut are staying here. I should be back soon."

Gordon nodded. "We'll look after 'em."

Knang strode down the hall ahead of Armin. He didn't argue. After all, she was the one with the gun, and the training and experience to use it if need be. His prideful wish to not need protecting could get them both killed in a situation like this. She was right not to indulge him.

As they went, the hallway's lighting became dimmer, flickering like ancient gaslights. The spot between Armin's shoulder blades burned with the sensation of something creeping up on him.

There's no one there. Ignore it.

He did, though it was difficult. He and his escort reached Mo's rooms without incident. Knang bypassed the auto-port with a distrustful scowl and banged her fist on the door. "Mo? It's Jem. Your boyfriend's here to see you."

Armin's cheeks went hot, but he said nothing. He didn't care if Mo teased him. All he wanted was to see Mo for a moment. Talk to him and make sure he was all right.

Only Mo didn't answer. Seconds crawled by. Mo's door remained closed, a blank gray barrier shutting Armin out.

Knang frowned. She lifted her hand to hammer on the door again.

"Wait." Paying no attention to her incredulous stare, Armin stepped up to the auto-port. "This is Dr. Armin Savage-Hall, invoking medical override to enter the quarters of mining specialist Maximo Rees. Acknowledge."

"Acknowledging medical override on the authority of Dr. Armin Savage-Hall," said the auto-port in its usual smooth, bland voice.

The door opened. Knang literally shoved him to the side so she could go in ahead of him. He understood—right now she was security, charged with keeping him safe—but it still rankled. His need to see Mo, to ensure he was safe and whole, had become desperate.

He saw the back of Mo's head over Knang's shoulder at the same time as she lowered her weapon with an irritated sigh. "Fucking hell, Rees, you had us worried sick, you bastard."

Mo turned from the 3-D display—frozen on a shot of static out of which an unidentifiable, amorphous shape attempted to solidify—and favored her with a crooked grin. "Sorry, Jem. I was watching the mermaid vids and I guess I was a little caught up." His gaze—strangely empty, without his usual spark of passion and rebellion—rose, roamed, and refocused on Armin. The grin widened. "Hey, Doc. I hope you didn't leave your work 'cause you were worried about me."

He had, of course, but that wasn't important. "It doesn't matter. I'm just glad you're okay. You didn't answer your com and I was afraid—" Armin broke off when he saw Mo's wrist. He went to Mo's side, snatched his hand, and pulled the injury into the light. "What happened here?"

"Huh? That?" Mo laughed and waved his other hand at the two side-by-side punctures on the inside of his right wrist. The wounds oozed little streams of blood from their macerated edges onto his pants. "Daisy bit me."

Knang wrinkled her nose. "Damn spider."

"How did that happen?" He knelt beside Mo's chair to inspect the wound. It was red and swollen, and an ugly bluish bruise stretched for about half an inch around both puncture marks, but there was no streaking, no odor, and no signs of putrefaction or infection.

"I was feeding her, and she bit me." Mo shrugged. "My own fault. I got too close. It happens."

He's lying. That fact blared like a trumpet in a harp solo. Armin had watched Mo feed Daisy before. He'd dropped the cricket through the barely open top of the cage, then snatched his hand back as though the spider might eat *him* if he didn't move fast enough. Even if he'd accidentally gotten too close somehow, Armin found it difficult to believe the Mo he knew—the one who strongly disliked spiders, if not actively fearing them—would be this calm about a bite.

He kept all of it between his ears because voicing his suspicions could only make things worse. Instead, he rose and went to retrieve the first aid kit from the wall niche beside the bed. "I'll clean and bandage that bite. Is Daisy still in her cage?"

"Oh, hell yeah. Not getting out of there anytime soon, let me tell you." Mo held out his wrist so Armin could clean it. "And she's been fed now, so she ought to be pretty docile for a while."

"I can take her back to my quarters, if you want." Knang eyed Daisy with blatant mistrust, but didn't take back the offer. "I won't be in there much—but hey, she'll be safe, and spiders don't need company."

For half a heartbeat, Mo's dark eyes blazed with a fierce, possessive light. Armin's chest tightened. Then Mo smiled, and he looked like himself again. "Thanks, Mama, but it's okay. She didn't mean to hurt me. And you know her bite isn't dangerous to humans anyhow. I'll be fine."

Knang's eyes narrowed. She took a step backward and stood watching Mo in silence. Her stance was relaxed, but her finger hovered near her weapon's trigger.

Armin felt her tense, vigilant presence at his back as he washed the spider bite with sterile saline, applied antimicrobial healing gel, and wrapped it in breathable, dirt-and-microbe repellent gauze. Lastly, he took the two sublingual anti-inflammatory disclettes from their waterproof pouch and handed them to Mo.

"Put these under your tongue and let them dissolve. They'll keep the swelling down and help the pain." As Mo popped the miniature discs into his mouth, Armin reached up to touch Mo's cheek. The skin there felt cool, the stubble rough against his fingertips. "Mo? Are you sure you're all right?"

Mo met his gaze, and for a heart-stopping second he saw all the things that might've been, all they could've meant to each other, if none of this had happened. He ached with the sense of lost possibilities. Then Mo blinked, a lazy sweep of his thick black lashes, and the moment passed.

His smile still in place, Mo bent and kissed his lips. Soft, sweet, tender, but detached, and the vague worry in his gut twisted tighter. "I'm fine. Just kind of fuzzy-headed from watching those damn vids a dozen times in a row." He gave Armin a playful shove. "Go on. I know you have shit to do."

It was true. Plenty of work still waited at the lab, and Armin could hardly expect his colleagues to handle all of it. But he didn't want to leave. Something about Mo felt off. He couldn't put his finger on it, but it made him want to stay. To protect Mo, somehow, from the wrongness he couldn't quite define.

Since he had nothing concrete to go on, however, he forced a smile, pressed Mo's hand, and stood. "Promise you'll com me if you need me."

"I promise." Mo's smile widened into the familiar little-boy grin that crinkled the corners of his eyes and made him look almost normal again. "My hero."

Jemima snorted. "Smart-ass."

Mo rose, yawning. "I'm gonna sleep for a while. I'll program you into the auto-port, Doc. Come join me when you're done."

The thought of sleep beckoned Armin like a lover. God, what he wouldn't give to lie down, close his eyes, and forget about everything for a while.

Knowing he'd see Neil's toothy, purple-eyed ghost in his nightmares alongside Carlo's mangled corpse kept him upright, open-eyed, and well away from Mo's bed.

"I'll talk to you soon." He touched Mo's hand. "Sleep well."

"I will." Mo yawned again, stretching his arms over his head. "Bye, Doc. Jem. Be careful out there."

With nothing left to say or do, Armin followed Jemima out the door. It slid shut behind them. He cast a glance at its featureless surface as they walked away, and felt hollow inside. Mo was uninjured. The worst Daisy's bite could do was make him slightly ill. They'd see each other again soon enough, and Mo was safer in his quarters than anywhere else on this pod.

So why did he feel like he'd just said good-bye?

The minute Armin and Jem left, Mo got moving.

Go now. Daisy's voice echoed in his head. *Mustn't waste time.*

Mo didn't bother to answer. The consciousness speaking through Daisy knew every idea and emotion, every question and fear tangling like snakes inside him. He pulled on socks and shoes, shrugged into a light jacket, and went to Daisy's cage. Following her silent commands, he lifted her in his palm and tucked her carefully into his jacket pocket.

If Armin and Jem saw him right now, they'd drag his ass down to medical isolation. Hell, not just isolation—heavy tranquilizers for now and hardcore psychotherapy once they got him upside.

The thought sent a hard chill up his back. The last thing he needed was to be locked up and helpless. Especially now that he was about to learn the secret behind this whole crazy business.

Cupping one hand protectively over Daisy's pocket, he opened the door, peered out, and hurried down the empty hallway.

He reached his destination without running into anyone, and disabled the security cams and alarms with disturbing ease. If they all survived, he'd have to find a way to tell Youssouf her security system sucked without confessing what he'd done.

Of course, that was one big fucking *if.* Him living to return to BathyTech in the first place was another. One he was trying hard not to think about.

A quick search confirmed what he'd already known. "We don't have anything for me to carry you in." Talking to Daisy—or, technically, whatever was communicating with him *through* Daisy—felt weird, but what else was he supposed to do? "Can you talk to me from the cart?"

No, she—it, whatever—answered inside his mind. *Share the suit. I can.*

In spite of whatever squick-suppressing drug she'd injected into him along with the knowledge serum, Mo couldn't help a shudder of revulsion. Picking her up was one thing. Even carrying her in his pocket, he could handle. But the thought of her in his walker suit, dragging herself along his nude body with her long, hairy spider legs, made his skin crawl.

She moved inside his pocket, reminding him that she heard his thoughts. *Do not be afraid. Soothe your fears, I will. Hurt you, I will not.*

Something in the cadence of the mental—*imagined? No, real, real*—voice eased the clammy-cold waves rippling over Mo's arms. He let out a short, sharp laugh. "Okay. Yeah. Okay."

Hurry. We must. They. Will. Stop you.

Part of him wanted to be stopped before he went too far.

He crushed the thought and its accompanying panic, hoping like hell Daisy hadn't picked up on it. *I want to know!* he screamed in his head, trying to drown out the traitorous stray whispers. *I need to know. I need to see. I need to learn. Show me.*

From Daisy he felt a wave of smug contentment, but didn't dare acknowledge his relief. Instead, he focused on the very real curiosity simmering in his gut. The lifelong desire to know things no one else ever had. To lay bare the secrets of the dark, even if they burnt his mind to a cinder.

Holding his breath, he opened the go-cart he'd spent so many hours in over the past few years. Nothing happened, and he let himself relax. Sure, he knew *how* to kill the alarm, but this was the first time he'd actually *done* it. He settled into the pilot's seat, opened the bay door, and dropped the cart into the black, icy deep.

The fact that no one had shown up yet to check the camera function told him nobody was watching the feeds. Blank screens wouldn't raise the same level of panic as someone taking a cart without permission—which was why he'd disabled the cams and alarms in the first place—but it should've meant at least one of the tech crew showing up to check it out. In fact, they should've caught him before he could get away, if they'd been paying attention. Meaning they weren't. Which he'd been counting on, of course. Things had gone to shit in there.

Judging by the poorly hidden fear in Armin's eyes, though, it must be worse than he'd thought. What had they found to make Armin look like that?

The more Mo thought of it, the more it bothered him. Maybe he ought not to be out here right now, chasing mysteries. Maybe he ought to turn around and go back, before anyone discovered him missing. Before they learned he'd stolen a cart and headed out into the deep alone.

Well. Alone except for the tarantula in his pocket. Like that was going to make him look anything but crazy.

He sat there in the pilot's chair, staring out at the organic detritus drifting like ash through the beams from the go-cart's headlights and waging mental war with himself. The soft touch on his ear startled him into a shout. If he hadn't been strapped in, he would've leaped out of his seat. As it was, his sudden movement knocked Daisy off his shoulder where she'd evidently climbed while he wasn't paying attention.

He'd been so distracted he hadn't even noticed. That *really* scared him. Distraction could be deadly out here.

Mo slumped, shaking in reaction. "Fucking shit. Don't do that."

If the entity borrowing Daisy's body heard him—or cared what he thought—it didn't let on. The spider clambered up Mo's leg, making him shudder, and onto the narrow shelf above the readouts. Its black eyes watched him with a weird purplish-blue glow and a spark of intelligence that definitely did not belong there. *Not go back. Others. Would not. Like it. Not understand.*

Mo rubbed at the ache in his temple. Much as he hated it, she was probably right. The damage was already done. When he went back, they were going to look at what he'd done, label him insane, and lock him up. They'd tell him it was all for his own safety. He might as well see whatever he'd come out here to see while he still had his freedom.

It's lying, whispered the part of him still able to think clearly. *Go back now, before it's too late. Find Armin. Talk to him. He'll listen.*

The presence in his head expanded in response to the thought. Grew heavy and smothering as toxic smog. He clutched the arms of his seat and fought to breathe.

Not go back, repeated the thing that wasn't Daisy, its voice deeper now, thick and sluggish as the liquid rock far, far beneath them. *Only forward.*

For the first time, Mo understood how little choice he had in what was happening.

Lucky for him, he'd always been good at rolling with the punches.

He sat back and breathed slow and steady until his confusion cleared and the tension seeped out of his muscles. Once his fear eased, it seemed obvious to him where he needed to go, so he brought up the 3-D map and entered the coordinates. Daisy crouched like a hairy little statue on the dash and said nothing, but Mo knew the instinct guiding him came from her. Or rather, *through* her. Somehow. Directing him away from the familiar terrain surrounding BT3, away from the vents, into unknown territory.

He peered out into the black water, watching the patterns of light and shadow play over the ripples of the ocean floor. Now that he'd stopped fighting the inevitable, a dark excitement familiar as a pair of worn jeans took over, making his heart pound and his armpits prickle with sweat.

He'd felt it before, countless times. The thrill of the new, the strange, and the illicit. The abandoned building hiding drugs and money, the dead man in the school basement, the subway tunnel where the gangs skinned people for fun. He'd thrown up when he'd seen the flayed, bloody corpses and caught the smell of raw meat, but finding the place after hours of exploration in underground gang territory had still given him the shock of discovery he'd always craved.

All his life, the things he wasn't supposed to know had called to him. He'd gone after them, he'd experienced them, and he'd learned. And now here he was, chasing probably the biggest revelation of all.

A few meters ahead, the sea bottom began a gradual downward slope. Richards Deep. Mo grinned. Why had he been afraid before? This was the best kind of adventure.

Whatever's down there, it's directly responsible for at least three deaths. Maybe more, if what's happening here is related to what happened on the Varredura Longa. This isn't a game. It's life and death.

Mo shook his head, irritated. His sensible side had never been this much of a problem before when he was out to satisfy his need to learn unknown things. And why did that damned inner voice sound so much like Armin?

Not hurt. The Daisy-thing spoke with a gentleness that magnified the alien grind of her voice in Mo's mind. *Only show. So much. To show. We have.*

Sensible-Mo didn't believe it. Adventurer-Mo, always the more dominant part, ground Sensible-Mo into nonexistence beneath his heel and smiled at the spider hunched in front of him.

Mo drove the cart down the slope and into the Deep for half a klick or so, until the seabed began to morph from mud and silt to rock, and the walls of the Trench started to rise around them. He stopped when his gut told him to, put the go-cart on trickle power and anchored it to the ocean floor. Daisy hopped onto his knee as he unbuckled, then climbed on to his shoulder. This time, her presence there felt right rather than creepy.

He didn't waste time wondering what that meant. He wanted to get suited up and head out ASAP. A sense of anxiety pushed on him, as if whatever waited for him in Richards Deep needed him to hurry. He couldn't imagine why, but keeping it waiting felt far more dangerous than going out there in the first place. Since his instincts had kept him alive when Dubai fell apart, he wasn't about to question them now.

Finding a way for Daisy to share his walker took more time than he liked. In the end, he was forced to put her in his helmet, since there wasn't room for her anywhere else, never mind the fact that she insisted on being able to see.

He scrunched his eyes and mouth tightly shut when the flow of Mist began and she inevitably freaked out. As far as he knew, this was the first time in history an arachnid had been subjected to Mist. He wasn't sure she would survive it. He held as still as he could while Daisy skittered around his helmet, shedding stinging hairs all over his face and hissing in his mind.

Goddamn. If he got through this experience with his sanity intact, he was never, ever going near another spider as long as he lived.

Finally, after what felt like years, Daisy settled down, both physically and in Mo's head. He opened his eyes, cautiously, one at a time. He could just see Daisy, huddled in a miserable little black ball near his chin. She didn't move, but Mo felt her presence in his mind. He decided to ignore the throbbing pain in his face and neck. She hadn't meant to hurt him. Everybody panicked the first time they had to breathe Mist, and spiders didn't even have the same respiratory system humans had. It must've been *way* worse for her.

Luckily for him, the suit's filter system had evidently taken care of the damn tarantula hairs. At least, he didn't seem to be breathing them along with the Mist. He didn't like to think about what those things could do to his lungs.

"All right there, Daisy?" He knew he didn't have to speak out loud. But it made him feel better. More normal. "Mist is always bad the first time."

All. Right. She sounded stiff, even more stilted than usual—and how weird was it that a fucking tarantula even *had* a usual speaking voice?—but calm, which was the important thing. *Must. Go. Must. Hurry.*

Amen to that. The tension he'd felt from somewhere beyond himself had grown more oppressive while he and Daisy had been preparing to walk. It pressed harder than the weight of the ocean.

Mo went through the safety checks as quickly as he dared, then pressurized the chamber, opened the moon pool cover, and leaped into the water.

Out in the ocean, Mo let the silent guides in his head lead him as he'd done in the cart. The lights from his wrists and helmet revealed wonders at every turn as he walked. Sure, it was only rock, rock, and more rock, but he'd never been in this part of the Deep. Every outcropping, undercut, and wandering narrow pathway through the rising stone walls was new to him. Virgin ground.

Had *anyone* walked this particular bit of seabed before? Maybe he was the first. A true explorer, blazing a trail. The idea made his pulse jump faster.

He wasn't sure how far he'd walked—he'd used nearly a third of the Mist he'd started out with, an uncomfortably large amount—when he caught a strange, inky radiance somewhere ahead. Frowning, Mo paced forward, studying the weird glow.

The closer he got, the more he realized it wasn't so much an actual light as a mental suggestion of one. It was as dark as the surrounding sea, illuminating nothing, yet when Mo switched off his walker lights, he found he could see in spite of the utter blackness.

Close. Anticipation threaded through Daisy's thick, crackling mind-voice. *You. Will. See. You. Will. Know.*

Mo ignored her. She'd done her bit, bringing him here. He didn't need her anymore. Whatever the big secret was, it was here, right in front of him. Almost close enough to touch. For the first time in all his years of grasping for hidden things, he was finally about to learn something no one else on Earth had ever dreamed of.

Excited now, his heart galloping and his cheeks flushed with heat in spite of the cold and the Mist, he broke into an awkward trot. Daisy bounced along the base of his helmet, her prickly abdomen scraping his throat, but he didn't care. Physical irritations were nothing. Knowledge was everything.

Each jostling step brought him closer, closer, closer to his goal. The black-lit horizon quivered and jumped. Shadows moved in the light that wasn't there.

As he ran on, the twisting, confusing dark became a narrow yet endless chasm opening practically at his feet. He stopped, sending a cloud of silt spiraling into the depths as if pulled.

Don't look, said the inner voice that was his own but sounded like Armin, because Armin had become important to him. *If you look, you can't unlook.*

No doubt. But Mo was a pioneer. A trailblazer. So he stood on the brink, he looked, and he saw.

He opened his mouth and screamed.

CHAPTER 11

Armin smelled the blood before they reached the final turn to the lab. Bile rose in his throat. "Oh no." He started to hurry ahead.

Jem stopped him with a strong grip on his elbow. "Uh-uh. You stay put until I tell you it's safe."

"But—"

"No buts." She pushed him flat against the wall. "Stay here."

She slipped into the intersecting hallway before he could answer. A second later, she let out a soft curse. He tensed. "Jemima?"

"Keep it down, will you?" She stuck her head around the corner. "Come on. But for fuck's sake, be quiet. I don't know what's going on, but it's bad."

Armin steeled himself against whatever he was about to see and followed Jemima out of his questionable hiding place into the lab corridor. Gordon lay facedown on the floor in a spreading red puddle.

"He's dead." Jemima glanced back at him, her face grim. "I checked, not that there was a lot of doubt."

Armin swallowed and looked away. "How?"

"Throat's slashed. Cut right down to the spine." Her restless gaze settled on Armin long enough for him to catch a glimpse of the terror she'd buried far below the grief and rage boiling on the surface. "I'm going in. You stay out of sight."

"Like hell." Armin crouched, plucked Gordon's weapon from his hand where his murderer had left it, rose, and glared at Jemima. "I know how to use a sidearm. And it's better for us to stay together, don't you think?"

She rolled her eyes. "Fine. I don't have time to argue with you. Just don't shoot anybody unless you have to, all right?"

He nodded. Evidently considering the question settled, she motioned him to the side, pressed her back to the wall, and entered the emergency code to enter the lab.

The door hissed open. Armin heard the unmistakable sounds of a fight.

Fuck.

Jemima peeked inside. She drew in a sharp breath and glanced at him. "You'll know who to shoot." She eased into the room and started firing before he could move.

His chest tight and legs shaking, Armin checked the safety on his weapon—it was off; Gordon must've at least tried to fire before he died—then followed Jemima inside.

He nearly tripped over something on the floor. He regained his balance, stopped, and stared, shocked. It was Poole, lying in a small lake of his own blood, a chunk of flesh torn out of his throat.

Armin backed away and looked around. Two women with horribly familiar elongated fingers and sharp, thin, translucent teeth lay nearby, both shot through the heart. One was twisted in a heap with her hair over her face. The other was sprawled on her back, blue-black eyes fixed on the ceiling. He recognized the woman Ryal Nataki had bitten and the miner who'd fought with him in the cafeteria before everything fell apart. It felt like ages ago.

Infected. Both of them.

One—Tsali, who'd volunteered as a security guard—held a knife coated with gore.

"Armin?" Mandala came out from behind the counter where she'd apparently sheltered. She was sweaty and disheveled, her dark eyes wide. She hurried over to him and grasped his hands in hers. "Are you all right? And you, Ms. Knang?"

Jemima brushed off the concern with a wave of her hand. "I'm fine. So's the doc. Gordon's dead, though." She nodded at Tsali's corpse. "I'm guessing she killed him."

"Yeah." Youssouf, looking every bit as mussed as Mandala, emerged from the rear of the lab, a scalpel in her hand. She tossed it on the counter, plopped onto a workstation stool, and wiped her dripping brow with her forearm. "Gordon was able to warn us before they got in. It probably cost him his life. If we get out of here, I'm giving him a posthumous award for bravery above and beyond."

"Thank you for showing up when you did." Mandala gave Jemima a tremulous smile. "You saved our lives."

"No problem." Jemima perched on one of the workstation stools, her gun in her hand and her eyes darting side to side. Still on watch. "Were you and the other doc fighting those two off by yourselves? Without weapons or anything? Where's Rashmi and Ling?"

Youssouf gestured toward the door. "They went to check out a report of someone trying to force their way into private quarters."

"We haven't heard back from them yet." Mandala let go of Armin's hand and paced back and forth, back and forth. "I hope everything's all right."

"They probably haven't had a chance to report in yet." Youssouf mopped sweat from her neck. "Especially if they had to handle a situation."

Meaning another infected person. Good Lord. Armin rubbed at the pain drilling through his right temple.

"Yeah." Jemima dropped her hand, hopped off the stool, and rested one hand on it. "I'll give 'em another ten minutes before I start worrying. Not that I can do anything about it."

She sounded unhappy. Armin sympathized. He hated being stuck in the lab when the whole pod was descending into chaos. But in the end, if a solution existed, it would come from here, in this room. From him, and Mandala, and Youssouf. So he'd keep his restlessness to himself and do his job.

"We need to do something about the bodies." Mandala nodded toward the corpses without looking at them.

Youssouf laughed, harsh and humorless. "You're right. Problem is, I'm fresh out of medical staff, except me. We can take 'em to the morgue, but it's gonna take me a while to get all the postmortems done along with everything else." She studied Poole's corpse with sorrow and fury churning in her eyes. "In fact, we don't have room for four more bodies in our morgue. No one seriously expected anything more than the extremely occasional medical death when this place was designed. Mass violence was never in the plan."

"I can imagine." Armin watched the fear, helplessness, and anger play across Amara's face and wished he could do more than feel bad for her. "Is there anywhere else we can take them?"

Mandala sat up ramrod straight. "There's a freezer right here in the lab. It's for samples that need to be kept in extremely low temperatures, of course, but I think under the circumstances we could make an exception."

"Dr. Jhut, I like how you think." Jemima set her weapon on the counter and strode over to the nearest corpse—Karen, the woman who'd fought with Ryal in the cafeteria, long ago in another life. "Doc Armin, you wanna help me move her?"

"Of course." Armin slid off his stool and went to help Jemima carry the dead woman.

Between the four of them, they got all the corpses into the freezer and the worst of the blood cleaned up in about forty minutes. That done, Armin fetched pouches of vitamin water for all of them from the lab's refrigerator, and they sat down to discuss what to do next. Jemima remained inside the lab at Amara Youssouf's insistence, her argument being that Gordon might not have died if he'd been inside instead of outside. Armin could tell Jemima didn't like it, but she was a soldier at heart and she obeyed orders.

Ling commed while they were talking. She and Rashmi had gotten another call while out on the first one. They were taking a long-toothed, glowing-eyed cafeteria worker to a makeshift lockup before heading off to investigate the second call—another complaint of someone trying to break into someone else's quarters. Armin got the gloomy feeling those calls would only increase.

They'd been brainstorming for nearly an hour before Mandala came up with their first truly useful idea. "Why don't we scan all personnel for signs of abnormal growths in the brain?"

"Hm. All of the infected people who we've autopsied so far have had abnormal growths in their frontal lobes." Armin scratched his chin, thinking over Mandala's idea. "It's hardly foolproof, though, is it? I mean, we don't know at what point in the contagion the growths begin to appear, or even if *all* infected persons would actually have them."

"Or if this is really a contagion at all, for that matter, though I think we all believe it is. In any case, we have to operate on the theory that it is." Youssouf frowned at the floor. "Well. I suppose it's a starting point. Blood tests wouldn't do any good, since none of the autopsies showed up any abnormalities in the blood. And we have to find a way to identify infected people if we ever hope to figure out how this thing is spread. Or *if* it's spread."

"So how in the hell do we scan everybody on this pod?" Jemima swept a hand toward the door, as if to indicate the population of BathyTech 3. "There's thirty people here. Or, well. There *were*."

A solemn silence settled over their little group at the reminder of those who had died, and of Hannah who lay in an upside medical bay, critically ill with an unknown pathogen.

Then there was Ashlyn, who remained missing. After two days of searching, no one had found a trace of her anywhere, though Youssouf had designated a two-person team to search the pod every twelve hours. Armin held himself personally responsible for whatever had happened to her.

"There's only one way." Youssouf cast a grim glance around the room. "We'll have to escort everybody to the med bay one at a time and scan them."

Simply thinking about it made Armin more exhausted than he already was. He scrubbed both hands over his eyes. "Dear God."

"It would take at least three to four hours. Possibly longer, depending on how quickly and smoothly we're able to get the staff through the process." Mandala leaned both elbows on the counter. "If anyone has a better idea, believe me, I'm all ears. I'm not in love with this course of action. But I think Amara's right. It's the only way."

"It's not ideal. But it's the best idea we have right now." Youssouf pressed both hands to her lower back and stretched. "Okay. We could sit here talking in circles 'til the end of time, but since that won't do anybody any good, I'm making an executive decision to go ahead and start scanning all personnel for these brain growths." She gestured toward Jemima. "Jem, you know this pod as well as anyone. Help me figure out the logistics so we don't miss anybody, will you?"

Jemima nodded. "Yeah. Sure."

"Great. Thank you." Youssouf stood, wincing when her knees cracked. "Damn it. I'm getting old. Armin, Mandala, I hate to say it, but we're going to have to scan Karen's and Tsali's brains to see if they have the growths. Might as well do that before we start on autopsies."

Mandala nodded, her mouth compressed into a thin line. Armin murmured his agreement. What else could he do? He didn't look forward to dragging the two corpses out of the freezer, taking them to the autopsy room, and performing the necessary tests. He'd much rather return to Mo's quarters and join him in bed. At least then he'd know Mo was safe. He wouldn't worry about him. But that wasn't possible right now. There was important work to do, and Armin was needed here.

"Whoa, hold up." Jemima glanced from Youssouf to Armin to Mandala and back to Youssouf with disbelief stamped all over her face. "Rashmi and Ling aren't back yet. They're probably gonna be chasing crazies for ages. Gordon's dead. That just leaves me. Do I stay here and stand guard, or go with you to the med bay?"

Uncertainty flickered through Youssouf's eyes. "Well—"

"We'll be fine," Mandala said. "If Jemima comes with us, that would leave you alone. None of us ought to be on our own right now."

"True." Youssouf scratched her neck. Studied the floor with creased brow and bottom lip sucked into her mouth. "I can lock the lab door using executive override. No one would be able to get in or out without my voiceprint."

Armin considered, and didn't like it. "You'd be safe, I suppose, but there's too much that can go wrong on both sides of the door."

"Yeah, I guess you're right." Youssouf sighed. "All right. You and Mandala take the bodies on your own. Jem and I can stay here and figure out a schedule. At least we'll get it done faster with the two of us together."

"Very well." Armin raised his eyebrows at Mandala. "Are you ready?"

She nodded, and the two of them headed into the rear of the lab to gather the bodies.

They'd just finished loading the dead women onto two hover stretchers when the lab's communication port burst into static. Armin spun around. "What the hell?"

An unfamiliar voice rose above the crackle and hiss coming from the com link. "*Peregrine* to BathyTech 3. Please answer. Urgent."

Youssouf was on it before the person on the other end had finished speaking. "Dr. Youssouf here. Who am I talking to and what's going on?"

"This is Shonda Wildcat, chief engineer. I'm comming at Dr. Ngalo's request. We've had twenty-four people develop signs of the same contagion you're dealing with down there. The doctor wants to know if you've made any progress in pinning down how it's spread or how to stop it."

Armin and Mandala glanced at one another. He saw a dread matching his own in her eyes.

Across the room, Dr. Youssouf shut her eyes and rested her forehead on the wall for a moment before answering. "Copy that, Wildcat. Actually, we've just been discussing that very problem. Tell Dr. Ngalo we haven't found anything better than our previous theory as far as how this thing's spread, but we do have an idea for how to screen people for infection."

"Okay. Let's hear it."

Youssouf explained what they intended to do, and how. To Armin, the heartbeat of silence on the other end when she'd finished felt distinctly skeptical.

"That's going to be exceptionally difficult up here." The engineer didn't sound happy. "It'll be hard enough for you down there. But we have five times the personnel you do."

"I know. But so far, the brain growths are the only abnormalities we've been able to find, other than the obvious physical changes." Youssouf sighed. "We're not even positive the growths will show on scan before the other changes start to show up. But it's the only thing we can think of. At least if we find an abnormal growth on someone's scan, we can go ahead and isolate them, and try to figure out a way to treat them."

"I have a feeling the treatment is going to be the hardest part." Wildcat sounded glum, not that Armin blamed her. "Okay. I'm being called back to work. Please com us if you learn anything new. We'll do the same."

"Will do." Youssouf frowned. "Hey, what's a chief engineer doing working in the med bay? Are they that low on medical personnel?"

"Yes. We're down to one RN and Dr. Ngalo. Everyone with any medical training at all is being drafted to help cover the med bay. Especially since all beds are full and then some." A horrific gurgling scream sounded in the background. "Shit. I have to go. We have to intubate Niro. Wildcat out."

The link cut off. The echoes of the shouts and that awful, wet howl rang in the sudden quiet.

After a few stunned seconds, everyone started moving again. Youssouf and Jemima settled at the workstation to hammer out a scanning schedule while Armin and Mandala prepared the two stretchers for transport to medical. No one spoke, but Armin knew the same terrible thought was foremost in everyone's mind, just as it was in his: if this thing had already begun spreading on the *Peregrine*, what hope did any of them have of stopping it before it got out of control? And if that happened, if the contagion took the *Peregrine* down and moved into the world beyond . . .

Armin rubbed his arms against the chill the idea brought with it. They'd all have to hope Dr. Ngalo, Captain Escalano, and the officers could keep enough control over their people to prevent panicked personnel from stealing a lifeboat and sneaking off to the mainland. This was no longer a simple matter of saving themselves here on BT3, or even saving those on the *Peregrine* they'd unwittingly involved by sending Hannah upside before they'd realized what they were dealing with. The top priority now was making sure no infected persons reached the continent. If that happened, the world as they knew it was gone.

Youssouf stopped Armin with a hand on his arm as he and Mandala reached the lab door. "Scan each other for growths once you've scanned the bodies." She dropped her hand. Her face was grim and lined, making her look her age for the first time in Armin's brief acquaintance with her. "After that, come straight back here. I don't want either of you interacting with anyone else."

Armin understood the subtext. If the scans showed that he and Mandala were uninfected—as far as they knew—she wanted them to remain so. Guaranteed.

It made sense. There was only one problem.

"I want to check on Mo after we've finished in the med bay. Please," he added when Youssouf's expression took on the sympathetic-yet-unyielding cast he'd seen countless times before in his career. Superiors always felt for you—or said they did—but were never willing to let you have what you needed until you persuaded them. "Hannah's pet tarantula bit him earlier, and I know they're not particularly venomous to humans, but I'm still worried. I'd like to make sure he's all right."

"He could bring him on in and scan him," Jemima suggested. "He'll have to be scanned at some point anyway. Might as well be now."

Youssouf threw her hands in the air. "All right. Fine. Check on Mr. Rees. *After* you get the scanning done on the bodies and on each other." She pointed at Armin. "But I want you to be very, very careful, do you understand? And I want you to bring Dr. Jhut back here to the lab first."

Mandala looked startled. "That's not necessary. In fact, I think I ought to go with him. It's safer for two than for one."

"I'm armed." Armin patted his pocket, where he'd stuffed the gun he'd taken from Gordon. "I'll be fine."

"Huh. Well, I'm not crazy about some upsider running around my pod with a weapon, but I also don't want to risk losing *both* of our two remaining scientists instead of just one." Dr. Youssouf aimed a glare at Mandala that made clear why she was the director of BathyTech 3. "Understand this. I'm only letting Dr. Savage-Hall check up on Mo because I get the feeling he would do it anyway." She held up a hand, silencing Armin's protest. "Yes, you would. Don't lie to me. You don't get where I am if you can't read people. Mandala, I guess if you really want to run off and help him I can't stop you, since I can't afford to put anyone in lockup for disobeying me, but I need at least one of you back here in the lab. That's all I'm gonna say." She pressed her thumb to the auto-port panel to unlock it. It slid open. The hall beyond was dim, the light yellowish. "Be careful, you two. Com when you get there."

"We will." Mandala led the way out into the hall, guiding the first stretcher in front of her. Armin followed with the second stretcher. Youssouf's stare burned into the back of his neck.

Getting to the med bay took longer than it should have, mainly because the lights had been quite faint all the way from the beginning of their journey to the end. They sputtered and flickered in a way that should have been impossible. Yet there it was. Whole stretches of hallway had gone entirely dark. In those spots, Armin was reminded of how very far they were from the world of light and warmth over seven thousand meters above.

Thankfully, medical still had full power, though the broken doors made Armin nervous. He and Mandala had to force the one that still moved out of the way in order to get the stretchers inside. While Mandala commed Youssouf to let her know they'd arrived safely, Armin rolled a crash cart in front of the opening. Mandala laughed, but the way he saw it, the dubious early warning they'd have when a hypothetical intruder had to roll the rattly, squeaky-wheeled cart aside in order to enter was better than nothing.

Scans showed the by-now-familiar growths in the brains of both dead women. Armin was relieved. It still wasn't definitive proof, but it helped support their working theory.

Scanning their own brains was more nerve-racking.

Mandala volunteered to go first. She stretched out on the scanning couch, as self-composed as always. "All right. I'm ready when you are."

Armin drew a breath, blew it out, and started the scanner. It circled Mandala's skull with a faint hum. A couple of minutes later, the scan machine let out a soft chime and retracted into the wall.

Mandala sat up, her face blank but her eyes glittering with anxiety. "Well?"

Armin studied the readout and grinned. "Nothing. You're fine."

She slumped forward, elbows on her knees and both hands over her face. "Oh, thank *God*. I was terrified."

"Well, now you know you're in the clear, so you can relax."

"I won't relax until this whole nightmare is over." Mandala stood and crossed to the scanner controls. "Your turn. Go lie down."

And now it was Armin's turn to be afraid. He obediently went to the couch and settled into the cushions, doing his best not to let Mandala see how his body trembled and his heart hammered. The body-conforming technology instantly hugged him in a firm but comfortable grip that prevented any movement while making sure there were no pressure points to cause pain or lesions. Since his apprehension wouldn't change anything, he shut his eyes and breathed and did his best to relax into the artificial embrace.

It was over more quickly than he'd expected. He jumped out of the couch the moment the chime sounded, and wiped the dew of perspiration from his upper lip. "So. What does it show?"

Mandala didn't answer.

Dread wound icy fingers into Armin's gut. Throat tight and legs shaking, he strode over to her side to look for himself. What he saw left him clinging to Mandala's shoulder so he wouldn't collapse.

An ugly gray-black mass sat like a fungus in the middle of Armin's left frontal lobe, its wormlike appendages penetrating deep into his brain.

CHAPTER 12

Armin stared at the readout for endless, sickening minutes, until the vile charcoal-colored blob burned itself into his retinas, tainting everything he'd ever seen or would see again for whatever remained of his life.

You are become Death, misquoted the invader in his brain. *The destroyer of your world.*

Armin swallowed the insane urge to laugh. He turned away from the image of the horror inside his head and the pity in Mandala's eyes and activated his com link. "This is Dr. Savage-Hall to Dr. Youssouf."

She answered immediately. "Youssouf here. What's wrong?"

Mandala gripped his shoulder. Her touch was comforting. He laid his free hand over hers. "We've done the scans. Karen and Tsali both had growths in their brains. Mandala's in the clear. But . . ." His throat went tight. He forced the words out anyway. "I have the growth."

She drew in a sharp breath. "Shit. I'm sorry, Armin."

Beside him, Mandala opened her own link to Dr. Youssouf. "I have a great many questions about this. The foremost being: when and how was Armin infected? Early on seems most likely, especially considering the size of the lesion in his brain, but if that's the case, why hasn't he shown any of the changes the other victims showed? Also—and to my mind more importantly—why hasn't he developed any symptoms of a large, rapidly growing, space-occupying brain lesion? Why didn't *any* of them? It might be possible that one of them would've had a tumor before all this started, and that it was therefore actually a slow-growing lesion, but for that to be the case with *all* of these people is impossible."

Armin touched his temple as the truth of that sank in. The human brain, trapped in its unyielding bony case, had nowhere to expand. A rapidly growing lesion tended to cause swelling and irreversible damage, with unmistakable accompanying physical symptoms. Loss of motor control. Seizures. Focal symptoms, very different from the hallucinations and psychosis exhibited by the victims thus far. If this thing had only recently taken root, yet had already grown to such an enormous size, he should've shown those symptoms. Hell, by all rights he should be dead.

Youssouf's voice over the com startled him out of his thoughts. "That's true. Besides which, these growths don't look like typical slow-growing tumors on the scans. They look closer to the high-grade malignancies. Damn it, that's a huge problem." She went silent for a second. "Is there any edema on Armin's scan?"

Mandala shook her head. "No. Just the growth. The surrounding brain tissue looks completely normal. Which I believe would rule out known varieties of malignancy, yes?"

"Not definitively. We'd need a biopsy for that. But on a practical level, I've never seen a lesion the size of the ones we've found present without any accompanying brain swelling." More thoughtful quiet from Youssouf. "Well. It's a puzzle for later. First things first. Armin, since you haven't shown any symptoms, you're obviously different somehow from the others. We need to figure out how. That might be the key to not only your survival, but everyone else's."

A thought struck Armin. "Not only that, but Mandala's been working closely with me the whole time and hasn't caught it. We need to find a way to figure out whether that's because it really is passed on when the victim's eyes begin glowing, or because she's somehow immune. Because I don't believe she ever looked directly at the stone, only its projected image."

Mandala nodded. "Correct. I don't know if we'll be able to do that, but we have to try."

"I'm going to isolate myself." Armin risked a direct glance at Mandala. She looked as calm and in control as ever, which made him feel better. "Can you come and get Mandala? She shouldn't have to go back alone. The lights are out here and there."

Mandala opened her mouth, no doubt to protest, but Jemima cut her off. "Rashmi and Ling are back. I'll send 'em over before they get called away again. Maybe the doc can go ahead and get their scans done, then one of them can stay with you and the other can come back with Dr. Jhut?"

Armin raised his eyebrows at Mandala. She nodded. "That sounds good. Send them on over."

"On the way," Youssouf said. "Hang in there, Armin. We're going to fix this. Youssouf out."

As soon as the connection cut, Armin headed for the isolation rooms in the main part of the med bay. He felt sick with fear and unfocused anger. He wanted to believe Youssouf was right and they could find a way to reverse what was happening to him. Realistically, though, he knew the odds were heavily against it. They would all pay lip service to curing the infected, because they must. But in their heart of hearts, they all had to know it wasn't going to happen.

He didn't voice any of his bleak thoughts. No need to make Mandala think he'd lost hope. Truthfully, he wasn't sure he had, even though he saw no reason to believe he'd ever leave BathyTech 3 alive.

Mandala trailed behind him. She didn't lock the iso room door behind him. "You haven't shown any of the signs. I don't see any reason to make you a prisoner here."

He smiled, keeping his gaze trained on the floor. Illogical or not, he didn't dare look her in the eye now that he knew. "Thank you for that. Promise me that you'll tell whoever is here after you leave to lock this door the moment I show any of the changes, though. All right?"

She didn't hesitate, for which he was profoundly grateful. "I will. For your safety as much as everyone else's." She stepped forward and planted one open palm on the glass. "But Armin, your case truly is different. For some reason, you have the growth—if it really *is* a physical growth—but not the psychosis or the changes we've seen in the others. I can't help but believe that if it hasn't happened yet, it isn't going to."

"I hope you're right." Something else she said made him look up long enough to catch the familiar glint of scientific excitement in her eyes. "What do you mean, *if* it's a physical growth? It's clearly not anything we're familiar with, but it's there. We all saw it on the scans."

"Yes, we did. But just think about it for a moment." She dropped her hand from the glass and tapped her fingers against her chin. "Like I said before, it's hardly possible that *everyone* who showed the lesions could have already had the exact same slow-growing tumor that just happens to look like a high-grade malignant tumor. So we must assume that the growths and the physical changes are related, and began concurrently. Which means the growths took root within the last week, at the outside."

Armin got it then, and understood the enormity of the questions raised

If this was a true physical growth, I should be comatose, or dead. Ergo, it isn't physical.

A wave of dizziness rolled over him. He stumbled to the bed, sat down, and rested his head in both hands. "If the growths aren't real in the physical sense, then what in the hell are they?"

Mandala let out a short, sharp laugh. "I have no idea."

The rattle of the crash cart effectively redirected the flow of Armin's thoughts. Adrenaline shot through him. He jumped up and lunged forward, fumbling for the door handle.

Mandala shook her head, her lips curving into an amused smile. "Relax. It's just our intrepid security team." She raised her voice. "Hold on a moment. I'll move that cart for you."

Relieved, Armin slumped against the wall. Christ. He should've known. He walked over to the sink and peered into the plain little mirror. His reflection stared back at him, eyes big and black and full of shock.

They didn't glow. Thank God.

Rashmi and Ling followed Mandala into the room. Ling nodded at him, her dark eyes cutting sidelong toward him for the briefest of seconds. Rashmi spared him a smile and a "hey" before moving on to the other side of the bay.

Being on the wrong side of a closed isolation door felt very strange. And lonely. With all the time in the world suddenly at his disposal, worry about Mo leaped from the back of Armin's mind to center stage. He activated his com link. "Dr. Savage-Hall for Maximo Rees."

He waited, watching through the open door across the room while Ling stretched out on the scanner couch. Mo didn't answer.

God. Not again.

"Mo, this is Armin. Please answer."

Nothing.

Armin waited. Across the med bay, Mandala finished Ling's scan and studied the readout.

Armin rubbed his eyes. "Armin Savage-Hall for Maximo Rees. Mo, damn it, *please*. I need to know you're all right."

The silence on the other end stretched on while Ling moved away and Rashmi lay down.

No one was watching. Acting on instinct, Armin opened the door, ran silently across the bay, and slipped into the hall.

All the way to Mo's quarters, through the stretches of deserted hallway dimly lit by guttering yellow lights, Armin questioned his spur-of-the-moment decision to sneak away from the med bay. Mandala's theory about the contagion—whatever it might be, exactly—being passed on through the glow in the eyes was the best one they had thus far. He told himself it was fine for him to do this, that he wouldn't pose any danger to Mo or anyone else since his eyes didn't glow. But they had no way to prove or disprove that theory. If Mo hadn't been infected, was Armin about to hand him a death sentence?

You've slept with him. Been intimate with him. And he's shown no sign of the changes.

The memory of Mo staring blankly at the frozen 3-D display, bleeding from a spider bite, prodded Armin like knives. Was that the first sign? Had there been signs before that? Signs he should've seen, but hadn't?

For the first time, Armin wondered if he'd gotten the contagion from Mo.

The worst part of that particular scenario was the illogical but unshakable idea that he'd failed to protect Mo from a danger he never should have had to face.

An abnormal gloom shaded the corridor outside Mo's door for several meters in either direction. Armin steeled his nerves and ignored it. He hammered his fist on the door, like Jemima had done before. "Mo? It's Armin. Open the door. Please."

No answer.

Armin didn't wait. "Auto-port. This is Dr. Armin Savage-Hall here to see Mr. Rees. Maximum urgency."

The auto-port answered in its usual bland electronic voice. "Mo is not in his quarters. Would you like to leave a message, Dr. Armin Savage-Hall?"

Not in his quarters. Christ.

Armin rested his forehead against the cool metal of the door. His stomach churned. "Where is he?"

"Mo has not informed this auto-port of his current destination or the time of his anticipated return. Would you like to leave a message, Dr. Armin Savage-Hall?"

Panic sparked at the edge of Armin's vision. He fought it back. "Yes. Message: Mo, this is Armin. If you come back before I find you or speak to you, please com me immediately. It's extremely urgent. Thank you. End message."

The auto-port chimed. "Message received. Thank you."

Armin turned and leaned on the wall, feeling at a loss. What now? Should he wait here? Go back to the med bay? Mandala would be furious with him. With good reason, yes. But that didn't make him more eager to face her.

No. He hadn't crept away like a thief only to slink back in defeat at the first sign of trouble. He'd broken every rule of safety and good sense because his gut told him Mo needed help. Needed *him*. He couldn't give up.

Digging deep for his determination, Armin shoved himself away from the wall and started walking. He had no particular destination in mind. He kept Mo front and center in his thoughts and let his feet carry him where they would.

Somehow, he wasn't surprised to end up at the aquarium.

As he pushed open the door, pictures flashed through his brain in vivid, super-saturated colors—bright blood on the white floor, Ashlyn's empty eye sockets, the sun glittering on the ocean's surface, Mo's face twisted in pleasure.

Mo's dark eyes gone blue-black, sparking purplish. Mo's fingers long and flexible; Mo's teeth sharp, thin, *wrong*.

Changed.

No. Please, no.

Then Armin was inside. The aquarium was empty.

His knees went weak. He sat down hard on the floor. "Thank God," he whispered. He wanted to find Mo. But not like that. Not changed.

Of course he still had to find Mo at all, and he wouldn't accomplish his goal by lingering in the places where Mo wasn't.

He rose to leave. A swift movement from beyond the dome caught his eye.

Only a fish, he told himself, even as he spun to see.

Technically, he was right. But mermaids weren't your average fish. And this one's milky eyes stared directly into his as if it could see inside his head.

In Armin's memory, Mo pounded hard and hot inside him, the cold floor dug into his elbows and knees, while a different mermaid watched him from the other side of the aquarium's GlasSteel wall.

Who do you think we are, Doctor?

He crossed the room and pressed both palms to the transparent barrier separating him from the creature. "What are you, really?" The thing outside stopped and bared its nightmare teeth as if it had heard his question. He wondered if it had. He leaned forward, staring directly into the mermaid's hazy-green gaze. "Can you understand me?"

The mermaid, predictably, didn't answer. But Armin thought he caught a faint purple-blue glint in the depths of its bulging eyes. Fear trickled like ice down his spine.

Something went *thud* to his right. Startled, he jumped backward, stumbled and fell, landing badly on his left hip with his left arm twisted underneath him. He ignored the sharp pain and glanced in the direction of the unexpected sound.

Another mermaid—bigger, heftier, wide eyes most definitely glowing like black lights—slammed into the dome as he watched.

Thud.

A noise like a shot followed. Little cracks webbed out from the point of contact.

Armin gaped, horrified. Outside, the big mermaid grinned at him.

Grinned. The light from the aquarium glinted off its long, curved teeth and the silvery scales on its tail.

No. Wait.

The light was coming from two different directions. Not only from the aquarium but from behind the mermaid also. From deep in the sea where there *was* no light.

He looked, saw two bright spots beyond the mermaid, and realized what they were.

Headlights. Moving toward the pod.

Oh, Christ. Mo.

Armin whirled and left the aquarium at a dead run.

He was halfway to the go-cart bay before he realized that the crack in the dome hadn't obscured his view of the go-cart. It had vanished like it had never been there. Maybe it hadn't.

Considering what it meant could happen later. Right now, he had more important things to think about.

He burst into the go-cart bay just in time to watch a cart approach the wide-open receptacle beyond the closed inner airlock doors. The outside doors had been left open.

The cart had blundered into the lock, churning up foam and waves, before Armin recognized the silence around him for what it was.

No alarms. The outer airlock doors gaping open should've had klaxons blaring throughout the pod, yet no one had heard a thing.

Armin couldn't help admiring Mo's ingenuity, even though he wanted to shake him and scream at him and make him understand how wrong he'd been to run away like that.

In Armin's head, Klaudia Longenesse drifted off into the dark to an unknown fate. He'd seen it a thousand times in his nightmares. Thank God Mo had been sensible enough not to go that route. Armin didn't think he could've handled it.

The inside airlock hissed open. Angry, terrified, and relieved, Armin rushed forward and threw his arms around Mo barely in time to catch him when he collapsed.

Come back. Come back to me. Mo. Mo. Wake. Up. Come back. Come. Baaaack . . .

A stinging smack landed on Mo's sore, swollen cheek. "Mo! Damn it, wake up. *Please.* Answer me."

The badly disguised panic in the familiar voice forced Mo's eyes open more surely than the slap to the face. Not that he appreciated being hit, but as tired and scared as he was right now? He could've ignored it.

He couldn't ignore Armin's fear, though. Especially when that fear centered on him. His safety.

"'M okay." Blinking against the painfully bright lights, he squinted up at the person-shaped silhouette hovering over him. If someone had to come meet him, he was glad it was Armin, for a hundred reasons he wasn't sure he wanted to unpack right now. "Armin. I know. I *saw.*"

Shocked silence. Not a surprise, but still an annoyance. Mo shoved Armin aside and tried to get up.

Only Armin's strong, sure grip kept him from falling to the floor again.

Goddamn it.

"They grow. In the dark." Mo nuzzled into Armin's neck. Inhaled his scent, sweat and musk and man. God, he wanted to curl up against Armin's chest and sleep for a year, but this was urgent. "They're coming for us. We have to go upside."

Armin's back tensed under his hands. "I need to take you to the med bay. Where is Daisy?"

Mo tried to remember. No matter how hard he thought about it, his mind wouldn't go back further than the thing that had sent him racing back here in a blazing panic.

"I don't know. She was in my helmet, but . . ." The implications of Armin's question finally sank in, and Mo frowned. "Wait. How'd you know Daisy was with me?"

"You've been bitten again. More than once." Armin brushed his fingertips over Mo's cheek—the one he hadn't slapped. The touch burned. "Also, you have a severe rash all over your face and neck. I'm no expert, but it looks very much like one caused by urticating hairs."

The memory of Daisy scrabbling around his helmet, hissing and scraping against him, flashed through Mo's mind. She'd panicked and brushed her abdominal bristles onto him when he'd started the flow of Mist.

He didn't remember being bitten, though. Had it happened later? After whatever it was he couldn't remember? The mysterious event that made him believe beyond the slightest doubt that the world as he knew it was over? That BT3 would become another Varredura Longa unless they all went to the surface right fucking now?

Christ. Forget Daisy, forget the bites and the rash—hell, forget his pounding head and roiling stomach—he had to convince Armin they had to leave, right now. All of them. Everyone on the pod. *Had* to. Nothing else mattered.

He let Armin manhandle him to his feet, since he couldn't do it himself. Why was he so fucking weak? But he protested when Armin dragged him to the bench beside the airlock and made him sit. "No. We have to go. Armin, please."

"We will. As soon as it's safe." Armin started working open the seals on Mo's walker suit. He didn't look at Mo's face, but kept all his attention on what he was doing. "Where are your clothes?"

"In the cart." Mo held up his arms and let Armin peel the walker off of them, since he didn't have the strength to fight. "Damn it, we're running out of time."

"We'll spare the time."

"But—"

Armin's strong fingers grasping his chin shocked Mo into silence. He gaped at Armin and did his best not to gasp in pain. A tiny sound escaped him in spite of himself, and Armin gentled his grip with a sympathetic flinch. "I don't know what happened to you out there. But whatever it was, it sent you back here confused, weak, and physically ill. Your entire face is inflamed from Daisy's hairs. The worst part is, you put her in your helmet on purpose." He dropped his hand and leaned closer, his black eyes full of horrified disbelief and still firmly fixed somewhere south of Mo's face. "A *tarantula*, Mo. In your *helmet*. *You* did that. Yourself."

Mo laughed. He sounded like someone had run his vocal cords through a cheese grater. Felt like it too. "Well. When you put it like *that*, it sounds kind of crazy."

The look on Armin's face said he was not amused. "I'm getting you out of that walker and examining you for any further self-inflicted injuries. Then I'm getting you dressed and taking you to the med bay. After that, you can tell me what exactly happened and what you saw." He pointed at Mo. "Stay put while I fetch your clothes from the cart."

Armin had never sounded so grim. Mo's heart sank. He knew Armin well enough by now to know they weren't leaving BT3 until Armin was damn good and ready.

Mo lifted his hips off the bench so Armin could ease the walker suit over his rear and down his thighs. "What about Daisy?"

Armin glanced up at him. "I'll look for her. But I'll be honest. She might not have survived."

Another image exploded behind Mo's eyes—his helmet falling to the go-cart floor in slow motion; Daisy curled up inside, unmoving.

Fuck. He wiped away the sweat beading on his upper lip and stinging his raw skin. Hannah loved Daisy like most people loved a fucking kitten. He'd never forgive himself if he'd gotten her killed.

He sat there with his bare ass on the cold bench while Armin went inside the cart. Watching Armin disappear into the dimness made Mo's heart race and his stomach churn. It felt bad. Dangerous. Like Armin might not come back.

Mo's lungs seemed to shrink, like he couldn't get enough air. He gripped the edge of the bench until the metal dug into his fingers, but it didn't help. The smothering feeling wouldn't let him go. Like he was seeing a preview of a future he could only prevent by walking an invisible tightrope without faltering. He hunched forward and fought back nausea.

A thousand years later, Armin emerged carrying Mo's clothes and helmet, and Mo breathed again. Mustering every ounce of strength in his body, he pushed off the bench, stumbled over to Armin, and wrapped both arms around him, clinging to him with a shaking grip.

Armin's breath hitched in Mo's ear. He slipped an arm around his waist. Kissed the side of his head. "It's all right, Mo. I'm right here. I'm not going to leave you."

A tight, sweet warmth closed around Mo's chest like a fist. No one had ever been able to see inside his head the way Armin did. He'd already become addicted to that connection. "I'm sorry." He wasn't really sure what he was apologizing for. Running off? Breaking the rules like he always had? Scaring Armin?

Yeah. Maybe that. He'd never cared that much about what other people thought, before. Armin was different. He was learning he'd do a lot of shit differently to keep from hurting Armin.

"Never mind that." Armin smiled at him and gently touched his sore face. "Come sit down. You can barely stand up."

Mo didn't argue, since Armin had the facts on his side. He let Armin help him back to the bench. "Did you find Daisy?"

In answer, Armin set the helmet on the floor. Poor Daisy lay on her back, her legs curled inward. She seemed smaller than before. Wilted.

Guilt and a surprisingly strong grief swelled in Mo's chest. "Shit. I *killed* her. What'll Hannah say?"

Armin didn't answer. The peculiar, heavy quality of his silence caught Mo's attention. He stared at Armin, who refused to meet his gaze. "I'm sure she'll understand." Armin lifted Mo's right foot and ran his hand up the back of Mo's calf. "Are you hurting anywhere? Other than your face, of course."

"No." Mo watched Armin examine his other leg. They hadn't known each other long, and Armin had his blank expression on, but Mo had studied his features constantly over the past few days, waking and sleeping, when he was aware of it and when he wasn't. His face had no more mysteries for Mo. "What happened?"

Armin was smart enough not to pretend he didn't know what Mo was talking about. "Hannah's worse. They had to sedate her because she became violent." He rose, pulled Mo gently forward, and leaned over to study his back. It must've looked all right because Armin didn't mention it. He settled onto the bench beside Mo and took his hand. "She's changing, the way Ryal did. The way they all did." He lifted his head but stopped short of meeting Mo's gaze. "They're doing all they can for her, of course. But it's up to us. We have to find a way to stop this."

"Jesus. Poor Hannah." Mo rubbed a hand over his chest. He ached all over, and he didn't know whether to blame spider venom or the triple blow of Daisy's death at his hands, Hannah's worsening sickness, and the thing he couldn't quite remember. The thing Daisy had died to show him.

Armin stood and started to reach for the pile of clothes on the bench. The strange, dull pain pooling in the frown lines around his mouth made Mo grasp his hand. Armin stopped and stood still, blinking at the floor.

Mo studied Armin with narrowed eyes. "What aren't you telling me?"

Armin squeezed Mo's hand hard and said nothing.

Fuck that.

Using Armin's grip as leverage, Mo pulled himself to his feet and examined Armin's stubbornly downcast eyes. His lashes cast long, thin shadows on his cheeks, and Mo's heart constricted. He wished he could wrap Armin around his soul like a blanket. Drown in him. Keep him forever.

He traced the line of Armin's jaw with his fingertips. "Don't keep me in the dark. That doesn't help."

"I know, but . . ." Armin swallowed. Licked his lips. Opened his mouth and shut it again.

A terrible dread oozed through Mo's veins like poison. "Armin. Look at me."

"I can't."

Oh no. "Why?"

"Because I have the growth in my brain. I'm infected."

The words felt like a gut-punch. Numb with shock, his throat too tight to speak, Mo wrapped Armin in his arms and held him close. Armin's heart thudded too fast against Mo's chest. After a second, Armin returned the embrace. His shoulders were tense, his fingers shaking where they dug into Mo's bare back.

"We can stop this." Mo stroked Armin's back, trying to ease away the fear knotting his muscles tight. "It's gonna be okay."

Armin laughed—a jagged, hopeless sound that hurt to hear. "I never would've pegged you for an optimist. I like it, though. I'm having trouble mustering any positive thoughts of my own right now." He nuzzled the side of Mo's neck, making his pulse run faster. "What makes you so certain?"

Mo thought about it. He still couldn't remember exactly what had happened, yet he'd come back from his adventure knowing in his bones that they held the key to their own salvation. All they had to do was see it for what it was.

"I don't know. But we can find out." He drew back and nodded at the helmet on the floor. "Everything that happened out there is recorded in my helmet cam. We can watch it in my quarters."

Armin nodded. Thoughtful, hopeful, the fear and sorrow edging back in the face of his scientific curiosity. "We really should get you scanned first."

Mo frowned. "Huh?"

"We're scanning all personnel for growths. It's cumbersome, but it's really the best way we have right now of knowing who's infected and who isn't." The corners of Armin's mouth tipped upward. "That's how I found out. Obviously, I haven't shown any physical or psychological changes. It's a bit of a conundrum."

"How do you know you're contagious?"

"I don't." Armin laid a finger over Mo's lips. "But I'm not taking any chances."

Mo raised his eyebrows. "Hate to point out the obvious, Doc, but you're here instead of in isolation, so . . ."

"Yes, well. You weren't answering your com. I had to see for myself that you were all right." Armin let out a laugh like broken glass. "You destroy my good sense, Mo. But I'd do the same thing again."

Because you're important to me, said the faint flush in Armin's cheeks and the way his body leaned into Mo's like a sunflower toward the light.

Something in Mo's chest drew tight. Since he didn't know what to say—and wasn't sure he could answer anyway past the sudden ache in his throat—he slipped a hand around the back of Armin's head and planted soft kisses on his eyelids. Armin's breath hitched. He smiled, and the warmth in Mo's gut grew.

He drew a deep breath. Let it out. "So. If you don't know if you're contagious, do you have any idea how this thing might be passed on?"

"Yes. That is, we have a working theory." Armin clutched Mo's hips, fingers clenching and relaxing, over and over. Nervous. "Mandala's theory is that it might be passed on via light wave radiation when a person's eyes begin to glow."

Mo ran that through his brain and came out the other side intrigued. "Huh. Interesting. You're pretty sure?"

"We're not *sure* of anything. But that theory fits the facts, yes."

Mo wasn't a scientist. But he kept up with enough journals to know the idea was unprecedented. He grinned, excited in spite of everything. "I'll get scanned later. Let's go check out my video first."

Armin's eyes widened. "But—"

"But nothing." Dizziness washed over Mo like a tidal wave. His vision sparkled. He hid it by sitting down. He needed to get dressed anyway. "If I go to the med bay right now, I'm gonna end up having to stay because Youssouf'll think I'm a danger to myself." He shook out his shirt and pulled it over his head. "And hell, I can't really prove I'm not, can I?"

"True. Though I don't believe you are."

Armin sounded amused. Good. That was way better than angry and defeated.

"Thanks." He reached for his pants, shoved his feet into them, and did his best to get them on without standing. Upright seemed like a good way to pass out right now. He swallowed bile and made himself keep talking. "So, yeah. I don't think we can spare the time for me to hang out in the med bay right now. We need to watch the video, then show it to Youssouf and Dr. Jhut if it's worth seeing. *Then* we can figure out what we need to do."

"Hm." Armin sat beside Mo, slipped an arm around him, and helped him lift his hips enough to pull his pants up that last little bit. "And what about you?"

The urge to play innocent was strong, but Mo knew better. He sighed. "Hannah has an antivenom kit in her quarters. You can use medical override to get it."

"I will, then." To Mo's surprise, Armin leaned forward and planted a soft kiss on his mouth. "Thank you."

"For what?" Mo stole another kiss, because Armin was *right there* and he couldn't help himself.

"For not being a stubborn ass. For letting me take care of you instead of fighting me." Armin smiled. He lifted his eyes, just for a second, and Mo caught a glimpse of those drowning-dark depths.

They didn't glow.

The halls between the go-cart bay and Mo's quarters were dim and deserted, thankfully. Mo didn't want to run into anyone. What the hell would he say?

Inside his room, he stretched out on the bed, sipped a pouch of vitamin water, and pretended not to worry while Armin went to fetch the antivenom from Hannah's quarters.

Armin's return after roughly ten minutes that felt more like ten years was a huge relief. Mo pushed off the bed, stumbled across the room, and draped his arms over Armin's shoulders.

Eyes averted, Armin let out a nervous little laugh. "What are you doing?"

"Shut up." Mo silenced the protest he knew was coming with a kiss. He cupped the back of Armin's head in one palm to hold him still, savoring the soft, wet heat of Armin's mouth and the slick push of his tongue. The scrape of stubble against Mo's raw skin hurt, but he didn't care. Armin's kiss hadn't changed. His touch hadn't changed. Nothing about him had changed, in spite of the thing growing in his brain, and that gave Mo hope.

When the kiss broke, Armin rested his forehead against Mo's. His eyes stayed shut, but he was smiling. "Did you miss me that much?"

"I don't like you being away from me right now. It scares me. It feels like you're not coming back."

Armin's smile vanished. His eyes opened and focused on Mo's chest. His unhappiness radiated through the tight muscles under Mo's hands, but Mo didn't regret his answer. If he demanded honesty from Armin—and he did—he had to offer the same.

"I wish I could promise I'd always come back. But we both know I can't do that. If I start changing . . ."

He didn't have to finish. Mo swallowed around the cold, bitter lump in his throat and nodded. "I know. Just promise you'll try."

"I can promise that." Armin's dark eyes flicked upward long enough to look into his for a brief second. Just long enough for Mo to see a bottomless anguish that pierced him deep. "And I want *you* to promise never to sneak off like you did today. I thought you were dead."

Shame brought a rush of blood to Mo's cheeks. He gritted his teeth through the intense burn, because he'd brought it on himself, and right now he thought he damn well deserved it.

"I swear I won't." He raked his fingers through Armin's hair. "I'm sorry. It was so weird. I felt like I *had* to. That's not an excuse. It's just . . . what I felt like."

"Well. It's done now, and you're back safe." Armin took his hand, led him to the bed, and pushed him gently to the mattress. "Now sit."

He watched while Armin sat next to him, opened the kit, and took out the little bottle of sublingual antivenom pills. He took the two tablets Armin handed him and tucked them under his tongue. He scrunched his nose as they dissolved and the bitter taste flooded his mouth.

Armin was already pulling on gloves and opening a bottle of clear liquid. "It's purified water with topical pain reliever in it," he explained in answer to Mo's suspicious look. He spread a plastic-backed pad on Mo's pillow. "Now lie down and shut your eyes. I'm going to wash your face with this and apply an anti-inflammatory cream."

"Oh, joy." Mo didn't look forward to it. But he did as Armin said, because the pain in his face and neck had grown so huge he wanted to run away from it. Since that was impossible, he was stuck with Armin's method.

Armin had a skilled, careful touch, and the stuff in the wash cooled the burn in Mo's flesh from *inferno* to *dying coals*. Still, by the time Armin patted him dry, his head and neck felt like one giant, swollen, throbbing ache. He dug his fingers into the bed and managed not to squirm while Armin spread ointment as gently as possible over his skin.

When it was over, Mo let out the breath he'd held for the last half a minute or so. Sweat gathered on his chest and fine tremors shook him from head to foot. He opened his eyes and blinked at the ceiling. "Fuck. Let's not ever do that again."

"We may have to do it again in a few hours, but hopefully it won't be as bad the next time." Armin rose, peeling off the gloves and tossing them in the trash. "I think you should rest for a while before we watch your video."

Rest. The mere idea dragged Mo's eyelids downward like a physical pull. Apparently his impromptu adventure had drained him more than he'd realized. His whole body buzzed with exhaustion. He wanted to give in to it more than he'd ever wanted anything.

Unfortunately, BathyTech had kind of a situation going, and if his walker vid could help fix it, then they were damn well watching it right this second. He'd hold his eyes open with his fucking fingers if he had to.

Since he didn't want to give Armin any more ammunition for his *making Mo rest* campaign, Mo merely sat up, shook his head, and smiled. "Naw, I'm fine. We need to go ahead and do this in case there's something important on there."

Armin's lowered brow and pursed lips said he knew exactly what Mo was doing, but he didn't argue. Mo was glad. He liked to think they were on the same page about what needed to be done.

He looked over at the dresser. His walker helmet sat there with Daisy's corpse huddled like so much trash in the lower curve. The thought of touching her dead body made him sick.

Because you killed her. You're racked with guilt.

But they didn't have time for his guilt, or his tiredness, or the nausea crawling up his throat. So he stood, shuffled over to his dresser, and picked up his helmet before he could change his mind. Armin opened Daisy's cage for him, and he slid her inside. Her body dropped to the bottom, brushing against the leaves with a dry whisper that broke his heart because it made him think of Hannah and how much Daisy's death would upset her.

If she survived. God.

Armin put an arm around Mo's shoulders. "Here. Sit down and let's get this done."

"Yeah." Mo let Armin lead him to the desk. He lowered himself into the chair and set the helmet on the sync plate. "Computer. Download walker video from today and display in 3-D, one hundred ten percent magnification."

"Yes, Mo."

There was a brief pause. Mo frowned. As short as the vid was, the download and display should've been instantaneous to the human eye.

Unless your eyes aren't entirely human anymore.

Sweat popped out on his upper lip and trickled down his back. Jesus.

The 3-D emerged from the desktop before he could think too hard about how much he might or might not be changing. Mo squinted at it. "Computer. Bring the room lights down to twenty percent."

"Yes, Mo." The lights dimmed until the alien vista of rocks and mud revealed in the glow of his helmet lights showed up clearly enough for them to see any important details on the display.

Armin leaned closer. His face shone with curiosity in the bluish glow from the vid. "Where is this? The location isn't displaying."

"I know. I have no idea why not." Mo sifted through his vague, scattered memories. "Richards Deep. Not where we found the rock, though. Someplace else. But I think . . ." He shook his head, as if he could rattle the missing pieces out of their hiding places and out into the open. "I don't know why, but I feel sure the area I was in connects to the place we found the rock."

From the corner of Mo's eye, he saw Armin's gaze cut sideways toward him. Wondering. Assessing. "Why did you go there?"

That was the hundred-million-dollar question, wasn't it? And Armin wasn't going to like the answer. Hell, Mo didn't like it either. But it was the only one he had.

"Daisy told me to." He made his confession without looking away from the display of his lights on the previously unseen path into Richards Deep. "When she bit me, I could hear her talking in my head, and she told me I would see things there that no one else had ever seen."

Armin didn't look at Daisy's still-open cage, but Mo could feel him wanting to. "Mo, you do know that's impossible, right?"

"Really?" Mo shot him a sidelong glance. "Bet you'd've said that about people growing pointed teeth and glowing eyes a couple of weeks ago."

A wry half smile twisted Armin's lips. "Touché. Still, you must admit it's pretty odd."

"Yeah. But I know what I heard." He'd hear Daisy's thick, cracked spider-voice in his nightmares for the rest of his life, feel the truth in his marrow when her venom flowed into him. "I remember thinking that something was speaking *through* her."

Armin rubbed his chin. "It could have been some sort of unusual reaction to the venom." He didn't sound like he believed that any more than Mo did.

"Maybe, but I don't think so." Mo examined Armin's profile, soft and ethereal in the cool light from the 3-D. "Daisy's eyes were glowing, Armin. And she had the longer legs and the teeth. Well, the fangs. I know that sounds crazy, but she did."

Armin swallowed, his throat working. "I don't quite know what to think of that."

"Yeah. I hear you." Mo felt a faint smile curve his lips. At least Armin hadn't dismissed what he'd said out of hand. "Maybe the vid'll help clear things up. Anything I saw ought to show up on there."

Since there was no arguing with that, they both watched in silence.

It went on for a long time. Eventually, Mo told the computer to speed it up, scanning for anomalous sounds or images. Even watching that way, they must've sat there for an hour and a half before something finally caught Mo's attention.

"Computer. Slow vid to normal." The display went back to normal speed. The lights on the video bounced, and Mo could hear himself panting. "What the hell? Am I *running*?"

"You don't remember?"

"No."

On the vid, Mo ran on. Safe in his quarters, he watched with a growing sense of familiarity as a weird light-but-not-light glowed black-on-black from the seabed. He grasped the chair arms hard as a feeling of impending revelation rolled over him.

"This is it." His voice sounded small and scared. "The thing. It's coming."

Armin said nothing, but he took Mo's hand, wound their fingers together, and held on tight. Mo clung to him, grateful for the human contact. It gave him an anchor in a universe that seemed to be drifting apart piece by piece.

On the display, a chasm gaped like a stony mouth. A darkness deep as the ocean poured out of it. Somehow, impossibly, the blackness illuminated rocky slopes, steps, and smooth inclines leading down into the unknown. Video-Mo moved closer. Looked down. Shapes drifted lazily in the space between the obsidian walls. Deep down, beyond the swimming silhouettes, the not-light radiated from a fuzzy blue-black point that defied focus. Mo's eye skidded off it like it wasn't there. As Mo watched, a new shape swam upward from the depths directly toward them, its long teeth bared and its green eyes aglow with purplish-blue sparks. Video-Mo screamed, turned, and ran the other way.

"Oh." Armin reached his free hand toward the 3-D, as if he could touch it. "Mermaids."

"Mermaids." Mo watched the helmet lights bob as he ran away. Something nagged at his mind, though he couldn't pinpoint it. "Computer. Go back two minutes. No, five."

"Yes, Mo."

The vid jumped back in time to Mo jogging along the underwater path. When he reached the edge of the chasm, he told the computer to slow the vid to one quarter speed.

Armin glanced at him. "What are you looking for?"

"I'm not sure. But I'll know when I see it."

He studied the vid in silent concentration. When he found what he was looking for, the slo-mo made it obvious. "Computer. Zoom in on upper right hand of screen. One hundred seventy-five percent magnification."

"Yes, Mo."

The object grew larger. Large enough to make out exactly what it was. Armin drew in a sharp breath. "Oh my God."

Mo nodded. "Yeah."

There on a ledge on the other side of the chasm lay a walker suit.

CHAPTER 13

Mo reset the video so they could watch the important part again in higher magnification. It didn't really help, though the sight of the mind-bending void just beyond his video self's virtual boots made his pulse race with a half-remembered terror.

Or was it anticipation?

"Who in the hell could it be?" Armin leaned over Mo's shoulder, staring at the body on the screen with intense concentration. "And how in the name of all the gods and devils did they get out there without anyone knowing it? And *when*?"

"Who knows? The only time the alarms were off was when I turned them off, and nobody would've had time to get out there without a go-cart. I don't know if they could get to that spot even *with* a cart." Mo stopped the vid and glanced sideways, admiring the graceful arch of Armin's neck. Maybe this goddamn contagion would magically go away and leave him alone. "But there's one way to find out who it is."

"Yes. Go get the body." Armin straightened up, both hands opening and closing, opening and closing. "It couldn't be Ashlyn."

He phrased it as a statement, but Mo heard the question behind it. He touched Armin's back. "She couldn't see. Even if she could find her way to the go-cart bay, she never would've been able to get the walker on and get outside."

Armin didn't answer, and Mo knew he was thinking of the missing walker suits on the Varredura Longa. If those crew members could take walkers and vanish into the sea in spite of having no eyes, Ashlyn Timms definitely could.

Mo hoped like hell she hadn't.

"Mo?" Armin's voice was subdued, like his mind was still on the body that might be Ashlyn's. "Why did you scream?"

Yes, Mo. Why?

His inner voice had started to sound as thick and cracked as Daisy's. Which couldn't mean anything good.

"I'm not sure. Everything's sort of a blur. But it's something to do with that chasm. That blurry spot at the bottom. I think it's connected to the mermaids, but I can't remember how." He thought for a second, putting himself back in that strange, surreal moment. "I think . . . I think that mermaid *spoke* to me."

From the corner of his eye, he saw Armin studying him with a palpable blend of curiosity and concern. "Did you happen to have the outside cam on as well? Maybe it would've picked up what the mermaid said, if you're correct. I know the built-in cam isn't configured to record sound outside the suit."

"No. There's no record of an outside cam vid. But it doesn't matter." Mo chewed his bottom lip for a second. This was going to sound at least as nuts as Daisy talking to him. But what the hell, right? Armin had gone along for the ride so far. Which only made him more perfect in Mo's mind. "I heard it in my head, Armin. It spoke to me telepathically."

Armin didn't answer. Instead, he looped an arm around Mo's shoulders, bent, and kissed the top of his head. For a small, painful moment, Mo was transported back to his childhood—before the blackout, before the deaths, before he'd learned to kill—to the time when his parents had kissed him like that before he went to sleep at night. His throat constricted and his eyes burned. Then Armin let him go, the moment passed, and he breathed again.

"The same thing happened to me. In the aquarium, right before I met you in the go-cart bay." Armin's voice was soft, uncertain, like he wasn't sure Mo would believe him. "I saw a mermaid outside. It looked at me, and . . ." He shook his head. His forehead furrowed. "I felt as though it could hear me. My *thoughts*. Its eyes glowed, like . . ."

"Like the one in this video," Mo finished for him.

Armin nodded, the movement slow, dreamlike. "It happened before too. The mermaid looking at me with its glowing eyes, as if it knew what I was thinking. After you and I were . . . together. In the aquarium."

Mo's heart lurched. "I remember. It was watching us."

Armin drew in a long, ragged breath, turned his head, and stared at the hollow of Mo's throat as if it held the answers to all his questions. "Was it real, Mo? Any of it? All the people in the bar, the way you and I danced, making love in the aquarium? Because it all felt so surreal to me, yet you remember at least that part, so I can't have imagined all of it."

The memory of Armin's cry when he came, ecstasy threaded with pain, set Mo's heart thumping. He ran a hand up Armin's side. "It was real. And, fuck, it was incredible."

Armin let out a faint, surprised laugh. Mo pulled him close to kiss him. "There wasn't anyone in the bar but you and me, though. What did you mean about all the people?"

"I was afraid of that." Armin's eyelids swept down and up again in slow motion. "I saw a bar packed with people, all dancing."

Mo stared at him. "So we both saw different things."

"It seems so, yes." Armin laid a hand on Mo's thigh, kneading the muscle as if the motion comforted him. "That bothers me. We both experienced the same event, but in different ways. I don't understand why."

Mo had a theory, and he figured Armin had the same theory, even if he wasn't saying it. "Do you think it has anything to do with the brain growth?"

Armin breathed. In and out, in and out. "I'm very afraid it might. Yes."

Silence fell. Mo grasped Armin's hip and clung. He felt as if the world had tilted beneath him. The parallels between this damned contagion and the glowy-eyed mermaids seemed obvious. How could it possibly be a coincidence? Especially since he'd been led out there to that chasm on purpose, to see the congregation of mermaids and the weird place in the depths where the eye couldn't focus.

The big question was, what did it all *mean*? How did those things come together to form an answer to what was happening here? Because, damn it, they *had* to.

"Those damned mermaids are involved in this whole thing somehow." Mo reached up to touch Armin's face, stroking the rough salt-and-pepper stubble shadowing his jaw. "I don't know how, or why. But they are."

"There's no direct evidence of that. But I think you're probably right. The glowing eyes . . ." Armin sighed. Raked gentle fingers through Mo's hair. "I'm going to com Mandala in the med bay."

"Okay." Now that he thought about it . . . "I'm surprised she hasn't already commed to yell at you."

The guilty set of Armin's features answered for him before he said anything. "She did, actually. While I was trying to get you to come around in the go-cart bay. I told her I was looking after you and to please cover for me."

"Oh." Mo thought about that. "She's gonna be *so* pissed off at you."

"Indeed. But it doesn't matter. You need medical care. You also need to get your scan. Then we need to show Mandala and Dr. Youssouf this video, and work out a plan for retrieving the body. I believe that's the first step in answering the questions posed by your video, especially when it comes to the mermaids and this chasm."

"Yeah. We'll do all of that."

Armin cast him a puzzled sidelong glance, but didn't comment on how disconnected Mo sounded. And Mo knew he did. Hell, he *felt* it. Felt like he was drifting away from the world he knew into someplace different. Better? Worse? He couldn't say. But he was helpless to stop it.

While Armin got yelled at by Dr. Jhut on the com link, Mo slow-moed through the vid again and stopped it at the edge of the pit. He raised the magnification higher. Zoomed until he saw nothing but the dark-lit depths. Stared and stared and stared until his eyes dried out and blinking hurt.

Far down, so deep it must be the Earth's core—or maybe another universe—the purplish-blue space twisted and writhed like a warning. Or an invitation.

Jem came to fetch them back to the med bay. Her mouth fell open when she saw Mo's face. "Jesus Christ, what happened to you?"

Armin, the useless rat, just crossed his arms and studied the floor. Mo sighed. "Daisy. Don't ask."

Jem shuddered. "I won't. Ew." She raised her weapon to the ceiling. "Now if you gents are ready, we'll get going."

She stepped out the door. Once she'd declared the way clear, she led Mo and Armin along the gloomy halls toward medical. "Everybody's there now. Youssouf's finishing up the scans since Dr. Jhut's busy analyzing those crazy brain tumors."

Surprised, Mo raised his eyebrows at Armin. "Didn't you guys already do that in autopsy?"

"Only in a limited way. We hadn't gotten around to full microscopic analysis." Armin rubbed his arms as if he was cold. "Do you know if Mandala's learned anything yet?"

Jem shrugged. "If she has, I don't know about it."

Silence fell. Jem marched along with her usual purposeful stride. Armin followed, clearly lost in his thoughts. Mo trailed behind the two of them and tried to ignore the lead weights dragging at his limbs.

"You're in trouble," Youssouf told Armin the second the three of them shoved aside the crash cart and filed through the crookedly half-shut med bay doors.

Armin's shoulders slumped. "I know. Mandala had some choice words for me. Not that I didn't deserve it, of course." He sighed, looking glum. "Is she too angry to speak to me?"

"You should know better than that." Dr. Jhut walked in from the autopsy room. She peeled off her work gloves and tossed them in the trash and peered at Mo with interest. "How on Earth did you manage to get a tarantula rash on your face, Mr. Rees?"

Mo's face flamed under the sudden scrutiny of not only Dr. Jhut, but Youssouf, Rashmi, and Ling. Damn it. "Long story."

Armin spoke before Youssouf could say anything. "It doesn't matter. I gave him antivenom and treated the rash and bites. The point is, he was out in Richards Deep."

Youssouf gaped. "You were *what*? Rees, for fuck's sake—"

"And," Armin plowed on, ignoring her, "he returned with video you need to see. There's a body out there."

The room went silent. Mo swallowed the urge to laugh. Armin did have a flair for the dramatic.

"A body." Youssouf stalked closer, until she was toe-to-toe with Mo. "Explain."

Mo held her grim gaze and fought the urge to fidget. When she spoke in that soft, measured tone, you knew you were in deep shit. "Yeah. Yes, ma'am. Well. That is, there's a walker suit on the other side of the chasm, and since you can't even open the suit without getting killed by the pressure right away . . ."

"Yeah, I know. You don't have to paint me a picture." Youssouf turned around and trudged back to the scanner. "Okay. First things first. Rees, let's get your scan out of the way so we'll know which side of the fence you're on. After that, I'll continue the scans while the two of you show Mandala your video."

"Oh." Armin blinked at the floor. Rubbed his neck. "Should she be exposed to me?"

Youssouf *pfft*ed. "We're all *exposed* to you right now, and have been for days, yet we don't have the growths. Crazy as it sounds, I think we're on the right track as far as it being passed on through light waves via eye contact only once the eyes begin to glow."

It *did* sound crazy. Impossible, for that matter.

It also sounded *right*.

Mo thought of the blue-black shine in Hannah's eyes and wondered how many people she might have infected, including him.

Youssouf beckoned him over. "Come on, Mo. Let's get this done."

He went. Putting it off wouldn't help. But it was like going to his execution because he knew what Youssouf would see.

Sure enough, when the machine chimed to tell him it was finished scanning and the image came up in glorious, irrefutable 3-D, Youssouf cursed and Armin turned away, arms crossed tight like he was literally holding himself together.

Mo rose from the scanner couch, his gaze fixed on the floor. When he was thirteen, he used to wish he could kill people with a look. Now, he'd rather not.

"Doesn't change anything." He went to Armin, pried his fingers loose from his upper arms, and took his hand. "Come on."

For the first time since Mo came to in the go-cart bay, Armin looked straight into his eyes. The fear and guilt there threatened to brim over and drown the world. Or at least the two of them, trapped by the aliens in their heads.

Mo forced a smile to keep the flood at bay. "It'll work out, Doc. You'll see."

Armin's anemic answering smile felt like a reward. "I hope you're right."

Mandala watched the entire video once, then repeated the pertinent portion at regular speed, and again in extreme slow motion. Armin chafed through it all, but said nothing. She had a sharp eye and a sharper mind. They could spare a few minutes to keep from missing anything important.

Finally, she halted the vid and sat back in her chair, studying the 3-D still with a frown.

"So?" Mo said when Mandala neglected to offer immediate feedback. "What do you think?"

She tapped a finger on her chin. "There's something not right about that suit."

Armin peered at the display again, more closely this time. The suit lay there just as it had before, a pale-gray sliver of humanity in the vast, cold emptiness of the deep. It looked lonely and forlorn.

"It's not right for it to be there at all." Nor was it coincidental, he suspected, though he didn't say so.

She wrinkled her nose. "You *know* that's not what I mean."

Mo narrowed his eyes at the display. "Damn it. I wish I could've gotten closer before. And if I magnify this any more I'm gonna lose resolution."

"It's just . . . something." Mandala sighed in clear irritation. "I simply can't put my finger on it." She tilted her head sideways. "Are any of the BathyTech suits missing?"

Mo shook his head. "Rashmi checked. They're all there. Which is weird, because where else would a walker suit have come from?"

"Of course, that also means it definitely can't be Ashlyn." Armin swiveled in his chair, glancing around the room as if she might emerge from a corner and laugh at him for being frightened. "Which means she must be on this pod somewhere. We simply have to find her." He knew he sounded stubborn and rather desperate, but he couldn't let himself give up on finding Ashlyn alive. He'd brought her here. It was his fault she was out there, mutilated and in need of help.

Mandala shot him a worried glance. "And yet we haven't been able to, no matter where we've looked, or how often. I can't imagine where she could be hiding, or *why* she would hide from us. I would say she's gotten out somehow, but I can't see how, when all the walker suits and go-carts are accounted for and her body is not lying below the moon pool or the airlocks. It simply doesn't make any sense. It's like she's vanished into thin air."

A heavy, brooding quiet descended on their little group. Armin hunched forward and rubbed his aching head. God, what he wouldn't give to go back in time, take his hard-won knowledge—such as it was—and redo everything that had happened since that first call from Dr. Longenesse. Maybe then the people on the Varredura Longa and here on BathyTech would still be alive. Maybe Neil and Carlo would still be alive. Maybe Mo wouldn't be infected. Maybe Ashlyn would be safe and whole.

Mo slid an arm around Armin's waist. He said nothing, but the warmth of his body and the back-and-forth rub of his thumb on Armin's hip were soothing. Armin leaned into him, grateful for his closeness, for his touch that offered support without words.

After a few silent moments, Armin rose and stretched until the blood thumped in his ears. "Well. We know the only way to solve this mystery is to go fetch the body, yes? So let's debrief Dr. Youssouf and work out a plan."

Mandala didn't budge. Neither did the bearing of fierce thought set into every line of her body. "Where does this chasm go?"

"What do you mean, where does it go?" Confused, Armin reached into the 3-D and moved it to show the ravine in question. "Where *can* it go? Deeper, that's all."

To Armin's surprise, Mo hummed in clear sympathy with Mandala. "I thought the same thing. There's a . . ." He squinted at the ceiling, one hand circling in the air as if attempting to conjure the word he wanted. "I don't know. Not a light. But kind of a light. Like it leads someplace it ought not to. You know?"

"Yes. I do." Mandala swiveled and pinned Mo with a direct stare, which he barely managed to avoid. Armin wanted to scold her, but didn't, since she was obviously going somewhere with this. "This area is unexplored? No one has been here before? You're certain?"

"Yeah. Well . . ." Mo gestured at the body on the ledge—which said it all, really. "But, yeah. There hasn't been any documented exploration of that area. Not counting whoever *that* is."

"Hm." Mandala turned her attention back to the frozen underwater display and tapped her chin again. "I have a very strange feeling about this whole thing."

"You and me both, Doc." Mo stood. His chair, sans wheels, scraped across the floor with a cringeworthy squeal. "I guess we ought to run this by Youssouf now. No point in twiddling our thumbs any longer, right?"

"Right. The sooner we get this settled, the sooner I can get back to my analysis of the brain lesions." Mandala brushed her fingertips along Armin's wrist without looking at him. "You two stay here. I'll get Dr. Youssouf."

Too restless to sit back down, Armin paced while Mandala left the little semienclosed alcove where the three of them had been huddled together for the last hour or so. Mo watched him for a moment, then came to him and gathered him in a tight embrace, one hand in his hair and the other splayed between his shoulder blades. Armin shut his eyes and let Mo's comforting warmth sink through his skin, wordlessly telling him everything would be all right.

For a moment, he almost believed it.

There was no real question over whether they should retrieve the body on the ledge. The problem, according to Dr. Youssouf, lay in who ought to go.

"Nothing against the two of you." She indicated Armin and Mo where they sat side by side on the desk in Gerald Palto's cramped office, the only truly private place to talk in the med bay. "But I don't want infected people working with uninfected on this. It's easy enough to avoid eye contact here in the med bay, or in the lab. Out there, the risk is *way* too high. When you're in a walker, you need all your concentration on the job at hand. Trying not to look your coworkers in the eye is nothing but a distraction."

Armin kept his agreement to himself. He'd realized immediately that he had very little say in the outcome of this particular argument. It was between Youssouf, Mo, and Jemima.

Mo sighed, his frustration plastered all over his face. "Who's gonna walk, then? You?"

She bristled. "It's been a while, but I used to walk every goddamn day just like you, hot shot."

"The operative phrase there being *used to*." Mo stared down at his hands, clenched together in his lap. "When's the last time you walked? Five years ago? The tech's changed. You know that. Everything's different now. It would take at least a couple of hours to bring you up to speed enough to be safe out there at all, and you'd still need a trainer with you at all times for a few days. You *know* we don't have that kind of time."

She scowled. "Damn it. Fine." She glared at Jemima. "Jem? What about your miners? Who's available?"

"Well. Me."

Youssouf groaned. "Are you serious?"

Jemima stuck her hands in her back pockets. "Yeah. Everybody but me, Rashmi and a couple of others have positive scans. And of course Rashmi, Hawk, and me are all on security, what with all the changed people who've had to be locked up, and Sully's got a broken ankle 'cause somebody from science who'd changed attacked her."

Armin glanced from Jemima to Youssouf, remembering at the last moment not to meet their eyes. "How many are infected now?"

"Seventeen staff have scanned positive for growths." Youssouf tapped a fingertip against the desk, her face grim. "All but four of them have shown changes already. Everyone who's changed is in a makeshift lockup, since this pod doesn't have the capability to force confinement to quarters by locking people in."

"Shit." Mo hunched forward. Shock leeched the color from his face, turning his skin an unhealthy grayish brown. Armin slipped an arm around his waist, offering what little comfort he could.

"Rashmi's helping Ling guard the med bay. Hawk's guarding lockup." Jemima glanced at Youssouf. "There's nobody else left who can walk. I suppose you could pull someone off security, but I really don't think that's a good idea."

Mo leaned against Armin. Fine tremors ran through his body, but his voice was steady. "Youssouf. Let me and Armin retrieve the body. We both have the growths, so we're not any danger to each other. Jem can drive the cart. We can stay in the back, so we won't be a danger to her either."

A muscle jumped in Youssouf's jaw. "And if you start to change out there? What then?"

"It's possible that they might," said Mandala, speaking up for the first time during this debate. "But if you want to be absolutely practical about it from the standpoint of general safety of the BathyTech pod, if they *are* going to change, the best place for them to do it would be with the two of them out in their walker suits away from the rest of us. Correct?"

Mo winced. "Ouch."

"Don't misunderstand me. I certainly don't wish such a thing on either of you. And I'm not certain that you will, if you haven't done it already. At least, it seems that everyone else who changed did so in a fairly short time." Mandala pushed away from the wall where she'd been leaning. Her face was thoughtful, her dark eyes sad. "But we can't very well ignore the practicalities of the situation, can we?"

Armin glanced at Mo, who smiled and shrugged. "She's right."

"I know." Armin yawned. God, how long since he'd slept? "Well. If that's settled, then, I think we ought to get on with it."

"Damn right. We've flapped our gums too long already." Jem crossed to the office door. "Let's go."

She strode out into the med bay without looking back. Youssouf planted her palms on the chair arms and pushed herself up as if doing so took all her energy. "Come on. No point in putting it off."

"Agreed." Mandala started for the door. "I'll finish up the analysis of the brain growths."

Armin followed Mo's broad back through the broken doors and into the sinister, flickering gloom of the hallway.

Luckily for everyone, BathyTech's walkers employed the latest in mapping technology created specifically for use at extreme depths. Mo's impromptu earlier walk had produced an impressively detailed 3-D readout of the seafloor.

Mo leaned forward and tapped the screen to the northwest of the chasm with the hand not absently kneading Armin's thigh. "This chasm can't be too far off from the areas of Richards Deep that we already know. Look. The place where we found that weird rock is just over here."

Armin stared at the digital readout of the newly discovered chasm, the place where they'd found the object, and the ominous blank space between them. Anything might be there. For the first time in his career, he dreaded what he might find.

The go-cart's com spat static, followed by Jemima's voice. "Coming up on our parking space, guys. Get ready to walk."

"Roger that, Big Mama." Mo rose. "C'mon. Let's get suited up."

Armin eyed the partial map as he followed Mo to the rack of walker suits. "It looks as though we're still a fair way from the chasm."

"I know. You saw how long the video was. I'm pretty sure that's 'cause I couldn't get the cart any closer." Mo stopped beside the suits and watched Armin with a solemn expression. "It's a long walk, Armin. And what's at the end isn't like anything you've ever seen. There's no shame in backing out if you're not up to it. I can retrieve the body on my own."

If someone else had said it, Armin might have taken offense. As it was, he'd learned enough about Mo to know he was speaking from concern for Armin's well-being and for the success of their current mission.

"I'll be fine." He stripped off his shirt and tossed it into the open locker beside his suit.

Mo kept his gaze locked on him while they both undressed and pulled on their walkers. It reminded Armin of the first time they'd walked together. Only a few days ago, but it felt like another life. A sense of loss he couldn't quite define stabbed him in the gut.

Before he could get his helmet on, Mo stopped him with a hand on his arm. Armin looked at him. "What is it?"

Mo leaned in and planted a soft kiss on his mouth. "I'm sorry all this shit happened. But I'm not sorry I met you."

Armin's heart turned over. He smiled. "I'm not sorry either." He stole a kiss of his own, light and quick, then stepped back. "Are you ready?"

"Ready."

They both put on their helmets. Armin started the flow of Mist and breathed deep until the wet, heavy gas filled his lungs.

The walk to the chasm took just over two hours. A long time, but not nearly as long as Armin had expected, given the length of the video from Mo's walker cam. For the first time, he wondered if time itself had actually changed somehow when Mo came out here before. It sounded like a ridiculous idea, but so did the hypothesis of an infectious disease being passed on via glowing eyes. And the concept of warped time wasn't entirely unprecedented, even if no one had applied it to these particular circumstances before.

They stopped a few meters short of the underwater gorge. Reluctance weighed on Armin, bowing his shoulders and binding his feet to the seabed. Nervous sweat prickled his armpits.

"Look at it."

Mo sounded reverent. Excited. Armin turned toward him. The helmet lights glittered in Mo's eyes. Armin's pulse jumped. Was that a purplish spark he saw hiding there?

Mo swiveled sideways and flashed him a grin, and the tightness in his shoulders eased a little. No. No purple in Mo's eyes. No blue. No glow. Just Mo's usual warm brown irises surrounding perfectly normal black pupils.

You're imagining things. Relax, before you get yourself and Mo both hurt.

In his enthusiasm for the adventure, Mo apparently didn't notice Armin's minor crisis. "Isn't it incredible?" Mo trudged toward the jagged rift, which spewed a weird, glowing darkness into the water. "I can't believe I was so afraid before. What was wrong with me?"

Logically, Armin agreed. He saw no valid scientific reason to fear this place. The readings for any sort of dangerous radiation were flat, and really, what else could hurt them here?

But this wasn't a place for logic. Instinct ruled here. And every instinct he had screamed at him to run.

Because he was a scientist, not an animal, he ignored his primitive inner voice and followed Mo.

Standing at the edge was far more confusing than lingering safely down the path from it. The strange, blurry spot at the bottom twisted the eye like a black light, only worse. It tugged at his mind when he stared at it. He got the oddest feeling that it was trying to pull him in. Hook him like a fish and swallow him whole.

He didn't look anymore. Especially after Mo extended the guideline from the closest suitable spot he could find to where they needed to be, and they adjusted their walkers' buoyancy to cross the chasm. The alien space churned black and bottomless below their feet.

Standing on the other side was a relief, even though the ledge was narrow and sloped slightly toward the pit. Armin steadied himself with a hand on the wall and told himself that half of this mission was now behind him. They only had to cross the strange ravine one more time.

Mo started toward the body, which lay a few meters away from where they'd crossed. "Walker One to cart, come in."

"Cart here. You there?"

"Yep. We're across the chasm and getting ready to retrieve. I'll com you again when we've got the body."

"Roger that. Out."

Mo cut the connection with Jemima. When he reached the body, he stepped carefully around it and knelt at the head. "Wait. Armin, there's nobody in here."

"What?"

"The suit's empty. Come see."

Armin closed the last few steps to the body and knelt as well, much less gracefully than Mo. He saw clearly now that the helmet was empty and separated from the suit. One side of the suit—the one they hadn't been able to see on video—was torn open. Armin laid a hand on one leg. It went flat, water jetting out of the rip in the side.

"What in the world happened?" he wondered out loud.

"That's the big question, isn't it?" Mo opened the cargo pocket in the side of his suit's leg and took out a large specimen bag. "Well, I guess we won't need the hover stretcher after all. We'll just put it in here. Help me, would you?"

"Of course." Armin took the legs of the suit and started to fold them in toward the middle. Then he saw the badge on the chest, and forgot how to breathe. "Oh. Oh Christ."

"Armin?" Mo reached over and touched him with the clumsy walker glove that allowed no human warmth to bleed through. "Are you okay? What's wrong?"

Unable to speak, Armin pointed to the two simple words on the front of the suit. Two words that changed everything.

Varredura Longa.

CHAPTER 14

I t was strange, Mo thought, how something as simple as the wrong name on a uniform could shift the whole universe off-kilter. He stared at the ordinary walker suit and wondered how it came to be so extraordinarily out of place.

The possibilities were fascinating. Exhilarating. He couldn't hold back a laugh.

It figured *that* would kick Armin out of his silence. He stared at Mo like he'd killed a basketful of kittens. "What in God's name could you possibly find *funny* about this?"

"Not funny. Exciting." Mo rolled his eyes at Armin's scandalized stare. "Come on, Doc. This walker ought to be somewhere in the ocean off Antarctica. Instead, it's on the other side of the damn world, in a part of the Peru–Chile Trench where no one's ever been before. Don't you want to know how it got here? Don't you want to know why it's *empty*?"

Armin's face came to life, going from stunned to angry in a heartbeat. "Of course I do. But I don't find this remotely exciting. It's horrific. And . . . and sad." He blinked several times in a row and turned to look out over the chasm. "This might have been someone I knew. If I'd only gotten there sooner."

Mo understood then. Armin still blamed himself—at least partly—for what had happened on the Varredura Longa. He still believed that if he'd dropped everything to rush straight to Antarctica when he got the call, he could've prevented everything that happened. The deaths. The mutilations.

The disappearances.

The memory of what Armin had told him played through Mo's brain as clearly as if he'd seen it himself: Dr. Longenesse, the research pod's leader, walking off into the deep with the unknown object in her arms.

"They never found the body," he mused.

Armin drew back like he'd been stung. "What?"

"Just thinking out loud. I'll explain when we get back." He didn't want to risk upsetting Armin. Not here, where their lives depended on staying calm and focused. He touched Armin's wrist. Armin peered at him with black eyes full of caution and pain, and Mo ached for him. "We're gonna take this suit back, and we're gonna figure out what happened to the person who was in it. That's the best we can do. Okay?"

Armin nodded. His skin was waxy and sallow in the weak glow of his helmet light. His eyes were dull, his normally expressive mouth a harsh line.

Mo recognized that look. He'd seen it plenty back in Dubai during those long, dark months of kill or be killed, of steal or starve. It was the look of a person pushed past his ability to cope. Eventually, Armin would come around, assimilate this new development and deal with it. Sooner rather than later, probably. Armin was strong and practical. He wouldn't let this get to him for long.

Right now, though, they still had to make it back to BathyTech in one piece. Which meant Mo would need to keep a sharp eye on Armin. Make sure his shell-shocked state didn't trip him up. Literally.

Mo lifted the empty helmet and tucked it into the bag. "I'll stow the suit. You let Jem know what we found, and tell her we're on our way back."

Relief washed over Armin's features. He didn't say why, but Mo could guess. If he was in Armin's place, he wouldn't want to handle the damn suit either.

While Armin commed Jem, Mo carefully folded the walker that ought not to be here and slid it into the bag on top of the helmet. Down in the chasm near his feet, in the murk that shone dark-on-dark against all logic and reason, the mermaids swam in patterns.

The guideline was longer on the trip back across. Longer and flimsier, gossamer thin, stretching in Mo's grip like spider silk.

He didn't like it. Was there something in the water here? Something that degraded the polymers? What if it broke? Walkers were *walkers*, not dive gear. They were built to stay on the bottom. They didn't have neutral buoyancy.

As if worrying about falling into a bottomless pit wasn't bad enough, there were the whispers in Mo's head.

Come with us, they hissed. *See what we see.*

Was it the mermaids? The abyss itself? Who knew? Certainly not Mo. All he knew for sure was that the voices came from outside himself. From everywhere and nowhere.

They sounded like Daisy's ghost—dry, cracked, insubstantial.

Dead.

Wrong.

Mo steeled himself against the silent entreaties to *look*, to *come*, to *see the wonders here*, and watched Armin's back instead. Armin, who was warm and real and alive, and needed Mo to make sure he stayed that way.

Armin had been there for him when he needed him. Been strong for him. Mo would not be anything less for Armin, who'd quietly come to occupy the central position in Mo's life.

The temptation to listen to the voices tugged at Mo's gut like a fishhook even after he and Armin stepped safely onto the solid rock ledge on the other side of the chasm. He called on every ounce of strength he possessed and ignored it.

When Armin started to turn and look, Mo stopped him. "Don't."

Armin's whole body trembled like he was fighting to keep from knocking Mo aside and flinging himself into the unknown. "I hear them. They're telling me to follow them. Down into the deep." He met Mo's gaze, his eyes wide and scared. "I want to."

Mo heard Armin's struggle as clearly as if he'd shouted. Was it wrong that knowing they were in this together made it easier to handle?

He grasped Armin's elbow as best he could with the clumsy walker glove and led him away from the edge of the ravine. "Me too. Let's go before we decide it's a good idea to do it."

Armin closed his hand around Mo's wrist, and for a strange, confusing moment Mo didn't know who was trying to stop who. Then Armin blinked, opened his fingers, and let his arm drift down, and the tension dissolved into the icy water. "Yes. Yes, you're right."

A tiny thread of disappointment wormed through Mo's insides. Because it wasn't nearly strong enough to overcome his relief, he adjusted the specimen bag's buoyancy to neutral and led the way down the path to the go-cart.

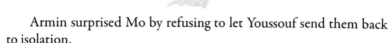

Armin surprised Mo by refusing to let Youssouf send them back to isolation.

"It can't be a coincidence that this suit came from the one other place where this same scenario may have played out before." Armin glared at Youssouf's collarbone, his spine stiff and his cheeks an angry red. "I need to be involved in this. I won't be shut out."

"Oh my *God*, I really don't need this right now." Youssouf sighed the sigh of the deeply put out. "Mo? Are you going to be a pain in my ass too?"

Mo didn't have to think about it. Of course he had Armin's back. "Yep. Sorry."

"No you're not." She sighed again and pressed the heels of her hands into her eyes. "Fine. *Fine.*" She dropped her hands, rose from Palto's worn-out desk chair—they'd gathered in his office again to talk, that being the only private spot—and dragged herself to the door like it was the hardest thing she'd ever done. "Mandala? What do you want to do with them?"

Dr. Jhut broke her frowning silence for the first time during this powwow to answer. "Well, we'll need to go over this suit inside and out for anything containing the DNA of whoever wore it. It has Dr. Longenesse's name on it, but under the circumstances I think we can't afford to assume it's actually her until we have more evidence. Anyone could have taken that suit." She studied Armin with obvious sympathy. "I know this is probably difficult for you, Armin. But I have to say, I'm relieved to have your assistance. The two of us can get any necessary microanalysis done much more quickly together than I could alone. Plus I think we need any and all ideas brought forward regarding what we're dealing with here. This event is completely unprecedented. I believe there's a great deal of value in being together in the same physical space, discussing the problem face-to-face." She glanced at Mo. "I'm including you, Mr. Rees. We need your insights as well."

"Hey, I'm always happy to tell people what I think." Mo did his best not to look directly into Dr. Jhut's eyes, but it was tough. She didn't seem worried about it at all. For a scientist and someone he'd found to be naturally cautious, it was out of character. Made him wonder about her. About what she believed when it came to whatever the hell was happening here.

"Very well. It's settled, then." Dr. Jhut pushed away from the wall and followed Youssouf out the door into the med bay. "Amara, I know you're not happy about this. But I promise you, it won't be a problem."

Youssouf cut her a sour look as the group left the office in a huddle. "You're right, I don't like it. But I trust your judgment. Just don't make me sorry for that."

Dr. Jhut smiled. "You'll have no cause to be sorry."

"Good. And make sure they stay in the lab." Youssouf half turned toward Mo and Armin, who were walking behind her and Dr. Jhut. "No offense meant, guys. I hope you know that. It's my job to make sure everybody in this pod stays safe. Which is why I'm staying here and working on a way to cure this thing."

A rare surge of affection toward his employer warmed Mo's heart. Youssouf was a tough old cookie, ran a hell of a tight ship, but she'd rather die herself than let anything happen to her crew. The way everything was unraveling between her fingers had to be killing her.

When they got to the autopsy room door, Youssouf clapped Mo, Armin, and Dr. Jhut on their shoulders and wished them luck, then stalked off to do whatever the hell doctors did when they were trying to cure something that wasn't even a proper disease. Mo picked up the specimen bag with the mysterious walker suit in it and followed Armin and Dr. Jhut toward the exit.

Jem fell in with them without being asked. "Because you need a bodyguard," she said before Dr. Jhut could turn a questioning look into an actual question. "Shut up and stay behind me when we get out into the hall. Rees, you take the rear position."

Mo resisted the urge to laugh at Armin and Mandala's identical irritated expressions. "Aye aye, Big Mama."

"You shut up too." She surveyed the group. "Everybody ready?"

Agreement all around. Jem nodded once. "All right. Let's move out."

Jem shoved the crash cart aside, and they all followed her into the hall. Someone pushed the cart back into position behind them, and Mo felt as cut off as if the bay door had actually closed.

Here, in the flickering dark of the corridor, the silence felt thick and breathless. Like something watched them from around a metaphysical corner.

Goose bumps rose up and down Mo's arms. He crept along behind Armin, eyes and ears wide open, turning this way and that in an attempt to look in every direction at once. All his senses seemed magnified—their footsteps loud as cannons, the smell of sweat from four unwashed bodies ripe and choking, his skin packed with too many nerve endings. His clothes scratched like sandpaper. Even the air burned. He traced the outline of the switchblade in his pocket and felt better, though he wished he hadn't left his gun in his quarters.

The strange sensations faded once they got inside the lab. Mo told himself it was a lingering side effect from the overdose of spider venom. He wasn't sure he believed it, but he was too tired—and, frankly, too fucking scared—to consider the possible alternative.

Something solid landed on his shoulder. He whirled around, heart thumping, thinking of Daisy.

Armin stood there, his hand still raised and a worried crease between his eyes. "Mo, are you all right?"

"Fine. You just startled me, is all. I was thinking." He forced a smile and clasped his shaking hands together. "So. What're we doing?"

Armin gave Mo a swift once-over. His frown deepened. "Actually, Mandala and I wondered if you would mind going over the video from the walker's helmet while she and I search the suit and helmet for DNA?"

"Oh. Sure, I can do that." Mo unclenched his hands and rubbed his palms on his thighs. The tremors had calmed down some, thankfully. Maybe Armin wouldn't notice.

Across the room, Dr. Jhut already had her gloves and mask on and the helmet in her hands. "I'll upload the video. You go ahead and bring up the interface."

Mo crossed to the nearest computer terminal and brought up the 3-D. "Computer. Display video uploaded from unknown walker."

"Yes, Maximo Rees." The terminal blinked red. Red. Green. "You will see *such thingssss, Mo. Such. Things.*"

Mo shut his eyes. *It wasn't Daisy. She's dead.*

But the mermaids were alive. And something had used Daisy to communicate with him.

Oh my, aren't you a clever one? Almost ready to choose your fate.

Choose his fate? He had no clue what that meant, but he didn't much like the pictures the voice in his head showed him. *Death or change,* it said. *There is nothing else, once you open your eyes. Once you know.*

Uneasy, sweat cold on his neck, he shoved the disturbing presence out of his head and opened his eyes again. The 3-D showed a blurry, yellowish still of a moon pool room.

His mouth went dry. "Armin?"

"Yes?" Armin started toward him, still pulling on his iso suit. "What is it?"

"Is this the moon pool on the Varredura Longa?" Mo pointed.

Armin stopped, one glove on and one still hanging from his fingers. "It's difficult to be certain, but it looks like it." He edged closer, as if the image scared him. Maybe it did. "Start the video."

"Computer, start video. One hundred and fifty percent magnification."

"Yes, Maximo Rees. Starting video with specified magnification."

The display expanded and began moving. The blurriness resolved into dim, blood-splattered clarity. Mo thought he saw a curled hand with a finger missing before the visual panned away.

Armin's breath ran out in a long *oh*, hissing into his mask. "That's definitely the Varredura Longa."

"Dear God." Dr. Jhut wandered over, her forehead creased in fierce thought. "This *must* be Klaudia. No one else that we know of left the pod after the slaughter."

"You're right." Armin rubbed a hand over his face. "But how did she end up in Richards Deep?"

"Computer. Pause." Mo glanced at the two scientists as the 3-D froze. "How do you know it's her? You already said it could've been anyone that took the suit. How do you know it's Dr. Longenesse?"

No one answered.

Scientists. Christ. "You guys want to wait and watch this after you've done your thing with the suit?" Mo turned from Armin to Dr. Jhut and back again. "It doesn't matter to me. Whatever you want."

They exchanged an almost-look. Some kind of scientific telepathy, no doubt, because they seemed to reach the same conclusion at the same time.

"It would be wonderful if we had that sort of time to spare, but we don't." Armin caressed the back of Mo's neck with his ungloved hand. "Go ahead and watch the video yourself. You have a good eye and a sharp mind. You'll do just as well as either of us would in catching anomalies."

"Better, most likely. He has far more experience with walker cams and videos than we do." Dr. Jhut cocked her head sideways and peered at the display like she wanted to jump inside it. "Mr. Rees, if you could mark any bits that you think we need to particularly study, that would be most helpful."

"Sure thing, Doc." Mo waved a hand at the both of them. "You two go on and get busy on that suit. I'll take care of this video. No problem."

Relief flooded Armin's face. "Thank you. Truly." He bent and planted a kiss on Mo's mouth.

It was a surprise, but a nice one. Mo opened up and let it go deep for a few long seconds before ending it. He grinned up at Armin as they pulled apart. "That'll keep me working for a while."

Armin walked away with sad eyes and a faint smile, and a sweet warmth spread outward from Mo's chest. If he could spare Armin a little bit of heartache by watching the damn video, he'd do it.

He was starting to think there wasn't much he *wouldn't* do for Armin.

All right. Time to focus. "Computer. Resume play."

On the 3-D, the unknown person lurched toward the moon pool and plunged in. Mo caught a brief glimpse of a body on the floor—its face a red mask, eye sockets black and empty—before the inky dark of the deep ocean blotted out everything else.

He expected the person in the suit to turn on the helmet lights. Or at least the suit's wrist lights. Instead, whoever it was plodded along in perfect darkness, breathing hard and fast and occasionally muttering, like she was talking to someone only she could hear.

The person on the display giggled, said, "Yes, yes, of course," and panted as if breathing had become incredibly difficult.

Mo marked the vid with a keystroke. Yep. Definitely a she. More confirmation for Dr. Jhut's theory that this was Dr. Longenesse.

The pained breathing continued for a good forty minutes, interspersed with occasional bursts of speech in French and German. Mostly single words, though a couple of times she blurted out entire phrases. None of it made any sense to Mo, even though he spoke both languages fluently, but he transcribed all of it for later review. Maybe Armin would understand what the hell she was talking about.

The darkness eased so gradually he didn't notice it at first. He only realized there was light coming from somewhere outside the unknown woman's suit when it struck him like a brick to the skull that he could *see* the faint slope of the seabed a few meters ahead of her feet.

"Computer. Increase magnification to two hundred percent." He spoke barely above a whisper, in case the woman on the vid said something important.

"Yes, Maximo Rees." The computer answered in a tone matching his. "She's almost there. Wait until you *seeeeeeee*."

Christ. Mo ground his teeth, ignored the thing whispering in his head and marked the video, because damned if the light wasn't getting stronger.

If you could call it a light. It looked more like the not-light in the heart of Richards Deep. The darker-than-dark blackness that somehow illuminated its surroundings like a million waterproof candles.

"Of course it's the same." Mo laughed, very softly so Armin and Dr. Jhut, several meters away on the other side of the room, wouldn't hear. He sounded more than a little hysterical, but he didn't care because this was fucking *huge*. "Come on, baby," he whispered. "Come on. Show me."

She did, unsurprisingly. He'd seen her future, so he knew she would. Still, watching her step over the edge of the slope, fall through the dizzy, chaotic whirl of whatever doorway led from there to here, and come out the other side into Richards Deep felt like witnessing history. Because it was.

He stared, captivated, while she shot upward through the canyon he'd gazed down into not that long ago. How, he had no clue. Walkers didn't have any source of independent propulsion. But there she was, rocketing through the water, past walls that reflected the bizarre negative glow, past the vague shapes of mermaids, to land on the narrow ledge at the top with a *thump* that jarred the video.

The display panned sideways. Two mermaid tails flipped away, almost close enough to hit the woman's face plate, and Mo got it.

"Jesus Christ. They carried her." The idea was completely insane. But he knew he was right. Damn.

"Mo? Did you find something we need to come see?"

Mo stopped the video manually to answer Armin. "This whole thing is shit you need to see. But no, don't stop what you're doing. I'll explain it later." He craned his neck to look over at where Armin and Dr. Jhut were peering at the walker suit through magnifiers, lab lights blazing all around them. "Are you finding anything interesting over there?"

Armin laughed. It was a strange sound, feverish and edgy, like he wasn't sure what to make of whatever they'd found. "Oh yes. It's interesting, all right."

"Finish reviewing the video," Dr. Jhut ordered before Mo could get up and follow his curiosity to their workspace. "We'll all share our discoveries when we've finished our tasks. I think we can all agree that it's better not to interrupt ourselves." She aimed a glare at Armin that said he'd better not argue. "I'm going to begin the analysis of the hair and skin samples. Why don't you start on the scales?"

Scales?

Mo gazed wide-eyed from Dr. Jhut to Armin and back again. "What d'you mean, scales?"

"We found a few scales inside the suit, along with human skin and hair." Armin shot Mo a look bright with discovery and horror. "We also found a few flakes of something we can't immediately identify. Something completely new, I believe."

"It could very well be skin infected with some sort of fungus. I want to perform a thorough analysis before we jump to conclusions."

We meaning *Armin*, judging by the tone in Dr. Jhut's voice. Not that Mo blamed her. He understood that they had to be sure.

But Armin didn't get this worked up over nothing. Which meant those unidentified flakes were probably more than some weird skin infection.

"Of course." Armin arched an eyebrow at Mo. "Perhaps the video will give us a clue as to what we're dealing with."

Mo snickered. "Subtle, Doc." He swiveled his chair back to face the 3-D display. "I'm on it."

He restarted the vid. Across the lab, Dr. Jhut and Armin went back to skin, scales, and the unknown.

Over the next hour or so, it seemed like all the best stuff was happening on the other side of the lab. Or at least, it sure as shit wasn't happening on Mo's side. He'd been watching unrelenting blackness and listening to the occasional nonsensical ramblings. Meanwhile, Armin and Mandala seemed to uncover one fascinating discovery after another. Or so he assumed, based on their agitated whispers and the way they hurried back and forth between their two stations.

What the hell was going on over there? What were they talking about? Did he really hear Dr. Jhut say something about *hybrid* something?

Did that mean what he thought it meant?

Death or change, said the mermaid in his head. *You can become so much more.*

The 3-D jerked. A strange, cracking, hissing sound came through the speakers. An even stranger silver-black blur—barely visible in the now-familiar negative light—obscured the display for a heartbeat, then vanished into the bottom left of the frame.

What the hell?

He stopped the vid and backed it up a few seconds. Stopped it again and went back five whole minutes, just in case, because he didn't know how long his mind had been drifting and he didn't want to miss anything important.

Familiar hands on his shoulders told him Armin had come up behind him in stealth mode. He tilted his head backward. "Hey."

"Hi." Armin, minus the mask now, bent to give him an upside-down kiss. "How's the video review going?"

"Okay." Mo straightened up, facing the display again as Armin sat in the chair beside him. "How about the microanalysis? Did you figure out the in between stuff?"

"Possibly. But we'll need to confirm our results." Armin leaned forward and peered at the display as if he wasn't sure he wanted to see what it might show him. "What have you found?"

On the surface, Armin sounded like his usual cool, scientific self. But eagerness and fear glittered like fireworks in his eyes, and Mo knew they must be on to something monumental. His pulse raced.

"Nothing definite yet. But something weird showed up just before you came over. I backed up and was about to watch it again." Mo slid a hand over Armin's knee. "You're just in time, if you want to watch it with me."

The muscles under Mo's hand tensed. "I'd like that. Thank you."

"Computer, resume video."

"Yes, Maximo Rees."

The computer restarted the vid without making any comments on it. Which was good, because if Armin heard the voice too, that would mean the *Death Or Change* squad had him in its sights as well, and the thought filled Mo with dread. Now that he'd known a life with Armin in it, he wasn't sure he could do without.

And wasn't it just awesome that he'd gone all needy over a man *now*, during a life-and-death crisis? Just his style.

The display remained unrelentingly black. The only way Mo knew it was moving was because he heard the woman breathing. Deep, gurgling breaths, heavy and pained like her Mist was getting low.

Maybe that was what had happened to her. Maybe she'd run out of Mist, ripped her way out of her suit in a panic and died.

Except that she never would've been able to get all the way out of her suit before being crushed by the weight of the ocean, even if she'd managed to tear her suit open in the first place, which was unlikely. Walkers were designed for toughness and flexibility. Human hands shouldn't be able to tear them.

In his mind's eye, mermaids deposited a woman in a walker suit on an undersea ledge and grinned at him with their long, sharp needle teeth.

He watched the blackness, listened to the increasingly labored breathing, and wondered.

A familiar fuzzy glow lit one edge of the 3-D. Mo sat up straighter. "She's back in Richards Deep."

Armin's cast him a sidelong look. "Where did she go?"

Mo glanced at Armin. The color had drained from his face, but he had his Scientist mask on, hard and cool and in control. Good. He was going to need it.

Mo turned his attention back to the video. "I don't know. It was too dark to tell."

They watched in silence for a couple of minutes. The dark-light outlined the edges of the canyon and the crooked, sloping ledge where they'd found the walker suit. The woman in the vid stumbled. The rocks rushed up to meet her face. Mo flinched, but she didn't hit. Instead, she floated. Floated forward, turned, landed on her back.

The whole time, she breathed like someone drowning. The vid moved in jumps and jerks.

"She's struggling." Armin grasped Mo's hand hard. "Is her Mist running out, do you think? Could that be what happened to her?"

"I wondered the same thing, but—"

The weird cracking sound Mo had heard before happened again. He still couldn't figure out what it was. Judging by the confusion on Armin's face, he didn't know either. The silvery thing whipped past, and the vid quieted. Mo opened his mouth to tell the computer to halt the vid. Armin shook his head. Mo settled back and they kept watching.

Nothing else happened. They no longer heard the woman's labored breaths. A few mermaids drifted overhead. One stopped and studied the walker, as if it found the thing interesting.

Eventually, Mo sped up the vid so they wouldn't have to watch nothing happen in real time for the next who knew how many hours. As it happened, they only sat through half an hour of triple-speed nothing before the video ended.

"Huh." Mo slouched in his chair, turning the whole thing over in his head. "The suit must not've been fully charged when she started out. The power should've lasted a *lot* longer than that."

"You're probably right. I expect she wasn't in the best frame of mind." Armin's fingers tightened around Mo's almost to the point of pain. Relaxed. Tightened and relaxed again. He hadn't let go this whole time. "In any case, power and Mist in the suit are both completely drained. That almost certainly played a role in her death."

"Where's the body?"

Armin sucked his bottom lip into his mouth. Let it go. "I don't know. I suppose she could've fallen into the ravine, even though I don't know how that would've happened without the suit falling in with her." He turned to look at Mo. "How did she get from Antarctica to Richards Deep, Mo? What did you see?"

A terrifying, exhilarating idea had been growing in Mo's mind as they watched that last stretch of quiet video and he'd mulled over what had come before. The intense gleam in Armin's eyes and the deliberate way he'd phrased his answer to Mo's previous question said he might be thinking the same thing.

"There was a ravine in Antarctica too. Not deep like the one here. But it had that same weird kind of light."

"Light, yet not light." Armin nodded, his gaze turned inward. Thinking. Processing. "Go on."

So he'd noticed its unnatural properties too. That made Mo feel significantly less unhinged.

"She walked from the moon pool to the Antarctica ravine in the dark and went right over the edge. Everything got all blurry and . . ." Mo circled his free hand in the air, searching for the words to describe it. "I dunno. It was pretty bizarre. You'll just have to see. Anyway, it was like that for a few seconds, then she came out the other side into Richards Deep, and . . . Well, this is gonna sound really strange, but I'm pretty sure the mermaids carried her to the top."

Armin let out a weak laugh. "Everything about this is strange. What happened after that?"

"She walked off into the dark. And kept on walking in the dark, until there at the end, which you saw. She must've gone off somewhere and turned around, since she ended up right where she'd started. At first she talked in French and German now and then, but she stopped after a while. It seemed like she had more and more trouble breathing."

"Her Mist was running low."

It was the most obvious explanation. But Armin sounded as doubtful as Mo felt. They regarded one another in solemn silence.

Across the lab, Dr. Jhut gasped loudly. Armin dropped his hand and jumped out of his chair. "Mandala? What's happened?"

She lifted her head from the microscanner. Her eyes were glassy. "Do you recall a little while ago when we were talking about those unusual organic samples from the suit and how they seemed to have characteristics of both the scales and the skin flakes?"

Hybrid, Armin and Dr. Jhut whispered in Mo's memory. His pulse sped up.

"Yes, of course." Armin cut a swift, wide-eyed glance at Mo. "You've learned something?"

"I think so. That is, if I have . . ." She trailed off into a high-pitched laugh at right angles with her usual cool, professional demeanor. "Christ, Armin. Whatever this came from is part human and part mermaid."

Shocked and fascinated, Armin hurried across the room to study the sample for himself. Sure enough, what he saw on the microscan was something entirely new. Pure elation ratcheted up his heartbeat in spite of all the horrors surrounding this particular finding. "Mandala, this is incredible. Absolutely unprecedented." He stepped back from the scanner and turned the grin he couldn't hide to his friend. "Congratulations, Doctor. You've just made history."

She stared at him as if he'd grown tentacles. He realized—too late, of course—that she hadn't even bothered not to look him in the eye. He dropped his gaze.

She didn't appear to notice. "You'll excuse me if I delay any celebrations until we all actually survive this nightmare, *Doctor*."

Behind him, Mo laughed. "Oh, come on. You made a huge discovery. Pat yourself on the back while you still can."

Armin bit the insides of his cheeks to keep himself from laughing in his turn. He rather enjoyed Mo's pitch-black sense of humor.

Mandala, however, did not. She made an impatient noise. "Good Lord. Is no one actually concerned with our survival? Do neither of you truly see the implications of this finding to our situation here?"

To his shame, Armin found that he hadn't thought of it that way. He'd thought of what might have happened to Klaudia Longenesse and of the scope of the discovery itself. But he hadn't yet applied it to their own plight here on BathyTech 3.

He didn't like what happened when he thought of it like that.

"You think people are changing, don't you?" Mo's voice was as serious as Armin had ever heard it. Wheels squeaked against the polycrete floor as he pushed back his chair. He stood, walked to Armin, and slid an arm around his waist. "Is that what this contagion thing is all about?"

God, what a terrible thought. Unfortunately, it felt right. Armin slipped his arm around Mo and leaned against his side.

"I'm not certain, of course. But I'm afraid it might be." Mandala peered at Armin as if she were trying to see through his skull. "I wish you would look at me. I don't believe I'm going to catch it from you. Your eyes aren't glowing, either of you, and I'm as certain as it's possible to be that that theory is correct."

Armin's stomach rolled. "You don't know that."

"No. I don't. But thus far I've seen nothing to make me believe there's any danger of infection—if that's the correct word at all; I'm not sure it is—via someone who's shown no actual symptoms. In fact, if we want to be absolutely strict about it, the only evidence we have connecting the brain growths to the changes the others experienced is strongly circumstantial. We have no smoking gun, as it were. It's all very strange, but one can't ignore the evidence."

Armin stared resolutely at the floor. "You're probably right. But I don't think it can hurt to be careful. I'd rather be overly cautious than not cautious enough when it comes to your life."

"I don't believe I'm being incautious, but I understand." She pressed her fingertips to her temples. "Well then. Mr. Rees, suppose we watch your video one more time? I think I'd like to see it."

Mo wrinkled his nose. "Okay, sure."

"I know you don't want to." Armin patted Mo's hip. "But I think I have an idea that will make it much more interesting and enlightening for us all."

To Armin's relief, he was right. The special filter he'd wanted to run the video through turned the permanent night of the deepest ocean to a blue-lit ghost world. Strange, cold, and uninviting—but visible, which was the point.

"I didn't know we had this." Mo pointed at the video, where the filter illuminated a narrow ledge winding through a previously unmapped portion of Richards Deep. "How the hell did you find it?"

"I actually had Dr. Youssouf install it before we arrived, in case we needed it for something like this. Dr. Longenesse invented this technology, back in our younger days. She was always the clever one." Talking about his friend and long-time colleague hurt. Especially when Armin thought he knew now what had happened to her. "Well. Anyway. There you are. Thanks to her invention, we're able to see what's happening to—" He stopped. Breathed. "To her. Assuming it actually is her."

Mo didn't say anything, but took his hand and laced their fingers together. Armin was grateful.

The three of them watched while the woman in the suit—*Klaudia; don't pretend it isn't her*—walked along the ledge in the cyan-tinged dark. Every once in a while, a mermaid emerged from the blackness ahead, as if leading the way. Their eyes shone a brilliant cobalt.

After a while, Armin felt a sense of familiarity creep over him. He studied the video with a frown. He couldn't help feeling he'd seen the spot before, though that was obviously impossible.

Unless . . .

The hairs stood up along his arms as the answer came to him. At the same time, Mo and Mandala sat ramrod straight in their chairs, all their attention on the 3-D as the woman in the suit reached out and placed a perfectly round, perfectly featureless black rock atop an outcropping on the wall.

CHAPTER 15

I f Armin was honest with himself, he had to admit he'd suspected this from the moment he first saw the words Varredura Longa on the abandoned walker in Richards Deep. Still, a suspicion he'd not consciously acknowledged didn't have nearly the same impact as seeing it happen right in front of his eyes.

Of course, knowing Klaudia had brought the object here and knowing *why* were two very different things. Learning the *why* promised to pose a much more formidable hurdle than finding out what had happened in the first place.

Mo sighed. "I wish you'd been able to recover the records from the Varredura Longa. Maybe we could figure out the reason why Dr. Longenesse brought that thing here."

"If there *is* one." Youssouf stopped pacing for the first time since she'd arrived in the lab to see the pertinent bit of footage for herself. "Who says she had an actual reason? If she was infected, she could've been acting on something her psychosis told her to do."

"I'd agree with you, except for the fact that this object—" Mandala gestured at the vault where the thing sat behind locked doors "—seems to be the trigger for the events both on the Varredura Longa and here."

Youssouf frowned. "I see your point about here. But how do you figure it set off what happened on the VL?"

A bitter half smile tugged at Armin's mouth. "They called us there in the first place to examine something odd they'd found in the ocean. It stands to reason that the object *is* that thing. Especially now that we know both objects are one and the same." God. For the first time in his career, he wished the puzzle pieces didn't fit so neatly together.

Mandala nodded, her brow creased in thought. "It's possible that her psychosis caused her to walk into the ocean with the object. But I find it very difficult to believe that a person suffering a psychotic break could find this portal—or whatever the hell it is—travel from Antarctica to here with an object she knew would cause the same havoc that destroyed the Varredura Longa, and deposit it in such a strategic spot: close enough to BathyTech 3 to easily retrieve with the go-carts and walkers. It's far too much to call it anything but deliberate."

Youssouf's shoulders slumped. "Good point."

"The mermaids are at the center of this whole thing." Everyone stared at Armin as if none of them had thought the same thing, which he found annoyingly disingenuous. He laughed, because it was either laugh or scream in their faces. "Please. All of you know it's true. The mermaids were in Antarctica. They're here. They carried Klaudia out of the ravine, for God's sake."

"We don't have proof positive yet that it was actually Klaudia," Mandala reminded him in her calm, remember-yourself scientist voice.

Armin rolled his eyes. "Compare the DNA tests on the skin and hair to her samples on record. We all *know* what you're going to find, Mandala. We *know*. You're the one who said it had to be her, for God's sake."

An uncomfortable silence fell. Mandala pursed her lips and looked away.

Armin went on. "The scales we found in the suit were mermaid scales. We've already posited that this contagion somehow changes human beings into mermaids. I don't think they can get any more involved than that."

Mandala aimed a cutting look at him. "I didn't intend to suggest that the mermaids were deliberately causing it."

"I know. *I'm* suggesting that."

Silence again, charged with the newness of the idea. Armin could feel the crackle of thoughts flowing as everyone in the room digested what he'd said and decided he was right.

Mandala broke the quiet. "I believe I'll run those DNA comparisons. We have to be certain about this." She rose and went for the stored skin and hair samples.

Armin couldn't argue with her logic, so he didn't try. He leaned against Mo, who sat in the chair next to his. God, he'd never been so exhausted in his life.

Mo draped his arm around Armin's shoulders. "So. What next?"

"Not a fucking clue." Youssouf plopped into the nearest chair, yawning hard. "I'm open to suggestions."

Everyone studied the floor. No one spoke.

The idea hit Armin hard enough to knock the tiredness right out of him. "The mermaids. Of course." He leaped to his feet and spun to face the group before any of them could ask the questions he knew were in their heads. "We should tag one of the mermaids and track it. We could see where it goes and what it does. If they're truly involved in this, or have created this contagion either purposefully or inadvertently, maybe tracking one will at least give us a direction for further investigation."

"Hm. Well, maybe we won't learn anything, but maybe we will." Youssouf rubbed a hand through her hair. "I think it's worth a try."

Mandala set the sealed DNA sample containers on the counter and crossed her arms. She didn't look pleased, but she didn't argue either. "How do we go about it?"

"It's no different from tagging any other animal." Armin went through it in his mind. Yes, it should work. "We find one, place the tracker, and let technology do the rest."

Mo let out a harsh laugh. "Something tells me putting on the tracker's gonna be a bitch."

"They're clearly a highly intelligent species, which makes it more difficult. But there are time-proven methods for tagging animals clever enough to catch on to your game. It won't be easy, but it *is* absolutely doable. I've tagged a great many animals in my day. I'm confident I can do it." Armin almost met Dr. Youssouf's eyes. He stopped himself just in time. "Amara, do we have the proper equipment here?"

She nodded. "Nobody seriously thought we'd ever need any of it. But BathyTech made sure we were fully stocked anyhow, just in case."

"Good thing for us, I guess." Mo rose slowly, both hands pressed to the small of his back. "Goddamn, I'm beat. I guess we have to do this right away, huh?"

"I think we should, yes." Armin glanced at Mandala, who was loading the last DNA sample into the tester, then at Dr. Youssouf. Neither disagreed with him, so he continued. "I'm sorry. I know we're all worn out. But if we're ever going to get control of this situation, we have to find out what, if anything, the mermaids have to do with it all. It's no good stumbling in the dark trying to find a solution when we're not even sure of the problem."

"I agree with you that we need to root out the cause of this . . ." Mandala started the testing machine, then lifted one hand and let it drop, as if she'd given up on finding the appropriate name for what was happening here. "This confounded situation we find ourselves in. However, I don't believe we can afford to simply wait and see what the mermaids choose to show us. If they indeed show us anything." She stood from the work station stool, one hand on the counter as if to hold herself up. Armin suspected she was as falling-down tired as he was. "I plan to do further testing on the samples we have, as well as the object. No, Armin, before you ask, I have no idea what else I can possibly test on the damn rock. But I shall see what, if anything, the samples suggest."

Youssouf eyed her with a tired smile. "I'd help you out, but I need to get back to the med bay and try to figure out if there's anything at all I can do for the folks who're already infected." She sighed. "Haven't had any luck so far, but you don't get anywhere by giving up."

"This is true." Mandala hid a yawn behind her hand. "If there's anything I can do to help, let me know."

"I will, thanks. Though you'll do a lot more good if you can work out how to keep anybody else from getting infected." Youssouf hauled herself out of her chair. "Well. Nothing gets done by sitting around talking about it. You boys get Jem and go catch us a mermaid."

Armin caught Mo's eye. Mo grinned. Armin grinned back. No one had ever tagged and studied a mermaid before. In spite of everything, Armin found himself looking forward to it.

Unfortunately, actually getting a tracker on one of the elusive creatures proved more difficult than they'd imagined, even taking the species' high intelligence into account. Armin couldn't help admiring them, in spite of his growing frustration.

"Fuck a goddamn *duck*!" Mo spun in his chair and kicked the bulkhead the third time the mermaid he'd targeted evaded the tracker.

Jemima, slouched in the pilot's chair next to him, shoved his knee. "Hey, leave the equipment alone."

"Yeah, yeah." He glared over his shoulder at the tiny mechanized dot on the view screen. It hovered in the water roughly thirty meters from the go-cart, waiting for further instructions. This spot, less than a quarter klick from the strange canyon, crawled with mermaids, but that only seemed to make them harder to catch. "How in the hell do they *know*? Every fucking time."

Armin shook his head. "Honestly? I have no idea." He patted Mo's knee. "Don't let it bother you. I didn't do any better than you did. Apparently this is the exception to the rule that automatic taggers are more accurate."

"Hm." Mo stood and started pacing. His long legs ate up the small space. "Hey, Jem?"

She half turned to roll her eyes at him. "What?"

"How much Mist we got in the walkers?"

"Enough for maybe four hours."

"That's all?"

She swiveled the rest of the way around to raise her eyebrows at him. "I got here the same time as you, Rees. You two were in such a tearing hurry you about fidgeted out of your skins waiting for me to do safety checks on the suits. When did you reckon I was gonna top up the Mist?"

"Point." He paced some more, his forehead furrowed so hard Armin wondered if it hurt. "Well, the go-cart tank's pretty full, if we need more. So I think we're in good shape. Shouldn't take that long anyway."

"What do you have in mind?" Armin asked, though he thought he knew.

Mo's mouth curved into a grim smile. "You and me are going walking."

"What, you think you'll be able to get a tracker on one of those slippery fuckers by hand when you couldn't do it with the auto-tagger?" Jemima made a dismissive noise. "Good luck with that, cowboy."

"Well, the automatic system's not getting the job done. Those damn things are too smart. Either we give up, or we try it the old-fashioned way." Mo trained his determined stare on Armin. "What about it, Doc? You coming?"

Armin's spirit leaped. Since the advent of the auto-tagger as everyday equipment six or seven years ago, he'd rarely gotten the chance to find and tag an animal using his hands, his eyes, and his wits. He missed it.

He rose, doing his best not to grin like an excited child. "I certainly am. Let's suit up."

"You two watch yourselves out there," Jemima called as he and Mo headed for the moon pool bay.

"Don't worry, we'll be careful." Mo turned to walk backward while he spoke to Jemima. "Keep the cart dark while we're outside."

She gave him a thumbs-up.

Shooting Armin a quick, enthusiastic smile, Mo faced forward again and picked up his pace. Armin followed.

"What makes you think we'll be able to accomplish this by hand when the auto-tagger couldn't?" he asked.

"I don't know if we can or not. It's like I told Jem, we have to try it this way or give up." Mo narrowed his eyes. His gaze focused somewhere in the middle distance. "But I was thinking, if the mermaids are really involved in any of this shit deliberately, maybe they'll approach us if we're out there in person. Maybe they'll *want* to get close. It's a long shot, but it's worth a try."

"That's actually a very good idea." Impressed, Armin touched Mo's arm as the two of them entered the moon pool bay. "You're a natural scientist."

"Computer, seal and pressurize bay." Mo crossed the room, stripping off his shirt as he went. "What makes you say that?"

"You have an affinity for this work. You *think* like a scientist." Armin skirted the pool to where the walkers hung in their protective niches and kicked off his shoes. "I think it's my favorite thing about you. I'm sorry that . . ." His throat constricted, holding the words inside.

Naturally, Mo heard what he hadn't said. The half smile on Mo's lips vanished. He threw his shirt into the open locker, closed the distance between them, and planted a gentle kiss on Armin's lips.

"This wasn't your fault, Armin. Not any of it. Especially not the things growing in our heads, or anyone else's."

Armin slid his fingers into the thick, dark hair at the nape of Mo's neck and leaned their foreheads together. Keeping him close while they were both still themselves. "I wish I could believe that."

"Why can't you?" Mo slipped an arm around Armin's waist. The other hand mapped the contours of his face as if memorizing him. "What could you possibly have done different?"

Armin turned his face into Mo's comforting touch. "What's happening here is directly related to what happened in Antarctica. The video from Klaudia's helmet proved it. If only I'd left immediately and gone straight down there when she called—"

"Then you'd probably be dead or missing along with everybody else on the Varredura Longa." Mo moved the arm around Armin, laid both hands on his cheeks, and stared into his eyes with an intensity that glued him in place. "You couldn't have stopped this, Armin. I'm glad you didn't go to Antarctica any earlier, because then I'd never have met you. And I'm *happy* I met you, no matter what else happens."

The certainly in Mo's voice brought a telltale sting to Armin's eyes. He blinked it away, smiling in spite of everything because the sense of belonging welling up inside him melted the icy dread for the first time in what seemed like forever.

"I'm glad too." Armin tilted his head to kiss Mo. *I wish this could last longer*, he said with the press of his lips and the sweep of his tongue. *I wish we could see the sun together, one day.*

They both knew it wouldn't happen. But he could wish.

Mo drew back with a small, wry smile. "Guess we better get busy. We still need to catch a mermaid."

Feeling melancholy, Armin finished undressing and began the process of getting into the walker. He watched without shame as Mo did the same beside him. God, but the man had a beautiful body. Almost as glorious as his mind. Armin wondered if it was wrong that what angered him most about this whole mess was that he and Mo would never have the chance for a future.

They'd only walked together twice before, but they already made a smooth, seamless team. They were ready to go in a matter of minutes.

Mo informed Jemima, the computer uncovered the moon pool, and they plunged into the sea.

Armin carried the tagger and trackers, since of the two of them only he had actual experience in hand-tagging. At Mo's suggestion, they kept their helmet and wrist lights on the lowest setting that still allowed them to see. With the go-cart dark and their walkers nearly so, they hoped to lure the mermaids close enough to tag.

Close enough to touch.

If only he truly could. But flesh-to-flesh contact with a mermaid at depth would mean a crushing, icy death. He'd take what he could get and be content.

He and Mo walked out to where the latest failed attempt at auto-tagging hung in the water. Armin had always thought the trackers resembled tiny electronic shrimp. When he'd first started using these new trackers several years ago, he'd foreseen losing a lot of them to sea creatures feeding, but that fear had proved groundless. Probably because the things didn't smell or taste like food, regardless of how they looked.

He closed his hand carefully around the curved little bit of hardware. "This one's already programmed. Might as well use it, if we can."

Mo took a slow step forward. "Heads up, Armin. I think you're about to get your chance." He pointed into the dark.

Armin peered along Mo's outstretched arm. A shape moved in the blackness. It grew more distinct, and Armin saw that it was swimming.

Fast. Toward them.

He made out the faint gleam of milky-green eyes a second later, and his heart jumped into his throat.

In his years as a marine geologist and biologist, he'd gone on hundreds of dives in all the world's oceans, and tagged more marine animals than he could count in a long Antarctic night. But none of those experiences had been anything like this one—a first, something historic, something no one else had ever done.

Also, the animals he tagged had never rushed at him this way, toothy mouths agape and eyes glittering with unfriendly purpose. It put him a bit off-kilter.

Mo hissed a sharp breath in his ear through the helmet's audio. "Doc . . ."

His tense whisper prodded Armin into action. He mounted the tracking device on the tagger without looking away from the creature swimming toward him.

It was slowing now, as if sensing his intentions. Its body language broadcast suspicion like a living radio.

In another time and place, Armin would have wondered how he picked up such a thing from a fish, no matter how bizarrely human it looked. But right now, the lives of everyone left on BathyTech 3—not to mention himself, Mo, and Jemima—might well depend on him placing a tracker on the creature approaching with more caution every second. So he shoved his curiosity to the back of his mind and followed the instinct telling him to concentrate on his fear.

He didn't like to call it that. He'd never been afraid of the ocean, or anything in it. Even the horrors he'd seen on the Varredura Longa had fallen squarely in the realm of man-made.

Then they'd found that damned rock that wasn't a rock here in Richards Deep. Reality had begun to crumble around him, and fear had spread through his soul like a stain. He wondered if he'd ever be rid of it.

For the first time in what seemed ages, he loosened his grip on the cold, sick dread inside him and let it rise to the surface. Let it raise his pulse and quicken his breath. Let it shine on his face.

The mermaid grinned, all sharp teeth and glowing eyes the color of rot. Its tail whipped. It swam forward with lazy grace. *No hurry*, it seemed to say. *You're not going anywhere, now, are you?*

He wasn't, though not for the reasons his target believed.

Armin laughed, because here he stood in the muck on the ocean floor, attributing deliberate, villainous strategy to a damned fish.

Mo cast him an appalled glance. "Not a good time to lose your shit, Doc."

"I know." Armin let the tracking delivery spear fall to the seabed and palmed the tagger portion with the tracker already loaded. The only way this was going to happen was if he could get close enough to do it with his own hands. "Don't worry. I know what I'm doing."

He could tell Mo didn't believe him. But Mo stopped talking and didn't interfere, so it hardly mattered what he believed.

Armin paced forward, one slow step at a time. He focused on his terror, his worry, his growing belief that none of them were going to make it out of this alive. The more the mermaid thought him defeated, the more likely it would come to him unsuspecting of his true motives.

He tried not to consider the implications of this animal having any inkling of his thoughts or motivations in the first place. That was a mental road to walk somewhere other than here, where nothing but his suit separated him from the pitiless sea.

He stopped roughly three meters from the creature. It kept coming, propelled by languid waves of its tail, until it floated close enough for him to see the imperfections in each tiny, flat scale on its too-human face. Its wide mouth opened and closed, opened and closed, like a filter feeder.

Armin wasn't fooled. This thing was a carnivore. A predator. Teeth like that were made for tearing flesh.

Looking into its eyes felt like drowning. But Armin did it anyway. He held the greenish gaze trying to invade him like a disease, let it have his fear and revulsion while he slipped his hand up, over, around, and attached the tracker to the base of the mermaid's dorsal fin.

With a screech he heard through his helmet, it jerked away from him, yanking him off-balance. He felt himself toppling.

Everything happened in slow motion. He saw the mermaid shoot forward, but couldn't move fast enough to stop it from sinking its movie-monster teeth into his right hand.

At first, Mo wasn't sure what had happened. Then Armin shouted, his voice full of surprise and pain, and Mo leaped forward to stop whatever the hell had made him sound like that.

Seeing the mermaid's teeth imbedded in Armin's hand stopped Mo in his tracks. "Shit." He fumbled for his stun stick. "Armin, hold still!"

"No!" The stubborn scientific determination Mo admired and hated gleamed in Armin's wide, terrified eyes. "Don't stun it! It's tagged! We don't know what the stunner will do to it."

Damn it. Mo lowered the stunner, but kept it in his hand. He wasn't about to risk Armin's life. Not for anything. Not even the lives of every other person on BathyTech. Hell, if it weren't for the self-seal suit fabric, the ocean would've already rushed in to stop Armin's heart with its cold. Mo would kill the mermaid in a heartbeat if that's what it took to keep Armin alive.

Mo knew what that said about him, but he didn't care. One thing he'd learned in Dubai was, when it came right down to it, people were no better than animals. You had to look after yourself and your people, because nobody else was going to. Armin was his now. His to protect. He'd keep Armin and himself alive first, and worry about the rest later.

The mermaid shook Armin's hand like a shark ripping its prey in half. Armin screamed, and Mo was done with being careful. He flung himself at the animal and shoved the butt end of his weapon into the nearest gill slit.

The creature let go of Armin with a high-pitched shriek that hurt Mo's ears, even through his helmet. It backed away. Blood drifted from its bared teeth in little red rivers. Its eyes glowed green and white and murderous.

Mo didn't dare look away. "Armin?"

"I'm all right." He sounded anything but, his voice weak and shaking. "The suit's already sealed itself. Not enough water got in to hurt me."

"What the fuck's going on out there?" Jem sounded scared and royally pissed off. "Rees! Report, goddamn it."

"Later." The mermaid tensed like a cat about to spring, and Mo did the only thing he could think of aside from stunning it. "Jem, lights, hit the lights! Now!"

Never in his life had he been so grateful for a strong, trusting working relationship. Jem didn't argue, or ask questions, or pull rank. She turned on the go-cart's outside lights, because she knew him well enough to know he had a reason for wanting them on.

Just like he'd hoped, the mermaid whipped around and hightailed it away from the brightness. Mo's knees sagged. "Thanks, Mama."

"No problem. You gonna tell me why I just did that?"

"Yeah, soon as I get the Doc back on board."

"Roger that. I'll get the first aid kit ready. What happened?"

"No, don't." Armin grasped Mo's wrist with his uninjured hand. In the white glow of the cart's lights, his face was pasty and lined with pain. "Jemima, I've just tagged that mermaid. It bit me, but I'm fine. I need you to keep an eye on the readout, and inform Dr. Jhut that we've completed the mission so that she can start tracking it. Will you do that?"

Jem's brief pause announced her disapproval as loudly as if she'd shouted it. "Whatever you say, Doctor. Out."

Mo slipped an arm around Armin's waist. Armin leaned against his side, nearly a deadweight in the water, and Mo tightened his grip. "Stay with me, Doc. We're going back to the cart." He picked up his pace, striding as fast as he could with Armin's feet dragging in the mud. "Hey. You awake?"

"Yes." Armin's voice was faint, but aware, and Mo could've cried with relief. "I . . . I feel ill. We should get back quickly." He breathed for a few seconds. In and out, too fast. "I'm sorry."

"Stop it. Hang on to me and save your strength."

Clutching Armin tight to his side, he made for the moon pool as fast as he could go.

He didn't relax until he'd heaved Armin over the edge into the bay, levered himself inside, and the computer had shut the pool's cover behind them. That done, he ripped off his helmet and gloves, tossed them aside, and crawled to where Armin lay motionless on the floor beside the pool.

Forcing himself to move slowly, calmly, carefully, he unsealed Armin's helmet and took it off. "Armin? Hey, talk to me."

Armin gave him a weak smile. His lips shaped Mo's name. Mo's throat clamped shut. His vision blurred. He bent and kissed Armin's cold, damp forehead.

He drew back, blinking against the sting in his eyes. "Let's get that glove off and see what we're dealing with."

Armin's chest shook. For a second Mo thought he was crying, and the world stood still. What would he do? What could he possibly say to make it better? The truth was he couldn't, and that fact destroyed him.

Then he looked into Armin's face and realized he was laughing. *Laughing.*

Damn that fucker anyway.

"What the hell's wrong with you?" He shot a swift glare at Armin, then turned his attention to the man's mangled, bloodied glove. "Shit. I'm gonna have to cut this thing off."

"Sorry," Armin whispered as Mo rose to fetch the first aid kit from the locker beside the door. "It was just . . . Incredible. So incredible."

"What? Getting your hand almost torn off?"

Mo hated his own scornful tone. He thought he knew what Armin meant. How many other people had ever touched a mermaid with their own hands? How many scientists would gladly suffer the same injury for that chance? Why was he being like this?

He turned back to Armin, the first aid kit in hand. Armin gazed at him with a shiny-eyed fondness that made him feel warm inside. "You know. You'd do the same, given the chance."

What could he say? Mo crossed to the pool and knelt at Armin's side. "You're right. I would." He laid both hands on Armin's cheeks and leaned forward, staring into his eyes. "But I still hate that you did it, because I don't want anything to happen to you. And I'm fucking scared to death of what this might do to you." He bent to kiss Armin's lips. A chaste but firm kiss, meant not to seduce, but to remind Armin that he was important to someone. When they drew apart, Mo thought Armin looked more like the man he had come to know. "Now hold still. This is probably not going to feel too good."

Armin sighed. "I don't expect it will. Do what you must."

He lay back on the floor, eyes closed. Mo opened the kit and prepared to go to work.

By the time the go-cart returned to BT3, Mo had Armin's wound cleaned and dressed as well as he could manage, and had bullied Armin into taking one of the broad-spectrum antibiotic shots included in the first aid kit.

Nothing he said could convince the stubborn bastard to take any of the pain meds, though.

"I need to keep a clear head." Armin spoke through clenched teeth, his upper lip beaded with pain-sweat. "I'll be fine."

"Since when does 'fine' mean you can't even stand up 'cause you're hurting so bad?" Jem wondered as she and Mo carried Armin into the med bay.

Armin pinned her with the same death glare he'd been using on Mo the whole way from Richards Deep to BathyTech. "Narcotics impede proper brain function. That is a known fact. Therefore, I will *not* be taking any. Why is that so damned difficult for you people to understand?"

Jem stared back, completely cool and unfazed. "Not all pain meds are narcotics, *Doctor*. If you think they are, then obviously the pain is fucking with your brain. Which is a known phenomenon, by the way. In case you didn't know that."

Armin rolled his eyes toward the sky more than seven thousand meters above. Mo swallowed laughter. He grinned at Jem, who winked at him.

They'd barely rounded the corner approaching the med bay when Youssouf came storming out. "How in the almighty fuck did you manage to get bitten by a damned mermaid?"

"I was tagging it by hand. It was the only way. They were wary of the auto-tagger." Armin nodded at his hand, draped over Jem's shoulder. "Mo washed it out and dressed it in the go-cart, and gave me an antibiotic shot, but they've informed me that I'm not allowed into the lab to watch the tracker until I let you have a look."

"And make him take something for the pain, would you?" Mo ignored Armin's scowl as he helped him through the door into the med bay. "It's hurting him really bad, but he won't take anything because he doesn't want it to make him fuzzy."

"Perhaps you missed the part where we are actually tracking a mermaid for the first time in history." Armin shoved free of Mo's grip and stood swaying in the middle of the floor, his black eyes blazing. "I *need* to be a part of this. I will not be pushed aside because of a simple injury."

"Fine. I'll give you something nondrowsy so you can concentrate without the pain distracting you." Youssouf went to the storage cabinet and started gathering supplies. "Anything else? You got any other problems with being treated for this bite?"

"No, he doesn't." Mo grasped Armin's elbow again. "C'mon, Armin. You're gonna sit your stubborn ass down and let the nice doctor fix up your hand so you can go play with the other scientists. Okay?"

"You're an annoying bastard," Armin grumbled, but he let Mo steer him to the nearest chair. He sat down and held out his hand for Youssouf to examine.

Twenty minutes later, Youssouf finally let Mo and Jem take Armin to the lab, after making him swear he wouldn't use his injured hand.

When they got there, Dr. Jhut waved them over without looking away from the tracking screen. "You absolutely *must* see this. It's fascinating."

Mo and Armin exchanged a glance. Excitement lit Armin's face, almost obliterating the pain-shadows.

Almost. Mo patted his pocket, where he'd stashed more pills for later. He'd force them down the stubborn idiot's throat if he had to.

Armin took the chair beside Dr. Jhut's and rolled it closer to the 3-D display. "What's happened? What are we looking at here?"

A pure-white octopus glided across the dark cube, and a thrill shot up Mo's spine as he remembered a TV show he'd seen as a child about the discovery of that particular species. *Antarctica.* He sat beside Armin, where he could see better.

"Your mermaid crossed into Antarctica about five minutes ago." Dr. Jhut cut them a look full of excitement. "So far, it's been in no particular hurry. It stopped twice while in the canyon in Richards Deep, for forty-five seconds the first time and two minutes seventeen seconds the second time."

Armin frowned. "What was it doing?"

"I'm not certain. Both times, at least one other mermaid was nearby, hovering in the water just as ours was doing." Her forehead creased. "Judging by the cross-movements I saw, I believe there may have been more than one, but I can't be positive."

"Gathering in groups. No one's observed them doing that before. Well, not until this canyon, anyway." Armin leaned forward, staring at the display like he was trying to teleport himself into it. "Were they communicating? That would definitely be new."

"If they were, it wasn't through vocalization." Dr. Jhut massaged her neck with both hands. She looked tired, but hell, so did they all. "Perhaps they use gestures? Their pectoral fins are very nearly prehensile."

"Or chemicals released into the water at short range." Armin rubbed his wrist above his bandaged hand. "Neither idea is entirely without precedent, even among marine life."

Mo thought about the voices in his head when he'd found that ravine in Richards Deep. The voices that seemed to come not *from* poor Daisy, but *through* her.

Death or change.

"They communicate telepathically."

Dr. Jhut and Armin turned to look at him at the same time—Dr. Jhut with a what-the-fuck frown, Armin with resignation.

"What in the world are you talking about?" Dr. Jhut's voice was sharp and clipped, her patience obviously hanging by a string.

Fine. Mo couldn't blame her. "I heard them. I didn't know it was *them* at the time, but they talked to me when I took the cart and went out to Richards Deep on my own. They led me out there."

Armin studied him with eyes full of understanding and fear, which surprised Mo not at all after what they'd both experienced in Richards Deep. "Do you mean to say they *wanted* you to find this . . ." He gestured at the tracker cam's display. "This gateway, or whatever you want to call it?"

"Yeah. They told me I'd see amazing things there. Things nobody else knew. They tried to get me to go in." Mo paused, thought about whether or not he should mention the next bit, and decided the time for keeping secrets was gone. "You know what I'm talking about. You heard it too."

Dr. Jhut's eyes went wide. "Armin? Is this true?"

Armin sighed. "Yes. I heard a voice in my head urging me to go into the crevasse. To follow the light and learn what it had to show me."

"Death or change," Mo whispered, very softly, for Armin's ears only.

Armin's jaw tensed. He touched Mo's knee, a brief brush of fingertips that said he understood what Mo was saying. Mo leaned closer and nuzzled Armin's ear because, Christ, he hated that these goddamn things were in Armin's head too.

"Well. Even assuming that I believe these mermaids actually communicated with both of you via telepathy—and I'm sorry, but that's a tremendous leap—we have no way to prove it. The sort of technology one would need to gather evidence doesn't exist. In the future, perhaps, but right now—" Dr. Jhut stopped, all her attention on the 3-D. "Something's happening."

Mo looked. The dark still stretched into infinity beyond their cube of visual, but he could see now. The same bizarre, backward illumination from Richards Deep filled this place. The tracker's cam picked up other sleek gray-white shapes slipping in and out of the blackness. Mermaids, filling a narrow chasm that seemed to reach to the center of the Earth. Their mermaid made a sharp turn, revealing a tremendous rock wall, gray and sleek as if it had been built and polished.

"Shit." Mo stared, impressed. "Where the hell *is* this?"

"This area is uncharted." Dr. Jhut pointed to the readout from the mapping software at the bottom left of the 3-D. "It's very deep. Almost eight thousand meters where our mermaid is, and it seems there's a chasm that may stretch deeper."

"A new deep-ocean trench." Armin laughed. "My God. We need to put together an expedition to study it."

"Let's get through this one first, shall we?" Dr. Jhut cast him a sour glance. "Look. There's an opening in the wall."

Mo got a glimpse of a long, jagged vertical crack, pulsing with a hard black glow, before the mermaid banked again and it veered out of view. He didn't need any more than that to know what it was, though.

"This is another gateway." Armin's words perfectly echoed Mo's thoughts. "Oh my God."

"I wonder how many there are?" Mo found the idea a little scary and a lot intriguing. "Could we use them? It could change everything."

Dr. Jhut held up one hand. "Let's not get ahead of ourselves. Just watch for now. Let's see where our mermaid goes, and what it does. We can decide what to do with the larger implications after we figure out why people here are changing, and what in the bloody hell to do about it."

She had a point. They shut up and watched.

Black-lit water and green-eyed, sharp-toothed mermaids streamed past. Another mermaid swam alongside for a minute, its muscular side undulating like a snake's. It pulled ahead just in time for Mo to see the vastness of the ocean vanish as their mermaid entered the crack in the wall.

Instantly, the sensible world gave way to chaos. The dark spun and sparked, twisted and pretzeled and turned reality inside out, and finally spat them into a spot Mo didn't recognize on sight, but whose coordinates he knew by heart.

"Jesus, it's in the fucking Mariana Trench." He glanced from Armin to Dr. Jhut and back. "Are you seeing this?"

Armin nodded without speaking. His face reflected the same shock Mo felt.

"This is . . ." Dr. Jhut leaned back in her chair, shaking her head. "It's unprecedented. I don't even know what to think."

"Of course this phenomenon must be studied, eventually." Armin glanced at Mo, then stopped and stared at the display again. "Wait. What's that?"

The *what?* on Mo's tongue died when he saw the small, round object on the trench floor. Their mermaid swam past it without stopping, but they all got a good enough look to recognize the way the impossible light reflected off the thing's glassy black curve.

A sudden white blur filled the display. The feed went dark.

Mo blinked. "What happened?"

"I have no idea." Armin touched Dr. Jhut's arm. "Can you get it back?"

She shook her head, fingers dancing over the controls. "No. It looks as though the feed's dead at the source."

Mo mouthed a silent *oh*. "So something's happened to the tracker?"

"It seems so, yes." She did something else. "I'm going back a bit in the record and slowing it down to see if we can tell what happened."

Mo rolled his chair closer to Armin's and watched, rapt, as the blur resolved itself frame by frame into a mermaid with hate in its eyes and long, sharp teeth closing around them like a living cave.

"My God. It bit off the tracker." Armin aimed a wide-eyed look at Mo. "Did you see that?"

"Yeah." Pulse thumping, Mo rested his hand on Armin's shoulder. "Why would it do that? Are they *that* smart, that they recognize a tracker when they see it?"

Dr. Jhut let out a soft laugh. "I have no idea what to even believe any longer." She backed up the vid and started the last few seconds once more, at the lowest possible speed.

"Wait, what's that?" Armin pointed to a fuzzy reddish spark on the attacking mermaid's upper lip. "Freeze it."

Dr. Jhut halted the playback. To Mo, it looked like nothing much. A trick of the light, maybe. But Armin paled when Dr. Jhut magnified the still. "Jesus, Mandala. Do you see?"

She nodded, grim faced. "Yes. We'd guessed, but still . . ."

"What?" Mo glanced from one of them to the other, confused. "What the hell are you talking about?"

"Look at the still." Armin gestured at the 3-D. "It's a ruby in that mermaid's lip."

Mo studied it. "Huh. Looks like it, yeah. That's weird."

"It's more than weird." Armin turned and met Mo's eyes. "Dr. Longenesse had a ruby stud in her upper lip. That mermaid is her."

CHAPTER 16

Like Dr. Jhut had said, the ruby didn't suggest anything they hadn't already guessed. But having it confirmed in such a concrete way left Mo reeling.

It had to be much worse for Armin and Dr. Jhut, who'd worked with Dr. Longenesse. Known her not only as a fellow scientist, but as a human being with strengths and weaknesses, friends and enemies and loved ones. How awful must it be to see someone you knew so radically changed?

Mo tightened his grip on Armin's shoulder. "Jesus, Doc . . ."

Armin's hand on his silenced him. "Mandala. Can we be certain?"

"You know we can't. Not short of capturing that particular mermaid and taking a DNA sample." She made a low, broken sound and hunched forward, covering her face with her hands. "And who knows if the DNA would even match any longer? God, Armin. What in all the hells is happening? And *why*?"

In Mo's head, the mermaids grinned and beckoned. *Death or change, friend.*

Since that didn't really answer Dr. Jhut's question, he didn't say it. They already knew people were changing. He wasn't going to make a bad situation worse by telling Mandala the mermaids said they had to change or die.

"I don't know." Armin put his arm around his colleague and hugged her, his head resting on the curve of her back. "But we won't give up until we solve this. All right? Promise me, Mandala. I can't do this without you."

She drew a deep breath. Blew it out. Straightened her spine. Her resolve seemed to have returned when she sat up. She gave a single, sharp nod. "We're all in this together."

She held out her right hand without looking away from the still of the mermaid's open mouth. Armin put his left hand on top of hers. Mo added his right hand. It wasn't much, but it was still a pact of sorts, and it made him feel better.

He stared at the blurred rapier teeth and the single red ember on the 3-D. *We'll stop you,* he thought at it. *You can't make us do anything. We'll find you, and stop you.*

The frozen image didn't move. Didn't speak. But Mo knew, somehow, that it mocked them anyway.

They decided, after some discussion, that their findings ought to be reported to Dr. Youssouf in person rather than via coms.

She wasn't overly receptive.

"Are you *fucking* kidding me?" She threw both hands in the air when Armin and Mandala both shook their heads. "Great. Just great. You've both lost it."

Armin swallowed his irritation. "Amara, the video from the tracker was rather obvious. The mermaid who bit the tracker off of the one I tagged had a ruby stud in its upper lip. Dr. Longenesse had a ruby in *her* upper lip. If you have another explanation for how a mermaid fish would have acquired such a thing, I'd love to hear it."

Dr. Youssouf scowled. "Just because I don't—"

The com from upside squealed, announcing an incoming message. The office went silent.

"*Peregrine* for Dr. Youssouf," said a staticky voice. "Please come in."

Amara lunged for the com link. "This is Dr. Youssouf. Who am I talking to?"

"Oh thank God." The voice breathed relief through the room like a perfume. "This is Dr. Ngalo. I'm afraid I have bad news."

Armin's stomach rolled. He was glad when Mo edged closer and slid an arm around his waist.

Amara cut a quick sidelong glance at them. Armin saw his own fears reflected in her eyes. "What's happened?"

A pause, short but eloquent. "Hannah Long died a few minutes ago. I'm so sorry, Doctor. We did everything we could, but nothing helped. She died of hypoxic respiratory failure, on one hundred percent oxygen through the ventilator . . . She wasn't able to absorb any oxygen at all. I can't explain it."

Dr. Youssouf closed her eyes. Beside Armin, Mo tensed and made a pained sound so soft Armin barely heard it. But he knew what it meant. Hannah had been Mo's friend. This must be devastating for him.

Armin wound his arm around Mo's hips and squeezed. He turned his face to Mo's, nuzzled his cheek, and kissed the sensitive hollow behind his ear. *I'm sorry*, he said with his touch, with his lips and the warmth of his body at Mo's side. *I'm here for you.*

Mo leaned his head against Armin's and thanked him with warm brown eyes and a long breath in his ear. Armin held him close and promised him without words that they would find the reasons behind this. That Hannah's death—and Ryal's, and all the others—would not go unresolved.

"Thank you for letting us know." Amara remained calm and controlled as a leader ought to be. She opened her eyes. They burned with anger and the need for revenge, though that need could find no real target. "What's your situation?"

"Not good. Whatever this is, it's spreading fast. And we're not even certain how or why." Ngalo paused. "If you have any new insights, this would be a good time to share."

They all looked at each other. Armin noted without much surprise that Dr. Youssouf no longer seemed worried about looking him and Mo in the eye.

Mandala was the one to answer. "We don't know anything for certain. You already know about the growths we've found, and our theories regarding light-wave spread." She paused. "We're still not certain why some people with growths have gone on to exhibit physical changes and psychosis, and others haven't. And we're not positive whether or not those without the physical changes can pass it on. We have a great deal more work to do in order to identify the specific trigger from dormant brain growths to active symptomatology."

Dr. Ngalo was quiet for a moment. Armin could almost feel her thinking. "What would you suggest we do, Doctor?" She sounded calm, resigned, doing what she must in order to save as many of her people as she could.

When Mandala hesitated, Armin jumped in. "Isolate anyone with growths in their brain, if you haven't already done so. If they start to exhibit physical changes, sedate them immediately. And cover their eyes. If our theories are correct, that will prevent them from passing on the contagion to others." They'd probably already done so, but it couldn't hurt to remind them.

"Oh." Mo sat up straight at his side. "I have an idea. It seems like the people who're infected can't breathe, right? Or at least Hannah couldn't."

"Many of our other infected patients are showing the same signs," Ngalo said. "I am open to suggestions."

Mo paused. Swallowed. "Hannah's lungs changed. Right?"

"That's correct, yes. Or at least that was my initial impression on postmortem scanning. I haven't had time to perform an autopsy." Ngalo paused. "Who am I speaking to?"

"Maximo Rees. I'm a miner. I was just thinking. Why not try Mist?"

"Mist?" Armin heard Dr. Ngalo's frown as clearly as if he could see her. "Why? We're already using liquid therapies. Not that it's made any difference. I can't image what advantage Mist could offer."

Mo leaned forward, his features alive with the force of his ideas. "I know it sounds weird. I don't imagine the gas mix is exactly what you'd normally use since it's meant for use at depth. But if nothing else is working, why not?"

Pregnant silence hung from the com. Armin nudged Dr. Youssouf, because Mo was right. If it kept someone from dying, it was worth a try.

Youssouf cut him an irritated look, but did what he wanted. "I think he's got a point. I don't want to go into the whole thing right now, but we have pretty compelling evidence that—"

Mandala kicked her. Youssouf stopped to glare at the other woman. Mandala shook her head. Youssouf turned to Armin with eyebrows raised. He also shook his head. Dr. Ngalo hadn't seen what they'd seen. If they told her what they suspected about the contagion changing people into mermaids, even after what had happened to Hannah, she'd cut them off entirely.

Youssouf licked her lips. "We. Um. Have evidence that this contagion changes the physiology of the lungs. We're not sure how yet, but it seems as though infected people have a harder time extracting oxygen from the air. You saw that with Hannah. It might be worthwhile giving the Mist a try. It might be easier to keep them oxygenated with a specialized depth mix rather than the usual liquid therapies."

It was true, as far as it went. A mermaid's respiratory system was radically different from that of a human being. Armin wished they could share the full truth with their colleague on the surface, but it was simply too risky.

Ngalo sighed. "Well, I'm ready to try anything at this point. Hannah's the first one we've lost, but she won't be the last if we can't turn things around quickly. We'll be in touch. Ngalo out."

"Yeah. Out." The connection cut. Youssouf rested her forehead against the wall. "Damn it. God-fucking-damn it. I *hate* lying to people."

No one said a word. Mo and Armin clung to each other as if their physical closeness would save them.

It wouldn't. Armin had begun to wonder if anything would. But Mo's warmth, strength, and vitality reminded him that they were both still alive. It gave him *hope*. And that was worth more than all the theories, ideas, and half-formed plans in the world.

Youssouf lifted her head. Her chin jutted out. Stubborn. Unrelenting. It made Armin feel marginally better.

"All right. Let's plan out our next steps." She shuffled over to the desk and fell into the chair. "Personnel with growths in their brains are isolated from those without. With the rather glaring exception of you two." She shot a cutting look at Armin and Mo. "We're gonna have to make plans for getting everybody off this pod safely, as soon as reasonably possible. Or at least getting the uninfected upside."

Armin was about to ask when she thought that might be, when Jemima burst into the office. It was so unexpected, every eye in the place turned to look at her.

"Boss, we got a problem." She clutched the door frame, her whole body radiating tension. It was so unlike her, Armin's heartbeat rose into the uncomfortable zone. "Some of the people in the lockup got out. According to the infected who stayed put, the ones who escaped attacked one of the others so the guards would have to open the door. They're loose in the pod."

Mandala's eyes widened. "How many?"

"Five."

Five too many. Armin felt sick.

Youssouf rubbed her eyes. "How long ago?"

"Not sure." Jemima looked at the floor. "They killed the guards. Neither of them had time to sound an alarm. Last time I was there was half an hour ago. It could've been any time between then and now."

Armin's heart sank. With changed people running free in the pod, how many more would they infect? Worse, would they do it deliberately?

Before Dr. Youssouf could give Jemima any direction one way or another, a low rumble shook the floor, the walls, the ceiling. Close behind it came an ear-splitting klaxon.

Armin gripped Mo's hand with all his strength as the floor vibrated under his feet. "What's happening?"

"No idea. But I'll find out." Rubbing her neck with her free hand, Youssouf paced the tight space between the desk and the wall. "Ling. This is Youssouf. Come in."

Several seconds of silence followed. Jemima cursed under her breath.

"Ling here," the woman answered finally. "We're investigating the explosion."

Rashmi broke in, his voice terse and clipped. "Youssouf, looks like the explosion came from the aquarium. We're compromised."

"Shit." Youssouf sat on the edge of the desk, her face grim. "Did that section seal off?"

"Yeah. But, boss, Hawk commed me and said someone broke into the explosives storage. What if—"

The answer to his unspoken question came in a horrifying *boom*, closer this time, sending dust rattling down from the ceiling.

Jemima lunged over to a panel on the wall and stabbed at a couple of buttons. A readout popped up, and she swore. "It's the go-cart airlock. Goddamn it."

The other side of the pod. Someone was deliberately, methodically destroying BathyTech 3. Armin swallowed bile.

Mandala stood and aimed a grim stare at Youssouf. "All right. We need to do our best to get everyone off this pod before whoever has the explosives destroys the whole thing. How long do you think we have?"

Youssouf shook her head. "I have no idea. It depends on how many explosives they've set. We didn't store a lot here, but there's only six sections to the pod, and they've already blown holes in two of 'em. Those two are closed off now." She peered at the rest of the group, solemn and fearful. "If they close off the section with the sub bay, we're fucked."

"Then we're out of time. We need to leave, right now." Mo stood, his hand still wrapped firmly around Armin's as if he never intended to let go. "I say we take whoever's not changed and any of the changed people we can get without going out of our way, and head for the *Peregrine*."

Armin stared at him like he'd never seen him before. "How can we do that? We'd be dooming the rest of the changed to certain death."

"They'll die anyway if we can't fix them. Maybe it's kinder this way." Mo's mouth twisted into a grimace. "It's not good, Doc. I know that. But what choice do we have?"

"He's right." Youssouf rose just as another rumble shook the walls. She cursed. "Rashmi! You still there?"

"Yeah, boss." His voice was fainter this time, backed by shouting. "It was the cafeteria this time. I'm gathering survivors and making for the sub bay. Ling's getting the folks from the med bay isolation and the rest of the security team's gathering the rest of the lockup. Tell me y'all are coming."

"Yeah. We'll be there in a few. Out." Youssouf rose. "Well. I guess that's it. Let's move out. We'll pick up anybody we meet on the way."

Mandala headed for the vault where they'd stored the object that had started all this. "We can't leave it." She dug the special box, goggles, and isolation suit out of the cabinet while she talked. "We must continue to study this thing if we're to find the solution to this problem."

"Fine. But the sub's not waiting for you. I got a whole pod full of people to think about." Youssouf turned toward Jemima. "Jem, get your ass to the sub. You're in charge of making sure everybody's loaded in an orderly fashion."

"On it." Jemima shot an indecipherable look at Mo and Armin on her way out the door.

Youssouf pointed at Mo. "Rees, you go help get the infected but unchanged onto the sub. Have 'em keep their eyes down, just in case. Get shirts, sheets, whatever you can find to cover their eyes once they're loaded. Armin, you're with him."

"Right." Armin followed Mo to the door.

Mo stopped at the doorway, patting the pocket containing his switchblade. "And the changed?"

She sighed as though the weight of the universe rested on her back. He supposed it felt that way to her. "If they leave you alone, leave *them* alone. Bring them if they're willing to come along restrained. If not, if they try to stop you, shoot to kill."

Armin stared at her, horrified. "Wait, you can't just—"

"We don't have time to argue," Mandala interrupted. She strode forward with the isolation box hovering behind her, the filter goggles shoved up onto her forehead and her suit still on. "Even if everyone who's changed shows up at the sub without us having to go find them, it's too dangerous to take them all with us. Maybe we can find a way to isolate some of them, but certainly not all. They could infect everyone on board." She squeezed his arm. "Let's go."

They went.

Armin and Mo got the unchanged infected to the sub without incident, while Youssouf's evacuation announcement went out overhead. They were a silent and subdued group, obedient as well-trained puppies. Grateful not to be left behind, most likely. Armin couldn't blame them.

None of the changed showed up. Nor did they see any on their way to the sub. Armin couldn't help but feel that was deliberate on the part of the changed. If they were truly becoming mermaids, what did it matter to them? They would live happily underwater.

He hoped for their sakes he was right.

Jemima was counting in another group when they got to the sub bay. She waved a hand toward a bin to her left. "Towels. Everybody take one and put it over your head. I know it feels stupid, but until the docs know exactly what's what with this freaky-ass infection, this'll keep folks with brain growths from spreading 'em by accident."

Armin snagged two towels from the pile, draped one over his head, and handed the other one to Mo. "We never found Ashlyn. Not even a sign of her."

"I know. I'm sorry." Mo donned his towel, took Armin's uninjured hand and laced their fingers together. "I just can't figure what could've happened to her. Especially with . . . well, you know."

Grief and guilt closed Armin's throat. Oh yes, he knew. Ashlyn's empty, bloody eye sockets would stalk his nightmares as long as he drew breath.

Youssouf came striding through the bay, herding a few stragglers ahead of her. "All right, people. This is it. We're all here. Get your butts on board and let's move."

Mo and Armin filed into the sub behind the last few personnel. Youssouf and Jemima followed. Armin heard the sub door clang shut behind him as he settled into the padded bench beside Mo, in the section assigned to the infected. It wasn't possible to divide the single space into separate areas to keep infected and uninfected away from each other, but at least they could try to keep the two groups from mingling.

He listened to Amara and Jemima go through the emergency evacuation process and felt truly calm for the first time since Ashlyn had scooped out her own eyes, then vanished. Their course for the immediate future had been set. They had to follow it, for better or worse.

Armin found a certain serenity in having no other choice.

Still, the clock was ticking, and everyone on board knew it. The atmosphere was thick with tension. It eased a bit when the sub sank through the pool into the open ocean and began rising.

Armin rolled up his towel enough to see what was going on in the sub. Beside him, Mo did the same. What else were they to do during the long trip to the surface? Both of them knew better than to look anyone in the eye.

Youssouf stood beside the hatch and scanned the crowd of frightened refugees. "It takes about four hours to reach the surface. Plus we'll have another couple of hours to get to the *Peregrine*. I suggest everybody try to get some sleep. They're short-staffed and pretty much running under emergency operations upside, so I don't know who all might be ordered into service as medical or security personnel once we arrive."

On the other side of the sub, Mandala leaned forward in her seat. "You'll need help here. I can—"

"You can get some rest, like I said." Youssouf aimed a wry smile at her. "Don't worry too much, this sub mostly drives itself. I'm gonna com the ship and let 'em know what happened, then all I have to do is keep an eye on our course."

Mandala didn't seem entirely convinced, but she subsided.

Armin wasn't fooled. He'd seen her go three or four days on nothing but caffeine and catnaps during projects she considered important, and she had that gleam in her eye right now. Though what she found immediately intriguing about this sub, he had no clue. Personally, he intended to follow orders and sleep. At least he felt relatively safe here, in spite of the handful of infected persons—aside from himself and Mo—on board. None had shown the slightest symptoms.

Worn out mentally and physically, he rested his head on the cushioned seat back, shut his eyes, and let his mind drift. The last thing he heard before spiraling into sleep was Dr. Youssouf on the com. "Youssouf to *Peregrine*. Come in, *Peregrine* . . . Youssouf to *Peregrine* . . . Youssouf to *Peregrine* . . . Come in . . ."

Some time later, Mo woke from a dream of darkness, cold, and exhilaration with a cramp in his neck, his towel wadded on his lap, and his left hand asleep. He eased his hand out from under his thigh, wondering how he'd managed to sit on it.

He was shaking out the painful prickling when Youssouf spoke from the other side of the sub. She sounded aggravated and more than a little suspicious. Since Mo knew better than to interrupt, he kept quiet and listened.

Youssouf was talking to someone on her com. "She was sleeping last time I commed. That was more than five hours ago. This is a goddamn emergency, and I have yet to speak to the captain of your ship. Wake her up."

A pause followed. Mo would've sympathized with the anonymous *Peregrine* crew member, under different circumstances. Youssouf was scary when she was mad, even over a com. As it was, he was on Youssouf's side.

"I'm sorry," answered a male voice after a couple of seconds. "But the captain said—"

"I don't care what she said. You go and wake. Her. Up. *Now.*" Youssouf jabbed her finger into the air with each word, as if the poor underling were actually there.

The guy didn't pause this time. "I can't do that, ma'am. I'm sorry. Dr. Ngalo's orders."

Youssouf's eyes narrowed. "What?"

"We've lost the first mate and all the other officers, ma'am. Dr. Ngalo is acting second in command. She said Captain Escalano was to get as much sleep as she needed now, while she could. And the doctor is coordinating everything for your arrival. She said you're all welcome here for as long as you need to stay. Dr. Ngalo says to tell you she has everyone who's showing symptoms securely quarantined, and everyone else is confined to quarters. She thinks we've turned the corner and she's getting control of it now, thanks to your information."

Youssouf's mouth twisted into a bitter smile. "Glad to help out."

"You really have. The doctor said she's sorry she can't talk to you herself right now, but she's in the middle of something."

"Oh, don't worry. I'll speak to her when we get there. Youssouf out." She cut the com link, sat back, and frowned at the ceiling.

Mo watched her, feeling as uneasy as she looked. "What's going on up there?"

She started. "Shit, Rees. Didn't notice you were awake." Yawning, she leaned forward again. "Sorry, I didn't mean to wake you up."

She didn't seem concerned about his lack of towel, so he decided not to mention it. "You didn't. I was already awake." Beside Mo, Armin shifted in his sleep with a soft, lost sound. Mo eased an arm around his shoulders, and he settled against Mo's chest. "Something's wrong up there, isn't it?"

"You mean other than all the officers being sick, or dead?" Youssouf sighed. Deep worry lines bracketed her mouth and dug between her eyes. "Yeah, I think so. I've known Rita Escalano for thirty years. There's no way she would go take a fucking nap during a crisis like the one happening on the *Peregrine* right now. Something's way, way off."

Mo didn't like anything about what she was suggesting. "You think the guy you were talking to . . ."

"Jankow. Security."

"You think he was lying?"

She nodded. "I have no idea if he's acting on his own behalf, or someone else's, but yeah. I think he was lying, at least about why he wouldn't let me talk to the captain. In fact, there's no reason why they should have me talking to a security guy in the first place."

Shit. Mo glanced around the sub at the handful of survivors sleeping on benches or curled on the floor, some peacefully, some not so much. They'd all thought they'd be safe on the *Peregrine*. Ngalo would have had them believe she had everything under control. But Mo knew enough about how ships worked to realize Youssouf was right. No captain would sleep while her ship was in danger, even if it meant using drugs to stay awake for days on end. Which meant Captain Escalano must not be physically able to talk to them.

Mo couldn't think of any possibilities that weren't damned bad.

"Why would anybody lie about that?" Armin twitched and moaned in Mo's embrace, and Mo rubbed his thumb in circles on Armin's upper arm, as much to soothe his own unquiet thoughts as to ease Armin's restless sleep. "I mean, even if Captain Escalano's incapacitated, I can't think of any good reason for Jankow or Ngalo or anyone else not to just tell you."

"Neither can I." Youssouf peered at him with a hard, grim expression. "That's what makes me nervous about it."

Mo didn't have an answer for that. He and Youssouf gazed at each other across the cramped sub, and Mo saw his own fears reflected in her face.

When they reached the *Peregrine* about an hour later, the sub bay was open to the sea, which was weird all by itself. Even stranger was the fact that no one had come to meet them.

"I don't like it." Armin hadn't moved from Mo's side, his body still pressed against Mo's as if he felt safer there, with Mo's arm around him and his hand on Mo's thigh. He'd discarded the stupid, useless towel as well. "Someone should have been here."

"I suppose if they're short of personnel, that's to be expected." Dr. Jhut sounded doubtful, as if she didn't believe her own words.

Mo shook his head. "Do you really think they'd let a sub full of people who could make their problem worse dock without an armed escort?" Fingers exploring the contours of the muscles in Armin's shoulder, Mo glanced at Youssouf, who was trying to stare a hole in the hatch and hadn't said a word yet. "Boss? What do you think?"

"I think if Rita Escalano was still in command of this ship, she would've had guns down here even if she had come herself and she was the only one." Youssouf turned, planted her hands on her hips, and studied what was left of the BathyTech 3 crew. She looked older than Mo could ever remember. Old, tired, and afraid. But no less determined for any of that, which made Mo glad for the umpteenth time that she was BathyTech 3's leader. "All right. Here's what I'm doing. Rita has a security-coded personal com link. If I can remember the code, I'm gonna try to raise her. If I can talk to her, fine. We'll find out what's happening on this tub. If not, it's my opinion that we'll have to act as though this ship is under hostile control."

The rest of the group sat in breathless silence while she tried to raise the captain. It took her several tries to get the code right. After that, she tried at least a dozen times to get Captain Escalano to answer.

After twenty minutes or so she gave up, her face gray. "She's not answering."

Given the conversation with Jankow and what Youssouf already suspected, Mo knew that couldn't mean anything good. He clutched Armin closer, nuzzling his hair.

Armin turned his head enough to kiss Mo's lips. His wide black eyes and the tight clasp of his hand around Mo's spoke as clearly as if he'd shouted. *I'm here. We're together. It'll be all right.*

Mo didn't think it would, really. But as long as he had Armin with him, he couldn't help hoping. He smiled his thanks, and wove his fingers through Armin's.

The sub's general com squealed, making everyone jump. "Doctor Youssouf? This is Ngalo. Please come in."

Youssouf's gaze turned steely. "This is Youssouf. What's happened to Captain Escalano?"

A heavy sigh on the other end made the com crackle with static. "I'm sorry, Doctor, but she died about an hour ago."

Shock rippled through the cramped space. Mo glanced at Armin. He was frowning hard, his forehead creased. Thinking, always thinking. Using that impressive brain to untangle all the knots in this crazy problem. It made Mo feel warm inside, never mind that this was the wrong time and place for those sorts of feelings.

Youssouf shook her head, her movements sharp, angry. "No. I talked to a security guard just about that time. Jankow, his name was. He said she was sleeping." She didn't even try to hide her suspicion. Ngalo must've heard it in her voice.

"She was, then, as far as he knew. Now, she's dead. She began showing symptoms and deteriorated so quickly there was absolutely nothing we could do." She paused. It seemed intended to convey frustration. Only it didn't. Mo listened harder, curious. "I know it's very strange. But this contagion has escalated alarmingly fast here. I believe we have it under control now, but it's been difficult, and we've lost a lot of people." Another pause. It felt almost, but not quite, sincerely grief-stricken. Fascinated, Mo removed his arm from Armin's shoulders to lean forward with his elbows on his knees. "I'm going to activate the guide lights for you. They'll lead you from the sub bay to the med bay, since I have no one available to escort you. I'm very sorry about that, by the way. I'm sure the captain would've done things differently. But most of our personnel are either dead or ill, and those of us who are left are making do as best we can."

To Mo's relief, Youssouf's expression didn't soften one bit. It didn't come through when she spoke, though. "I'm sure you are, Doctor. Guide lights would be much appreciated. My crew and I will be at the med bay as soon as we can." She cut a thoughtful glance at the men and women huddled together with shoulders hunched and eyes downcast, some still with towels over their heads and others having thrown them aside. "In the meantime, is there anywhere I can safely isolate about a dozen people?"

She didn't explain any further, and Ngalo didn't ask. Which only made Mo more suspicious. "Of course. Our engineer's lounge should do for now. I'll put on red guide lights for your isolation patients and whoever you send with them, to lead them there. The lights to the med bay will be white." Another pause. This time, Mo swore it felt triumphant. "I'll give you green lights as well, to lead the rest of your personnel to the nearest crew quarters area. They can bed down and get some rest, if they like."

"That's fine. Thanks. We'll see you shortly. Youssouf out." She cut the connection and faced the crowd of terrified people, all of them murmuring among themselves. "Shut up and listen. None of you are leaving this sub. You got that?"

Everyone here had worked under Youssouf long enough to know better than to question her when she spoke in that iron tone. But these weren't ordinary circumstances, and a few—particularly among the uninfected—wanted off the sub more than they feared their boss's anger. They called out questions—*Why not? What's going on? Who's gonna stop us?*—until Youssouf stepped forward, unholstered her weapon, and bellowed, "Enough! Next asshole who speaks is gonna get shot in the fucking knee!"

Everyone went quiet so fast Mo's ears rang. He did his best not to smile. A lot of people wouldn't be able to get away with that. Youssouf did because her people knew she meant it.

She swept her glare around the space like a spotlight. "All right. If you idiots are done with your bitching, I'll explain the plan to you."

No one spoke. Mo glanced over his shoulder at Armin, who stared back as if looking through him.

Worried, Mo leaned back and touched his thigh. "Hey. You okay?"

Armin started. His eyes focused, and his lips curved into a distracted half smile. "Yes, fine. What—"

Youssouf cut him off. "I'm leading a small squad to the med bay. Jem, Ling, and Mo, you're with me. Armed, safeties off, eyes and ears open. You see someone changed, you shoot. Got it?" She didn't wait for any of them to answer, but pointed to Rashmi. "You're in charge of security here until we get back. Mandala's executive officer until then. You'll answer to her. Understand?"

Rashmi nodded. "Roger that."

"Good man." Youssouf looked around. "Understand this, people. I want every single one of you alive and well. That's why I want you *here*. I don't know what's happening on this ship. Maybe exactly what Dr. Ngalo said. Maybe not. If not, I want to be ready to run if we have to."

Youssouf stepped close to Mandala to speak low and urgently in her ear. Jem strolled over and handed Mo a Triton semiautomatic. "Your weapon, soldier."

"Thanks, Big Mama." He gave it a quick once-over. It was nice, one of the newer models. Life was looking up.

Until Armin peered at him with troubled eyes and downturned mouth, put his arms around him, and rested their foreheads together. "You're infected. You should be staying here with us." He didn't say *with me* out loud, but Mo heard it in his angry, wounded tone. "Why is she making you go?"

"Because I'll kill people if I have to. I won't hesitate. She needs that right now." Youssouf hadn't said, of course, but Mo knew. She didn't hire people without a full background check. "Don't worry. I'll be back. We all will."

The furrow that dug between Armin's eyes scolded Mo for promising things he might not be able to deliver. But Armin only nodded and squeezed Mo's hand, because he was human, and humans—weak, sentimental creatures that they were—needed something to hang on to. Even if it was a lie.

Though Mo fully intended to make good on his word.

He cupped Armin's face in his free hand and kissed him. "See you soon, Doc."

"Soon." Armin dropped his arms and rose to his feet. "Be careful."

"Always." With one last, lingering look at Armin, Mo pointed his weapon at the ceiling and joined Youssouf beside the sub's exit. "I'm ready when you are, boss."

"All right, then. Let's move out." Youssouf drew her weapon. "Follow the white lights, boys and girls."

Jem took point without being asked. She opened the hatch, swept her gaze and her gun both in a wide arch around the sub bay, and barked, "Clear." She moved into the bay and jogged toward the corridor lined with tiny white lights along the floor.

The rest of the group followed, with Ling bringing up the rear.

Mo cast a backward glance as he crossed the bay. Armin was watching him, dark eyes focused somewhere in another universe. Then Rashmi shut the door, putting a slab of thick gray metal between Mo and the man who'd become uncomfortably important to him.

It felt like the worst sort of metaphor.

Ignoring the unfocused dread prodding at the back of his brain, Mo turned his attention to the job at hand.

No sooner had the hatch shut behind Mo and the rest of the group than Ashlyn's voice crept into Armin's head like a thief. *He's gone, Doctor. Gone. He's not coming back. He's going to die. They're going to rip his organs from him and feast on them. They're going to take his eyes, those beautiful eyes, and eat them, suck out the juice like grapes.*

Armin squashed the mental images that sprung up in spite of his best efforts not to listen. It wasn't Ashlyn whispering to him anyway. Couldn't possibly be Ashlyn, never mind how the voice sounded in his mind. She'd always been standoffish, but she'd never been cruel.

Between his ears, the thing pretending to be Dr. Ashlyn Timms laughed at him. *You've no idea what plans we have, my friend. Such great plans. We will change this little world of yours.*

A vision of vast black seas exploded behind Armin's eyes—oceans spanning entire worlds, deep and crushing, cold as space. In that endless void swam things whose shape and substance defied description, whose thoughts cut like razor wire and left his psyche slashed and bleeding.

The vision vanished in the space of a heartbeat, but it took no longer than that to imprint on Armin's soul. He sat there shaking inside, stunned to the marrow. Was this what they were faced with?

Yes, my friend. Our universe is so much richer than this one. So much wider, and darker. When you are one of us, you will see.

If it weren't for the events of the past ten days, he'd have believed himself delusional. As it was, he feared something far worse. Was this the beginning of the change? Would the world look different to him when his eyes began to glow? Would he develop a taste for blood and death when his teeth became wicked spikes?

Would the desire to learn all the secrets the voice in his head promised—the desire he kept shoving aside, because it felt so wrong—finally overcome his fear?

He rubbed his arms. God, he was cold. Funny, how BathyTech 3 had never seemed as dank and chilly as this ridiculous submersible did even though the sub currently sat on the ocean's surface, during the middle of spring, not far from the equator.

"Armin? Armin. Are you all right?"

It took him a moment to realize this voice was Mandala, speaking to him in the more conventional manner, in the here and now. He forced a smile. "Yes, I'm fine. Just thinking."

"Hm. If you say so." She took the seat beside him. "I don't like one bit of this. I wish we were well on our way to land. But we must take care of things here first. Otherwise it's all useless, really."

"Yes. I suppose it is." Armin imagined the mermaid contagion spreading beyond the *Peregrine*, to the South American mainland and beyond. Millions could die.

Unless it evolved. Unless it found a way to produce mermaids who could live out of the water.

In that scenario, Armin foresaw the end of everything.

We will change this little world of yours.

He lowered his voice to a whisper. "I'm hearing things, Mandala. I hear Ashlyn in my head."

Mandala, consummate scientist that she was, studied him with a keen eye and a neutral expression. "Is that your only symptom?"

Who do you think we are, Doctor?

Because he had the feeling the two voices weren't actually different, he answered, "So far, yes."

"And what has she said?"

He raised an eyebrow at his colleague and friend. "*She* didn't say anything. It must be my imagination."

"I suppose." Her eyes had a thoughtful shine.

"You suppose?"

She sighed. "Armin. When you hear the voice you identify as Ashlyn, what does that voice say?"

He leaned back in his chair and stared at the ceiling. "That we're foolish to believe we're going to get out of this alive. That the mermaids have great plans for the world. That . . ." He breathed in. Out. He sounded weak and shaky, and he hated it. "That they are going to kill Mo and feast on his organs."

Silence fell. Around them, their fellow submersible prisoners talked in low, fearful voices. To Armin, they sounded like the damned praying for redemption from a false god.

He'd begun to believe she wasn't going to answer by the time she spoke up. "I'm no psychiatrist. But to me, this doesn't sound as if you're changing. It sounds like someone who's been through a great deal and is suffering a severe stress reaction, in which your subconscious is reciting your worst fears."

Armin smiled. "I'm not sure I believe that. But I choose to accept it because I like it much better than the alternative."

"Good." Mandala cut him a sly sidelong grin. "Believe everything I say. I'm smarter than you."

This time, Armin laughed out loud. "That you are." He grasped her hand. "Thank you."

"Anytime."

A brain like hers would taste so sweeeeeeet, breathed Ashlyn in his mind. *If only she accepted. But a seed cannot grow in barren soil.*

He held on to Mandala's hand. He didn't know what that meant. But if the mermaids thought they were getting Mandala—or Mo, or anyone else he cared about—they were wrong. He'd stop them if it was the last thing he did.

I was here, you know, the impossible Ashlyn taunted. *I hid right here in this sub, after I left medical. I thought I'd be safe here. But I wasn't. They had me anyway. They had me all along, from the moment I saw the egg.*

Armin's breath froze. The egg? God, that must be . . .

Oh yes, yes indeed. I was right, you see. The egg holds the seeds. Seeds of darkest light. They enter through the doorways of the eyes, and grow. Ashlyn sighed in his mind, a long, gurgling, horrific sound. *The choice was already there. Death or change. There is no other way, once the seed takes root.*

Christ. Armin clung to Mandala's hand like a lifeline. She was right. This was nothing but his guilt talking. He blamed himself for what happened to Ashlyn, and this was the punishment his subconscious mind devised for him.

It *must* be. The alternative was too terrible to bear.

Ashlyn's new voice laughed at him, a rough, vicious rasp with all the humanity hollowed out of it. *Poor, deluded Armin. We'll have you too. You're ours already. You just haven't accepted it yet. But you will.*

A shriek from across the sub startled Ashlyn out of Armin's head. Grateful, he blinked and focused on the commotion.

Mandala was already over there, her arm around a young man who looked one more scare away from catatonia. The woman beside him was talking fast, one hand gesturing wildly, the other holding something Armin couldn't quite see.

He stood. Took a few steps forward. And turned away, shaking his head, when he saw the soiled gauze bandages dangling from the woman's fingers.

It couldn't be. It simply. Could. Not. Be.

He sat down again and stared at the wall directly ahead of him, muttering *no no no no no* under his breath. If he didn't see, didn't hear, then maybe reality would change.

Don't fight it, Armin. Let us in. You can't even imagine what you'll learn once you change.

Ashlyn's plea was gentle this time, soft and sweet as a lover's. It made her easier to resist. Armin hardened his soul against her, against the change, and felt her anger pummel the primitive centers of his brain.

From the corner of his eye, he saw Mandala approaching him, her mouth downturned and her face troubled. Fear closed around his throat like a noose. He didn't want to hear about the concrete proof that Ashlyn had hidden in this sub. That she'd removed her bandages at some point, then vanished all over again. If his psychosis was clairvoyant, he'd rather not know.

Before she reached him, a loud *clang* hit the sub's hatch. The handle moved and started to turn.

Everyone stilled. Every voice went quiet. Not only was it too early for Youssouf and the others to be back, but they would have commed first, or at least announced their presence from the outside. In fact, only those who meant harm would try to come in without announcing themselves first.

Rashmi, stationed at the hatch, engaged the lock, then aimed his weapon at it. "Doc?"

"Don't open it," she said. "Not until we know it's our people."

Armin felt the tension level in the sub diminish a bit. Mandala had never acted as a captain, but she possessed a calm authority that tended to put people at ease.

Mandala approached the hatch, shoulders straight and head high. She hit the com link to the outside. "This is Dr. Mandala Jhut, acting captain of this submersible. Announce yourself, please. What is your name and your intention?"

Silence. No one spoke, to answer Mandala's question or otherwise.

After several long minutes, Mandala turned away. "Well. Whoever it was, it seems as though they've gone. Perhaps they thought the sub was empty, and they'd loot it for supplies." She shook her head. "Despicable behavior. I shall certainly report it when we reach civilization."

The handle rattled again. Rashmi aimed his weapon. The hatch vibrated under two hard blows, then flew entirely off its hinges and landed on him. The thick metal slab flung his hands to either side, open and twitching. His gun clattered harmlessly away. Blood and worse things leaked in sluggish rivulets across the sub's floor, staining the shoes of those too shocked to move their feet.

In the stunned quiet following Rashmi's death, Armin looked up, into the sub's open hatchway, to see what had come for them.

Peregrine's passageways looked like those on BathyTech 3. The lights flickered yellow, dim and sickly, casting no shadows and illuminating nothing. The ladders weren't any better, most of them either barely lit or pitch-dark.

Mo couldn't think of a worse omen. Not that he believed in that sort of shit.

Youssouf stopped them a few meters short of the med bay. "Okay, people. I don't know what's in there, but I'm betting it's not good. Be ready for anything. Including exactly what Dr. Ngalo said. Got it?"

Affirmatives all around. Mo drew a deep breath and smelled blood. He made sure the safety on his weapon was off.

They approached the med bay in an armed huddle. Youssouf hit the outside com. "Youssouf to Ngalo. We're outside. Let us in."

Nothing. Mo aimed from the hip, ready to hit the first threatening thing he saw between Youssouf and Jem. He felt better when he saw Jem doing the same thing.

Mo was ready to say fuck it, take the sub to the mainland, and appeal to the Chilean government to make the damn ship disappear when the doctor finally answered. "Ngalo here. Thank God you're here. Please come in."

The monitor beside the hatch went from yellow to green. Youssouf glanced behind her—surveying the troops—then swung open the hatch.

Mo caught a glimpse of shining blue-black eyes and rapier teeth before Jem's shot caught what used to be Doctor Ngalo smack between the eyes.

The changed doctor fell to the floor, dead. Youssouf stepped around her and entered to the left. The rest of the group fanned out across the med bay bulkheads like they'd been soldiering together forever, weapons live and aimed, gazes scanning for more poor bastards like Ngalo.

"That *was* Ngalo, right?" Ling edged to the desk and around to the other side. "Shit. Three dead. Eviscerated. And their *eyes* are gone, what the *fuck*, man?"

Mo kept his weapon up and his attention on the apparently empty space ahead while Youssouf knelt to check the one Jem had killed. "It's her, all right. Still got her badge on." She stood, gun aimed at the ceiling. "I knew this stunk to high heaven. Goddamn it."

"Mo. Ling. Check the rest of the bay." Jem jerked her chin toward the half-closed curtains on the other side of the desk. "If there's survivors, we need to take care of them, one way or another. Understand?"

They nodded in tandem. Mo liked having Ling with him. He knew they were on the same page. They'd both lived through a lot. They didn't have to discuss it to know who to protect, and who to kill.

As it turned out, that wasn't an issue. Jem had already shot the only living being left in the med bay. Everyone else was dead—some cleanly, some not so much. Which accounted for the stench of blood Mo had picked up from outside the med bay.

"No survivors," Ling reported after their sweep. "Looks like one or two might be missing. But there's nothing alive in here other than us."

"Missing." Youssouf turned in a slow circle, studying the floor, the ceiling, the cabinets, every spot that might hide a person. "You checked everywhere?"

"Every possible spot, yeah." Mo followed her gaze to a small medication refrigerator. "Even that. No one's there. Not that anybody could hide in there and live."

She didn't snap at him, or even give him one of her *shut the fuck up* looks, which told him how serious their situation must be right now. "Okay, here's the plan. I'm going down to the engine room. I'll destroy the cooling system, and let the core go critical. The rest of you, go straight back to the sub. I'll give you as long as I can, but I can't promise anything. You'll need to be quick. Make for the mainland. BathyTech has a research installation in Chile. You know the place, Jem?"

To Mo's surprise, she nodded. "I know it."

"Good. Report everything that's happened to BathyTech central command while you're on the sub, then head straight for the research installation. Command'll get the Chilean government involved, if necessary."

Mo watched her with an unexpectedly strong pang of sadness. "What about you?"

"I'll make for the lifeboats." Youssouf gave him a crooked smile. "If I get to 'em in time, maybe I'll see you in the mountains."

"I'm bringing up guide lights to the engine room." Jem did something at one of the computer terminals. "Hope you like blue."

"Right now, blue's my favorite color." Youssouf crossed to the hatch. Mo covered her while she opened it. The passageway outside was as silent and empty as before. Youssouf stepped through. The others followed. "If there's a problem with the sub, com me. I'll com you if I think there's anything you need to know urgently. Use text codes, not voices. Otherwise, it's complete radio silence. Got it?"

"Got it." Jem shut the hatch. "Be careful."

"You too." Youssouf positioned her weapon and strode along the passage, following the blue lights.

Mo turned and followed Jem back the way they'd come. They'd traveled a couple of eerily silent passageways and slid down one dark ladder before Mo realized that none of them had even questioned the idea of destroying a ship full of people without regard to who was changed and who wasn't. He wondered what that said about him. About all of them.

As they descended the second ladder from dimness into near-blackness, the skin pebbled on the back of Mo's neck. He swept up his weapon, searching for a target.

He didn't need to speak. Jem and Ling, evidently feeling the same gut-level warning he did, had their weapons up. The three of them stood back to back to back, peering into the dark. Waiting.

Mo felt the attackers coming before he saw them. A wave of destructive purpose slammed into his mind with tsunami force. He staggered, shook himself, and recovered in time to shoot the first shining-eyed, white-skinned, needle-toothed face that emerged from the gloom. It splattered red and gray on the walls and floor. The body—male, wearing an engineer's uniform—collapsed.

More followed, snarling with their viperfish teeth, grasping for Mo, Jem, and Ling with long, thin, jointless fingers as flexible as tentacles. Their eyes glowed blue, purple, and black. Mo fired again and again and again, along with Jem and Ling.

For a little while, the passageway rang with weapons fire. Then the changed finally stopped coming, and the quiet seemed deeper than before.

Jem counted the bodies sprawled in a soup of blood, brains, and bits of skull. "Seventeen. Jesus fucking Christ."

"Yeah, well, these creeps're no match for a good piece." Ling patted her Triton.

Mo had his doubts about that. Sure, they died when you shot them. But he couldn't shake the feeling that these guys hadn't been trying to kill them. Not that he was anxious to find out what would've been done to them if they'd been caught.

Jem cast an anxious glance around them. "We need to get going. All the gunfire's bound to draw more of those fuckers."

She didn't need to argue her case. The three of them moved out.

They ran into two more groups of the changed—five and three—before reaching the sub bay. Just like the first group, the smaller ones seemed intent on *catching* them rather than killing them. Neither succeeded, though one of the group of five managed to nip Ling's arm before he died.

"Why weren't they trying to kill us?" Ling wondered as they approached the sub bay. "It doesn't make any sense."

"None of this shit makes any sense. Stop trying to understand it and just deal with what comes up." Jem stopped at the end of the passageway and peered into the bay. "Oh. Fuck."

Mo's pulse shot up. He sidled up next to Jem and leaned over to look.

His stomach dropped into his feet. Bodies lay scattered over the sub bay floor, some ripped open, others slashed neatly across the throat. Blood splattered the floor, the walls, even the ceiling.

The sub was gone.

CHAPTER 17

Mo heard Jem talking. Giving orders. Laying out a plan for dealing with this latest disaster.

He ignored her and strode into the bay, his weapon ready to fire at anything alive that wasn't one of their people. "Armin? Where are you?"

He picked his way through the dead without looking at their faces. His heart thudded fast enough to make him sick. Fuck Jem's plans. He'd just appointed himself the finder of survivors.

"Armin!" he called again, louder this time. "Answer me!" He crossed the bay. Aimed his piece at a locker and opened it. Moved on when he found only dive gear. "Armin, damn it—"

"Mr. Rees, over here."

Dr. Jhut's voice hit him like a million volts. He whirled and jogged to a passageway on the other side, where she stood outlined in feverish-orange light. "Jem! Dr. Jhut's alive. Over here."

She gave him a thumbs-up and tapped on her wrist com. Mo hoped she was messaging Youssouf.

He reached Dr. Jhut and looked around. "Are you okay? Where's Armin?"

"I'm fine. Just a bit bruised. Armin's in there." She gestured to a vent in the bulkhead. "He and I were hiding there with a few others. There aren't many of us left. They took most of our people, and killed the rest."

Mo wanted to shout with relief that Armin was safe. But it seemed they all had bigger things to worry about. "Who did?"

"Changed people. I assume they were ship's crew, once. But they were far gone." She rubbed her arms. The horror of what had happened was etched into the new lines in her face. "They broke into the sub. Literally knocked the hatch loose. It landed on Rashmi and killed him."

"Oh damn." That hurt. Rashmi had been a good miner, a good friend, and a good person. He hadn't deserved to die that way, squashed like a fucking bug.

"I know. I'm sorry." She touched his arm in sympathy. "After that, they herded some of us out into the bay and started killing. Armin was kept in the sub, but he rushed out, grabbed me and the man next to me, and simply ran for it. I don't think they expected it, honestly, because there was sheer pandemonium for a while. Several others were able to escape from the sub and from the ranks of those they were attempting to kill. Once it became apparent that we couldn't rescue anyone else, we hid in the ventilation duct. I suppose they weren't keen on trying to reclaim any of us because they simply shot the ones they wanted dead, dragged the others into the sub, and left."

Ling aimed a fierce glare at the slice of empty ocean visible through the open bay doors, as if she could bring back their people with the power of her mind. "What the hell do they want with the sub?"

Dr. Jhut shook her head. "I have no idea. But I couldn't help noticing that the ones they killed or attempted to kill were all uninfected, and the ones they took all had the growths."

They kept Armin in the sub. He's only safe now because he ran. The nearness of Armin's escape made Mo weak in the knees. He knew he should feel worse about so many others being taken or killed, but all he could think was, *Thank God Armin's safe.* He didn't like where his mind went when he thought about why the changed would want to take only those who had the growths.

Jem walked up, her weapon aimed at the ceiling and her gaze roaming. "Okay, Youssouf's sabotaging the cooling system now. She's gonna try to meet us at the lifeboats, but she said don't wait for her under any circumstances. She doesn't want anybody still here when the ship blows." She leaned down to squint into the vent shaft. "C'mon out, folks. We all have to take a walk now."

A few scared, dirty, blood-spotted refugees crawled out of the vent shaft. Dr. Jhut soothed them and helped Jem gather them into an easily defensible huddle. Mo frowned. Where was Armin?

He emerged after the others and stood studying them as if they were a separate breed. Worried, Mo touched his dust-smeared cheek. "Hey. You okay?" He took Armin's elbow and got him moving when Jem gave him the stink eye.

Armin looked startled, as if he hadn't seen Mo approach. He let Mo lead him like a child. "Oh. Yes, I'm fine." His eyes widened, finally focusing on Mo. "My God, what happened? Are you hurt?"

"Not even a little. But you should see the other guys." Mo grinned.

Armin stared, obviously not finding Mo's lame little joke at all funny. "They were going to take me."

He said it like he was discussing a new breed of bacteria, not his own attempted kidnapping. That worried Mo a lot. Once a person checked out emotionally, their risk of checking out physically went way up. Mo had seen it happen more than once. He didn't want it to happen to Armin.

Luckily, Jem let him get away with acting as rear guard so he could keep an eye on Armin. Ling walked the middle, while Jem took point. Dr. Jhut worked her way through the ranks as they went, easing everyone's fears as much as possible, keeping them moving along and especially keeping them quiet. Mo wasn't convinced silence would help them any, but it couldn't hurt. At least they'd be able to hear any potential attackers coming. He hoped.

Dr. Jhut also dropped back every few minutes to check on Armin, for which Mo was grateful. He wasn't sure what was wrong with Armin, but something was definitely not right. And the more Mo watched him, the more it became clear—to Mo, at least—that this was no simple posttraumatic reaction. It was something else. Something deeper. More sinister. Meaning Mo wasn't letting Armin out of his sight for one minute until he figured out what was broken, and fixed it.

As their group neared the lifeboats, the changed rushed them from side passageways in ones and twos. Jem, Ling, and Mo shot them without any trouble. To Mo, the whole thing felt like a performance. Like the changed were attacking this time not to capture or kill, but because it was expected.

"I don't like it." He filed on deck behind Armin and Dr. Jhut. "What've they got up their sleeves?"

Dr. Jhut pursed her lips. "Perhaps they already have what they wanted and they were simply doing what they could to keep us from escaping."

"Yeah, well, they did a piss-poor job of it." Mo turned to face the passageway they'd just exited while Jem and Ling helped the refugees into one of the lifeboats. "They had to know that if they hit us one or two at a time, they'd just get killed. So what the fuck?"

"They have plans." Armin's voice was soft and slow, with a singsongy rhythm that raised goose bumps up and down Mo's arms. "You can't stop them. But they don't want you. Not yet."

What he said made Mo feel cold all over. Not because Armin sounded unhinged, but because, for reasons Mo couldn't pinpoint, he didn't. His words rang true.

Mo helped Dr. Jhut into the boat, then Armin. He glanced around the deck before climbing in himself. "I don't see Youssouf anywhere. Jem? Have you heard from her?"

Jem shook her head. "Haven't heard, haven't seen any sign of her." Her fingers clenched her piece and released, clenched and released, so hard her knuckles paled each time. "I commed her just now. Sent her the radio silence code for mission accomplished. She didn't answer."

So that was that, then. Dr. Youssouf's life had ended here, on a dead ship, saving her people from something none of them really understood. He wanted to scream for everyone they'd lost, for the unfairness of it all. He wanted to find those half-human fuckers and tear them all apart with his bare hands. But he couldn't. All he could do was run, protect what was left of the BT3 crew, and hope he lived to take revenge one day.

With everyone on board, Youssouf likely dead, and the ship's engine hopefully on a course for nuclear meltdown soon, there was nothing to do but leave. Jem ordered everyone to secure themselves, Ling unlocked the boat, and it fell into the ocean with a bone-rattling thump.

Ling took the helm and set a course for the coordinates Jem gave her on the South American coast. Mo had never been to BathyTech's rumored research facility in the wilds of Chile's coastal mountains, but he was relieved to be going there. Isolated—and preferably heavily guarded—was exactly what they needed.

They'd been riding the heavy Pacific swell for nearly two hours when a *whump* almost below the range of hearing hit Mo's eardrums. Several minutes later, their lifeboat rose on a tremendous wave. Then another, and another.

No one said anything, but they knew it meant Youssouf had succeeded in her mission and the *Peregrine* was gone, along with anyone left on board.

The boat's small population seemed to take a collective breath. Mo saw the same thought in every suddenly hopeful face—*It's over. Nothing left to hurt us now.* All around him, the handful of survivors from BathyTech 3 settled down to rest.

Because he hadn't shaken the sense of something lurking around a corner, he sat with his Triton across his knees and guarded Armin's restless sleep.

In Armin's dreams, he cut through the deepest, coldest water as if it were a warm summer afternoon. The tarry blackness became a universe of gauzy watercolor, blues and purples and softest grays. He swam, his body sleek and powerful, his eyes finding each particle of light with marvelous efficiency. He snagged an octopus with his teeth. Its intelligence exploded into his mind as its sweet, rich blood poured down his throat. God, how had he never known this before?

You can have this for always. This, and so much more. More than you ever imagined. Soon now. We're coming for you, Armin. We're coming.

Ahead, a crack opened in the seafloor. Shadow poured out like a negative of sunlight. It called to Armin with a promise of knowledge—dark things, hidden things, all the answers to all the questions mankind had feared to ask since the beginning of time. Armin swam toward it. To dive into it, give himself to it, learn all that he'd never realized he needed to know.

He was close now, close enough to look into the void and see . . .

The world shook, the darkness of knowledge vanished, and he was back in his human body, sitting on a utilitarian bench, blinking in the blue-tinted dimness of the *Peregrine*'s lifeboat. Confusion gave way to a curious blend of disappointment and profound relief.

He looked up at Mo, who stood beside him with weapon drawn, his entire body tight and alert. "Mo? What's happening?"

"Kevin Bhagat just went batshit and jumped overboard." Mo glanced sideways at Armin with wide eyes full of the fire and steel Armin so admired. "He was changing. I saw it. We all did."

The *I know you know what's happening, now tell me* remained unvoiced, but Armin heard it nonetheless. Smiling, he stroked the hard, graceful line of Mo's thigh. "I'm going to miss you."

The considerable force of Mo's full attention zeroed in on Armin. Dropping his weapon, Mo sat beside Armin and grasped his shoulders. "No, you're not. Because I'm going to be right here with you. I'm not going anywhere. And I'm not letting you out of my sight." His eyes narrowed, his keen gaze drilling through flesh and bone into Armin's core. "Whatever you think they're gonna do to you, they're not. I won't let them."

My hero. Armin wanted to laugh at himself, but his heart hurt too much.

Across the boat, a woman screamed. Everyone scrambled over one another to get away from the other woman—only a girl, really, she couldn't have been older than twenty-two—suddenly lunging at everyone in sight. Her long, waving fingers and shining cobalt eyes told the tale. Jem put a bullet in her head.

Armin felt his fate approaching. Too fast, too fast.

His pulse hammering in his ears, he splayed his hands on Mo's cheeks and captured his mouth in a kiss that said everything he hadn't put into words and now never would, because he was out of time.

Ten days. Such a short time to learn to love someone. Yet there it was. He hoped Mo would understand, eventually.

Mo made a small, helpless sound in his throat. His arms went around Armin's waist and he kissed him as if he knew it would be the last time.

Armin's chest tightened. He liked to think that if things were different, they would have been happy together.

When they drew apart, Armin peered into Mo's eyes—those beautiful, dark eyes he wished he could look into forever—and smiled. "We'll see each other again. I promise. And then you can decide for yourself. Because you *will* have to decide, eventually. You know that."

Mo's features twisted with a pain Armin understood perfectly. "Death or change. No, Armin, don't."

But it was already too late. Armin had felt her coming. Now she was here.

The heavy reinforced canvas arching over the wooden lifeboat, protecting them from the sun, ripped like paper. He didn't resist when the cold, inhuman fingers snaked through behind him, wrapped around his upper arms, and dragged him up, through the hole in the canvas, over the side and into the sea.

He heard Mo scream, the sound muffled by the growing weight of the ocean as strong mermaid arms dragged him down, down, down. *Armin*, Mo howled, like his world was ending. *Armin, fuck, come back, bring him back.* The water distorted Mo's face into a rictus of agony, his eyes and mouth empty black holes. He struggled against the vague shapes holding him back.

Armin was grateful to the others in the boat—probably Jemima and Mandala—because he knew that without them, Mo would be over the edge and following him into the depths. Trying to save him, even if it meant his own death. And it would. He wasn't ready yet. They would kill him.

For a moment, Armin watched Mo's silhouette recede and allowed himself to mourn what they would never have. When he could no longer see even the shape of the boat on the surface, he turned away at last. He set his face to the deep and the white-skinned, eyeless thing who'd forced him to choose between death and this strange new form.

It all happened so damned fast. One second Armin was sitting there beside him, saying things Mo wished like hell he didn't understand, black eyes full of a sadness and resignation that shook Mo to his bones. Then the mermaid tore through the canvas and took Armin into the sea. And all of Mo's screaming and cursing and pleading hadn't stopped it.

He hadn't protected Armin at all. He hadn't saved him. Armin was gone.

Gone.

Mo felt like he'd been scraped hollow. He knew they still had to reach the Chile coast. That they still had work to do. A contagion to understand. A cure to find.

Right now, he didn't care. All he wanted was to jump into the cold Pacific water and follow Armin down.

He would have, if Jem, Dr. Jhut and a few others hadn't stopped him.

They'd *stopped* him. Kept him from taking Armin back from the monster who'd stolen him.

"Why?" His voice came out rough and cracked, his vocal cords ruined from first screaming Armin's name over and over, then simply screaming because he couldn't stop. "I could've saved him. Why'd you stop me?"

Dr. Jhut wouldn't look at him. Silent tears rolled down her cheeks. He didn't know if that made him angrier, or if he just felt worse. She'd known Armin a long time. Letting him go must've been awful for her. So then, *why?*

Jem sat next to him, her shoulder pressed against his arm. "You know why."

His breath ran out like he'd been kicked in the chest. He closed his eyes and hunched forward, resting his forehead on his hands. Yeah, he knew. Armin's choice had been change, not death. He wondered if the thing Armin had become was still *Armin* inside. If he would even recognize Mo. If he'd keep that last promise to come back. To see Mo again.

The soul-deep ache that had burrowed deep into Mo's gut when Armin went purple-eyed and sharp-toothed into the sea tore at his insides with renewed vigor. He squeezed his eyes shut tight and wondered if he'd ever feel normal again.

The boat sailed on, making its way toward the Chile coast. No one spoke. Still in shock, Mo figured. When he couldn't stand the closed-off interior of the lifeboat any longer, he straightened up, stood, and walked out into the open prow. No one stopped him, though Jem followed. Ready to keep him from jumping overboard, probably.

He cracked a tiny smile. It was a little late for that.

He went to the edge and squinted out across the ocean. A storm in the distance formed a dark-gray shadow on the horizon. To him, it looked like his Armin-less future.

We'll see each other again, Armin's memory told him. *I promise.*

He'd promised. Why had he done that?

I'm going to miss you.

The suspicion Mo had felt before and pushed away came roaring back.

We'll see each other again. I promise.

"He knew," Mo whispered into the salty breeze.

Armin had known this was going to happen. And he'd tried to tell Mo as best he could that it wasn't the end.

Maybe he ought to wish Armin was dead instead of changed. But he didn't. He found a strange, driving hope in knowing Armin still lived. Somehow, somewhere, even if he was never able to keep his promise.

You can decide for yourself.

Death or change. Your decision.

Yes. His decision. He could wait.

Jem approached him, cautiously, her concern stamped all over her face. "Hey. I'm sorry, Mo. I know you two . . ." She made a vague gesture with the hand not holding her weapon. "Well. Anyway. I'm sorry. You okay?"

He peered at the ominous blackness of the approaching storm. Maybe they'd all drown in the resulting high seas. More likely, they'd come through it, to fight through another day, and another, and another. It might not be easy, but nothing worthwhile ever was.

"Don't worry," he said. "I'll be fine."

CHAPTER 18

The machine chimed. Mo waited for the couch to roll out of the scanner—state of the art, courtesy of the Chilean government, like all the equipment at BathyTech's facility here in the Chile mountains—then hopped down onto the floor. He raised his eyebrows at Mandala, operating the controls from behind a lead-infused window. "Well?"

She shook her head and thumbed on the intercom. "It's still there. Just as robust as ever."

Mo sighed and hung his head to hide his relief. After nine months, the growth in his head hadn't shrunk even a millimeter. All the other infected that hadn't eventually changed—seven; admittedly not much of a sample, but still—had shown shrinkage in their brain growths by the three-month mark. Some shrank faster, some slower. Most were entirely gone by now. His was the only one still completely unchanged even though he himself hadn't changed either.

It drove Mandala batty, mostly because it threw a monkey wrench in her working theory that the change required not only knowledge and acceptance of the oncoming change, but darkness and the pressure of the deepest ocean to complete itself safely. She'd also theorized that sunlight and pressures of sea level or less killed the growths if no signs of change showed up within a certain amount of time. The first two of their group who'd changed had died, before Mandala started putting them on Mist and keeping them in a pressure chamber like the ones used to treat the bends. It worked, at first. In the end, though, nothing would do but releasing them into the ocean. She did it, because she disliked murdering test subjects more than she disliked having more mermaids out there.

Mo, as per his lifelong pattern, had to be the one to screw things up.

Not that it mattered to him. He was only biding his time here. Helping Mandala while he waited for the only thing that mattered to him.

He tried to look contrite. "Sorry. I swear I don't mean to be a problem."

She laughed, soft and affectionate. "Come on through. Let's discuss it."

He didn't much want to. But he owed her that much. She'd cut herself off from family, friends, and her former life to solve this problem. The least he could do was discuss his unique case with her when she asked.

Not that it did much good, if he wasn't entirely honest.

She wouldn't understand, said the Armin-voice he'd heard in his head a lot in the past few weeks. *She's brilliant, and her theory is correct. But you can't tell her. She would try to stop you.*

As usual, hearing Armin talk to him again soothed him. Made him feel warm and safe. Made him sure he was doing the right thing by keeping his silence and waiting.

He pulled on his shirt and crossed into the dim little room carved out of the rock of the mountainside, where Mandala worked the controls of the brain scanner. "So. What's up, Doc?"

She ignored him. He hadn't been able to get so much as a sharp look out of her with his silly jokes for ages. "You *will* inform me immediately if you start to exhibit symptoms, correct?"

"You know I will." Not true. "The last thing I want is to turn into one of those fucking monsters that took Armin. I'd rather be dead."

Which wasn't true or untrue, exactly. It didn't matter to him. All that mattered—all he'd thought about for nine long, lonely months—was Armin.

"Hm." She tapped her chin with her index finger. "I want to talk about Armin for a moment."

Coming so hard on the heels of his own thoughts, her words threw Mo off guard. His heart thudded hard. "Why?"

"Because I need to confirm some things, and you always evade these questions." She swiveled her chair to stare straight into his eyes. "I know this is difficult for you. I know how you felt about him. It's difficult for me too. He was my friend for many years. But Mo, if I'm ever to stop this thing, I need you to help me. Will you do that?"

Shame heated Mo's cheeks. They'd been monitoring communications, and they knew the mermaid contagion had spread, in spite of everything. While they'd been battling the changed on the *Peregrine* and making their way to Chile where they all still hid from the world, another scientific expedition had recovered the object they'd spotted in the Mariana Trench while monitoring the tagged mermaid, and the whole thing had played out again.

Not that they knew anything beyond the finding of the object and the fact that everyone involved in the expedition had vanished. BathyTech had later funded a joint rescue and recovery expedition with the Hong Kong–based company that had sent the original expedition, but they didn't find anything at all except an abandoned long-term submersible. Not even any bodies this time. They'd pieced together the rest based on their own experiences. The news had nothing but speculation.

To Mo, it felt like a plague of mermaids, spreading across the globe in secret. Their group here in the Chilean mountains was doing its best to understand it and stop it, with support from BathyTech and the government of Chile, but it was an uphill battle.

At least the threat was confined to the deep ocean. It wasn't much of a positive, but it was something.

He made himself answer because Mandala deserved that much. "I saw him change. Just like you did. Just like Jem did. His eyes glowed. His fingers got long and flexible. His teeth . . ." Christ. This was harder than he'd thought it would be. He breathed in and out. In and out. Mandala waited. "All the changes were there. And . . . and I'm pretty sure he knew it was going to happen. A few minutes before, he told me he was going to miss me."

Mandala's brow drew tight. She looked sick. "He told me he heard Ashlyn talking to him, in his head. He said she told him they had great plans for the world, and they couldn't be stopped." She let out a weak laugh. "I told him it sounded like his guilt talking. My God."

Mo's knees gave out. He plopped onto the floor. "So we were right. They really *do* communicate telepathically."

"It seems so. Perhaps the growths also function as facilitators for telepathic communication, although I have no idea how one would even begin to test that idea." She watched Mo with an uncomfortable intensity. "Did you see the mermaid who took him?"

He nodded. "Did you?"

"It had no eyes."

He'd never heard her speak quite like that—shaky, afraid, but still curious. They regarded each other with solemn understanding. So now they knew. The creature Ashlyn Timms had become had spoken to Armin telepathically. Had told him she was coming for him. And then she had.

It confirmed the theories Mandala had developed over the months of observing infected people change, or not change. The growths were the key. They only seemed to take root in the right sort of brain, though Mandala was stumped trying to work out what the right sort was. All she knew for sure was that hers wasn't it. Neither was Jem's. Once a person consciously recognized what the growth meant, they had a choice to make—accept, or not.

Change, or die.

Hannah had died because she hadn't known, and never had the chance to do what was necessary for her to live as her body became something unhuman. But the voices that had spoken to Mo and Armin had lied. You could kill the contagion—you could *live*, and remain human—if you got to the light and the open air in time. If you stayed down, there was only change or death.

Mo believed Armin had chosen the change not because he wanted it, but because he found it preferable to death, and he hadn't known there was any other way. It made him sad for Armin, for all he'd lost with that decision, and furious with Ashlyn for presenting him with what amounted to a false choice.

"Why did she choose the change?"

Mo looked over at Mandala. She was frowning at the wall. "Who? Ashlyn?"

"Yes. She was so strong. So practical. She cut out her own eyes so it wouldn't happen to her, for God's sake, I simply don't understand." Mandala sighed and rubbed her neck with both hands. "Oh well. I suppose you can never truly know what's in a person's heart. They can surprise you in wonderful and terrible ways when times are at their darkest."

Oh, yes, Mo knew that well enough.

He clambered to his feet, took Mandala's hand, and gave it a comforting squeeze. "Well. You've got a direction. Your theory's sound, in spite of my brain trying to fuck it up. That's good, right? Maybe you can save the world after all."

She flashed him a wan smile. "Well, I'm not sure how much of a difference this new information makes, but one can hope." She pressed his fingers with hers, then let go. "You'd best get started if you're going to make it back to your cabin before dark. Unless you'd be willing to stay here at the compound this time?"

A swell of affection warmed him. Mandala wasn't an easy person to get to know, but they'd become friends over the months, and he cared about her. It felt nice to have someone worry about his safety.

"I appreciate it. But I'd rather get back to my own bed. Thanks anyway."

She nodded, obviously unsurprised. They had this same exchange every month when Mo made the journey inland from his one-room shack on the coast to the BathyTech research facility to get his brain scan. She asked him to stay, at least overnight, and he said no thanks. It had become a routine for them, comforting in its own weird way.

Mandala rose to walk with him down the dank, narrow hallway to the exit. The armed guard opened the door to let them through.

She touched his arm at the top of the steep stone steps. "Same time next month, then?"

"Wouldn't miss it," he lied. Smiling, he leaned down to kiss her cheek and give her a hug. "Call me if you need me."

"Of course. You do the same."

He felt the weight of her gaze on his back as he descended the steps. She watched him until he rounded the first hairpin turn. She would have kept watching, he knew, if he hadn't been out of sight at that point.

She probably knew he was keeping something from her. But he doubted she had any idea what.

He really ought to feel worse about that than he did.

We can't always avoid hurting those we care for. What must be, must be, nevertheless.

Mo stopped, one hand on the cold stone at his side, and peered out over the sheer peaks and hidden gorges as if Armin were hiding there. "When?"

Soon. Very soon. Can't you feel me near you, love?

Fear, anticipation, and happiness so pure it hurt expanded in Mo's chest until he couldn't breathe. He shut his eyes tight. Tears leaked out to trickle down his face.

I feel you, Armin. He pressed a hand over his heart, as if to hold Armin there where he belonged. *I'm waiting for you.*

Armin's scent curled around him on the mountain breeze. He opened his eyes, half expecting to see the man himself standing there.

The path was empty. But Mo could *feel* Armin's essence infused into him, and it gave him strength.

He made his way down the series of switchbacks to the valley floor with a clear mind and a heart at peace for the first time since Armin's glowing eyes sank into the Pacific.

Three days later, Mo woke deep in the quiet hours of the night from a dream of walking into darkness, with the echo of Armin's voice in his ears.

It was time.

Throwing back the covers, he rose from his cot, pulled off his clothes, and walked naked from his shack in the deep V of the cliffs to the little hidden beach about one hundred thirty meters away.

A full moon hung low in the sky in the west, turning the swells silver. The surf was calm, and Mo waded out until the water reached his waist. It was cold enough to make him shiver, but he didn't want to return to shore. What was the point?

I'm here. I'm ready.

In answer to his thought, a shape broke the surface a meter or so away. It was sleek and white, with long, sharp teeth and black eyes.

Not greenish white. Black, like Armin's. Like in his dream, a million years ago in another life.

Mo's breath froze. His heart galloped so fast it made him dizzy. The mermaid rose. *Stood.* It stared at him with those eyes black as the deep.

"Armin?" Mo whispered, though he knew the answer.

The creature—*Armin*—lifted an arm and touched Mo's cheek with tentacle fingers.

Arms. Fingers. Legs. *Breathing the air.* A whole new evolution.

Yes, Mo. I am new. We have evolved.

Evolved. God.

Have you decided?

Had he? He'd thought so. But now . . .

Evolution. Breathing air. Soon, they'd overrun the planet.

Mandala had to know this. He had a responsibility.

The thing who'd been Armin—*I loved you, Armin, God*—moved closer. The black eyes were sad. *Too late. Cannot be stopped. Not now. It has begun.* His long, long fingers stroked Mo's hands, the touch so soft, so gentle. *You are here, in the sunlight world. You do not have to change, or die. You can live, and remain human. Your choice is truly your own.*

Rage shot through Mo's blood like a summer storm and died away just as quickly. It wasn't fair that he should have to make this choice. But life wasn't fair. Nothing was fair. Everybody did the best they could and lived with the consequences.

He stared into Armin's bottomless eyes. "I've made my decision." He waded closer, reached out, and touched the cold, cold skin of Armin's strange new face. "Life isn't life without you. My decision was made the minute you went overboard nine months ago. I'll be with you, whatever it takes. Whatever I have to be."

A pulse of mingled grief and joy flowed into him through the strange connection between himself and Armin. *You've chosen. Now let it happen.*

Mo's pulse jumped with an explorer's excitement as Armin took him beneath the waves and he felt his body begin to shift. He'd always loved an adventure. And he'd never been afraid of the dark.

Dear Reader,

Thank you for reading Ally Blue's *Down*!

We know your time is precious and you have many, many entertainment options, so it means a lot that you've chosen to spend your time reading. We really hope you enjoyed it.

We'd be honored if you'd consider posting a review—good or bad—on sites like **Amazon, Barnes & Noble, Kobo, Goodreads, Twitter, Facebook, Tumblr,** and your blog or website. We'd also be honored if you told your friends and family about this book. Word of mouth is a book's lifeblood!

For more information on upcoming releases, author interviews, blog tours, contests, giveaways, and more, please sign up for our weekly, spam-free newsletter and visit us around the web:

Newsletter: tinyurl.com/RiptideSignup
Twitter: twitter.com/RiptideBooks
Facebook: facebook.com/RiptidePublishing
Goodreads: tinyurl.com/RiptideOnGoodreads
Tumblr: riptidepublishing.tumblr.com

Thank you so much for Reading the Rainbow!

RiptidePublishing.com

ACKNOWLEDGMENTS

Many thanks to my editor, Del, for her technical expertise and assistance on this book. She helped me *so* much in working out the tech-related kinks! Any remaining oopses are solely my own.

ALSO BY
A L L Y B L U E

For a complete booklist, please visit www.allyblue.com.

ABOUT
THE AUTHOR

Ally Blue is acknowledged by the world at large (or at least by her heroes, who tend to suffer a lot) as the Popess of Gay Angst. She has a great big suggestively shaped hat and rides in a bullet-proof Plexiglas bubble in Christmas parades. Her harem of manwhores does double-duty as bodyguards and inspirational entertainment. Her favorite band is Radiohead, her favorite color is lime green, and her favorite way to waste a perfectly good Saturday is to watch all three extended version LOTR movies in a row. Her ultimate dream is to one day ditch the evil day job and support the family on manlove alone. She is not a hippie or a brain surgeon, no matter what her kids' friends say.

Website: allyblue.com
FB profile: facebook.com/AllyBlue.author
FB fan page: facebook.com/pages/Ally-Blue/98548113963
Twitter: twitter.com/PopessAllyBlue
Pinterest: pinterest.com/popessallyblue/
Tumblr: therealallyblue.tumblr.com
Yahoo group: groups.yahoo.com/neo/groups/loveisblue/info
Goodreads: goodreads.com/author/show/34997.Ally_Blue

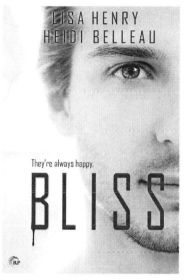

CPSIA information can be obtained at www.ICGtesting.com
Printed in the USA
LVOW12s1048030515

437050LV00005B/698/P